Fillies

and

Females

Bev Pettersen

Cover art design by Vivi Designs
Editors: Pat Thomas & Rhonda Helms

DEDICATION

To my son, Hans, who provided
computer support and jokes
when desperately needed.

Also available from

Bev Pettersen and Westerhall Books

Jockeys and Jewels

Color My Horse

ACKNOWLEDGEMENTS

Sincere thanks to Brenna Pettersen, Barb Snarby, Becky Mason, Patricia Thomas, Lauren Tutty, Anne MacFarlane, Julianne MacLean, Virginia Janes, John MacKinnon, Audrey Milford, and Liana Mason. You made a bumpy road much smoother.

CHAPTER ONE

Becky pushed the empty wheelchair through the crowded owner's box and wished, once again, she were invisible. She kept her face carefully neutral, trying to hide her discomfort.

Accompanying her employer to the track wasn't her usual duty but the weekend nurse was sick, and Martha would have been devastated if she hadn't been able to attend this long-anticipated horse race. Not that there was anything wrong with horses—Becky quite liked them—but the people who thronged these glamorous affairs made her edgy.

All the usual society types attended. Few would refuse an invitation to watch the Lone Star Derby from a swanky skybox stocked with an array of food and liquor as well as Martha's illustrious friends. However, some of them weren't very friendly. Becky gripped the rubber handles just as a lady with molded cheekbones and an equally molded dress stepped sideways, cutting off her path and forcing the chair to bump the wall.

"Hurry, Becky. Over here!" Martha Conrad called, her voice shrill with impatience.

"Do you want to switch chairs?" Becky asked, once she finally maneuvered the wheelchair to Martha's side.

"No, I just want my binoculars. You packed them, didn't you?"

Becky gave a reassuring nod and unzipped the side pocket on the back of the wheelchair.

"This is so nerve-wracking." Martha clutched at her neck, fretfully fingering a striking string of pearls. "I wish Malcolm were here."

Her thin chest flailed and Becky edged closer, her own hands tightening with concern. Martha had been devoted to her husband and was reluctant to sell the race stable after his sudden death. But maintaining the operation was stressful, even with excellent staff, and doctors had warned the excitement was dangerous for her weakened heart.

"There's our colt now." Martha's voice steadied, her words even carrying a familiar hint of sarcasm. "Look, Ted. Hunter's the horse with number one on the saddle cloth."

Martha's nephew glanced at the string of horses with such indifference, Becky wondered why he'd bothered to come. Maybe like her, Ted was uncomfortable with crowds, although in his case it seemed based on apathy rather than insecurity. His reaction didn't bother Martha one bit, since scores of enthusiastic guests were already murmuring their admiration.

Martha's horse, Code Hunter, seemed to know he was being scrutinized. He arched his neck and strutted like a rock star. Becky edged closer to the balcony, fascinated by the horse—his confidence, his bearing, his legitimate blue blood. Malcolm Conrad had spent twenty years developing Thoroughbreds with both speed and stamina, and Hunter was the result of his breeding program. In four starts the colt was unbeaten and if race odds were any indication, he'd win again today.

"An impressive animal." Ted glanced down at Martha. "But he should be, considering the money Uncle Malcolm wasted."

Disapproval edged his voice and Becky averted her head, pretending absorption with the post parade. His tone bothered her, but she'd learned it was safer to remain silent.

Silence also made it easier to observe others and when she peeked back at Ted, his taut eagerness surprised her— boredom or disapproval were his usual expressions. He'd been visiting Martha more frequently since Malcolm's death and his pale blue eyes, so devoid of emotion, always made her uneasy. He resembled a detached businessman rather than what one would expect of Martha's sole heir.

A lady giggled, and Becky's thoughts scattered as new energy zapped the skybox. *He's here.*

"Oh, gracious. My trainer has arrived. Over here, Dino!" Martha waved, abruptly the picture of health, and her seventy-four-year-old voice bubbled with fresh excitement.

The crowd parted as Dino Anders strolled through the middle of the room. He didn't wear his usual cowboy hat, and his hair was dark and windswept. A sports jacket was slung over his shoulder, and a crisp white shirt emphasized his tanned face and easy smile.

Becky gulped. He was movie star gorgeous, and in a moment he'd be beside her. She studied the tips of her thick-soled shoes, hoping this time she could control her blush, control her squeak. Maybe this time his friendly attempts at conversation wouldn't make her freeze.

But it wasn't only her. Even worldly Martha wasn't immune to the Dino effect. "How's my lipstick, dear?" she whispered.

"It's good." Becky grabbed a tissue and blotted a corner of Martha's lined mouth. "Now it's even better."

Martha gave Becky a conspiratorial wink, cupping her mouth so Ted wouldn't hear. "I may be old but I'm not dead."

A moment later, Dino's deep voice sounded beside them. "Hello, Martha. You're looking very elegant today."

Martha giggled as he leaned down and kissed her rouged cheek. "I assume there will be a win picture with Hunter," she said. "Can you promise me a trip to the winner's circle?"

Dino straightened, his smiling brown eyes studying the horses warming up on the track. "Can't guarantee it, but Hunter's training great. Should run well."

"Of course, if he doesn't," Ted said, edging closer, "it's obvious the stables should be sold." He gave Martha's shoulder a solicitous pat. "Racing was Uncle Malcolm's passion, not yours. It's crazy to chase his dream at the expense of your health."

Becky blinked in dismay. It was no secret Ted wanted Martha to sell but this was the first time he'd stated his opinion in public, and it was thoughtless of him to be so blunt. She sensed Dino's similar disapproval, could feel his pulsing resentment even though he stood several feet away.

However, Dino's easy shrug revealed nothing. "Then let's hope Hunter wins today," he said, "so nothing needs to be sold. You're nervous, Betty. Have you made a big bet?"

It took several seconds before she realized Dino was talking to her. She looked into his teasing eyes—they reminded her of warm caramel with gold flecks. And the way he smiled. He never remembered her name, yet always smiled with such warmth it made her knees wobble. No wonder the other nurses all clamored to escort Martha to the races.

She paused, moistening her mouth so it wouldn't squeak. "My name's Becky," she finally said, "and I don't bet." She forced herself to hold his gaze, to smile, to keep her head up like Martha advised, but it no longer mattered. A brunette with bold eyes and bright lipstick swooped in from the other side and grabbed his arm.

Dino turned to the lady and tilted his head, listening as she asked him about race strategy.

"Since Martha's horse drew the rail," he said, "our jockey will take Hunter out quick, grab the lead and hopefully hold off the closers. With any luck, we'll all meet in the winner's circle." His voice rippled with lazy amusement. "That's the plan anyway."

He sounded relaxed, unconcerned that a horse he trained was running in the biggest three-year-old race in Texas. Didn't seem to notice he was the center of attention, especially with the women, although even the men eyed him with expressions ranging from admiration to envy.

He'd easily blown off Ted's rude comment, and she sensed nothing now but the fascinating whiff of leather, soap and virile male. God, she wished she could be so comfortable.

She stared through the spotless glass panel, nails pressed into her palms, while the horses circled the gate. Dino was too close for her to really relax, but she had no more worries. His greetings were always unfailingly polite, but her replies never came quickly enough. He wouldn't speak to her again today, not with the lipstick lady hanging on his arm. At least she could retreat into silence and enjoy the race. No one in this group ever talked to her—no one except Martha and Dino.

Chatter softened as the horses disappeared behind the starting gate. Guests pressed closer to the balcony, attention shifting from their drinks to the track. Hunter's jockey wore the bright silks of Conrad Racing Stable, a vivid yellow with a black diamond, and horse and rider were easy to spot. An assistant starter led them into their slot.

Soon. The race would start soon. The air crackled with expectation, and she leaned forward, forgetting her shyness, caught up in the emotion.

"He's in the gate," Dino said, his big body motionless.

Martha reached up and clutched Becky's hand. Ted gestured at a waiter.

Two horses left to load. Anticipation pricked the air, and the raucous crowd at the rail stilled. Becky bent closer to Martha but kept her gaze fixed on the one hole, praying Hunter would break clean. *Gate to wire, please.* If the race were too close, it would be stressful for Martha. Already she could feel the trembling of Martha's hand, the tissue-thin skin of her fingers.

Even Becky's heart pounded. She bent down, pretending to adjust the pillow behind Martha's shoulders but really just wanted to be close. If she was this nervous, how was Martha feeling? This couldn't be good, and it was the type of situation the doctors warned to avoid. "Deep breaths," Becky whispered, trying to hide her concern. "Hunter will do fine."

The nine horse balked, and two gate attendants rushed forward and pushed the reluctant colt into his slot.

"The horses are in," the announcer blared.

Crack! The gates snapped and ten horses burst out. Five strides and Hunter grabbed the lead. A bay horse joined him at the hip. However, Hunter was clearly in control. Becky blew out a relieved sigh, surprised to realize she'd been holding her breath. Hunter's jockey kept a tight hold, carefully rationing the colt's speed as the two horses pounded into the first turn, followed two lengths back by the rest of the pack.

She wanted to jump up and down, but Martha had a death grip on her hand so she forced her feet to remain still. But— oh no. It looked like the bay was catching Hunter. "Go, Hunter!" she yelled, unable to remain silent.

"Our horse is looking good, Betty," Dino said. "Jock's just rating him. The first quarter was almost twenty-four seconds, so he should be able to hang on."

Oh, God. Dino was talking to her again, despite the gorgeous lady who clung to his arm. And he'd called Hunter 'our horse.' Warmth lapped through her chest, even though it was rather irritating he never remembered her name. They'd met on nine previous occasions, six times at the races and three times at Martha's house—although of course she hadn't been counting.

She yanked her head back to the throng of galloping horses. Hunter had opened up a three-length lead and gaily led the group around the far turn and into the stretch. The colorful jockey crouched over Hunter's bobbing neck, urging him toward the wire. Someone yelled in Becky's ear, and Martha's fingers tightened their grip. Oh, wow. He was going to win easily. But then, inexplicably, the colt quit. She watched in shock as the bay horse surged past, then another horse in red blinkers, then seven more. Oh no, this was awful.

Hunter had finished last.

The room silenced, so tomblike the only noise was the rattle of ice as the bartender mixed a drink. Becky was reluctant to look at Martha, knew she'd intended this party as a coronation, not a humiliating defeat. And the trainer! She felt Dino's raw disbelief and wanted to reach over and give his hand a consoling squeeze.

No one moved, except an expressionless waiter who delivered Ted an icy martini.

"Well, that's racing," someone finally said with a forced laugh.

"Your horse tried hard, Martha," another voice said, too hearty to be genuine.

Dino leaned over Martha's shoulder, so close Becky caught the subtle hint of his aftershave. "Very sorry," he said gruffly. "Not the result I expected, or the one you deserve. I'll check on Hunter then ship him back to your stable. Obviously he needs time off." He kissed Martha's cheek and strode from the room.

Betting stubs fluttered to the floor as disappointed guests drifted from the railing and rushed to refill their drinks. Everyone had expected a trek to the winner's circle, followed by indulgence in the ritual champagne. Even Martha's water glass was empty, except for one lonely cube of melting ice.

Only Ted had the luck to replenish his martini. He'd signaled the waiter just before the race, as though aware they wouldn't be drinking champagne—which was impossible. The man was a hospital administrator, not a psychic. Her gaze lifted to his face and she froze, stunned by his expression.

She jerked her head away before he caught her watching. But goose bumps shivered a trail down her back because she was an expert at reading emotion, and his expression as he stared at Martha had not been that of a solicitous nephew. In fact, it had been undeniably malicious.

Dino rushed through the crowd milling in front of the grandstand, his jaw rigid. He prayed Hunter was okay, although the colt had looked healthy when he galloped past the finish line, merely exhausted. Exhausted and beaten.

An attractive reporter with clacking heels rushed to intercept him. "Dino," she called, "your horse was favored to win. What do you think contributed to his disappointing finish?"

"No idea." He glanced over his shoulder, searching the returning runners, worried about Hunter. "I'm on my way now to check him."

She pressed closer, hungry for details and ignoring his hint. "It's no secret Malcolm Conrad's goal was to win this race with a homebred. Considering Hunter's last-place finish, what do you suppose he'd say if he were alive?"

Dino almost winced, remembering his promise to Malcolm. But he hid his regret behind a rueful smile. He couldn't recall this reporter's name but he did remember her paper; they targeted the negative aspects of racing rather than the many positives. And while she was merely trying to pump out a story, her questions still stung.

Malcolm would have been devastated at this result, as was his loyal wife. The shock and disappointment on her face had cut to the core. He'd truly expected to give her a win today. Hunter's gallops, his works, even his attitude had all pointed to a monster race. Yet the talented colt had run like shit.

Not entirely like shit. He blew out a sigh, reaching for any bright spot. The first part of the race had been beautiful. However, by the eighth pole Hunter had quit running, and the finish line was the only place that mattered.

The reporter waved her notepad, and it was clear she wasn't going to let him escape without some sort of comment.

"Well, ma'am," he said, "I think if Mr. Conrad were here, he might say horses are like people. They have good days and bad. That's what makes them so interesting. And just like us, they have to keep trying."

She smiled back but clearly wasn't satisfied. "Still, you must view this loss as a major setback? Especially considering rumors that Mrs. Conrad intends to sell?"

Dino's chest tightened a painful notch, but he forced a chuckle. "If I listened to every rumor, I wouldn't have time to train. Now I really must go and check my horse."

She nodded, pressing a gold-embossed card in his hand. "When you're not so busy, give me a call. I'd love to hear the whole Conrad story. Any day...or evening," she added with a throaty laugh.

He subtly checked the name on the card. Danielle Whitlock. A definite looker, but he knew he'd never make that call. Too fancy, too forward and he'd had his fill of aggressive women. He slipped the card in his pocket, his mind already on Hunter, nodded politely and continued past the security guard and onto the track.

And there was his horse. Trotting evenly but with heaving flanks and lowered head. Nothing wrong with his stride. However Hunter looked exhausted as did his dirt-smeared jockey.

"What the hell happened out there?" he asked as Brad leaped off and unbuckled the saddle.

"No idea." The jockey shrugged, his voice heavy with disappointment. "He just ran out of steam. I pretty much had to carry him home."

Frowning, Dino wiped Hunter's flaring nostrils, checking for blood. Found nothing but caked dirt. Still, bleeding in the lungs would make a horse quit and although Hunter had never bled before, the colt seemed oddly distressed.

He passed the reins to Hunter's solemn groom. "Cool and bathe him. We'll have the vet run some tests. I gotta figure this out."

And he had to figure it out quickly. Martha was on the brink of selling, no doubt encouraged by her hovering nephew. Yet her horses were just peaking, and he sincerely believed Hunter was destined for greatness.

One bad race should be forgiven. Horses like Hunter didn't come along every day...and neither did jobs with established race barns like Conrad's.

Anxiety churned in his gut as he followed the beaten horse back to the barn. More than ever, he wished Malcolm was still around. He missed the man. Missed watching race video, sharing their analysis, sharing their dreams. And if Martha let the stable dissolve, he'd be out of horses, out of money, out of a job.

Chirp. He flipped his phone open then wished he'd checked the display when he heard his ex-wife's smug voice.

"I see the race is over," Laura said. "So, do you have my money?"

"Nope." His hand tightened around the phone. "And since you're watching television, you know the results. Obviously, I'll need more time."

"You were supposed to have the down payment this week. I have another buyer so if you don't want the ranch, let me know." Spite sharpened her words. "Or maybe you'll finally admit I was right, and you can't make any money training horses."

"Gotta go," he said quietly. "My lawyer will be in touch." He closed the phone, determined not to let her barbs tank his already-shitty day.

He trudged past another security booth. Waved at the gray-haired guard then followed the horse path onto the backside, where long wooden barns stretched in rows. The horses he trained were stabled in barn sixteen, although some of his operation was conducted at the Conrad facilities. One temperamental filly even shipped in on race mornings. It was an excellent setup—good horses, good facility, good purses— but with Malcolm's death, the elite operation had suddenly turned fragile.

He sighed, his steps slowing. Martha had to be convinced not to sell. It would be a tragedy to quit and let her husband's hard work dissolve. At the very least, she should finish the Lone Star meet so she'd receive better prices. Sure, she'd had a heart attack and wasn't feeling sprightly, but if watching the races was too stressful, she and her disapproving nurse could just stay away.

He'd get the horses winning again. Christ, he'd promised Malcolm. Resolve lengthened his stride, and he brushed aside a prick of guilt. Keeping the horses for another two months was definitely for Martha's benefit, and he wasn't being selfish, only sensible.

CHAPTER TWO

Becky sorted medication tablets, keeping a careful watch on Martha and Ted. The disappointing race had taken its toll, and the waxy color in Martha's cheeks was worrisome. The way Ted lingered by her bed, harping about Hunter's poor race, didn't help either. It was late and Martha needed sleep, not a reminder of the horse's lackluster effort.

"It's clear you should sell this place," Ted went on, leaning over Martha's pillow, seemingly in no hurry to leave. "Those horses suck away your health. My friend runs a gated retirement facility. Doctors on site twenty-four seven. They accept only the cream of society."

"You're very thoughtful, but good gracious, I'm tired." Martha yawned, her voice trailing off. Her eyelids flickered twice then closed.

Ted sighed with exasperation. Becky ignored his grating presence, continuing her count of pink and blue pills.

"She always falls asleep when I'm here," he said. "If *you* were any kind of nurse, you'd talk some sense into her."

Okay. Obviously he was talking to her now. Becky's hand tightened around the cap of the prescription bottle, but she lifted her head and met his gaze. "Martha needs her sleep, but I agree that racing isn't beneficial."

"Damn right. It almost killed her today. And it was embarrassing watching that nag stumble around the track. The quicker she sells, the better." His voice lowered. "At least you understand the situation. I'll have my secretary collect some brochures on Autumn Acres. Please ensure Martha reads them."

He smoothed the collar of his shirt, looking much more satisfied, although his smile didn't reach his pale eyes.

Ping. Becky fumbled a pill in rare clumsiness and stooped to retrieve it, grateful for any excuse to look away. He strode from the room without another word. It took a moment for her hands to steady, and she snapped the top back on the container, irritated he made her feel like a helpless teenager all over again.

She'd been with Martha for three wonderful years, but today was the first time Ted had even deigned to directly address her. Obviously he was taking an increased interest in Conrad affairs, although when Malcolm was alive his visits had been thankfully brief.

She sighed, knowing it was silly to have an aversion to a man simply because of his pale eyes—eyes that reminded her of another time, another place. She rattled the medication jars back onto the shelf and shoved away the memories.

"Is he gone?" Martha whispered. She twisted her head and checked the doorway, her gray hair fanning the pillow.

"For now." Becky tried to frown at her manipulative patient, but her lips twitched and it was impossible to keep from smiling. "You won't be able to pull the old sleep trick much longer though. Here, drink this."

Martha scowled but accepted the glass and swallowed the colorful pills. "Ted's like my sister. Rather bossy, but at least he cares."

"Yes, and I'm afraid this time he's right." Becky's voice turned serious. "You shouldn't watch any more races, at least until you're stronger." Regret shadowed Martha's eyes so Becky quickly added, "We could always drive over to the gallop track and watch the horses here on the property."

Martha sniffed. "Better than nothing, I suppose. But watching them train at home isn't nearly as exciting as racing at Lone Star. I simply don't understand what happened to Hunter. Malcolm bred that horse for endurance. He should be able to get the distance. And Dino is a top-notch trainer. He knows how to condition a three-year-old." She reached out and grabbed Becky's hand. "I don't want to sell the horses, not until Malcolm's breeding program is vindicated. And I don't want to look at Ted's silly brochures. Not yet."

"Then don't," Becky said, alarmed by the odd note of helplessness in Martha's voice. "Selling is your decision. But you should probably stay away from the track."

"You'll have to go for me then." Martha's grip tightened around her wrist. "Watch the horses. Keep an eye on things. Malcolm always said absentee owners created problems."

"But I don't know enough!" Becky's voice rose. It wasn't the horses that scared her but the people, and her pulse kicked at the thought of seeing Dino every day. Having to talk to him. She didn't like to be around men, any sort of men, but especially not big, confident ones.

"You've learned a lot in your time here, and your resume said you went to a riding camp. That's one of the reasons we hired you. Now I want you to do this one small thing." Martha softened her grip and gave Becky's hand a knowing pat. "Don't worry, dear. Dino won't bite. He's a kind man, and his flirting is harmless."

Harmless maybe, Becky thought, wringing her hands. But for someone with zero social confidence, dealing with Dino's charm was like having a root canal. Everyone gravitated toward him. Entering his sphere was like being on stage. The mere thought of visiting the track without Martha as a buffer made her stomach cramp.

"Yes, well, glad that's settled." Martha closed her eyes with a satisfied smile. "I'll be able to sleep now."

Becky yanked the nightstand closer to the bed and plunked a water glass next to Martha's bible. This was not good. Once Martha made up her mind, she was like a rhino. *I need you to do this one small thing.* Maybe it seemed small to Martha, but it didn't feel small to her, and the panicked thumping of her chest wasn't at all reassuring.

CHAPTER THREE

"It's a good thing you drive so slow. At least we won't scare the horses." Martha blew out an impatient sigh. "No chance of that, not at this speed."

Becky stopped the Mercedes, ignoring Martha's criticism as a chestnut horse cruised around the training track. The rider was tiny, with a blond ponytail that bounced beneath a white helmet, and horse and rider moved with fluid grace. "What horse is that?" She twisted further in the driver's seat, craning to see.

The Conrad stable was huge, and although she'd visited the barn and private track many times before, she rarely came in the morning when horses trained. That had been Malcolm's passion, Malcolm's domain. He'd always been the one to accompany Martha.

"That's Echo Beach, a three-year-old filly." Martha's voice swelled with pride and she lowered the window, letting in a rush of warm air. "Malcolm said Echo's quirky and doesn't like to travel, but she's one of our best. Dino wants to enter her in a six-furlong sprint next week."

Which meant he might be around today, Becky realized. Dino spent most of his time at the Lone Star track, but if this filly was racing soon... Her fingers tightened around the steering wheel, although she managed to keep her gaze from darting to his guesthouse. "How many days a week is Dino here?" she asked, surprised her voice sounded so level.

"As much as necessary." Martha shrugged. "Slim manages things—under Dino's direction—but Dino always comes for the works."

Becky peeked over her shoulder. Several dusty cars sat in the parking lot, along with a rugged truck that carried the Conrad logo. She knew Slim, a short graying man who didn't talk much and who'd been with Conrad's for years. Despite his crustiness, she was fairly comfortable with him. *Please, let it be Slim who drove that tough-looking truck.*

"Look at the stride on that filly." Martha's head craned out the window.

Becky leaned forward, intrigued despite the yawningly early hour. As long as there were few people around, it was more enjoyable to sit in the car and watch the beautiful horses than sit in the house and worry about Martha.

"See that!" Martha gestured, her voice rising.

Even Becky recognized the horse's effortless burst of speed. The rider waved a whip, buried herself in the horse's neck, and the filly scorched around the track. "I think she'll win any race she runs," Becky said, staring in awe. "How could she lose?"

"She does look good." Martha oozed satisfaction as she leaned back and raised the window. "Drive over by the rail and see what Dino says."

"He's h-here?" Becky's voice cracked and she raised a hand to her mouth, pretending to cough. Martha already thought she was absurdly tongue-tied around men. She'd tease unmercifully if she knew Dino's presence left Becky's brain paralyzed.

"Of course he's here." Martha huffed with impatience. "That was a work—a fast gallop, not a conditioning session. Like I said, he always comes for an important work."

"I see." Becky peeked in the mirror. Maybe she should have put on some makeup. Not for Dino of course, merely as a confidence boost. But it was only seven a.m. Who wore makeup this early?

She glanced sideways, her mouth twitching. Clearly Martha did. Rouge had already settled into her wrinkled cheeks. However, she still looked regal. Nothing scared Martha. Although since the double whammy of Malcolm's death and her subsequent heart attack, she'd grown more fragile. Now she needed moral support, and Becky's job had evolved into companion as much as a nurse.

Becky edged the Mercedes beside the tough truck with a jutting trailer hitch and resolutely squared her shoulders. If Martha wanted her to learn about race horses, she'd do that. And she'd force herself to talk. No big deal. People did it all the time.

Martha's door abruptly clicked open. Dino's heart-stopping grin appeared, his eyes shadowed by the brim of his cowboy hat, and Becky's resolution snagged in her throat.

"Did you see that, Martha?" Enthusiasm filled his voice as he swung the door wide and smiled down at Martha. "Four furlongs in forty-six seconds. Filly's not even blowing. Looks great for Saturday."

"Excellent." Martha took his hand, accepting his help as she maneuvered out of the car. "I, however, won't be able to attend. Ted and Becky don't approve. Apparently my stuttering heart can't handle all the excitement."

Becky slid from the driver's seat as Dino's gaze swung in her direction. His smile remained but his disapproval blasted across the roof of the car, making her want to shrink back into the seat. She ignored him, pretending to watch as Slim slipped a lead line on the returning filly.

The rider vaulted off, removing her helmet and shaking out her ponytail as she sauntered toward them. "Hello, Mrs. Conrad," she called, perky and pretty. "Remember me? I'm Stephanie." She reached out and shook Martha's hand. "Glad you dropped by. We all miss Malcolm, but he'd be very happy to see how this filly has developed." The blond rider was older than she first appeared, probably in her thirties, with laugh lines that fanned her eyes. "Let me know if you stay here tonight, Dino," she added. "I can pop over later."

She included Becky in her friendly wave and walked away with only the slightest of swaggers. Anyone who could ride like that probably deserved to strut a bit. She had a whip stuck in her back pocket, well-worn chaps fringed with leather, and a pink protective vest. Five-foot-nothing, a full six inches shorter than Becky, yet she walked as though she were invincible. Becky squared her own shoulders and peeked at Dino.

He nodded but wasn't looking at Stephanie, his attention still focused on Martha. "Let's go in the office and grab a coffee." He slipped a supportive hand beneath Martha's elbow. "You can see

Hunter too. He shipped in last night. I'm going to throw out yesterday's fiasco. Give him a month off. Then find another race."

"Did the vet check him out?" Becky heard Martha ask as she trailed the mismatched couple into the barn. Dino's height and broad shoulders dwarfed Martha, emphasizing her frailness, although the man's virility probably overpowered most people. He'd slowed his long stride to fit Martha's ambulatory shuffle, and his jeans molded to his lean hips like a second skin.

Gosh, this was perfect. Now she could stare all she wanted. He didn't seem so threatening when he wasn't trying to engage her in conversation. And no wonder women clung to his arms. The T-shirt hinted at ridges in his back, and she could easily imagine him shirtless, looking like one of those muscled magazine men.

His body alone would make up for any deficiencies of character, although he didn't seem to have any. Always cheerful, never condescending, one of the few people who always acknowledged her...and she really shouldn't be ogling his ass.

She jerked her head away, concentrating instead on the unique smell of horses, hay and leather. So welcoming, so soothing—the smell alone sparked a nostalgic rush. Straw rustled as horses poked curious heads over stall doors, checking her out as she walked down the aisle and acting just like the animals she remembered from camp.

A horse nickered, not a feed-me call but a soft, throaty sound that beckoned like a siren. She paused. The horse stuck a head over the door and nickered again, watching her with soulful, brown eyes. Had to be a girl. No boy could possibly have such beautiful eyelashes. The mare had dark-tipped ears, black hairs on her white face and the most elegant head Becky had ever seen.

"That's Lyric," Dino said, glancing over his shoulder as though sensing her interest. "Bred here but retired now."

"She's beautiful," Becky said, forgetting her awkwardness. "May I go in?"

He hesitated but must have seen the longing on her face. "Yeah, okay. But be careful. She nips. And don't touch her belly. She'll kick. She's also an escape artist, so watch the door." He gave a wry smile. "Actually that mare is quite tricky. Let me help you."

"No, I'm fine," she said quickly.

He lingered for a moment, but it was obvious he wanted time alone with Martha. A slow nod, and he turned and continued down the aisle.

Becky slid back the bolt. The mare watched with hopeful eyes then, exactly as he'd warned, charged forward, trying to barge past. She yanked the door shut just in time. Lyric flattened her ears and swung her head, threatening to bite.

She laughed, remembering a cranky mare from camp behaving exactly the same way. That horse had merely craved attention though and, like a kid, her nasty mood was only a front.

"Don't be silly," she scolded, scratching the mare's jaw.

Lyric's ears flicked but moments later she lowered her head and sighed, her breath sweet with the smell of alfalfa.

Becky sighed too, almost able to imagine she was thirteen again. Subsidized camp had been a refuge from the foster homes she'd bounced through. No one yelled at her or chased her or worse, and she'd been allowed to sleep in the barn with kind counselors and kinder horses—the only time she'd ever experienced any real security. Except now, with Martha.

A voice sounded in the aisle but she remained in the stall, engrossed with scratching Lyric. The mare forgot to pretend she was cross and stretched her neck, grunting with pleasure.

The voice moved closer, speaking low but with urgent undertones. She peered over the stall door. Recognized Slim but his back was to her, a cell phone pressed against his ear.

"Hunter's here, but no problem. I'll look after it," he said before closing his phone.

"Hi, Slim," she said.

He jerked around.

"I didn't mean to surprise you," she added quickly. "Dino said it was okay to go in the stall."

"Fine with me so long as you don't get kicked." Slim shoved the phone in his pocket. "That mare's poison. Where's Dino?"

"In the office. With Martha."

He grunted but said nothing. She'd always been able to relax during past meetings with Slim, but now he scuffed the floor with his boot and his discomfort was contagious. The silence stretched.

"I saw the race yesterday," she said brightly, stepping into the aisle and pushing the door shut before Lyric could rush past. "Heard Hunter shipped back already."

Slim jabbed a thumb. "Yeah, want to see him? Third stall from the end. Heard he ran a clunker. Guess that means Mrs. Conrad will sell soon?" His voice rose with worry, and Becky's empathy swelled. Naturally the man was concerned. His job was at stake, and she'd heard his daughter was confined to an institution.

"I don't think any sale decisions have been made," she said, following the direction of Slim's thumb to where an imperious head stared down the aisle. Hunter still looked cocky, not at all like a horse that only yesterday had been beaten twenty lengths. Confidence was a wonderful thing.

She trailed Slim as they approached the colt but slowed when she saw the fluid that trickled from Hunter's left nostril. "Is something wrong with him?"

"Why do you ask?" Slim's voice chilled.

"There's some discharge. I just wondered if he was sick."

"He's fine. A bunch of dirt was kicked in his face yesterday. Better back away though. Colts bite." He motioned her down the aisle. "Come on. Let's see what's happening."

She followed him into Dino's office where Martha was tucked in a corner chair. Her color was good, her eyes bright, and clearly whatever she'd discussed with Dino hadn't been too upsetting.

And the office smelled enticing. Becky stepped past Slim, lured by the smell of hickory coffee. Martha had insisted they rise early, and there hadn't been time for their usual breakfast of green tea and toast. Becky didn't particularly like green tea but Martha was on a strict diet, so now her mouth watered at the smell of fresh coffee.

Dino lounged in a chair behind the desk and gestured at the coffee maker. "Help yourself. You too, Slim. Come hear the news. Now that Martha can't attend the races, she's appointed a watchdog."

His voice hardened, and Becky tried not to flinch beneath his cool stare. Gone was the congenial man she'd always seen at the track. Now his eyes were dark and formidable. How had they ever reminded her of sweet caramel?

She walked to the coffee machine, relieved her hand didn't shake as she filled two cups and passed one to Slim. Hostility always bothered her, but this was unwarranted. She wasn't really a watchdog...well, maybe a bit. But so what? Dino was only racing horses; she was trying to save Martha's life.

She raised her head, guessing her cheeks were beet red but determined not to shrink. *He can't hurt me.* He didn't run a foster home, couldn't give orders and, like her, was only an employee. Besides, Martha's wellbeing was more important than a bunch of horses galloping in a circle.

"It was a joint decision that Martha avoid the track," she said. "Ted and the doctor feel the same way." She had to speak uncharacteristically loud to be heard over the whir of the air conditioner. "Especially after Hunter's poor race yesterday," she added with a spark of alacrity. Hunter *had* run like shit, and Dino was the trainer.

His mouth tightened. Oh, damn, now she'd really made him mad. She took a hasty sip of coffee.

"So you're not selling the horses yet, Mrs. Conrad?"

She'd forgotten about Slim's presence, and thankfully his worried question drew everyone's attention.

"No," Martha said with a reassuring smile at Slim. "But I want to ensure everything runs smoothly. Want to know what's happening." She turned her attention back to Dino. "And I expect you both to accord Becky every courtesy."

"Certainly." Dino tipped his hat. "It will be our pleasure." But his words were clipped and it was quite clear, at least to Becky, that her company would be far from pleasurable.

Dino watched the silver Mercedes inch from the graveled lot. Hell, the little nurse drove like an old lady. In some respects, she seemed older than Martha. Luckily not all the live-in nurses were so staid. A couple of them had been downright neighborly and one of them, the lovely Greta, had spent a few steamy evenings in his guesthouse.

He rubbed his jaw, trying to remember when Greta had left. Three months ago, maybe four. Hard to remember. Martha always had two or three nurses and while the pretty ones never seemed to stay long, the Brown-Betty nurse hung around forever. He still wasn't sure of her name although she'd shown some unexpected spunk in his office. She'd surprised him, and women rarely surprised him.

"Cute little thing," Slim said behind him.

"Who?"

"Well, I'm sure as hell not talking about the old lady."

"Don't call her the old lady," Dino said absently. "Martha's our employer. And is the nurse's name Becky or Betty?"

"Betty, I think. I can ask the housekeeper. Jocelyn knows everything."

Dino shrugged, his thoughts already switching to horses. "What did the vet say about Hunter?"

"That everything's fine." Slim hooked his thumbs in his jeans and tugged his sagging pants into position. "You staying here tonight?"

"Yeah, got a dinner at the big house with Martha and Ted."

"How long before she sells?" Slim asked.

"If we get some wins, she'll probably hang on. Hope so anyway." A muscle ticked in Dino's jaw. Martha wasn't the only one who needed a win. His salary was fair, but he relied on the fat race bonuses. Laura wouldn't wait much longer for the down payment. "Keep a good eye on Echo. We need a win from that filly. Malcolm never wanted her stabled at Lone Star so we'll haul in Saturday."

Slim grunted but didn't look happy. Lately he'd been edgy and even more morose than usual, if that was possible. And the way his pants hung, the man was losing a lot of weight.

"How're things?" Dino asked, eyeing his foreman with concern.. "How's your daughter?"

Slim shrugged but worry creased his leathery forehead, and he fiddled with his belt buckle. "We're surviving. Wish I could afford a better place for her."

Dino blew out a sympathetic sigh. It was common knowledge Slim had an adult daughter who'd been injured at the track and was now stuck in a wheelchair. Damn bad luck, as by all accounts she'd been a helluva rider. "We've got good horses racing for big purses," he said. "Should be better cash flow soon. I'm sure Martha's lawyer can set up a trust account. Give you some peace of mind."

Slim stared glumly at the dust left by the crawling Mercedes. "I'd need ten winning seasons to be able to give Jilly what she needs. Not much chance of that, not with Malcolm gone and Mrs. Conrad on the brink."

Dino shook his head. He didn't consider himself materialistic, but money definitely smoothed out a lot of problems. Ten winning seasons—hell, no wonder Slim was sour.

"Got a good buddy in New York," he said, then paused. After all he didn't know Slim *that* well, had only worked for Conrad's the past nine months. However Malcolm had held Slim in high esteem, and he couldn't stand by and watch a man struggle. "Mark trains for a sheikh," he continued. "I can give you a reference. You'd make better money up north."

Slim jerked around, his eyes widening. "Mark? Mark Russell? I heard of him. Damn big of you. But I've got things worked out."

"Good," Dino said. "And hopefully the filly will make us all happy on Saturday."

Slim nodded and trudged toward the barn, head down, shoulders hunched. But he didn't look like he had things worked out, and Dino didn't like unhappy staff. Slim was a longtime Conrad employee and his skill at picking out yearlings was unquestionable. Lately though, the man had been a tad impatient with the horses.

And what the hell had he meant when he'd called the nurse cute? It was difficult to see anything the way she hid behind those shapeless clothes, that long hair. And she wasn't very friendly. He'd attempted conversation before, trying to coax out a smile, but she'd always shut him down.

Sighing, he reached down and scooped up an errant piece of baler twine. Clearly he'd have to try harder. For some reason Martha trusted the quiet nurse which made her goodwill all the more critical.

CHAPTER FOUR

"Maybe you should go to bed early tonight," Becky said, her eyes narrowing as she absorbed Martha's pallor. The early-morning excursion to the stable had left Martha exhausted and despite the brave makeup, her cheeks were now pasty, her breath labored. Becky checked her blood pressure and marginally relaxed. "Not so bad. I think a good night's sleep will help. But you should go to bed right after dinner."

"You'll miss me, won't you dear?" Martha spoke so quietly, Becky had to strain to hear.

"You mean when I drive to Lone Star tomorrow, all alone, not knowing anyone or even where Dino's barn is?" She forced a cheerful smile, hating to think of Martha's mortality. "Of course I'll miss you."

"You've become much more than a nurse, much more than a companion. You're like a member of the family."

Becky's heart wrenched. In reality, this lady was the only family she'd ever known, and the thought of losing her was terrifying. She squeezed her eyes shut, hiding her shimmering emotion, and kissed Martha's clammy forehead. "That's why, in spite of my fear and ignorance, I'm going to be the best darn horse reporter you ever had."

"Horse reporter." Martha gave a wan smile. "I suppose that's a good name. Just watch the horses. They'll tell you how they're feeling. I still can't understand why Hunter ran such a poor race." Her hand clutched at her throat. "I want to keep going until the Lone Star meet is over. Need to make sure Malcolm's name isn't forgotten. He wanted that so much, wouldn't want me to sell yet." Her voice faltered. "But I won't make the scheduled dinner tonight."

Panic jerked Becky upright. "But it's too late to cancel. What about Ted and Dino? They'll be here soon."

"You can cope, dear. You're much braver than you think. And Jocelyn has the kitchen under control."

"But you need me with you." Becky's voice squeaked and she swallowed, trying to ease her tight throat.

"The night nurse is very capable. You know that. You hired her. Just enjoy the wine. It's a lovely Beaujolais—your favorite. By the way, Ted is bringing some documents." Martha's voice turned smug. "And he'll be extremely disappointed when I'm not there to sign them."

Becky groaned. "Is this another trick to avoid Ted?"

"Of course not. I'm tired. You said so yourself."

Becky eyed her suspiciously. No doubt Martha was pale, but she was also wily and the prospect of dealing with Ted's displeasure—all alone—made her gut wrench. She'd have to face Dino too, although that thought caused an entirely different type of quivering.

She took another quick gulp. It was shaping up to be a very stressful night. Unfortunately there probably wasn't enough wine in Martha's expansive cellar to make it any fun.

CHAPTER FIVE

"This is unacceptable." Ted topped up his wine and, for the third time that evening, ignored Becky's empty glass. "Mr. Anders and I both expected to meet with Martha. If she's too tired to eat, obviously involvement with horses must be curtailed. You should have known better than to drag her down to the barn."

Becky picked up the bottle and refilled her own glass. Ted's mouth had been flapping throughout dinner, but it hardly bothered her anymore. Even his pale eyes failed to rouse her usual aversion. The man was a total pain. No wonder Martha always pretended to fall asleep—unlike Becky, Martha was limited to a strict diet and unable to find refuge in wine.

Another fifteen minutes and she'd escape. Could pretend Martha needed checking, even though there was another night nurse.

"Martha didn't seem tired when she was at the barn this morning," Dino said from across the elegant table. "And watching Echo gallop around the training track won't cause a heart attack. It's certainly not Betty's fault if she's tired."

Becky's initial gratitude flipped to irritation when Dino once again mangled her name. "Thank you, Dano," she said.

But he didn't catch her deliberate mistake; his steely gaze was locked on Ted.

She fingered the stem of her glass while the two men sparred, their hostility blatant. Neither had shown her much attention so her conversation had been limited to the briefest of replies.

Fortunately there was always unending wine at Martha's formal dinners. She'd been able to sit and sip and study Dino.

He wore a dark sports jacket and white shirt, and she blew out a sigh of appreciation. She may not enjoy talking to good-looking men, but she definitely liked looking at them.

Ted abruptly tossed his napkin on the table, still staring at Dino. "You should know I brought along papers for Martha to sign. The quicker she sells the property—and every horse on it—the longer she'll live. And that's really what we want, isn't it?" He turned to Becky. "At least you do, right?"

"Of course," she murmured.

"So you'll help me convince her?" Ted asked.

Becky's gaze darted to Dino's alert face and then back to Ted. She stopped twirling her glass and squared her shoulders. "What Martha really wants," she said, "is to have a few more wins with the horses Malcolm bred."

"That's ridiculous." Ted snorted. "We already saw Hunter in action. How many more debacles do we need? I question your nursing competence, Becky."

"Easy," Dino said.

One word, but Ted immediately paused. "You must understand," he shot Dino a wary look and lowered his voice, "Uncle Malcolm had a dream but so does every owner. There's no reason to believe this crop of horses is any better than last year's. Aunt Martha shouldn't waste any more time. I really thought she'd be more sensible after that animal's performance yesterday."

Dino crossed his arms, his shirt tightening. He must go to a gym or carry a lot of water buckets. It was clear he was more than capable of keeping puny nephews in line, and also clear he wouldn't let Ted ride roughshod over anyone. Earlier he'd even stopped Ted from scolding the cook.

"I do understand your concern," Dino said, his voice surprisingly amiable, "but not your authority. I work for Martha, not you. And she has some promising horses that I intend to race. And win."

"Then it's both your fault if the old lady keels over," Ted snapped.

Becky's hand jerked, splattering red wine over the tablecloth, and Dino shot her a reassuring smile. However, when he looked back at Ted, his voice was as tight as his arms.

"I realize Martha suffered a heart attack, but she's agreed not to watch any more races. Besides, she's already selected a very competent stand-in." His gaze met hers again, and his mouth curved in that irrepressible smile. He even gave her a conspiratorial wink.

She smiled back, suddenly very glad he was here.

"Excuse me, please." He pulled out his phone, frowning as he checked a text message. He abruptly rose from the table. "Sorry, I have to go. Loose horse. Slim just noticed the empty stall." He paused, his enigmatic gaze settling on her face. "Are you coming? So you can report to Martha?"

"What? Oh, of course. Good night, Ted." She shoved her chair back and bolted after Dino, glad for any excuse that kept her from being stuck alone with Martha's nephew. "What horse is loose?" she asked, trying to keep up as he strode down the hall to the foyer.

"Lyric."

"But I'm sure I closed the door..." Her voice trailed off in dismay.

"You weren't the last person in her stall," Dino said. "I helped Slim and Stephanie with night feed." He swung the heavy door open with easy strength. "And I know I shut it," he said grimly.

Dino flicked on his high beams, scanning the sides of the road as he searched for movement. Most loose horses would hang around the barn, looking for a way into the feed room, but Lyric had always been a rebel. She'd escaped one other time and been caught two miles away, dangerously close to the highway. He squeezed the steering wheel, trying to block images of a horse loose in traffic. Martha didn't need any tragic accidents.

He glanced sideways. Becky—Ted had distinctly called her that—was perched on the edge of the passenger seat, face pressed against the side window. At least she provided another set of eyes. He hadn't the heart to leave her alone with that prick, Ted. She'd drained her wine as though it were water and clearly been uneasy throughout dinner, although she'd had the guts to defend Martha's interests.

Ted was a manipulative asshole and to blame a well-meaning nurse for Martha's declining health was petty and cruel. He couldn't condone petty and cruel. "See anything yet?" he asked, realizing his passenger hadn't spoken a word since she'd scrambled into his truck.

"Nothing yet, but at least she's white."

"Technically, the mare's gray," he teased, trying to loosen her up. "White thoroughbreds are rare."

Her head swiveled in the darkened truck, and she stared at him through the gloom. "She looked quite white to me."

"Her muzzle and the tips of her ears are black so she's considered a gray."

"Okay," she said. "But I'm still looking for a white shape in the dark."

He smiled despite his anxiety, relieved to hear her lilting amusement and happy that she would actually talk to him a bit. His good humor remained when they reached the pulsing interstate and saw no sign of a runaway horse, gray or white.

"Thank God," he said. "Doesn't look like she came this way. Slim and Stephanie probably caught her on the lower road."

"Dino..." Horror thickened Becky's voice, and he jerked around.

For a second he stopped breathing, his air escaping in a ragged hiss. Unless it was a moving rock, Lyric was grazing on the narrow median of the highway. He flipped on his emergency flashers, swerved up the ramp and jammed the truck onto the gravel. "Wave at the oncoming vehicles," he said. "Try to slow them down."

He grabbed a halter, clumsy with urgency. Pushed open the door, leaped over a soggy ditch and scrambled up the bank.

Cars rushed past in both directions, lights cutting the night, but thankfully there were no thundering transport trucks.

"Hey, girl," he said softly.

Lyric raised her head from the clover, blinking, as though surprised and not entirely happy to see him.

He tucked the halter behind his back and edged closer. "Good girl," he soothed.

She sidled away, dropping bits of grass in her hurry to escape.

He followed, talking softly, trying not to rush as a big truck rumbled over the hill. She was on the very edge of the median now, nose down, still hunting for the choicest morsels but prudently keeping her distance. Dammit. She'd never been an obliging horse.

The truck whizzed past. She didn't move and he exhaled a long breath. He circled, trying to herd her down the ramp, but the crafty mare pivoted and walked along the median, so nonchalant a stranger would assume she regularly grazed in the middle of the dark highway.

He edged closer, keeping his crooning low and unhurried. Only two feet away now, almost close enough to touch. But when he reached out, she snorted and wheeled, tail raising like a banner. A car whizzed past, noses pressed against the windows, and the driver...oh shit, no—

Honk!

Lyric flinched then bolted, kicking up clumps of grass as she galloped down the meridian and across the road. Hooves clacked on the concrete. A car swerved amid squealing brakes and stinking rubber. She vanished into the ditch.

A pickup skidded to a stop. "Need some help?" a man called as he flung open his door.

"Yeah. Loose horse," Dino said. "I'll try to herd her up the access road if you can block her from running back onto the highway."

The man said something, but Dino couldn't wait and scrambled back down the bank. A white shadow stood unmoving in the narrow ditch, barely twenty feet away. At least she'd stopped galloping and was off the road. Now he only had to keep her moving in the right direction.

"I've got her," a quiet voice said.

He paused, had forgotten all about Becky. She probably thought the mare would behave like an obedient dog off leash. He shook his head, fear making him impatient. "There's another guy coming to help. We're going to chase her down the road. Try to herd her toward the barn."

"But I've got her. I tied my shirt around her head. It has long sleeves."

He blinked, absorbing her words. The white shape hadn't moved so maybe Lyric really was caught. Hard to believe though. He edged closer, straining to see. Looked like a shirt was wrapped around her ears, across her nose, with a sleeve acting as a makeshift lead line. The perfect halter. Even better, the mare seemed submissive, as though she didn't intend to fight the restraint. But the shirt meant...

He edged around the mare, peering through the gloom. Yes, Becky's bra gleamed whitely in the night, a perfect match with the mare's coat. Surprisingly lovely breasts. He could see the swell—

He jerked his head back and whipped off his jacket. "Here. Put this on. I'll hold her. Good job," he added. "She's not an easy horse to catch."

"You caught that horse?" a concerned voice called from the top of the ditch.

"Yeah, buddy. Thanks for stopping." Dino stepped sideways, blocking the man's view of Becky, protective despite the darkness. The jacket rustled and he glanced down at her, dwarfed now in his dinner jacket. Even with heels, she only reached the top of his chest. Heels, and they had a two-mile hike.

"Can you drive a standard?" he asked as he slipped the halter on Lyric and untied the life-saving shirt.

"No."

"Then you'd better wait in the truck. It's quite a walk. I'll have Slim pick you up."

She clasped the jacket together with both hands and peered toward the highway, where several guffawing men had gathered. "I don't want to stay here." Her voice carried a note of panic. "I'd rather walk with you."

"Sure. Whatever you want." He passed her the twisted shirt.

"Thank you. For what you did. For using your shirt like that." He swallowed, shoving aside the image of her chest bared beneath the moonlight, exposed except for her bra. She always wore such baggy clothes. Weird she'd hide such lovely curves.

He turned Lyric and headed along the private road to the barn. Conscious of Becky's heels, he kept a slow speed. But the mare, ever perverse, chafed at the pace. Without racing or a foal, she was bored and a pain to handle. Probably needed some sort of job.

He glanced sideways. Becky hadn't complained but was clearly struggling to keep up. No doubt she'd have a few blisters by the end of this night. "Have you ridden before?" he asked.

"A bit. A while ago."

"Why don't you mount up? Give Lyric a job, seeing as her shenanigans dragged us out here."

He half expected a refusal, but the expression on her face was one of pure delight. She still clutched his jacket though, holding it together with one hand and gripping her rolled-up shirt in the other. Impossible to ride like that.

"Here. Stick your shirt in the pocket." He stopped the mare, reached over and buttoned the jacket, trying to ignore her sexy cleavage. "Now you don't have to hold it shut. It's dark anyway." But his voice thickened because it wasn't that dark, and there was something intimate and rather appealing about her being wrapped in his long jacket, smiling shyly as she awaited a boost.

He slid his hand along her leg, grabbed her knee and lifted her up. "Hold onto the mane," he said, impatient with his reaction. Thirty-two years old and he'd seen his share of bare skin. Besides, this lady was nothing like his usual girlfriends.

Lyric tossed her head as though protesting a rider but jigged for only a moment then settled into a long, ground-sweeping walk.

"Everything okay?" he asked, checking over his shoulder.

"Oh, yes." Her teeth flashed whitely. "This is lovely. Her back is nice and warm. And my feet don't hurt anymore."

And that was the most he'd ever heard her say. Friendly darkness always made women relax, something he'd learned when he was thirteen and had charmed the pants off Annabelle Lewis. Not that he was going to make a move on Becky. No way. But she definitely had plenty of spunk beneath that reserved exterior. What made her tick? She obviously had some experience with horses.

"Where did you learn to ride, Becky?"

Her throaty laugh surprised him. "Camp. And now my name is Becky, not Betty?"

He grinned in the direction of her flashing white teeth. "You're definitely a Becky. Bettys don't ride horses in the dark. With no shirt," he added.

"You have experience with that?"

"Some," he said candidly.

She turned silent. He assumed his honesty had sent her retreating into her shell but when he glanced back her face was lifted, eyes squeezed shut, and she was doing something with her arms. Raising them to the sky?

Her spontaneity was at such odds with her colorless appearance, he swallowed his chuckle and turned away, feeling like an intruder and not wanting to dampen her delight. She looked like a night pixie, and he completely understood her euphoria. It was always magical riding a good horse under the stars. Nothing matched it.

He stared straight ahead, conscious of her every motion but afraid she'd stop if he looked back. Flat, easy walking. A fat moon smudged the horizon, and the only sound was the rhythmic crunch of Lyric's hooves and Becky's soft, feminine breathing.

He didn't know how long he walked before she broke the silence.

"We used to sneak out and ride like this at camp. I think the counselors knew, but they never got mad."

"Your parents didn't have horses?" he asked.

"I didn't have parents." She spoke without pity, but there was a lifetime of sadness in her voice. "What about you? Always had animals?"

"Yeah. Grew up on a small ranch. Lots of work. Always wanted brothers and sisters to help with the chores. The best time of my life though. I love that place."

"Your parents still live there?"

"No, my ex does." Unlike Becky, he couldn't keep the bitterness from his voice. "Better hold onto the mane. A vehicle's coming."

Headlights pierced the dark. Lyric tensed then stumbled, and he tightened his hold on the lead as the truck rumbled alongside.

Slim lowered the window and stuck out his head. "You caught her. No problem?"

"Nope," Dino said. "How'd she get loose?"

"Don't know. Must have worked the latch free. I'll add a snap. You know what she's like."

"I know I don't want any more incidents like this." Dino spoke evenly, aware Becky was listening, all ears for Martha. The smell of diesel stained the air and Lyric pawed, impatient to keep moving. "We'll talk back at the barn," he added, tossing Slim his jangle of keys. "Ask Stephanie to pick up my truck. It's parked by the highway."

"Close call then?" Slim asked, his voice thick with emotion.

"Too close," Dino said.

CHAPTER SIX

Becky yawned, waiting while Dino bandaged Lyric's legs. The wine, food and adventure left her sleepy, but she didn't want the night to end. Riding a horse again had stoked her confidence, and it had been a treat walking under the stars, with only a beautiful horse and Dino's deep voice for company.

He was truly a nice man, she decided, as he wrapped the mare's legs in thick, blue bandages. Definitely not as scary as she'd first thought. In fact, he was easy to talk to, almost as easy as Martha, and in the dark she'd been able to forget he was so darn good looking.

Even without his hat he resembled a cowboy—or perhaps an outlaw—his hair a little too long. And the way those ripped arms worked over the mare's legs, his shirt hugging the ridges, well...she wouldn't have minded if the walk had lasted a few hours longer.

"There you go, sweetie."

The affection in his voice made her jerk to attention. She blinked with shock, then realized he was talking to Lyric.

"Come closer, Becky," he said over his shoulder. "I'll show you how to wrap. Martha will probably ask if her horses are bandaged for their workouts."

She stepped closer, glad he couldn't see her flush. Of course he wouldn't call her sweetie; she knew that.

"This is a standing wrap," he went on. "I rubbed her legs. Slim will remove them in the morning. We want to support her tendons after the adventure. Tomorrow you'll see five of Martha's horses on the track. Three of them will have rundown tapes but they'll be lower—see, down to here. They keep dirt from irritating the heels. What time are you coming?"

"What time does it start?" She hoped he'd say late morning.

"Training hours are six to ten. I usually take the young horses out first, but tomorrow I'll hold off for you."

She forced a nod. Lone Star Park was a forty-five minute drive from the Conrad Stable and she'd only been on the backside once before, with Martha and Malcolm. It had been a daunting place, full of brash men and brasher horses.

And this time she'd be alone. Fear wormed through her, and she fidgeted with a button on his too-large jacket, growing even more panicky when she realized her chest was exposed, almost to the top of her bra.

"Come by barn sixteen. But be there by seven at the latest," he said, seeming oblivious to the amount of skin she was showing. "There's an owner's pass in Martha's car. It will get you into the lot. Are you cold?"

His eyes narrowed on her jacket, *his* jacket actually, and she tugged it higher. She never showed cleavage, always covered herself to the neck.

She stepped back, face hot with embarrassment, and pulled her wrinkled shirt from the pocket. "I'm fine. I'll go put my shirt on and return your jacket."

"Don't rush on my account. It looks much nicer on you."

She flushed but there was nothing threatening in his voice, just a simple statement, maybe even a compliment. He smiled, not even looking at her chest, and slowly her fingers uncurled.

A truck roared outside, a door slammed, and they both turned. Seconds later, a bright blond head appeared in the aisle. Stephanie, but not dressed to ride. Tonight she wore black jeans and a scooped purple shirt that clung to her curves. *She* definitely wasn't shy about showing cleavage.

"Here're your keys, Dino." She tossed him a rattling key chain. "Looks like Lyric was lucky. We saw her tracks all over the median." She raised an amused eyebrow at Becky's clothes. "Guess Lyric wasn't the only one who got lucky."

"Actually Becky used her shirt to catch Lyric," Dino said. "And she may be working herself into a new job if my current staff can't keep the horses safe."

"Aw, I'm sorry." Stephanie's smile faded. "I don't think I left Lyric's door unlatched, but I was in her stall. I'm sorry," she repeated.

"Sorry doesn't help. There'll be a staff meeting, Wednesday at two. You'll also be seeing Becky around more often. Martha isn't well enough to watch the gallops, even on the training track, so she's taking Martha's place."

"I see." Stephanie shot Becky another curious glance. "Are you coming down here tomorrow? I'm galloping five, including Hunter."

"No," Becky said, "I'll be at Lone Star tomorrow."

"So Martha's real sick?" Stephanie tilted her head, eyes troubled.

"Her heart is weak," Becky admitted, "but she wants to keep the horses racing. Finish what Malcolm started."

"You could take a camera," Stephanie said. "Show her video and stuff so she feels closer to the action. That might help." She nodded at Becky's grateful smile then turned to Dino. "I'll wait for you at your place. You won't be long, will you?"

"No, Slim can drive Becky home. I'll be there in a few minutes."

Becky's smile slipped a notch, and she scratched Lyric's neck. She hadn't expected Dino to drive her home. It had already been a wonderful evening, and he deserved the company of a gorgeous lady like Stephanie.

However some of the magic faded from the night, and she was relieved only Lyric could see her forlorn face.

CHAPTER SEVEN

The screech of whinnying horses blasted through Becky's bedroom, yanking her from a deep sleep. She groaned and jammed a pillow over her head.

Martha thought it fitting that Becky use Malcolm's shockingly loud alarm clock. "It gives the proper start to an exciting horse day," she'd said. But the shrill horse calls were more jarring than any buzzer, and it didn't feel like a good way to start any sort of day.

Becky stumbled from the bed, found the relentless clock and flipped the switch. Five-thirty. Dino wanted her at the track by seven. Time for a quick shower and a check of the nurses' rotation. She'd munch an apple in the car.

Thirty minutes later and freshly woken by the shower, she poked her head in Martha's bedroom. A sleepy-eyed nurse padded to the door. "Don't worry," the nurse whispered. "Deb is on days this month. Mrs. Conrad will be fine."

Becky nodded in relief. Deb was one of Martha's favorites—or at least one she tolerated with minimal criticism. She backed from the bedroom, grabbed her camera and some fruit, and slipped into the Mercedes.

The drive was mainly interstate, and she reached Lone Star in forty minutes, following directions already programmed into the GPS. The sharp-eyed guard in the security booth checked the owner's tag dangling from the mirror and moments later she crunched onto the graveled lot of the backside.

So far, so good. She cracked open the car door, her confidence stalling as she peered through the misty dawn. Rows of barns extended in orderly lines and a string of horses pranced along a walkway. A man with wet jeans led a dripping horse in circles. A boy whizzed past on a rusty bike, headset clamped to his ears and singing fearlessly.

People and horses bustled in all directions. Even the animals seemed to know where they were going. She sucked in a resolute breath and grabbed her jacket, forcing herself to leave the cocoon of the car. Spring mornings were cool so she had an excuse to bundle up. She zipped the jacket to her neck.

Mud squelched as she edged along the row of barns, checking the numbers posted at the end of each door. Two, five, six—at least she was going the right way. A horse and rider trotted past. She stepped back, unsure if the rider was too busy to give directions.

"*Buenos dias*," someone called and she jerked sideways but they weren't talking to her. In fact, no one seemed concerned with her presence. Slowly the tightness in her shoulders eased.

A man in a cowboy hat sauntered past with a steaming coffee and a friendly smile.

"Can you point me in the direction of barn sixteen?" she asked, staring wistfully at his coffee.

"Dino Anders' barn? Sure." He jerked a thumb over his shoulder. "Four down on your right. The one with the big green hammock."

"Thank you," she said, continuing in the direction of his thumb jab and wondering where he had bought that big coffee.

And there it was. Barn sixteen. Two horses circled on a mechanical contraption with protruding arms. A groom led another horse around a ring of sawdust. Bright flowerpots hung from hooks on the side of the barn, and an orange clothesline sagged with wet bandages. A wide hammock stretched invitingly between two trees. No sign of Dino.

She slowed, not sure now where to go. But at that instant, Dino stepped outside, looking like an old friend in a strange land, and her heart thumped with relief.

"Hi, Becky. Ten to seven. You're on time." He smiled with approval. "We've got five of Martha's ready now so we can walk over to the gap."

"What's the gap?" she asked, trying not to gawk, but his denim shirt clung to his broad shoulders and she didn't want to look too closely at his lean hips, at the thick leather belt and rugged buckle. My God, he was sexy. It was surprising the girls here managed to do any work.

"The gap is where the horses go on the track," he said. "This way."

He'd already turned and headed along the road so she rushed after him. His stride was long, and he didn't seem inclined to slow but his very purposefulness put her at ease. She was huffing when they reached the track. It was a lot of walking to watch a bunch of horses gallop.

She glanced across the infield. From this side the clubhouse looked tiny, but the horses and people seemed bigger, more real. Like she'd slipped through a secret door and now peered through the back of a mirror.

Horses pranced through a gap onto the oval and she was close enough to reach out and touch each gleaming coat. Emotions were palpable—the focus of the riders, the optimism as each handler released their horse, the concentration of the trainers. Several people lounged at the rail, many empty-handed but some with notebooks and cameras. The air on this side was even different, and the primal smell zapped her with bone-deep excitement.

"Wow," she breathed, sucking it all in.

Dino glanced down. His eyes were shaded by his cowboy hat, but his smile was slow and understanding. He turned to his horses and called out a change of instructions. She watched, transfixed, as fearless riders guided their charges around the oval. Some horses squealed and bucked when they first entered the track. Others trotted off in workmanlike fashion, and another tossed his head up and down as though his mouth hurt. Each horse acted differently, wrapped in their own personality. She was so enthralled she forgot her own nervousness, forgot her numbing attraction to Dino, forgot even to ask which horses were Martha's.

"That's one of ours coming now," Dino said. "I'm trying to teach him to run straight. He's green and lugged out his last start."

The rider flagged the horse's outside eye with his stick—it seemed the colt was running straight as an arrow. She turned and looked at Dino. "That looks pretty good, doesn't it?"

"Not bad," he said with a smile. "Now watch the chestnut. She's been sticky about switching leads. Cost her a win last month."

Becky leaned over the rail, studying the chestnut and the beautiful symmetry of her slim legs. She hadn't realized race riders worried about which leg was leading, but obviously horses stayed balanced and would run more efficiently if they could change leads on cue. "How does the jockey get a lead change?" she asked.

"Weight shift," Dino said. "Or sometimes a tap on the shoulder."

And there it was. The chestnut switched leads and ran the turn like a train, like a big, unstoppable express train. "This seems like a very good training day." She tilted her head, smiling impulsively at Dino, unable to curb her enthusiasm.

"Yeah, this is a pretty good day. But you never know with horses. Sometimes they regress. Hunter had been scorching around the track. I was positive he'd win Sunday." He gestured over his shoulder. "Want to go the kitchen and grab breakfast?"

"Definitely," she said quickly. She hadn't realized there was a restaurant on the backside, but it was a sure bet they served something tastier than green tea and apples. Must have been where that man had bought his coffee. This day was getting better and better.

They walked along the gravel road, past lines of sweaty horses and smiling grooms. Several people called out Spanish greetings, and it was clear Dino was well liked and not just by women. She swerved to avoid a puddle, and he casually looped his arm around her waist and steered her onto dry ground.

"Watch your step," he said, keeping his hand on her hip.

She stared straight ahead, trying to act casual, trying to ignore the heat of his fingers but was so acutely aware of his touch she could barely breathe. And then they passed the puddle and he lowered his arm, and she really wished he had driven her home last night.

"Did you get up early and drive in?" she asked, thinking of Stephanie.

"Yeah. Usually when I train at Lone Star, I stay in my apartment, but there's been a lot of upheaval since Malcolm died. Slim and I are still working things out. That's the kitchen."

He gestured at a square building with a long walkway. Luxury cars and dented trucks were crammed, side-by-side, in a small parking lot. Dino opened the door, and she stepped past him into a room bursting with Stetsons, conversation and a sizzling grill.

A dark-haired lady with a purple riding vest paused by the door. "It's Monty's birthday tonight. You coming by the bar?" She shot Becky a curious glance.

"Yeah, Angie, I'll be there." Dino barely paused as he scooped up a tip sheet and angled into the food lineup. "What would you like?" he asked Becky.

"Coffee, scrambled eggs and bacon, white toast, please." She fumbled for her money, trying not to stare as Angie swung the door shut. The woman was gorgeous with a graceful neck and exotic eyes. If she were a foot taller, she'd be a good candidate for a super model.

Dino's warm fingers covered her hand. "Put your money away. I've got it," he said, his attention on a comment in the tip sheet. "Code Hunter throws a clunker that's typical of stable," he recited. He crumpled the sheet in a ball and tossed it into a waste bin. "Christ, don't let Martha see that," he added, still scowling. "Where will you be for Saturday's race?"

Becky's face flamed. He didn't realize he was still holding her hand, but his touch made her skin tingle. "Don't I have to sit in the owner's box?" she asked.

"Not if you don't want to." He dropped his hand, turned his attention to the cook and rattled off a slew of Spanish. Said something that made the cook laugh, then turned back to her. "You can watch from the rail with me. I only go up to the box for Martha."

"Okay." Her chest warmed with relief. She wouldn't have to listen to stiff conversation by status-conscious people; she'd be able to get close to the horses. And she'd be with Dino. Suddenly Saturday seemed a very long wait.

"The rail it is then," he said. "And if we win, it's easier to walk to the winner's circle."

She nodded happily, not even trying to flatten her smile. "How many of Martha's horses are running?"

"Two. Echo, the filly you saw galloping yesterday, is in the feature race. There's also a cheaper allowance horse running. Not a homebred." Someone called a greeting and he waved, then glanced back at her. "We'll haul in the morning of the race. Echo gets worked up when she's away, and Malcolm always wanted her to sleep at home."

"I can understand that," she said. "Sleeping in a strange place would make me edgy too."

"Luckily some girls don't mind." He grinned as he passed the cashier some crumpled bills.

There was no doubt what he meant, and she waited for a jolt of discomfort. Surprisingly it didn't come. Her mind felt sharp too, not tangled with anxiety. Odd. Sexual innuendoes by men who looked and talked like Dino usually turned her into a mute rock.

She placed some napkins on the tray, waiting while he talked with the cashier. He was nice to everyone. Really nice too, no cheesy smile or fake interest. He actually wanted that cashier to have a nice day.

He carried the tray to a table. She quickly added some milk to her coffee and followed. After a childhood of bare necessities, she'd always appreciated food, and everything here smelled wonderful. Probably had been a year since she'd enjoyed a big breakfast—Martha was on such a strict diet that green tea and dark bread were standard fare.

She sat down, taking a moment to savor her heaping plate— the fluffy eggs, crisp bacon and toast soaked in butter. White bread too, not a grain in sight.

Dino generously laced his eggs with salsa. "Nice to see you know how to eat. I usually feel like a pig around women."

"I hear you are," she said, then froze in horror, shocked by her impulsive words. She, who was never impulsive. *Please, God. Maybe he didn't hear me.*

But he stopped dumping salsa on his eggs and his eyes narrowed. "What did you say?"

"Nothing," she mumbled, pretending absorption in the packet of strawberry jam. "Want any jam?"

"What did you say?" he repeated.

His voice lowered and she shot a quick look at his face. He wore his tough look now, the one that had made Ted quail, and she wanted to sink through the floor.

"I believe you called me a pig," he said softly. "I'd like to know what you mean."

Her chest tightened but oddly the wave of panic she'd expected didn't come. He wouldn't hurt her, and it wasn't just because they were in a public place. She still felt comfortable with him even though she'd obviously annoyed him. But how could she admit she was bothered by Stephanie, Angie, and even the spike-haired woman at the next table who eyed him like he was an item on the menu?

"I'm really sorry." She took a nervous sip of coffee. "Actually what I meant was that I'm a food pig and I can't wait to eat." She picked up her toast, unable to meet his eyes. "Gosh, this looks good. It's been a while since I had a real breakfast."

"Martha's rich as Croesus and doesn't feed you?"

She nodded eagerly, glad they were on a safer topic. "I live in her house. It's only fair I eat and drink the same food."

He raised an eyebrow. "I doubt Martha drinks a bottle of wine every night."

"I only drank a lot because Ted was there," she admitted. "He makes me nervous."

"But I don't? And *I'm* the pig?"

She blew out a sigh. He was a smart guy and obviously wasn't easily distracted. "Well, there are all kinds," she said, her mind scrambling.

"Like what?" His hand covered hers.

She wiggled in the chair but at least he was smiling again, as though amused by her discomfort. Unfortunately the touch of his hand sent her senses blasting into overdrive.

"Before you eat, let's hear it," he added. "What kind of pig am I?"

He'd tilted forward. She stared at his beautiful mouth but couldn't formulate any words, and her pulse pounded so erratically beneath his thumb, he had to feel it. "A woman pig," she squeaked.

He stared at her for a long moment. His thumb stroked the back of her wrist and she was certain he wasn't even aware of it. He followed her gaze, quickly released her hand and leaned back. "I like women," he said. "Doesn't make me a pig." He didn't seem annoyed or even fazed; if anything, he looked confused.

"Guess the definition depends on numbers. Like did you sleep with more than one woman in the past month?" She smiled, surprised she was able to tease. "Maybe more than two?"

"Eat your food," he said, no longer meeting her eyes. And she could have sworn she'd made him blush.

Dino strolled down the raked aisle, checking every stall, enjoying the orderly atmosphere. All the horses looked healthy, eyes and coats gleaming as they tugged at their noon hay. Good appetites meant happy horses. They'd been happy on the track too.

Becky would only have positive things to report to Martha. She'd been surprisingly observant. Had even noticed the head-tossing gelding, something Suzy had missed. He paused and turned back to the groom who lingered in the gelding's stall. "Suzy, vet's coming by tomorrow," he said. "Might be wolf teeth. Next time your horse is uncomfortable with the bit, check his mouth."

"Sorry, boss. I should have noticed. He was hard to bridle too." She flipped her ponytail over her shoulder and stepped up to the front of the stall. "Was that Mrs. Conrad's granddaughter with you earlier?"

"No, that's Becky, her rep. She'll be coming by the track a bit."

"Then the rumors are true? Conrad stable is for sale?"

"Not yet. Not if we please Becky."

"Oh, we're good then." Suzy's face brightened with relief. "You're the perfect man for that job."

"What do you mean?"

"You know." She giggled, smoothing her T-shirt. "You're real popular with women."

He scowled. First Becky. Now Suzy. Unbelievable. Since his divorce, he'd enjoyed many women, but he didn't consider himself a hound. And he was always honest, always kept it casual and never, ever dated anyone who worked for him.

He dragged his hand over his jaw. At least he never dated anyone like Suzy, not girls who worked directly for him. Maybe there'd been a few who worked indirectly with him. Yes, Stephanie worked for Conrad Stables, and there had been Greta and a few other nurses. But they didn't work for him. And it had been fun on both sides. No promises, no commitment. He was careful to avoid needy or bitchy women. One disastrous marriage was quite enough.

Suzy flashed a knowing smile, and his scowl deepened.

"That bucket is dirty and there's a manure stain on your horse's belly." His voice flattened. "And soak his hay. You should always do that when a horse has a sore mouth."

She ducked her head, color climbing her neck, and he felt like he'd just scolded a puppy. But damn it, she was barely twenty. What did she know? Still, Becky had accused him of being a pig, only hours earlier, and she was plenty observant. She didn't talk much, but he could see the wheels moving behind those intelligent brown eyes.

She'd loosened up too and turned into a real chatterbox, at least around him. He'd been slightly disappointed when she left after breakfast although the prospect of her visits had originally left him resentful.

Lyric's night rescue must have cracked her shyness. Clearly she'd enjoyed being on the mare's back. It was crazy she couldn't ride regularly, especially since Martha's manor was surrounded by horses. Actually there was no reason why she couldn't ride Lyric. The mare was always well behaved in the paddock.

Besides, with Echo racing in a week, he intended to spend more time at the Conrad barn. He could help Becky with the first couple of rides. Smooth her way with Slim. The man was a capable horseman but sometimes resented visitors—clearly he also felt pressure to win. It didn't help that Ted was pushing Martha to sell. But a good race from Echo would improve everyone's mood. Improve everyone's finances too.

He continued his barn check, stopping to adjust a sagging hay net and wishing Hunter had performed better. There would have been a lot less pressure if the colt had won. He was confident in his training program and accepted that horses were rarely predictable. But it was disconcerting that his hopes of regaining the family ranch now depended upon a flighty filly and the reports of a bashful, brown-eyed nurse.

CHAPTER EIGHT

"You shouldn't have rushed back," Martha said as Becky fluffed the pillows, propping them behind Martha's head. "I happen to know Dino is excellent company."

Becky tidied the already immaculate bedside table, conscious of Martha's probing eyes. "Yes, he's good company but I thought you'd want to hear about your horses."

"Of course I do," Martha said. "What did you think?"

"Dino's barn is well kept, clean and even more organized than the barn he manages here. All the horses look great. I saw five on the track today, including the two names you wrote on the list. Three wore rundown bandages. One of them has a sore mouth but they all galloped well, really well."

"Who has the sore mouth?"

"The bay gelding that's a half brother to Hunter. Dino says it's wolf teeth and told someone called Shane to call the vet."

"Shane is Dino's assistant, another nice man." Martha reached over and squeezed Becky's hand. "I appreciate you checking the horses, and it's good for you to get out. You need to find a real life, especially since I won't be around much longer."

Becky's throat constricted so tightly she couldn't speak, could only pat Martha's hand. "You have lots more time," she finally managed. "A little heart attack but you're only seventy-four. You just have to be cautious. And I brought some pictures and video and on Saturday, I'm going to figure out how to place a bet for you."

"Video isn't the same as being at the races." Martha sighed in frustration. "I'm supposed to rest but it's boring in the house. Malcolm and I used to drive around, checking the grounds before going to the track."

"Would you like to go for another drive around the estate?" Becky asked. "Maybe check out the pastures and the training barn? We could visit Hunter. And Lyric."

A smile creased Martha's face. "You like Lyric, don't you? Did you know Dino called half an hour ago? Suggested you be allowed to ride that mare."

Becky's eyes widened. It had been a rare day of fun to leave the estate and join Dino at the track. And now he was arranging for her to ride Lyric, the most beautiful horse in the barn. She clasped her hands, trying to maintain her composure, trying to concentrate on what Martha was saying.

"Give you a chance to ride." Martha said. "So, do you want to ride with Dino once in a while?"

"Ride with D-Dino?" Her voice cracked, and heat rushed to her cheeks as she stared at Martha. Not only ride beautiful Lyric but accompanied by Dino? Not Slim. She must be hallucinating.

"Guess you won't have to watch me nap anymore." Martha smiled ruefully. "I can't think of a nicer man to go riding with. He put a smile on Greta's face too. But do be careful, dear."

Becky realized she was gaping and snapped her mouth shut. She had to say something though and prayed her tone was casual enough to fool Martha. "Don't worry," she said. "I'd never fall for anyone like Dino. I'm not his type, completely the opposite of Greta."

"You mumble a bit and certainly hide behind that mane of hair. But a cut and highlights would help." Martha leaned forward, staring at Becky's face. "Your eyebrows need shaping as well. And makeup—a lady should always wear makeup. But your bone structure is okay. And you do have lovely hands."

Becky smiled despite her thrust of pain. Even Martha—who liked her—thought her plain. And that was a good thing. Exactly what she wanted. It was best not to draw attention, and Lyric certainly didn't care about her looks.

She glanced down, ruefully waggling her fingers. At least Martha said she had good hands. For riders, those were more important than a pretty face.

Becky stared over the lonely oval. "The track looks deserted."

"It is deserted," Martha said. "Horses are trained in the morning. They're used to a schedule. Grooms leave about eleven and return at four, but Slim is generally around."

"Can we take a look at Lyric?" Becky asked. "And of course Hunter and Echo too," she added, realizing Martha was more interested in her racehorses than the retired mare.

"I own this place," Martha said. "We can do whatever we want. But park close to the front door or else drive around to the side entrance. I don't want to walk far, and those clouds look like rain."

Becky edged the car close to the front door. She supported Martha as she inched from her seat, and they entered the barn at a sedate pace. The aisle was spotless but empty. Horses poked heads over their stall guards, studying them with hopeful interest.

"That looks new." Martha pointed to a shiny snap that reinforced the bolt on Lyric's stall. "She escaped once last year and almost caused an accident. Malcolm said she's a magnet for trouble. I'm glad Slim is being careful."

Becky averted her head. She hadn't told Martha about the mare's latest escapade, deciding it would only cause unnecessary worry. It was unfortunate that Lyric—the horse most likely to head to the highway—had managed to get loose, but tragedy had been averted.

Lyric nickered and Becky stepped closer, pleased the mare remembered her. "I'm going to ride you, beautiful," she murmured. "I'll brush you and learn how to wrap your legs, and maybe you won't want to run away."

"Let's visit another stall. Lyric nips." Martha gestured impatiently. "Echo and Hunter are our best horses. I pray Echo runs well on Saturday."

Becky gave Lyric an apologetic pat then supported Martha's elbow as they shuffled to Echo's stall. The filly nudged Martha's hand, clearly anticipating a treat.

"Malcolm and I always brought peppermints." Martha's sad smile twisted at Becky's chest. "We used to visit them everyday, just the two of us. Such fun." She propped her purse on top of a hay bale and shuffled through the contents, finally extracting two pink mints which the filly deftly lifted from her hand. "Please win on Saturday, girl. Help justify this place. Ted promised he'd help look after things, but his insistence on selling is wearisome."

Becky's throat tightened. Martha sounded so vulnerable; the heart attack she'd suffered following Malcolm's death had definitely changed her psyche. Ted shouldn't be pushing her so hard. He never would have dared if Malcolm were alive...or if Martha was her usual domineering self. Becky knew she was only a nurse, knew it was safer not to get involved, but she'd never been able to turn away from someone in need.

"From now on," anger thickened Becky's voice, "I'm going to speak up when Ted is pushy. I won't be quiet."

Martha gave a wan smile and continued down the aisle, seeming to be amused by Becky's impulsive declaration. They both knew her habit was to duck confrontation.

Hunter stuck his head out, not deigning to look at them, but instead staring over their heads. That horse didn't duck from anything. Despite losing on Saturday—losing badly—he clearly still considered himself king of the barn.

He didn't smell like a king though. Becky wrinkled her nose, distracted by the odor. "He looks good, but he doesn't smell like the other horses," she said.

"I don't notice anything," Martha said. "Probably he's on a different type of feed."

Becky didn't say anything more, just took Martha's arm and helped her shuffle down the aisle. But she didn't think the smell clinging to Hunter was feed related. It reeked like something bad, something rotten.

"I'm sorry, Ted." Becky gripped the phone, enunciating clearly into the mouthpiece. "Martha has retired for the evening. She won't be able to see you until Sunday either, the day after the race. You're welcome to leave any documents with Jocelyn. But as you noted, Martha needs rest. That's why her bedroom is now off-limits to everyone but medical staff."

Becky moved the phone six inches from her head, enjoying Martha's delighted smile as they both listened to Ted rant about overstepping nurses and their fragile job security.

Once he slowed, Becky pressed the phone back to her ear, recalling Dino's rationale. "Actually my job is to look after your aunt," she said. "I regret you don't approve but *she* pays my salary, not you. See you on Sunday." She snapped the phone shut, blew out a big breath and sank into the closest chair.

"Well done. Surprisingly well done." Martha settled against the pillows with a complacent smile. "Thank you. He won't be able to complain after Echo wins on Sunday. You were quite brave. I know that was difficult for you."

"I'm braver on the phone," Becky admitted. "It's tougher to look someone in the face. Especially someone with pale eyes like Ted's."

"Why's that?"

"Beats me." Becky rose and circled to the medication table.

"Then just look at his forehead," Martha said.

"What?"

"If people's eyes intimidate you, just look at their forehead."

"That might help." Becky nodded. "Thanks."

"After seventy-four years, you learn a few tricks." Martha waved her hand in dismissal, but pleasure flushed her cheeks. "Now pass me my purse. I want to bet a few dollars. I'm also going to call Dino and remind him Echo absolutely must win."

Becky reached for the purse. She'd been thinking of Dino all evening, wondering where he was, what he was doing. Martha might even ask her to make the call, and if so, she wanted to thank him for arranging the rides on Lyric. She paused, her arm outstretched.

Martha's purse was missing.

She sighed and lowered her arm. "Sorry, but I think your purse is still in the barn. By Echo's stall."

"Will you get it for me?" Martha's voice fluttered with agitation. "I'm sure the workers are all very honest. However, a lonely purse is tempting."

"Sure." Becky turned toward the door. "Be back in fifteen minutes."

She hurried to the garage and backed out the Mercedes. Raindrops pelted the windshield and she adjusted the wipers, craning to see the dark road through the beading water. Vapor lights lined all the Conrad roads but, although decorative, the white light wasn't very functional.

The trip to the barn usually took a quick four minutes, but tonight the drive seemed foreign in the soggy darkness. She parked near the back of the barn which had a shorter walk to the side door and less chance of being drenched. Hopefully the staff door wasn't locked.

She closed the car door, ducking her head from the stinging rain, and splashed toward the barn. The slick knob stalled for a moment, then turned beneath her hand. She slipped inside.

It was pitch dark, and she fumbled for a switch, trying to remember the layout. Feed room, office and bathroom were on her right and past that were the long rows of stalls. Only about ten feet through the blackness, and she'd be in the aisle with its friendly night lights.

Cautiously she edged along the wall, hand extended, still feeling for a switch. Felt nothing except the rough wall. Didn't matter though. She'd almost reached the corner and the muted lights of the aisle.

"Should have fucking killed you."

Her heart thrust against her ribs. She froze. Obviously a joke. Sounded like Slim, but those furious words had to be a mistake. She peeked around the corner, straining to see and blinking at the sudden light.

Slim stood in the aisle, legs jammed wide. He held a bay horse—Hunter. She recognized the colt's expression, still imperious despite the chain twisted over the top of his tender gums. Slim poked at the horse's left nostril with what seemed to be a wire with a light on the side.

Uncertain, she backed against the wall, nervously tucking her wet hair behind her ears. Nobody else was around this time of night so whatever Slim was doing, he clearly believed he could doctor the colt alone.

Or else he didn't want anyone to see.

The thought crept into her brain, unwelcome and chilling. She backed up, legs stiff as she fumbled along the wall, silently retracing her steps. Finally the door handle poked her back. She scooted outside and retreated to the security of her warm car. Hit central lock and sank against the seat.

One thing was certain. She did not want to walk into the barn now. The purse would be safe until morning. But if she didn't return with it, Martha was bound to fret.

A drop of water trickled down her forehead. Maybe she could wait for Slim to leave and then grab it. However, if he saw her car, he'd wonder why she was sitting alone in the dark. And probably he was just checking Hunter's runny nose. Yesterday there had been discharge, and today there'd definitely been a rotten smell. If he was looking for infection, she should offer to help or at least make her presence known. But she'd enter through the front door. Let him know she was coming.

Yes, that's exactly what she'd do. Slim probably wasn't doing anything wrong, and besides, she was tired of tiptoeing around men.

Pumping up her resolve, she started the car and circled to the front. Parked beside the wide doors and made a show of backing up. Slow, awkward, slow. Made sure Slim could see her flashing red lights. But her heart didn't slow; in fact, it raced. Probably caused by the cold rain but she prudently slipped the phone in her pocket before unlocking the car door and entering the barn.

"Hello," she called, hating the tentative squeak in her voice. "Anyone here?"

Slim materialized in the aisle, his voice gruff. "Yeah. What'cha doing here so late?"

"Martha forgot her purse. Did you see it?"

"No." He immediately turned helpful. "Where'd she leave it?"

"On the hay by one of the stalls. Hunter's, I think," she added impulsively, watching his expression.

"I haven't been by his stall," Slim said, averting his head. "Just dropped in to check Lyric. Make sure she doesn't escape again."

Becky shoved her hands in her pocket, disturbed by his blatant lie. The feel of her phone was reassuring, and she forced a tight smile. "Okay, I'll go look." She stepped past him, forcing her feet to walk nonchalantly down the aisle.

Horses stuck their heads over stall doors, acting the same as they had a few hours ago, but now the barn felt creepy. And Slim's shadowing steps made the back of her neck prickle. Whatever he'd done to Hunter, he obviously didn't want anyone to know. He'd waited until the barn staff had left, had even lied about being near Hunter's stall. Her legs turned cold, clumsy, and when Lyric greeted her with a soft nicker, she paused, grateful for the excuse to quit walking.

"There it is." Slim pointed at the purse lying on the hay bales between Lyric and Echo's stalls. "Thought you said it was by Hunter?"

"I can't tell the horses apart." She shrugged and grabbed the purse, tucking it beneath her arm. "Where's Hunter again?"

"Further down."

She scanned the aisle, her gaze swinging toward the back entrance. The area that she'd been standing in was definitely shadowed. No way Slim could have seen her. And the sound of the rain had surely muffled her car.

"Why is Hunter the only horse to have his halter on?" she asked, careful to keep her voice casual.

"It shouldn't be." Slim walked toward Hunter's stall. "Damn Cody forgot to take it off. I'll get it."

Hunter flattened his ears and struck at the stall door as they approached, the noise so sharp, she flinched. His ears pinned and his eyes rimmed with white.

"He looks mad," she said. "Usually he just ignores people."

Slim's gaze sharpened on her face. "Thought you couldn't tell the horses apart?"

"I can't," she said. "I've just never seen any of these beautiful animals so angry." She edged away from Hunter's teeth, trying not to wrinkle her nose at the unpleasant smell. Besides, Slim was still staring and it seemed a good time to skedaddle. She focused on a brown spot on the left side of his forehead, just below the rim of his cowboy hat, relieved to avoid his squinty eyes. "Glad I found the purse. Martha's waiting so guess I'll see you tomorrow. What time does Stephanie gallop?"

"Late. Nine-thirty. Dino wants to watch too." Resentment flashed across his face, but she didn't want to stay and analyze. She just wanted to leave.

She backed up, nodding every step, then turned and rushed down the endless aisle, away from Hunter. Away from Slim. Everything was fine. No need to hurry. But she felt Slim's narrowed gaze pinned to her back and by the time she reached the door, she was almost running.

CHAPTER NINE

Dino adjusted the speaker on his truck phone as he finished rattling off instructions to Shane. "Soak his foot and have the farrier put on some bar shoes. Horse can walk the shedrow for the next few days."

He cut the connection and concentrated on the flowing traffic, satisfied with the morning training. He'd left Lone Star earlier than usual so he could whip down to Conrad's and watch Echo work. And if Becky dropped by, he'd have time to give her a quick lesson.

Judging from her bareback ride, she had good balance but it was probably safest if she stayed in the paddock. Lyric hadn't raced for several years and was often cantankerous. However, there was no reason why staff shouldn't enjoy a retired horse. It'd be good for the mare, and Becky needed a break from her boring life in Martha's mausoleum. He'd already glimpsed the personality she kept under careful wrap, and there was a lot more spirit there than he'd originally guessed.

Martha had been keen on Becky riding too, although she wouldn't tolerate any accidents. "Becky's much more than my nurse," she'd said, "and I won't be happy if she's not around to cater to me."

Selfish old harridan, he thought with affection. At first he'd considered the flamboyant Martha and self-effacing Becky to be an unlikely pair, but Becky definitely had a spicy side. Getting to know her was like peeling an onion. He had an abrupt image of peeling clothes and shook his head in disgust. She already thought he was a sex addict, and although he didn't usually give a rat's ass about people's opinions, he did care about Becky's.

He drove onto the luxurious Conrad estate, past the shimmering lake and along the tree-lined drive. The south road led to the broodmare barn, and the north curved to the race barn. The grounds were always impeccable. It was apparent there was no lack of groundskeepers. The race stable employed six workers, including Stephanie and Slim, but they only concentrated on the racehorses; the broodmares and grounds were someone else's responsibility.

"Shit!" He rounded a corner and jammed on his brakes, flinging up a spray of gravel and almost clipping a man draped over a tripod.

"Sorry. Didn't expect any cars," the man called from the middle of the road. "We're almost through. One more minute."

Dino nodded and checked his watch. Nine-thirty. Of course, Slim would wait, but Dino hated to upset a training schedule. And lately Slim had been prickly. Obviously he missed Malcolm, probably more than Dino did.

The surveyor made a last adjustment, gave an apologetic wave and dragged his equipment over to a white panel van.

Dino lowered his window as he edged past. "Road work?"

"Just a cost estimate. They're widening the road for a golf course."

Dino jammed against the seat, shocked into silence. A golf course. Jesus. But it made sense. Vast property, lots of water, close to the city—probably more profitable than racing horses. But his stomach jerked in protest, and seconds later his shock morphed into anger.

Martha had assured him she wasn't selling, at least until after the Lone Star meet. He'd assumed there'd be plenty of opportunity to earn his bonus. Had even turned down another job offer, mainly because of her assurance as well as his promise to Malcolm. Big mistake. He rubbed his knuckles, fighting the urge to drive his fist into the steering wheel.

He'd miscalculated. Badly. Should have left when Malcolm died but had stayed with Martha out of misguided loyalty. Maybe that's why she'd sent Becky in her place. Maybe she was busy selling horses. Maybe Echo wasn't even running on Saturday.

Gravel ricocheted beneath the truck as he sped up the driveway and rammed to a stop by the barn. "Horse is tacked up," Slim called from the doorway. "Meet you at the rail."

Stephanie appeared, perched on Echo, and the filly looked so stunning, pride momentarily replaced Dino's frustration. Damn, but Malcolm bred good-looking horses. Too bad he wasn't still the owner. Too bad Martha and Becky couldn't tell the truth.

His scowl deepened as Becky emerged from the barn, obviously still pretending it was business as usual. She wore her typical baggy clothes, although today she seemed taller. Maybe it was her hair, no longer loose, but neatly captured in a ponytail, shiny and glinting beneath the sun. She was definitely the type of person who grew on you.

His scowl faded, the tension seeping from his shoulders. This shit wasn't her fault. But why the hell was Martha foisting Becky on him, wasting everyone's time, pretending she wanted to race even though surveyors were already hired?

Becky passed him a coffee, and he automatically nodded his thanks. Must be the nurse in her, wanting to look after everyone. And he did love a coffee by the rail, treasuring moments when he could relax and enjoy the simple beauty of a galloping horse.

"Thanks," he said, smiling in spite of his disappointment. "I brought something that will go well with this."

He reached into the cab and extracted a bag of cinnamon buns—something he'd picked up when he'd been in a better frame of mind. But her face lit with such delight, his mood softened. Quite likely she had no idea what Martha was planning.

"Oh, my gosh," she said. "That's great."

He smiled, momentarily forgetting Martha's treachery and his precarious employment. "There's enough for two each and if you're still hungry, you can have one of mine. Come on. Slim's waiting by the rail."

Her gaze darted to Slim, and she tugged nervously at her lower lip. "Can I talk to you in private? About Hunter?"

"Yeah, sure." He blew out a sigh, guessing she was going to announce Martha had a buyer for the colt. "But not yet. Tell me after." He grabbed her elbow and guided her to the rail, unwilling to hear bad news just before an important work.

"You all look like this is a party," Slim said, eyeing the brown bag. "Got one in there for me?"

Dino passed him a cinnamon bun. "Filly looks fit. You and Stephanie have done a good job."

Slim shrugged but his mouth curved in a rare smile, and they munched companionably beneath the rising sun. Stephanie trotted by, yelling something about bad calories, and Echo looked so eager Dino's tension eased. It was a beautiful morning and if the filly won on Saturday, Martha might decide to race the rest of the meet. A few good races and he'd have enough for the down payment. He just needed some time.

He glanced at Becky, watching as she licked some frosting from the top of her lip. "I'd give you another," he said, "but Lyric might complain if you weigh too much. Better save it for after your lesson."

Her head shot up, the glow on her face momentarily stunning him. Damn, she was pretty.

"I'm riding?" she asked. "Today?"

"Yeah," he said gruffly, still studying her face. "If you're free. Thought I could hang around and help."

"What about your horses at Lone Star?" Slim asked.

Dino dragged his gaze off Becky and glanced at Slim. "Shane has everything under control. He's almost as competent as you." He meant it as a compliment, but Slim didn't crack a smile.

"There is something I need your help with," Slim said slowly. "I asked the local vet to scope Hunter, but he put me off. Now I think Hunter's got some sort of cold. He won't let me handle him. I think he might need a round of antibiotics."

Dino stared at the man, too shocked to hide his anger. "Goddammit! You told me the vet checked that horse?"

"Got Hunter mixed up with the other colt that ran Saturday. Just a mistake. I'm real sorry."

Slim tugged at his hat, looking so embarrassed Dino bit back another curse. Slim rarely made a mistake. And the man was worried sick about his daughter; it was only fair to cut some slack. But if Hunter needed antibiotics, it would definitely delay his next start.

"I'll look at Hunter after the work," Dino said, his voice clipped. He clamped his jaw and glanced at Becky. Now that he was already pissed, he might as well get her bad news too. "What do you want to tell me about Hunter? Did Martha sell him?"

"Sell him? Of course not. I just had a question..." Her voice trailed off as she glanced at Slim.

"Okay, shoot."

She gripped her coffee and darted another look at Slim, so uneasy he was swept with a surge of protectiveness. Obviously she thought it was a stupid question and clearly was intimidated by Slim's presence.

"I remember now," Dino said smoothly. "You wanted to ask about riding out alone. Well, that's a definite no. But you can ride Lyric anytime as long as you stay in the paddock."

He winked, turning his back so Slim couldn't see, and she gave him such a grateful smile his chest swelled.

"Riding Lyric is a bad idea," Slim said.

Dino wheeled, irritated at the man's rudeness. "I think it's an excellent idea. And so does Martha." He hardened his stare until Slim averted his head. But then the galloping filly grabbed his attention, and he forgot about Slim as Stephanie cruised down the backside. He tilted his wrist, adjusting his stopwatch, his attention on the filly. Echo moved fluidly, ears pricked, as though awaiting a signal.

He'd told Stephanie to run when she hit the quarter pole, and they watched in silence as the filly reached the marker and took off.

Echo's neck extended, her stride lengthening. She carried her head unusually low when she ran, but it was clear she was keen to motor. Stephanie crouched over her withers, barely moving as the horse charged around the turn, hooves pounding as she straightened for home. A slight tap from Stephanie and she smoothly changed leads, hitting another gear and powering across the finish line.

Dino stopped his watch, staring with glee. "A shade over forty-eight. What did you get?" He looked at Slim who nodded in agreement, still studying his own stopwatch. "Perfect. Martha will like this." He turned to Becky who was still draped over the rail and staring at the receding filly. "What do you think?" he asked, unable to keep the satisfaction from his voice.

She looked at him with eyes that glowed. "I think Martha will be delighted. Echo looked so strong and happy to be running. Will Stephanie ride her on Saturday?"

"No. She quit jockeying after she had her baby. She's strictly an exercise rider now. Prefers the relaxed atmosphere here."

"She has a baby?" Becky asked. "Is she married?"

"Divorced."

He glanced down the track. Stephanie turned the filly and headed back, her smile unmistakable. A good sign. Steph was a savvy rider with great instincts and if she was happy with the horse, it boded well.

Usually it boded well. Stephanie had shared his opinion that Hunter would win last week, and they'd both been dead wrong about that one. He suppressed a spike of uncertainty.

Echo trotted up in a swirl of dust. "This filly's ready to fire a big one." Stephanie's breath came in short gasps as she unsnapped her helmet. "I want to send a bet down. I'm guessing we were bang on the forty-nine seconds you wanted."

"A little quicker actually," Dino said, "but it all looked good." Stephanie had a stopwatch in her head. The time was a bit faster then he expected, but the filly had galloped easy and would have plenty left for the race.

Slim looped his lead through the bridle and she vaulted off, while Echo pawed and jigged as though eager to run another quarter mile.

"Save your energy, girl." Dino patted her damp neck. "You'll need it for Saturday. Make sure she's on the grounds by seven on race day, Slim. I'll have a stall ready." He turned to Becky. "Want to tack up Lyric now?"

She nodded, her face still shining as she admired Echo. "This is going to make Martha so happy. I can't wait until Saturday. Looks like she can't lose."

Dino smiled, but a horse race was never a sure thing, and much depended on luck. Yes, Echo looked like a winner—but so had Hunter. A lot was outside his control. The only thing a trainer could do was get the horse to the starting gate—happy, healthy and ready to run.

"Lyric's on the hot walker," Slim said. "No one told *me* she was going to be ridden today."

Dino swung around, stunned by the man's rudeness. Malcolm had held Slim in high esteem but a poor attitude was never acceptable.

"I'll show Becky how the hot walker works," he snapped. "And you and I need to meet later, at noon, to make sure everyone is in accord."

"Everyone is in accord, boss," Slim said quickly. "Just saying Lyric's on the walker. That mare's been standing around for years. Might do her good to be ridden. It's not like she's my horse."

Dino glanced at Becky, afraid her enthusiasm might be dampened by Slim's surliness. Usually she was so quiet. But she wasn't ducking her head now. In fact, she stood firmly on his right, facing Slim with squared shoulders. He sensed she was trying to look tough but the effect was ruined slightly by her pink lips, sweet, vulnerable lips smudged with a spot of white icing.

"Let's go to the hot walker, Becky," he said, clenching his hand, resisting the impulse to wipe away the icing. But, Jesus, he couldn't stop staring at her hot little mouth. He looped his hand around her hip and tugged her away from Slim, then lowered his arm, annoyed by his compulsion to touch her. "You have icing on your face," he muttered.

She swiped at her lips as she trotted beside him, clearly oblivious to his thoughts. "I thought a hot walker was a person?"

"That's one kind," he said, staring straight ahead. "But there's also a mechanical hot walker. You probably saw them at Lone Star. You clip the horse on and they walk around in a circle. Saves time and labor."

"But I didn't see anything like that here," she said.

He let his gaze slide back over her face. She looked different today. Must be her hair. Usually it flopped around her face, but today the ponytail held it back. She really was damn cute.

He jerked his head away, pointing at a large circular roof, which always reminded him of a fairground ride. "The hot walker here is different. Deluxe. Sides are enclosed, and horses are loose in individual sections. It's safer and the timer can be programmed."

"How long was Lyric in there?"

"Press the third button on the right and check the memory. It tells everything."

Becky walked up to the controls, stood on her toes and peered at the steel box. "Thirty minutes. Will she be too tired for me to ride?"

The wind grabbed her bulky shirt, exposing an inch of creamy skin on her back. He wished the wind would push it higher. Wished she'd at least tuck it in, so he could check out her curves. Ever since he saw her shirtless, he'd been intensely aware of her femininity.

"Will Lyric be too tired?" she repeated and he jerked his brain back, irritated. Maybe he *was* a pig. My God, this woman was practically a nun, and he was mentally undressing her. She wasn't even his type. Someone's type, but definitely not his.

"No, that's a good warm-up," he said, his voice thick. "Now press the red button, tuck your shirt in and grab your horse."

Her nose wrinkled in confusion. "Tuck my shirt in?"

"It's safer." He kept a solemn expression. "Horses. Moving equipment. You never see a cowboy riding in a flapping shirt, do you?"

"No, I guess not." She reached down and tucked the end of her oversized shirt into her jeans.

He crossed his arms, watching with appreciation as her curves emerged. "You look really nice," he said impulsively.

She froze. Her gaiety vanished and her face turned so pinched, he wished he'd kept his mouth shut.

"Sorry, Becky." He raised his hands. "I was out of line."

But she stared as though he were some kind of sex offender, and he felt like a piece of shit. "Look, I apologize," he said. "Sometimes I have a big mouth. But you look nice today…and I thought you should know."

Her face slowly relaxed, and she stopped looking like a helpless bunny poised for flight.

"Come on," he drawled, trying to hide his remorse. "Press the red button and get your horse."

She stepped into the compartment, clipped the lead on Lyric. He resolutely kept his eyes off her cute little butt. Lyric was surprisingly obliging, not even trying to push past and escape.

"Tie her to the ring in the stall and brush her. But don't clean her hind feet. She kicks. Call me when you need help."

"Where will you be?" she asked.

"With Hunter. I want to see what Slim's talking about."

She nibbled at her lower lip, as though deep in thought. No sign of any icing, but her mouth had a really cute shape that made his thought career.

"So why would he be doing that?"

"What?" He jerked his head up. Saw the question in her eyes and guiltily realized he had no idea what she'd just asked. Christ, maybe he really was an oversexed asshole.

"Why would Slim look up Hunter's nose with a flashlight?"

"Probably to check if there's mucous," he muttered. "The smell means Hunter has an infection. I'll take a look."

"Slim didn't see me watching last night but it looked like it was a hard job, checking Hunter's nose. Want me to help?"

He didn't often need help with a horse, and he definitely didn't want her running back to Martha with crazy snot tales, but she looked so damn sweet. "Yeah, definitely." He cleared his throat. "First, tie Lyric in the stall. Do you know how to tie a quick-release knot?"

"Sure do." She led Lyric toward the barn and he followed, permitting himself a quick sweep of her beautifully shaped butt. Rounder than most of the female riders but absolutely perfect for palming. He jammed his itchy hands in his pockets.

"What'cha looking at, boss?" Stephanie called. "New filly on the grounds?"

His mouth tightened. Becky and Lyric disappeared inside the barn and he yanked his gaze off the door and looked at Stephanie. "Just studying Lyric's conformation," he said. "Wondering why she tripped the other night. We trainers are paid to be observant."

Stephanie grimaced and opened her car door. "Yeah, tell me about it. My ex was a trainer too. He studied a lot of conformation, not always equine."

"We trainers are often misunderstood."

"I've heard that before too." Stephanie snorted. "Long hours, endless worry, fickle owners. Your ex didn't even like racing. No wonder your marriage busted up."

He adjusted his hat, uneasy with the conversation. Laura's cheating no longer left a sour taste but the fact that she lived in his family home certainly did. She'd always hated living in the country but now was too contrary to leave. A few wins though and he'd be able to pay her price. Buy it back. "I'll be around tonight if you want to drop by and watch some replays or something," he said.

"Gosh, you're a smooth talker." Stephanie slipped into the car. Her car roared off as he walked into the barn.

He walked down the cool aisle, pausing as Becky struggled to tie Lyric. He stepped into the stall and shortened the rope. "Should be shorter. And make sure you stick the end in the loop so she can't undo the knot. She's a smart one." He patted the mare on the neck and headed down the aisle, his thoughts shifting to Hunter.

The colt stuck his head over the stall, seeming in fine health, but when Dino buckled the halter, the smell of infection almost made him gag. "Damn," he muttered as he slid his hand in Hunter's mouth checking for sharp teeth. Nothing obvious. The smell seemed to come from the nose.

Light footsteps sounded, and Becky peeked over the stall door. Maybe she could help after all.

"There's a rubber flashlight hanging by the tack room," he said. "Can you grab it?"

She nodded and rushed off. Hunter was unusually resistant, tossing his head and flattening his ears, and Dino led him further into the stall, trying to reassure him. Finally the colt let him touch his nostrils without fighting.

Becky returned, wide-eyed, and passed him the light.

The smell was stronger on the left and he used his finger to probe the nostril wider. "There might be some blockage," he said over his shoulder, "but it's hard to see. You're a nurse. Is that snot?"

She stepped closer. He tugged her to his side, afraid the colt might strike her. She seemed oblivious to the danger, her face rapt with concentration as she peered up. He kept his hand on her hip, ready to push her away if the colt reared. "I can reach up there," she said and her little finger disappeared into the horse's nose.

Hunter flattened his ears but stood obligingly. They all stared as a chunk of yellow appeared between her index and middle fingers.

"Dammit!"

"What is it?" She stared at the object he'd pulled from her hand.

"A goddamn sponge." Anger shortened his words. "Poor horse. Running his guts out and unable to breathe. That explains a lot. Slim noticed the smell last night. Sponge must have caused the infection."

His mouth clenched. "Some asshole at Lone Star sponged my horse. I'll increase security at the barn. Tell the state agency. But damn, that race can't be rerun."

"Guess it's a good thing Echo is shipping in on Saturday," Becky said. "She won't be around the track very long."

"Yes, that's a very good thing," he said.

A horse clopped down the aisle and he glanced over the door. Cody, the head groom, accompanied by Slim, led a cooled-out Echo back to her stall. Slim saw their faces and hurried toward them.

"You checked him out?" Slim asked. "Is it an abscess?"

"No. Look what Becky pulled from his nose."

"Well, goddamn." Slim fingered the stained sponge in disbelief. "I haven't seen anything like this in years. Guess Hunter did pretty well, running on limited air. Echo is shipping in Saturday morning. Do you have good security?"

"There'll be a groom posted by her stall. No one will get to her." Dino's fists clenched as he fought a bitter sense of violation. "Guess I better tell Martha."

"Maybe not," Becky said, sounding subdued. "This is so vindictive. I think it would upset her."

"But she needs to know why Hunter ran poorly." Dino crossed his arms. "And I think it would strengthen her decision to keep racing."

"And I'm thinking of her health. So it's best not to say anything." Becky raised a stubborn chin and crossed her own arms, and he wondered why he'd ever thought her meek.

"She's right," Slim said. "Guess it's more important to think of Martha than to make a public excuse."

"I suppose," Dino said slowly, not liking how the two had aligned against him. He also didn't like the idea that he was the selfish one. "Is your horse groomed?" he asked abruptly, resigned to the fact that no one else would ever know why Hunter ran so badly.

"I'm going to brush her now." Becky lowered her arms, peering up at him with grateful eyes. "And I really appreciate you not saying anything to Martha. That's big of you."

He gave a rueful shrug—he didn't feel big at all—and he wasn't sure if he was keeping his mouth shut for Martha. Or for Becky.

A grin split Becky's face. She stared between Lyric's ears, trying to follow every one of Dino's instructions. *Sit up. Heels down. Shoulders back. Don't hang on her mouth.* The Western saddle felt bulky compared to an English saddle, but it was amazing how the mare moved forward with little leg pressure. It would be much easier to ride in a more familiar English saddle though.

"There's an English saddle kicking around in the tack room," Dino said, as though reading her thoughts. "I'll dig it out for next time."

His hip was propped against the rail, cowboy hat pulled low. He looked like her private Marlborough man, chewing on a piece of hay instead of a cigarette. And he was the nicest, easiest-going person she'd ever met. Amazing that only a week ago, she'd thought him intimidating.

"This saddle is fine," she said, unable to stop smiling. "Everything's perfect."

"Must be boring though, going around in circles." His grin was slightly wicked. "And you're doing great. Time for a real ride." He tossed away his piece of grass and headed for the barn. "I'll grab Hank. Your smile tells me you have a need for speed."

"No," she called quickly. "I don't have that need."

But he'd already vanished into the barn.

Her fingers tightened around the reins. She was confident riding in the paddock, but those open fields looked scary. The only trail riding she'd ever done was on an ancient gelding, and

Lyric was a totally different animal than the bombproof camp horses.

Minutes later, Dino led a rangy chestnut from the barn and smoothly stepped into the saddle. "Let's go," he said.

"How do I get out?" she asked.

"Either jump the fence or lean down and open the gate."

She eyed the imposing white fence. "Does this horse know how to jump?"

"Probably not." He chuckled. "The racetrack is pretty flat."

Becky tightened her mouth and guided Lyric to the gate then reached for the latch. But Lyric sidled away, and she only grabbed air. She turned Lyric and tried again. This time she touched the latch but couldn't keep the mare from moving forward.

"Use your leg to push her over and check her with the bit," Dino said, still grinning but making no move to help.

Gritting her teeth, Becky tightened the reins and bumped the mare with her leg. Lyric edged sideways. "Please don't move," she whispered, aware Dino was laughing and probably had never been entertained by such an inept rider. Even Slim hovered by the barn door, a half smile on his face. She stretched, lifted the latch and the gate suddenly swung open.

"Yay!" Flushed with triumph, she waved an arm. The sudden gesture spooked Lyric who leaped forward, bouncing her from the saddle. She grabbed the mare's mane and desperately hung on, frozen with fear. Then somehow Dino was beside her. He snagged a rein and brought Lyric to a plunging halt.

"Good job with the gate," he said, his eyes twinkling, "but best not to make sudden moves around horses, especially racehorses. Now get your butt back in the saddle, tighten that helmet and sit up."

He sounded so bossy, she considered giving him a salute but was rather grateful for his deft snag. Besides it seemed unwise to wave her arm again. "Isn't it against the rules for you to ride without a helmet?" She raised an eyebrow at his cowboy hat.

"I only take this hat off for special occasions," he said. His deep smile was so intimate, heat rushed to her cheeks and it had little to do with the hot sun. She dipped her head, adjusting her reins, not sure if he was teasing or flirting. Men like Dino didn't flirt—not with her—but there was definitely an undercurrent. Besides, she hadn't asked him to hang around and go on a trail ride. He'd offered all by himself, and that fact alone left her buoyant.

"There are some oak trees on that hill," he added. "We'll ride to the top. The view reminds me of my ranch."

He was clearly an accomplished rider and looked like an extension of his horse, completely relaxed even though Hank was obviously keen to run. She hoped he didn't expect her to go too fast. Lyric was definitely happy to be out—the mare pulled impatiently at the bit, as though afraid Dino's horse would get in front. Both horses flattened their ears, with Lyric even reaching over and trying to bite Hank, warning him not to pass.

"Aw, hell." Dino shook his head. "They're warmed up and you look comfortable. Let's just let them run."

"What do you mean?" Her voice rose an octave.

He just grinned and eased into a canter. Lyric stopped fighting the bit and smoothly moved alongside Hank. And suddenly they were galloping.

Becky's heart shot into her throat but Dino was beside her, looking in complete control, and she remembered how easily he'd snagged Lyric. Besides, it all felt perfect. Wind whipped her face as the horses galloped up the hill, and her worries about falling off blew away.

The hill was long and smooth and eventually Lyric's stride slowed. Dino checked Hank so she tightened her own reins, and soon both horses were trotting and blowing with distinct satisfaction.

"There. They'll walk nice, now that they rid themselves of some energy," he said.

"You mean we can't gallop anymore?"

He chuckled. "I knew there was a wild woman hiding under there. No wonder Martha said to take you up here."

"She asked that?"

"Gave me specific instructions. As long as you checked out okay in the paddock."

Becky straightened Lyric's mane, her fingers clumsy with embarrassment. Dino had been *ordered* to take her riding. No doubt he'd prefer to be with Stephanie. She'd heard them talking outside the barn about meeting later. "I'm fine now," she said. "And this horse seems well behaved. No need for you to stay."

"And let you have all the fun? I don't think so." His smile was so genuine, she didn't feel quite so badly. "Look at that." He gestured beyond the ridge. "Nothing prettier than Texas land. Last time Malcolm and I rode up here, a bunch of turkeys flew out and scared my horse."

"Did you fall off?"

"Nope." He looked so amused by her question, she had to laugh. But she checked over her shoulder, not quite as confident of staying on if Lyric shied from any noisy birds.

"Where exactly were those turkeys?" she asked, tempted to grab the saddle horn. However, he seemed to think she was braver than she was, and she didn't want to hold the horn and show she really was a chicken.

"Over by the cottonwoods," he said. "We won't ride down there. The river bed's too rocky."

"It's beautiful." She looked away from the river, studying the ridged hills. "Is your ranch like this?"

"Mine is drier, more rugged. And it's not mine yet. My ex got it in the settlement."

"What did you get?"

"A nice colt. But he broke down in his second race." His face shuttered, and it was clear he wasn't going to speak anymore about the subject. "Time to turn around," he said. "You're welcome to ride Lyric any time, but don't leave the paddock unless Slim or I are with you. You can lead her out for walks though. She'd love the chance to graze."

Becky gave Lyric's neck another exuberant pat. What freedom. She could saddle up and ride in the paddock and even lead Lyric out to nibble clover. Almost like having her own horse, something she'd dreamed about when she was a kid but always knew was an absolute impossibility.

"Thanks," she said, but her throat seemed thick and she didn't think he'd heard. "Thank you very much, Dino," she repeated, making sure she enunciated clearly. Martha would be proud.

"No need to thank me. And it might make Lyric happy. Improve her disposition." He frowned. "That mare seems to have fallen through the cracks. Don't think she ever made it to the broodmare barn. Or maybe they bred her a few times and it didn't take."

"Take?"

"Get pregnant," he said. "Maybe she's barren. I don't know why Malcolm kept her in the race barn."

"Maybe Lyric didn't like the stud? Or the stud didn't like her?"

"Studs aren't usually fussy, Becky," he said.

His lips twitched and it was clear he was trying not to grin. Beneath her, Lyric pranced, obviously sensing Becky's embarrassment, and she tightened the reins. "Can we go a little faster?" she muttered.

"Nope. We need to cool them down. We shouldn't teach a horse to gallop home either, especially a racehorse. Besides," his grin escaped then, a high wattage smile that made her heart leap, "Martha would fire me if you were hurt...I wouldn't want to see you hurt either."

He was staring at her, his brown eyes oddly serious. His beautiful stud eyes, she reminded herself.

"So the race is on Saturday?" she asked, reaching for something to change the subject. "And Slim will haul Echo in early?"

"Yeah. You can drive along with him. Make sure the filly arrives ready to win."

"What time will Slim leave?"

"Five-thirty. But I'll take you for breakfast once you arrive. You can have all the coffee and bacon you want." His slow smile made her heart flutter. "And I promise not to tell Martha."

"Gosh, you really know the way to a woman's heart." She was relieved her voice sounded so flippant.

CHAPTER TEN

Martha sniffed and pushed her plate away. "I'm tired of fruit and whole wheat bread."

"Try the cottage cheese. This new brand is very creamy." Becky forced herself to take another bite, swallowing her guilt along with the truly bland breakfast. Tomorrow she'd be treated to a wonderful meal at the track. Poor Martha would be stuck with cottage cheese and tea.

"What are you smiling about?" Martha clinked her spoon in irritation.

"Nothing really." Becky gave up pretending the cottage cheese was edible and reached for her water glass. "Thanks for telling Dino I could ride Lyric."

"His idea, not mine. He always likes my nurses, although he's never taken any of them riding before." She tilted her head. "He's a very kind man. Maybe if you fix your hair, wear a little makeup, different clothes—"

Becky leaned forward and gently squeezed her hand. "It's okay, Martha. My goals in life don't include a man."

"I've noticed that. Although I don't understand why." She gave a long-suffering sigh. "Malcolm and I were so happy. It would be nice to see you settled before I go. Has there ever been a young man in your life?"

Becky toyed with the glass, her finger leaving a rounded smudge in the condensation. "Just one and it wasn't serious." Not on his part anyway, she thought wryly. And she didn't want to think about Craig and his repulsive hands, the click of the camera, the bright lights. "I'm not keen on men, Martha," she added quietly. "The foster homes never worked out. There was some trouble. I ran away when I was seventeen." She glanced up, gauging Martha's expression. No disgust only genuine concern.

"And then what?" Martha asked.

"I found a job cleaning at a rehab center. Took nursing courses at night. It took a while." She lightened her words with a forced smile. "But you know all that. You've seen my resume. I'm content with my life."

"Content isn't the same as happy. You need more than a crotchety old lady. And some men are a lot of fun."

"I'm sure they are, but that's not what I want. And thanks to you, horses are back in my life. That's more than enough fun."

"Are you planning to ride again today?"

Martha's voice carried a hint of wistfulness, and Becky paused. The morning was still cool and the thought of riding was tempting, but Martha appreciated her company. Another nurse was on duty but Becky was being paid to be a companion now, not a nurse. She certainly wasn't going to ride if Martha wanted her around.

"Because I insist you go down to the barn," Martha added. "I want you to check on Echo, since I've promised Ted that filly will win on Saturday." She waved her hand. "Now run along. I need to nap and I can't have you bumping around, keeping me awake. Just be back in time for lunch. That other nurse is fine but much too serious."

Becky stared for a moment, then leaned over and gave Martha an impulsive hug. "You really are the kindest lady."

"No, I am not," Martha said. "We both know I'm rather selfish. And why don't you wear a little lipstick?"

"Dino probably already left for Lone Star," Becky said, not thinking.

"Ah-ha." Martha cackled. "I knew it. He's an impossible man to ignore, even for you."

Flustered, Becky shook her head. "I'm not ignoring him. But I'm not interested. Not that way. I was only thinking if he wasn't there, I'd have to ride Lyric in the paddock."

"Of course." But Martha's eyes twinkled and she suddenly looked ten years younger. "Well, maybe Slim or Stephanie will ride with you."

"Maybe they will." Becky tried to inject some enthusiasm in her voice. She figured it would be more fun to ride alone than without Dino. It wasn't that she liked him—she had too much sense to fall for a man like that—but he knew so much about horses and he made her feel special. She wasn't deluding herself. He'd never be interested in someone as plain as her; he was just naturally nice.

"Wouldn't hurt to put on a little makeup though," Martha said. "The horses won't mind."

"Maybe some lipstick," Becky said. Heck, even Stephanie wore some sort of pink lip gloss, and she rode horses all morning.

Martha gave a smug smile.

"Just to protect me from the sun," Becky added quickly.

Becky parked in the empty visitors' lot at the side of the barn, not quite ballsy enough to park in front, not without Martha. On the training track, a gray horse trotted along the outside rail. Obviously Stephanie was on the job. Slim wasn't in sight but his truck was in the staff lot, squeezed between two compact cars. No sign of Dino's truck. Obviously she'd missed him.

She entered the rear of the barn. Hunter glanced at her then stared over her head at something he deemed more important. She took a cautious sniff as she passed but there was no sign of decay, only the wholesome smell of horse and hay.

Lyric's stall door was open and she jerked to a stop. Had the mare escaped again? No. She blew out a whoosh of relief. The halter was also gone so likely Lyric was merely on the hot walker.

She scooped a lead line off the rack and hurried to the walker. Lyric was one of two horses circling inside. Safe and exactly where she should be. Becky flipped the switch and stopped the walker, following Dino's instructions. She stepped inside and hooked the lead on Lyric's halter. Gave her a quick pat...then stiffened in shock as drops of sweat beaded the air.

The mare was soaked. Sweat drenched her neck and belly, the smell overpowering, and her nostrils flared pink. Becky gulped. Was this normal? Lyric hadn't been at all sweaty yesterday—even after the ride. Maybe she was sick.

But the other horse in the walker—a chestnut filly that looked like Echo—appeared similarly hot. Odd, because Echo's race was tomorrow, and she'd heard Dino order only two jog laps today. Becky stopped Lyric by the control panel and pressed the button to resume motion, hoping Echo wouldn't mind being alone, although judging by her lather, it was also time for the filly to leave the walker.

On impulse, she pressed the timer. The red display beeped then flashed: two hundred minutes.

"Wha'cha doing?"

She swung toward the curt voice, her heart pounding with guilt. "Hi, Slim. I was wondering if it was all right to leave Echo in here alone."

"I'm just coming to get her. She's jogged her two laps and had a twenty-minute cool-down on the walker. Heard you're driving to the track with me tomorrow?"

Becky nodded, trying to keep her eyes from skittering back to the display panel. Dino had shown her how to work the buttons, and the numbers showed the horses had been walking for two hundred minutes—not twenty.

"Better be on time." Slim frowned, glancing down at his ever-present clipboard. "I won't wait if you're late. Filly has to be on the grounds by seven."

"I'll be on time," she said, knowing she had to tell Dino about Slim's behavior. And she definitely didn't want this crusty man to join her on a trail ride; it would be more enjoyable to ride alone in the paddock. Besides, Lyric's head was unusually low, and the mare wasn't even pulling at the lead. Seemed like a good day to practice opening gates.

She tugged on Lyric's lead and the mare followed. So did Slim.

"Forgot my lead line." He jammed a pen in his back pocket and brushed past her. A picture fluttered to the ground.

Becky stopped Lyric, scooping up the photo before the mare ground it into the dirt. A young woman's face stared back. A face with a slack mouth and dull eyes. Oh, God. She'd cared for many patients like this at the rehab center, and they always tugged at her heart.

"Slim," she called, flipping the picture over, feeling intrusive. "You dropped something."

He turned and scooped the picture from her outstretched hand, carefully wiping off a speck of dirt. "Thanks," he said, sticking it back in his pocket. "Need any help saddling?"

"No, thanks."

"Dino told me to help with her hind feet."

"It's okay. I can do it." But she remembered Lyric's protest yesterday when Dino had handled her hooves, and her voice lacked conviction.

"Dino gave an order," Slim said as she led Lyric into the airy stall, "so I have to clean her back feet. I assume *you* can look after her front?"

"Yes, you can assume that, Slim." His sarcasm made her speak more forcefully than usual. She even stared at him the way Dino did when he was annoyed, although she did cheat a bit and locked her gaze on his forehead. It was a huge coup when he was the first to look away.

"Let's get this done," he grumbled, pulling out a hoof pick and grabbing Lyric's hind leg. When she swished her tail in protest, he smacked her. He tried again, and the mare slammed her hoof against the wall.

"Quit," Slim said, slapping her again. The sound was loud in the serene barn, and Becky stiffened. She'd already noticed Dino handled the horses differently, with far better results. He hadn't had any problem checking Hunter's nose either, not like Slim's tussle that rainy night when he'd thought he was alone. Still, Slim was the barn manager, and both Martha and Dino considered him an expert.

Lyric turned, her soulful eyes holding Becky's. Her mute appeal reminded Becky of a needy patient, and it was impossible to remain silent.

"Dino says that with some horses, you shouldn't push them too hard," she said. "What kind of horse is Lyric?"

"A bitch, that's what kind." Slim stepped back and kicked the mare in the belly. Lyric pinned her ears but grudgingly let him lift her hind leg. "See. You have to show them who's boss." He deftly cleaned her feet. "Just make sure you kick with the side of your foot. Otherwise you could break some toes."

"I don't think I'll be doing much kicking." Becky eyed Lyric's flattened ears with alarm. It was a good thing she was riding in the paddock, because the mare now had a very sullen look.

"Suit yourself. Just don't touch her flank." Slim tossed the hoof pick in the grooming kit and stalked from the stall.

Becky sighed but finished grooming with no mishap, then tacked up the mare and led her outside. Lyric immediately brightened, but Becky gulped in dismay. How was she going to climb on? There were no mounting blocks anywhere, nothing like the big ones at summer camp. Yesterday Dino had given her a leg up, but she didn't want to ask Slim for any more help.

She tried mounting from the ground, but her foot didn't reach the stirrup—failed by a full six inches. Either her legs had to grow or she needed a stirrup extension. A clump of baler twine hung on a hook by the door. She scooped up a piece of twine and tied it on the left stirrup, adjusting it until the length was right. Perfect. Now she'd be able to scramble into the saddle unassisted.

But it still wasn't easy. Lyric kept sidling toward the grass, forcing her to hop on one leg. Her frustration grew. Two grooms rushed past, but as usual they didn't look her way. To her left, a horse walked off the track and she realized Stephanie had finished with her mount. Damn, she didn't want to look like an idiot in front of the capable gallop girl.

Pumped with resolve, she led Lyric onto the manicured lawn. The mare buried her nose in the lush grass, happy at last, and there was ample time to stick a toe into the loop of twine and scramble up. It wasn't pretty but she was on. She rewarded Lyric by letting her eat another moment before pulling her head up and heading to the paddock.

Luckily the gate was open and she was able to walk in with little effort, other than kicking it wider with her boot. Not a stylish technique but effective.

"Nice day, isn't it," Stephanie called, walking past on a sweaty chestnut. "This is my last horse of the morning but days like this, I could gallop ten."

Gallop ten? Becky's legs still ached from yesterday's ride. She couldn't imagine being fit enough, or skilled enough, to gallop ten horses.

Stephanie pulled the chestnut to a sudden halt, her eyes narrowing. "Do you know there's a piece of baler twine hanging from your stirrup?"

Becky's face prickled with embarrassment. "It's my mounting rope," she muttered.

Stephanie's melodious laugh filled the air. "Better than a leg up. But if you ride on the trail, be sure to unfasten it. Dangling ropes are dangerous. By the way," she rose in the saddle, digging a hand in the pocket of her jeans, "can you place some bets for me tomorrow? Dino was in such a hurry, I forgot to give this to him." Her impatient horse sidled to the left, and she turned him in a circle. "Never mind. I'll come back after I take Chippy to his groom. He's eager for his bath."

Becky forced a smile as Stephanie headed to a waiting groom, ignoring the painful twist in her chest. She didn't want to think about Dino and Stephanie. Setting her mouth, she guided Lyric alongside the gate, determined to learn how to open it when mounted. Fortunately Lyric was happy to stand still, seeming to doze while Becky leaned down and practiced with the latch.

Steps sounded as Stephanie walked up, balancing a Styrofoam cup and some crinkled bills. She'd replaced her helmet with a pink ball cap and looked fresh and energetic, despite just galloping twelve hundred pounds of eager horse. "I've never seen that mare so quiet," she said.

"She's tired. She was on the hot walker with Echo."

"Oh, that Echo." Stephanie's voice rose with excitement. "She felt great again this morning. Put twenty dollars on her nose for me and another two dollars to win on Arctic Chip. Chippy's the horse I just rode. He's racing tomorrow too."

"You're not going?"

"No. I make it a firm policy to stay away." Stephanie's smile faded as she sipped her coffee. "I really miss it but my daughter is only two. She needs me healthy. And this is a relaxed job. I come at seven, gallop some nice horses and leave. And when I get the urge to jockey again, I think of Jill."

"Who's Jill?" Becky straightened in the saddle, letting the gate swing shut.

"Slim's daughter. She was hurt riding Lyric at Lone Star." Stephanie's eyes darkened. "Jockeying is dangerous, but the reality hits home when it happens to someone you know."

Becky glanced down at Lyric's lowered head, trying to imagine the mare racing. Hard to picture, especially now when the mare was so relaxed. Her ears were tilted and she rested a hind leg, not even twitching when Stephanie passed Becky the money. "Guess that explains why Slim doesn't like Lyric," Becky said ruefully.

"Oh, he likes all the horses. But he and Dino have different styles. Dino is a race trainer. Doesn't want his horses too submissive. They need that extra fight to dig deep and gut out a win. Slim is more old-fashioned and likes control."

"Was Lyric feisty when she raced?"

"Definitely, but she knew her job. Her last race, she took a bad step. Three horses went down. Jill was just unlucky." Stephanie glanced toward the barn, her voice lowering. "Slim's been grumpy lately but like everyone, he's worried about Martha selling. It'd be tough for all of us, even Dino, to find jobs that pay this well."

"Plus Dino and Slim each get a house," Becky said, unable to resist probing. She'd never been in either of the ranch-style guesthouses. Dino's was larger, but they both looked beautiful, typical of everything on the Conrad property.

"Yeah, it would be a dream to have one of those. Dino has a small apartment close to Lone Star but he's staying here more often since there are three horses in training—Hunter, Chippy and Echo. Although he didn't sleep here last night...too worried about the horses at Lone Star after that sponge was found in Hunter."

Stephanie's face darkened, but Becky's disgust about the sabotage was tempered with guilty relief. Dino and Stephanie hadn't spent the night together after all.

"It's hard to fix a race with all the drug testing," Stephanie went on. "And now with a twenty-four hour guard, there's no way anyone can touch Dino's horses."

"You think someone at the track doesn't like him?" Becky asked.

Stephanie shrugged. "It probably wasn't personal. Dino's a good trainer and well-respected. But Hunter was the favorite. When someone stuck that sponge up his nose, they created a sweet betting opportunity. Everyone wants to make money." She waggled a finger. "As do I. So don't forget to lay my bets, because Echo feels like a rocket."

Stephanie's confidence in the filly was reassuring. Martha was meeting with Ted a day after the race, and a win by Echo would prove the horses were worth keeping.

"Gotta go." Stephanie turned toward a dented blue hatchback. "But you look bored sitting on that horse. Next week I'll go on a trail ride with you."

"I'd like that," Becky managed. Usually retirees were her company of choice, not dynamic women like Stephanie. But she hadn't felt at all uncomfortable, had even enjoyed the conversation.

Maybe being on Lyric's back made her bolder, or maybe it was the horses in general. Not worth analyzing right now though. It was too beautiful to worry about anything. The sun was shining, the breeze was fresh and Lyric was being so sweet and cooperative, she deserved a treat.

Becky leaned forward and scratched the mare's shoulder, promising to bring her back a generous bunch of carrots. Lyric had given her another wonderful ride even though they'd only walked a grand total of thirty feet.

"Don't stare." Martha opened her eyes and scowled. "I'm not dead yet. But sitting at the dinner table makes me sleepy. From now on, I'll eat in my room."

"Does this sleepiness have anything to do with Ted's visit on Sunday?" Becky asked, refreshing the water glass.

Martha harrumphed deep in her throat. "Of course not. I don't run from anyone. Although how my sister managed to have such a boring son is beyond comprehension. Ted probably won't stay long on Sunday, especially if you talk about how beautiful Echo looked in the winner's circle."

Becky smiled, her anxiety over Martha fading. Ted's visits were never pleasant but Martha seemed unfazed, and Ted obviously thought he was fulfilling a family duty. Maybe he'd shut up about the business of selling. His tactless comments stung and placed unnecessary pressure on all the Conrad staff, especially Slim whose mood grew darker every day.

"Do you know Slim well?" Becky asked impulsively. "I heard his daughter used to ride."

"Jill? Yes, she rode some of our horses right up until her accident. So glad you don't race, dear. It's much too dangerous." Martha picked up a straw and jangled the ice in her glass, her voice turning pensive. "Such a tragedy. I remember poor Malcolm being unable to sleep. Refused to go to any parties either."

"I imagine Slim and Jill also had a tough time." Becky couldn't keep the dryness from her voice. "Do racetracks have insurance?"

Martha abandoned the straw and waved her hand in dismissal. "I'm sure they do. Malcolm was going to check the situation once everything settled. But let's not talk about that sad business. Tell me about Echo."

"She's feeling like a rocket, according to Stephanie."

Martha sniffed. "Hope that girl didn't get her too tired. The race is tomorrow."

"Dino's instructions were to jog around twice."

"Good. That's what Malcolm would have done too. So you'll drive down with Slim? You can use the owner's box. Remember, you're representing Conrad Stables so be sure to dress up. I want you to look fabulous in the winner's circle."

That meant her brown cotton pants and white blouse, Becky thought with a pang. She didn't usually care about clothes, but it was doubtful Martha would approve of her attire.

Martha leaned forward, a knowing gleam in her eyes. "If you don't have anything suitable, there's still time to shop. A friend of mine owns a lovely boutique. I'll have them pull some appropriate things. Size seven?"

Becky started to nod, then stiffened. "What makes you think I can't shop on my own?"

Martha snickered and reached for her phone.

*

Multi-colored bags filled the passenger's seat. Becky couldn't stop peeking. Granted, she wasn't keeping all those beautiful clothes despite Martha's generosity and the insistence of the sales clerks. Only one outfit was required. However, Martha's instructions to the owner had clearly taken precedence over anything Becky said.

She'd never shopped in such an upscale boutique, and it had been weird to have two hovering attendants who seemed to know more about her size and style than she did.

It was fun though and now she knew exactly what to wear tomorrow. In fact, she couldn't wait for the race.

Clothes did make a difference.

She drummed the steering wheel in happy rhythm to the radio and detoured down the Conrad's lighted driveway toward the stable.

One last stop. A promise to be kept.

The car eased off the smooth concrete and onto the gravel road. The decorative lamps didn't throw much light, and she strained to see. Slim's truck was already hooked up to the horse trailer, an imposing silhouette, primed and ready for morning. Beyond the trailer, both Slim and Dino's houses appeared as dark blotches without a thread of light. The illuminated dashboard read nine o'clock.

She parked in the deserted employees' lot close to the wide end doors. Grabbed the carrots from the floor of the car and headed for Lyric's stall, relieved that nightlights illuminated the aisle. Lyric stuck her head over the door, blinking curiously. Hay protruded from her mouth, and when she gave a welcoming nicker, soggy green clumps dropped to the floor.

Becky pulled out a carrot and stepped into the stall, smiling as the mare pushed greedily at the bag. "You were such a good girl today." She scratched Lyric's silky neck, enjoying her enthusiasm. She wasn't sure how many carrots she could safely feed a horse. Dino had said only two apples a day, but she'd forgotten to ask about carrots.

Lyric seemed to think she could handle the whole bag, and it was incredible how fast she could gobble. Becky distracted her by dropping a carrot in her feed bin, then backed from the stall and carefully secured the safety snap.

She moved toward the adjoining stall, carrot in hand, surprised when Echo didn't stick her head out. She and Lyric were good buddies, and Becky had assumed Echo would hear the crunching and insist on a treat too.

She peered in the stall, calling to the filly, but the chestnut just stood in the far corner, flicking curious ears. "Come on, girl. I know you're resting for the race but look what I brought." She waved a carrot.

Echo edged forward, seeming surprised to have a visitor. She gave the carrot a suspicious sniff then took a tentative bite. Becky held the end while the filly chewed—painfully slow—and Becky curbed her impatience even as she marveled at the contrasting eating styles. Lyric ate like a glutton, while Echo was a nervous nibbler.

"Good thing that's a carrot in your hand, not coffee. Caffeine will test."

Becky turned toward the familiar voice. "Hi, Slim. I thought you were asleep. Just stopped in to see Lyric."

"That ain't Lyric. That's Echo."

"Yes, but I thought Echo would want a treat too. Although she doesn't appear to have ever tasted a carrot."

"A lot of horses never have." His mouth curved in a half smile. "You should have seen Lyric the first time she ate a carrot. Peppermints are better anyway," he added. "Easier to carry, and they don't get moldy. We should leave now and let that filly rest. Silly to bother her before a race."

"Oh, of course. Sorry." Becky turned away, feeling like a chastised kid, but Lyric nickered as she headed down the aisle, and the mare's affectionate display more than compensated for Slim's rebuke.

A shrill whinny abruptly blared from the dark. Lyric thrust her head further over her door and responded with an earsplitting bray.

Becky winced and followed Slim down the aisle and out of the barn, away from the noisy mare. She lingered by her car, straining to see the whinnying horse who had so disturbed Lyric. The noise didn't come from the pasture but from the east, from the direction of the hot walker.

"Do you think someone forgot a horse on the walker?"   She glanced at Slim who waited by the front of the car.

Sighing, he stepped forward and yanked open her door. "No one forgot anything. I put a horse out that had a touch of colic. You get going now. We have an early morning, and I can't wait if you're late."

She slid into the car so quickly she bumped her knee against the steering wheel. *Colic.* She remembered walking a horse late into the night because of that. All the counselors had been worried the horse would roll and twist a gut, and everyone had been exhausted the next morning. The horse, however, had been fine.

She hesitated a moment then lowered her window. "Do you want me to stick around and help?"

He leaned down, his voice softening. "It's okay, Miz Becky. Appreciate your offer though. You go home and get some rest." He rapped his knuckles on the car. "And I can wait a few minutes if you're late. Five or ten maybe."

CHAPTER ELEVEN

Becky perched on the seat in Slim's truck, trying to act casual, but the thrill of riding shotgun—hauling real live racehorses—left her bouncing like a kid. She glanced over her shoulder for the hundredth time. The trailer was still there, still attached, and if she really focused, a horse's pricked ears were visible through the window.

She couldn't tell if it was Echo or Chippy, the gelding also being shipped. They were eerily similar, both chestnuts with no white markings. In fact, when Slim had led the horses up the ramp she hadn't been able to tell them apart.

"Do you get excited before a race?" she asked, trying once again to coax words from Slim. It was like pulling teeth though, and she had new empathy for people who'd tried to draw her into conversation. Being on the other side wasn't fun either. "Everyone must get a little excited," she added with a smile, remembering how Dino's lazy grin always made people relax.

Dark circles lined Slim's eyes, but his expression softened. "I don't get excited now but the way you're hopping on the seat reminds me of Jill when she first started."

"How old was she?"

"Fourteen. Couldn't get her apprentice license until she was sixteen so she started galloping at Conrad's. She was always excited when a horse headed for the track. Girls and their horses, you know." His voice caught. His knuckles whitened around the wheel, and the truck's speed increased.

Becky's throat tightened as brittle silence filled the cab. Poor Slim. "It has to be the most exciting thing in the world, to get a horse ready to race." She stared straight ahead, realizing he was swiping his eyes and aware he wouldn't want an audience. "I wouldn't be able to sleep if Lyric were running today," she added, pretending to adjust her seatbelt.

"Guess they're like your kids," Slim said slowly, his voice gruff but steady now. "And don't forget, they behave like kids too. You never know what a horse is going to do."

"Maybe, but Stephanie thinks Echo deserves a big bet." Becky patted her stylish new purse. "I'm going to bet too."

"Yeah, well don't bet the farm." Slim gunned the truck and trailer past a pokey Cadillac. "The more you need a win, the worse a horse runs. And the old lady really needs this win, right?"

"Martha likes to win, just like everyone else." Becky shrugged, reluctant to admit how important the race really was. Ted's visit tomorrow would definitely be more tolerable if Echo galloped home with a stakes win.

Slim grunted as he eased onto the turnoff to Lone Star Park. "Dino will be happy. We made good time this morning."

Her breathing quickened at the mention of Dino, and she checked the garment bag hanging in the cab. At least she had stylish clothes to wear for the race although Martha had insisted she wait and change after lunch. "You'll never stay clean otherwise," Martha had said. "But you can wear your new jeans in the morning. And that cute little jacket."

Thank God for the advice. Martha had been right. Hay already stuck to her jeans; it was impossible to stay clean around horses.

Slim greeted the guard at the security booth, flashed some shipping papers, and was waved through. They rumbled onto the backside of the track. Excitement pulled her to the edge of the seat.

The sun barely cut the dawn mist but already eager horses filed to the track, ears pricked, helmeted riders perched on their backs. Bustling grooms toted buckets, hoses and pitchforks, and several horses circled on slow-moving hot walkers.

Horses filled every nook and cranny, and she couldn't contain her delight. A spotted pig trotted across the gravel, chased by a white-haired man, and even Slim smiled.

"The track is hectic," he said, edging the rig past a line of horses. "But it's always fun. I worked here until my wife died."

Fun didn't adequately describe it. Magical, maybe. Becky craned her head as a gray horse, lathered with soapy suds, opened his mouth and played with water jetting from a hose while his proud groom grinned. "It's another world," she breathed.

"Yeah, but Conrad's is less stressful. Comes with vacation, and the regular hours give me more time to visit Jilly. You do what you have to do." Emotion thickened his voice, and he gave a self-conscious cough. "Now you have a good time—but we're busy, so don't expect me or Dino to hold your hand."

"No, of course not." She swallowed further questions about the track and straightened in the seat. They'd almost reached the shedrow, and she knew the way to the gap. She didn't mind standing by herself and watching the horses. In fact, she couldn't wait to wander around the backside.

Slim eased the rig to a stop. She opened her door and jumped to the ground. A young woman walked out of the shedrow leading a bay horse with red bandages. She was tiny, pretty and flirtatious, and giggled at something a blond man said.

And then Dino appeared. His eyes locked with hers, and his welcoming grin tugged at something in her chest.

"Hi," he said.

She heard Slim behind her complaining about traffic but Dino only nodded, his warm gaze still on her face. "You look nice today," he said softly. His eyes slid over her new jeans and then back to her face. He squeezed her shoulder before walking past and opening the side door of the trailer.

She drew in a quivery breath. Some day maybe, she'd get used to his touch. Now she no longer jumped; she merely turned dewy.

"Horses travel okay? What the hell—" Dino's voice sharpened, alarm pinching the corners of his eyes as he swung toward Slim.

"It was an uneventful trip," Slim said, shrugging in confusion.

"What's wrong?" Becky stepped closer, trying to peer past Dino into the trailer.

"Hopefully nothing," he said, still studying Echo. "But she looks subdued. Usually she's a tiger when she hits the track. Did you check her temperature, Slim?"

"Didn't see the need." A mottled red climbed Slim's neck and he crossed his arms over his chest. "Filly was fine when I loaded her."

"We'll check her out," Dino said. But his expression was grim as he wheeled away from Slim and motioned at a red-haired groom. "There's coffee in the office, Becky. End stall. Give me a few minutes before we go eat."

Under his critical eye, two grooms unloaded the horses. Chippy, the chestnut gelding, looked great, prancing and calling to a horse in the adjoining barn. But Echo's head dragged, as though uncaring where she was or who she was with.

Dino swore, Slim shook his head and the red-haired groom looked worried. They all ignored the gelding and filed into the barn behind the sedate filly.

"Chippy never gets that kind of attention, but he's always happy," the second groom said as he led the perky gelding.

"He looks a lot like Echo," Becky said.

The groom chuckled. "Yeah, until you look underneath. Chippy's definitely a boy. And he couldn't keep up to Echo unless she was wearing gumboots. He's a low-end claimer. She's a stakes winner."

Becky struggled to remember the various types of races. Claiming was the lowest level but she'd only ever accompanied Martha to stakes races, the highest rung of competition. Martha had pinned all her hopes on Echo. In fact, she hadn't even mentioned Chippy, although Stephanie had sent along a two-dollar bet for the gelding.

Chippy strutted into the barn, pulling on his lead and calling exuberantly to the other horses. Definitely a big difference in the two horses. Echo was apathetic, while Chippy looked ready to party.

She trailed the gelding into the barn. Dino, Slim and the blond man she'd seen earlier were conferring and she walked down the aisle, feeling much more confident than the day of her first visit. Dino had said there was coffee in the last stall, and she soon saw what he meant.

The stall was actually a tack room with three chairs, a folding card table and a profusion of charts and pictures tacked on the wall. Half-filled coffee cups littered the desk, serving as weights for stacks of paper.

A coffee machine gurgled on top of a compact fridge. She poured herself a cup of dark coffee. Checked for milk but only found mismatched medicine bottles and three cans of Coke. She closed the fridge, took a cautious sip and was immediately reassured. The coffee was excellent.

She wandered to the wall and studied the win pictures. Martha and Malcolm grinned back at her, along with Dino and a group of well-dressed strangers. The caption read: *Echo Beach, Lassie Juvenile Stakes, $100,000 purse.*

Echo looked energetic in this picture. Her head was high even after running seven furlongs, and she bore little resemblance to the horse that had just stumbled off the trailer. Dino obviously had reason to be concerned.

Becky peered out the door. Slim was leaning over Echo's stall, intent on something, but she couldn't see Dino. A scrawled note was tacked to the office door. 'No coffee or pop in aisle.' She left her cup and walked toward Echo's stall.

Dino had his ear pressed to Echo's stomach but straightened and gave Becky a reassuring smile before turning to Slim. "Gut sounds normal. No temp. She eat up this morning?"

"Yeah. Licked the feed tub clean. Like I said, she was fine when she walked on the trailer."

"We'll leave her alone for an hour and re-assess, but I don't like what I'm seeing." Dino rubbed the back of his neck, his voice troubled. "Might have to scratch."

"Scratch?" Becky's voice rose in dismay. "You mean she won't run?"

"Not unless she's feeling a hundred percent," Dino said.

"But Martha will be disappointed."

"We're all disappointed." His authoritative tone invited no argument, reminding her that he was accustomed to making tough decisions. "Shane's finishing up the set and joining us in the kitchen. Come on. I'll buy you both breakfast."

"Can't." Slim jammed his hands in his pockets and turned away. "Gotta make some phone calls. See some people."

Dino nodded and turned to the red-haired groom. "Don't leave this mare alone, Red. Not for one minute. I want to know everything she does."

"Sure, boss." The groom brandished a wrinkled notepad. "She won't fart without me writing it down."

"Good. And tell Shane to meet us at the kitchen." Dino glanced at Becky, his voice lightening. "Let's go then. Been looking forward to breakfast with you."

He was looking forward to breakfast with her? 'Me too,' she wanted to say. But her tongue felt awkward.

"I'm eager to see if you can eat as much as last time," he added.

Her happiness flattened, replaced by a rush of disappointment. She wasn't as slim as the women he was accustomed to, and she did love food, but it was demoralizing that her healthy appetite was what drew his attention.

"Maybe if you didn't hang out with so many skinny riders, you'd realize how normal people eat," she said.

"Relax. I'm kidding you." And his warm eyes did look teasing. "Want to drive or walk?"

"Walk. I like seeing all the barns."

"Good. I like that too." His smile was so infectious, her disappointment slid away. They stepped from the barn and into the slanting sun. She slipped on her sunglasses and walked beside him, enjoying his commentary on the other barns and horses.

A gray filly was entered in the same race as Echo. They lingered, watching as a groom led her around the sandy tow ring.

"That horse is sure feeling good," Becky said as the gray squealed and kicked out in a series of playful bucks.

"Yeah." Dino gave a rueful sigh and turned away. "How did Echo really look when you left Conrad's? Were you there when Slim loaded?"

"Yes, and she was full of energy. It was Chippy who was quiet."

"Odd," Dino said. "Chippy loves traveling. Can't run very fast, but sure thinks he can. You positive it was Chippy, not Echo?"

Becky frowned as she pictured the horses. It had been dark, and she wasn't quite certain she could tell them apart. "Pretty sure." But she wrinkled her nose, wishing she could be more help. Dino was definitely worried about the filly's condition. "Maybe Echo just needs a strong coffee."

Dino chuckled. "Coffee tests."

She blinked in confusion. "Slim said the same thing. What does that mean?"

"After a race, the winner and a random horse have to give a urine sample. Ten drops of coffee and a horse will test positive for a stimulant."

"What happens then?"

"Trainer's in big shit." Dino took her elbow and guided her up the walk to the kitchen. "And that's never good, so Echo has to get on the muscle without any help from me."

His hand was large and warm and as usual, just the touch made her stomach do funny flips. "I see," she said, determined to keep talking intelligently even though her body had turned traitor. "What does 'on the muscle' mean?"

"Hot to trot. How a horse should look before a race. How Lyric felt right before we galloped up the hill."

He released her elbow, pulled open the door and thankfully her brain cleared. "I see," she said. "Well, it seemed Echo was on the muscle this morning, and Chippy wasn't. But Slim had to tell me the horses' names. All I know about Echo is that she eats carrots slowly."

"I never thought of Echo as a slow eater," Dino chuckled, "but maybe she is, compared to some ladies I know."

She jabbed him in the ribs. He didn't seem to notice, and she rubbed her elbow. Clearly that jab hurt her more than it hurt him. He was rock-hard, like one of his conditioned Thoroughbreds. Probably had one of those washboard stomachs, conveniently designed for women to rub their fingers over, the type of stomach she'd never experienced before, had never even touched—

"You have a wistful look," he said, still smiling. "Thinking of pancakes?"

"You guessed it," she said, but a hot flush climbed her cheeks.

*

Dino shook his head as he checked the dozing filly. "You mean she's been lying down the whole time?"

"Yeah, boss, but she's not sick or in distress." Red flipped open his notebook. "Vitals are good. She's just dog-tired."

Dino yanked his Stetson lower, hiding his expression. He trained a few laid-back horses who could nap through any commotion, but Echo wasn't one of them. Normally she'd be pacing the stall, primed and eager to run. Once she'd even jumped over her door. Her excessive energy was one of the reasons he and Malcolm had never stabled her at Lone Star. Obviously she wasn't in any shape to race today.

Damn, this sucked. Martha needed the race, needed the encouragement a win would give, but a bad race from a classy filly like Echo would be worse. And it certainly wouldn't help the horse and whatever health issues she was fighting.

He blew out a reluctant sigh. "We'll have to scratch. Call me when the vet comes. Are Becky and Shane back from the kitchen yet?"

"Haven't seen them," Red said.

Dino sighed again and stalked from the barn. Slim was slouched in his pickup, oblivious to events. Dino rapped his knuckles on the window. The man twisted, fumbling with his cell. He said something in the phone then cut the connection and opened the door.

"You look guilty," Dino said. "Must be hitting on my ex-wife."

"I don't even know your ex," Slim said, scrambling from the cab.

"Slim, I'm messing with you." Dino shook his head in exasperation. The man was so uptight, he seemed ready to explode. Didn't seem to be sleeping either. His eyes were baggy and his jeans sagged. "Just wanted to let you know I'm scratching Echo," Dino added mildly.

"What! You can't scratch her."

Dino stiffened, surprised by the man's passion. Usually Slim was taciturn, but now he was downright animated. "Wouldn't be fair to run," Dino said. "She's been lying down for the last couple hours. That's not normal. Not for her."

"The filly's fine." Slim slammed his truck door. "And the old lady really needs the win."

"Martha," Dino automatically corrected. "And I thought you of all people would be glad to scratch. Safer for the horse, safer for the jock. "

"No one ever worried about Jill." Bitterness laced Slim's voice, and he jammed his phone in his back pocket.

"I know you're worried about paying for your daughter's care," Dino said. "But if we have a few good races, Martha will hang on. Maybe she won't sell at all. And it's better to scratch than have a bad race."

"Doesn't matter what we do. We all know she's going to sell. Especially with that nurse poking around. Running back and spreading stories."

Dino flexed his hands but couldn't control the tightness of his voice. "Please refer to our employer as Martha. And the nurse's name is Becky who, by the way, supports what we're doing. She's potentially one of our biggest allies. We have to be nice to her."

"Yeah, well, I still don't think you should scratch."

"Then it's good you're not the one in charge." Dino's jaw hardened. He twisted, pausing when he saw Becky only ten feet away, coffee cup gripped in her hand. Her eyes were a stormy brown, and she looked disappointed, almost hurt.

"You heard?" he asked. "We're going to scratch."

She nodded, stiff with disapproval, a stark contrast to the lady he'd earlier shared breakfast with, the lady who'd gaily devoured a stack of syrup-soaked pancakes. He liked her smile way better than that closed stick-up-the-ass expression. And since she'd seemed to really care for the horses it was disappointing she'd still want to race Echo.

"Sorry you made a wasted trip." He crossed his arms, surprised her reaction bothered him. Owners and their reps were an odd bunch. He'd thought she'd approve of the scratch. Report favorably to Martha. But now it appeared her interest in the horses' health wasn't totally genuine.

"The trip wasn't a waste," she said. "I can still watch Chippy."

"Yeah, race three. Only a claimer though."

"Chippy doesn't know that. I imagine he'll be happy if he wins."

"Yeah, he probably will." He studied her cautiously, uncomfortable with the bite in her voice. Lately, she'd dropped that aloof air and he liked it. He didn't want her mad, and he especially didn't want her mad at him. "There's no choice here but to scratch," he added. "Martha might give you some grief, but I can call and explain."

"It's okay. Shane already told me something must be wrong. That Echo is usually hyper at the track."

"Which is why she shouldn't run. But maybe you can still enjoy a few races."

She nodded but her voice remained cool. "After you left the kitchen, Shane and I walked around the backside and went over the *Racing Form*. He gave me lots of betting tips. Told me what to look for."

"Yeah. You two were gone awhile." Dino checked his watch, surprised at his irritation. He'd asked Shane to show her around but hadn't expected them to buddy up for half the morning, and clearly her mood had drastically altered. Shane was a born flirt. Maybe he'd come on too strong. "Shane is going to be busy with Chippy now," he said evenly. "Want to watch the race from the rail or should we go up to Martha's box?"

"Dino!" Danielle rushed toward him with a reporter's single-minded zeal, camera man tagging behind. "Heard a rumor you might scratch," she called.

Amazing how she could sniff out stories. And how willing she was to take advantage. He crossed his arms and forced a polite nod. Didn't want to give her any encouragement. She'd cornered him at the bar a few nights ago but her ruthlessness turned him off. Her type always had an agenda, and they tended to turn nasty when things didn't pan out.

"I have to consult with the owner now." He edged toward the barn. "We're still deciding."

"Okay but talk to me first." Danielle flashed him a confident smile. "And I'll buy the drinks next time."

"Sure," he said, keen to get back to the privacy of his office where he could call Martha. "You two coming?" He glanced back at Becky and Slim.

But neither of them moved. They stared at Danielle as though mesmerized.

Dino paused. The reporter was gorgeous and always impeccably dressed, but surely they could see she was poison. He definitely didn't want her chatting them up, wheedling out information. So far though, she hadn't acknowledged their presence, had even turned her back as though they were inconsequential.

The sides of his mouth twitched. If she knew Slim and Becky were from Conrad's, she'd be all over them, including them in her lethal charm. They didn't need that. He didn't want Becky even breathing the same air as Danielle.

Protectiveness filled him. He cupped Becky's elbow and herded her toward the barn. "We need to call Martha before she hears the scratch on the news," he whispered. "I'll talk to Danielle later."

"I'm sure you will," Becky said, her tone flat.

He scanned her face. As usual, her chestnut hair was loose, partially hiding her expression, and he fought the impulse to tuck it behind her ear. She was so cute when she wore a ponytail, when she showed her face. Why had he ever thought her plain?

"What I mean is," he said, choosing his words carefully, "we have to watch what we say around that kind of reporter, that kind of paper. They're more interested in gossip than horse racing. They like trouble. And that's the last thing Martha needs. Just leave Danielle to me."

"Of course," she muttered.

He realized he was still holding her elbow even though they were safely in the barn. Reluctantly, he lowered his hand. "Look. I just don't want her to badger you or Slim about the Conrad operation."

Becky rolled her eyes. "She didn't seem interested in badgering me. Or Slim. Just poor little you."

"That's because she doesn't know who you or Slim are. And quite frankly, I don't like her badgering." He winked. "Let's hide in the office."

He checked over his shoulder for Slim, but the man wasn't in the shedrow so he closed the office door and pulled out a chair for Becky. "I'll call Martha now. How's she feeling?"

"Tired, a little apathetic." Becky sat down, her voice thickening. "Hard to get her to eat."

It was clear she doted on Martha, clear they shared much more than a working relationship. "How long have you worked for her?" he asked, still holding his phone.

"Three years."

"I've been with Conrad's almost a year but don't remember seeing you much."

"Maybe you didn't notice me." She stared at him with level eyes. "Another nurse, Greta, worked weekends and she enjoyed going to the races."

He yanked his hat lower, remembering the nubile Greta and some other things she'd enjoyed. "Were you around when Slim's daughter had her accident?" he asked, keen to change the subject.

"No. I never heard much about Jill."

He sighed and pressed Martha's number. Something was bothering Slim, and the fact that he still wanted to run Echo was disturbing. A good horseman should never dismiss a horse's lethargy. If Slim had personal problems, he needed to sort them out.

A polite voice answered the phone but advised Martha was unavailable, and Dino cut the connection. "Martha's unavailable," he said. "I should have let you call. Maybe you'd have been put through."

"No. Martha told Jocelyn to always put your calls through if she's awake. Unavailable means she's sleeping."

"Who's Jocelyn?"

"The housekeeper. Been around forever." Becky rolled her eyes. "You probably don't remember *her* name either."

Dino shifted on the chair. He never forgot a horse's name but sometimes people names didn't stick as well. "I couldn't hear what you were saying earlier," he muttered. "And no one ever said your name. I'm sorry for calling you Betty."

"Pardon. I can't hear you."

"I'm sorry I called you Betty," he repeated.

The muffled sound alerted him, and he glanced up and caught her laughing. Her eyes danced, her lips tilting in a mischievous smile. He leaned forward, absorbed by her mouth, knowing that if she had smiled at him like that before—just once—he never would have forgotten her name.

A rap sounded on the door.

"Come in," he drawled.

Shane stuck his head in. "Vet's here, boss. I can take Becky over to the grandstand if you want. Catch a few races before Chippy runs."

Dino glanced at his watch, surprised it was almost post time. He still had a lot to do in the shedrow, and Becky would have more fun by the grandstand. But had Shane bothered her earlier?

Shane stepped further into the office and smiled at Becky. Her stylish jeans were much different than the baggy brown pants she usually wore. Trust Shane to notice a pretty girl. Dino had never worried about casual liaisons before but now he wondered if his old boss in New York had experienced the same irritation when he'd flirted with women.

"Becky's here on business," Dino said, shooting Shane a warning frown. "Conrad business."

"And it will be my business to escort Ms. Becky to the races." Shane tipped his cowboy hat with an exaggerated flourish, stepped forward and offered his arm.

Dino watched in amusement, remembering how she shied away from physical contact, much like a spooked horse. It had been days before he could even touch her elbow. Shane's flirting might work on the backstretch girls but it wasn't going to do anything for a cautious girl like Becky. She needed groundwork, a lot of trust, and certainly wasn't ready to cuddle up to any guy. No doubt, she'd choose to stay in the office with him, and that was just fine. He didn't mind making time. In fact, he was glad she was tagging around with him.

He leaned back in his chair, propped his boots on the desk and waited for her polite excuse. But she rose, linked an arm through Shane's and his jaw dropped when the pair waltzed across his office floor and out the door.

CHAPTER TWELVE

Becky propped her elbows on the rail as the gleaming horses entered the paddock for race one. This was way better than being stuck high up in an owner's box. Here she could get close and really see the animals. It would be much easier to pick a winner.

The first horse was beautiful, a well-muscled bay with a white blaze and cocky attitude. Looked like a good bet.

But then number two pranced past, a compact chestnut chomping at the bit, clearly eager to run. He didn't look like a horse anyone should bet against.

She flipped open her program. The race was short, only six furlongs, so maybe the second horse would be the better bet. But her interest leaped to number three when he strutted past, close enough to touch, a white-faced bay with rippling muscles and a haughty expression.

The horse had a groom on each side, and he wasn't as nicely built as the first two but something about his eye grabbed her attention. Supreme confidence. That was it—the same look Dino had—as though he had no doubt everyone would love him. This horse wasn't wasting any energy, unlike the chestnut. He strode past with a free-striding walk, his swishing black tail the only sign of impatience.

The crowd murmured as the number four horse jigged past, shaking his head and fighting his handler. Already a white lather coated his neck and glistened between his muscled hindquarters. Not a good sign. She grabbed her pen, preparing to draw a line through that entry, but paused when she saw his race history. Even though he was over-excited, he'd won or placed in his last five races. No way could she toss him.

"See any you like?" Shane asked.

"Every single one." A frustrated sigh punctuated her words.

"Don't decide anything yet. The favorites are eight and eleven, just walking in now."

She rubbed her forehead. This was much easier when she only had to bet on Martha's horse. Each runner here looked better than the last. It was impossible to pick only one.

"Guess it's easiest to bet on the nicest name," she said in dismay.

Shane chuckled. "That's one method. But in the kitchen earlier we talked about the top four. So you already have it narrowed down on paper."

"So you're saying don't look at the other horses?"

"I'm saying it's best to focus on the four you know can win. Not the ones that catch your eye in the paddock."

She nodded, grateful for the tip. Shane was a nice guy. His hat was almost as rakish as Dino's, and he shared that cowboy charm. Her brain didn't fog when he touched her though, so it was easier to think. When he grinned, his mouth looped in an endearing smile which she suspected drew a fair share of feminine attention.

She was amazed more single women didn't come to the track. It was the perfect hangout with gorgeous horses and rugged men. What more could a girl want? And she was enjoying herself way more than on the occasions she'd been dragged to Martha's elite skybox. Of course, the new clothes helped.

"Oh, no." She glanced down in dismay. "I forgot to change and my clothes are still in Slim's truck."

Shane gave her a quick appraisal, followed by an approving wink. "I think you look just fine."

"But Martha insisted I dress up in case we won. Guess it doesn't matter now that Echo is scratched. I won't have to go for a picture." She turned, scanning the trainers in the saddling enclosure, sparked by an idea. "Maybe that's another way to bet? Wouldn't the trainer who expects to win be dressed the nicest?"

Shane's chuckle drew the attention of the sun-glassed man standing on her right.

"That's a new theory," the stranger said. "I usually bet on speed, breeding and jockey-trainer percentages, but I go to the races a lot and have to admit I've never seen that trainer in a suit before."

"That's Old Spud." Shane leaned forward, nodding. "You're right. Spud doesn't usually dress like that. I'm shocked he even owns a suit."

Becky ran her finger down the program. The number six horse was a gray she and Shane had discounted earlier, but the fact that the trainer didn't often dress up must mean something. She smiled at both Shane and the helpful stranger. "That's my horse then. And I like his name, Liverpool Lou. Plus he's gray and has that winning look."

"Don't know about the winning look," Shane said. "He hasn't won in six tries although he's dropped in class and his breeding is top notch. I saw his dam run. Pretty good mare. She was a gray too."

"Yeah, I remember that horse." The man on her right shoved his mirrored sunglasses higher on his nose. "Won some black type races. I was here when she leaped the fallen horse and won from way back. Three jockeys went down that day."

"Yeah. One of the jocks was Jill Barrett," Shane said. "Damn shame."

Becky glanced at the gray horse being saddled. So the gray's mother had raced against Lyric. Had also been involved in Jill's accident. Maybe even caused it. A chill ran down her neck and despite the warm sun, she shivered. Everything in the horse world seemed intertwined.

Shane turned from the stranger and lightly touched her shoulder. "Want to go up to Mrs. Conrad's box or watch from the rail?"

"The rail," she said quickly. She'd never had this much fun at the races. Everyone in this section was so nice.

The stranger with the sunglasses had been shuffled sideways by a stocky man in a striped shirt who gave an apologetic smile as he squeezed in beside her. "How's the four horse look?" he asked. "My cousin said if the horse was calm in the paddock, he'd be a cinch to win."

"He's pretty lathered up," she admitted.

The man sighed. "Thanks. That's all I wanted to know."

"You're observant," Shane said. "I don't even remember the four horse." They both looked across to where the saddled horses awaited their jockeys. "Let's get our bets down and find a good spot to watch."

The pari-mutuel line moved fast, and Becky made her bet and tucked her ticket into her back pocket. Six dollars to win on Liverpool Lou, the six horse. She'd never bet in her life, and although the minimum wager was two dollars and she was usually very prudent, six dollars on number six sounded lucky.

Shane pressed a plastic glass in her hand and gave a boyish grin. "I know your type is used to champagne but here in the cheap seats, we prefer beer."

Her type? She'd never been slotted as the champagne type, doubted many men even bothered to slot her, and she gave Shane a grateful smile before taking a sip. The beer was cold and foamy and surprisingly good. She hadn't had a beer since she was sixteen, when one of the other foster kids had sneaked a case into the basement.

"The beer company is giving away souvenir hats so I grabbed you one. Thought it might fit if you stuck your hair out the hole in the back—you know, like girls do. But maybe you don't like hats? Or the color?"

He looked so uncertain she quickly accepted the ball cap. The caption read 'Cold Beer, Hot Fillies' and she jammed her hair under the pink cap just like Stephanie did. "Thanks, Shane. It's perfect." She tilted her head, smiling and feeling unusually jaunty.

He stared for a long second. "You look real pretty," he finally said. "Think I'll grab us a couple more beer."

Becky adjusted her hat, smiling as she watched him ease past a short lady with an oversized purse. A handsome cowboy had just told her she looked pretty. Yes, this was definitely a great place to hang out.

She tilted her head, letting the sun kiss her face, and resolved to bring Martha down to the rail once her health improved. Clearly, it was more fun here than perched in an owner's box, isolated from the action. Easy to maneuver too.

The horses paraded past the grandstand and her number six horse remained cool, calm and confident. It seemed she'd picked well even though the gray's odds were ten to one—much higher than the popular Conrad horses which were usually sent off as heavy favorites. Obviously not many bettors followed her dress-up theory.

She glanced around, searching for the gray's trainer and his unusual suit. Jerked in surprise when she spotted Slim leaning on the rail, less than ten feet away. He had his phone clamped to his ear and didn't notice her. "Nothing else I can do." His voice rose. "Filly's been scratched."

She tucked a strand of hair behind her ear, feeling like an eavesdropper but conversely straining to hear.

"Maybe she's too tired," Slim said. "Hard to judge. Didn't expect the scratch." His voice rose in agitation. "No way."

Cursing, he snapped the phone shut. A teenager on her left shot a curious look at Slim but Becky kept her head averted and pretended to watch the horses warm up. Obviously he'd been talking to someone about Echo. Not Dino or Martha. He'd never talk to them in that tone.

"Big lineup," Shane said, yanking back her attention. "Hats are all gone too." He handed her another frothy beer. "Hey, Slim," Shane called. "Did the vet scratch?"

Slim jerked around, staring at them for a moment. "Yeah." His gaze flickered over Becky. "So there's no sense hanging around here. I'm going to haul the horses home after the third race. Meet me at the shedrow then, Becky."

"But the feature race is the seventh," Shane said. "And the eighth race will be good too. A horse Dino once trained is the favorite. You two should stay for the afternoon. Let me buy you a beer, Slim."

"Can't," Slim said. "Got horses to feed."

"But whoever was going to feed when we planned to stay for Echo's race can still feed," she said impulsively. "So there's no need to rush back."

"That's right." Shane gave an enthusiastic nod.

Slim stared at Becky, ignoring Shane. "Unless Dino tells me to stay," he said, "I'm leaving after the third. So you best be ready."

Becky flushed and took another sip of beer, wishing Slim wasn't quite so difficult. It seemed a shame to leave after three races, although if Martha didn't have any horses running, there was no real reason to stay.

Shane gave her a commiserating look and rolled his eyes. She dipped her face in the beer, hiding her expression. However the cold beer tickled her nose, and she could feel a giggle bubbling in her chest. And then she did laugh—partly at Shane, partly at Slim, but mainly because it was a great day at the track.

Dino watched Red lead a strutting Chippy into the saddling enclosure to join the horses entered in race three. Red nodded approvingly. "Chippy's on the muscle today, boss. He dragged me over here."

"Good." Dino rubbed the back of his neck, trying to ease his tension. A win in a claiming race wouldn't compensate for Echo's scratch but might help Martha's outlook, enough to keep her stable intact a bit longer.

Still troubled, he scanned the spectators ringing the paddock, searching for Chippy's owner—owner's rep actually. But Becky and Shane weren't in sight. Maybe they'd decided to watch from Martha's box, or maybe Becky didn't really care about watching a low-level claimer.

He turned back, greeting the valet as Red guided Chippy into his slot to be saddled. Chippy pawed when Dino placed the saddle on his back, always a good sign for this particular gelding. Chippy didn't have much speed but never lost for lack of try.

Sometimes inexpensive animals had bigger hearts than their more regally bred counterparts. Until a horse's first race, it was always a mystery what was inside, kind of like a woman you were just getting to know. Sometimes, no matter how hard you tried, things didn't work out.

He sighed, trying to shake his odd melancholy. Still, events seemed to be tilting the wrong way. First there was Hunter's shocking loss and the despicable sponging, then Echo's scratch, and soon he'd have to admit to Laura that he still didn't have the money. Maybe she was right, and he wasn't good enough to make a living as a trainer.

At least Shane looked happy, the way he always looked when parading around with a new woman. He glanced past Shane in abrupt concern, searching for Becky's familiar long hair. Was she in the clubhouse? Shane shouldn't have deserted her. She wasn't comfortable with Martha's friends, and Dino wanted her to have fun, not hide behind that aloof pretense.

And if Martha hadn't invited other guests to the box, Becky would have to sit alone, sipping wine with only a waiter for company. He stared up at the boxes, trying to spot her. Shane was still smiling as he pulled a pink-capped girl into the paddock—a spot reserved for owners and trainers. Dino fought a flare of irritation and jabbed his thumb at the sign, 'Paddock entry restricted.' Frowned again at Shane and the girl beside him.

Sucked in his breath, gut slammed. The girl was Becky and without the hair to hide behind, she was stunning. He shouldn't have let her go off with Shane. Her cheeks were all rosy too, like she'd been drinking.

"Did you two get your hands on some wine?" He crossed his arms, studying her too-bright smile.

"No wine," she said. "Just beer."

"Aren't you going to clean Chippy's feet, boss?" Red called.

"Of course." Dino dragged his gaze off Becky's mouth. "Give me the hoof pick."

He checked over his shoulder, watching as Shane guided Becky into the owner's spot. Shane was acting way too familiar with an owner's rep. As Dino's assistant, the guy should know better. It was always bad business to fool around with owners.

Dino's scowl deepened. Becky's arm was still linked through Shane's, whose own hand was conveniently in his jean pocket. So technically Dino couldn't yell at Shane. And he certainly couldn't yell at Becky. Still, their closeness was disturbing.

"Going to stretch Chippy's legs, boss?" Red asked.

"Always do," Dino said, bending back down and stretching the horse's front legs. At least Becky looked happy. But why was she so comfortable with Shane? He was just a kid, only twenty-four. At that age, guys had a hard time thinking of anything but sex. And Becky was so innocent. Probably far too trusting.

"Shane!" He jabbed his thumb. "Look after Chippy now. And go back with him after the race."

"Sure, boss," Shane said, stepping forward,

Dino strode across the grass to Becky. "Everything okay?" he asked cautiously. "You having fun?"

"Sure, I even got a new hat. First present I ever got from a guy."

"I'm sure you'll get lots more," he said, unable to drag his eyes off her mouth. "Come on," he said gruffly. "Let's go over by the rail."

"Aren't we going to figure out our bets? Shane told me exactas pay the most, but I only have Chippy so I need to pick a second horse." She wrinkled her nose, looking genuinely perplexed as she studied the trainers. He'd never noticed the smattering of freckles on her nose...its cute little tilt.

"None of those people are really dressed up," she added. "A sports jacket and jeans are a bit ambivalent, don't you think? Like you might win but you're not really certain."

"What are you talking about?"

"That's how I pick my horses. By how the trainers are dressed." She blushed but patted her pocket. "It's an excellent system. I already picked the winner in the first two races, but Shane said if I could pick the top two, I could bet the exactas and make even more money."

"Shane's been doing a lot of talking," Dino said but he turned back and studied the trainers. He knew most of them, and everyone looked typical except for old Ben Mason, who usually wore a stained straw hat. Today though, Ben's felt Stetson gleamed whitely in the sun.

Dino pulled the *Racing Form* from his back pocket and checked Ben's horse, Total Surprise, number one on the program. The gelding had run against Chippy three races back and finished in the money. With this group of horses, they should both be fighting for a piece of the purse. And Ben always liked a nice hat for a win picture.

"You might check out the one horse," Dino said. "Total Surprise."

"Definitely not." Becky shook her head. "That trainer isn't a bit dressed up."

"For Ben, he is. And he wouldn't risk getting his best hat dirty unless he had a shot at the money."

"See!" Her face brightened. "You *do* know the clothes system. Think Chippy and Total Surprise will come one, two?"

She sounded like a hardcore bettor, and he smiled at her enthusiasm. "All I know is that Chippy is feeling great, and Total Surprise is the same caliber of horse. Plus, Ben is wearing a real nice hat."

"Okay, but which horse will come first? Shane said I have to put them in the right order or I don't win a cent."

"Just box them. It'll cost you a little extra, but you'll cover your ass." His gaze drifted down to her rounded bottom, and he jerked his head up. "Want to watch from Martha's box?"

"Gosh, no. I love the rail. The people are much nicer down here."

"Maybe it's because you're smiling."

"It makes a difference, doesn't it," she said, her expression suddenly so vulnerable he felt bad.

He reached up and gently stroked her cheek. "Yes, I generally find it does, honey." Her eyes widened but he let his finger touch the side of her mouth before lowering his hand. He looked over her head as Shane boosted the jockey onto Chippy's back, and Red led the prancing chestnut toward the track. "Do you want another beer?" he asked. "Maybe another hat?"

"I think one cap is enough. But I would enjoy another beer."

He bought two beers while she detoured to the betting window. Then they slipped into a prime spot near the finish line. Chippy was warming up well, not fighting the escort pony although he tossed his head, clearly eager to enter the gate.

"Horse has the desire but unfortunately not much ability," Dino said. "Too bad he can't run like Echo."

"I can't tell those two apart," she admitted. "I thought it was Echo in the hot walker this morning."

"Chippy was in the walker?" Dino stiffened. "Today?"

"Slim said he was just stretching Chippy's legs before the trailer ride."

Dino turned and studied Chippy. The hot walker was unusual but Chippy looked good, so whatever Slim had done seemed to have worked. Too bad Slim hadn't done the same thing for Echo.

The starter called the horses. One by one, the runners disappeared into the gate.

"Let's hope the seven horse comes out blazing," Dino said. "Chippy needs a fast pace."

"What about Total Surprise?" Becky asked. "Is he a closer too?"

"Ben's horse has the same style as Chippy," Dino said, "but he's in the one hole. Sometimes when you're stuck on the rail, you have to throw away caution and go for it." She met his gaze but quickly looked back at the horses. "And sometimes caution is a good thing," he drawled.

"Horses are in the gate!" the announcer blared. The crowd stilled, air thickening with anticipation. *Clang!* The gates opened and nine horses burst out.

A good start. Martha's distinctive yellow silks were visible. Chippy galloped smoothly and had come away fifth. As expected, the speedy seven horse led the way, and Total Surprise was tight on the rail, running second.

Becky jumped, bumping his arm with every bounce. Pink stained her cheeks as she strained to watch the pack of galloping horses. He wrapped his hands around the rail, determined not to touch her again, afraid he might scare her.

He stared at the horses, trying to concentrate on the race and not the woman beside him. The seven horse had opened up a five-length lead while Total Surprise still hugged the rail in second, and Chippy plugged along in his usual steady fashion. Might be okay. The time of the first quarter was a blistering twenty-two seconds, the half in forty-five. Already the seven horse weakened.

The pack relentlessly closed the gap on the faltering leader. As the horses rounded the turn and entered the stretch, Total Surprise grabbed the lead with Chippy running third.

Come on, fellow. Dig deep. Dino's grip on the rail tightened as Chippy battled with a gray storming up on the outside.

Chippy's ears flattened as he fought to fend off the wave of horses. Inch by inch he pulled away, closing ground on the leader. You can do it, boy, Dino willed, watching Chippy inch up to the leader's shoulder, then to his nose. The two gallant horses crossed the wire as one.

"Wow!" Becky said as the tote board flashed 'Photo Finish.' "That was the best race I've ever seen. Even better than the stakes races. I couldn't see the numbers though. Who was the horse beside Chippy?"

"Total Surprise." Dino grinned. "So if you boxed your bet, you got the exacta. Good job."

She nodded but her expression turned wistful. "It's a shame one of them has to lose. They tried so hard. I couldn't help but cheer for them both. And that old trainer wore his best hat. He'll be disappointed if he doesn't win."

Dino gave her elbow a quick squeeze. "I know how you feel. But I want to win too, so save your cheers for me. Beside, it'd be nice to have a picture with you in it. Now finish your beer because I think Chippy got it on the nod."

Her eyes widened although he didn't know why. From their vantage point at the finish line, he was quite confident Chippy had won. Another two feet and he would have been certain. The horse had a big heart, and even though it wasn't a stakes race and didn't count toward his training bonus, he'd receive a percentage of Chippy's winnings.

"Martha isn't going to like this," Becky said. "She wanted me to dress up for the winner's circle. I brought new clothes but forgot to change."

"Martha doesn't hang this type of picture," he said. "Only stakes races go on the wall."

Her eyes widened with indignation. "But these horses tried every bit as hard, maybe harder."

"Sure they did. But Chippy isn't a homebred. He's by some obscure Canadian stud."

"I see." Her expression turned glum. "So no matter what Chippy does, he'll never be important because he wasn't bred by Malcolm?"

"Exactly. And only horses born at Conrad's are retired there. That's why Lyric can stay."

"That's sad. I wonder if Chippy feels second-class, like an orphan."

"That's crazy." He started to laugh but sobered when he saw her expression. She really looked worried. "Horses don't think like people, Becky. And no one is second-class unless they believe that themselves. Chippy is a very confident, happy horse."

The crowd roared, and he swung around to check the board. The flashing red numbers showed Chippy on top. Excellent. "Come on. We won." He grabbed her arm, hustled her past the security guard and into the winner's circle.

Minutes later, Red led in Chippy, followed by a grinning Shane. They clustered around the bright-eyed horse. Dino scanned the throng for Slim, but the man was nowhere in sight so he turned his attention back to Becky, enjoying her delight as she was presented with a wooden plaque with ornate gold lettering.

"Can I pat Chippy now?" she asked once the photographer lowered his camera.

"Yeah and don't forget to thank the jock," Dino said. "Brad gave him a good ride."

Brad leaped off Chippy's back, teeth gleaming against his dirt-smeared face. He said something to Shane then grinned as Becky stepped up, patted the horse and extended her hand. Whatever he said made her smile, and she surprised Dino by leaning over and kissing Brad's muddy cheek.

The jock grabbed his saddle and sauntered to the scales while Becky watched him with a rapt expression.

"Jesus, Becky," Dino said. "Don't look at the jock like that. He's already too cocky."

"Where's he going?"

"To weigh out. Then to the jock room to change his silks for the next race."

"He just looks so...fit."

"Of course he's fit. He's an athlete, one of the top riders at Lone Star." Dino put his hand on her hip and guided her out of the winner's circle. She still had a dreamy look, like she wasn't even seeing him, and he had the urge to dip his head and kiss her. Make her notice *him*.

"I don't think you should have any more beer," he said, using the streaming crowd as an excuse to keep his hand around her waist. "We'll go to the backside after the stakes race. And you'll have to change your betting system. This is a big race so every trainer will be dressed up."

"But I have to go." She shrugged. "Slim wants to leave now."

"And I want you to stay," he said.

CHAPTER THIRTEEN

Chippy stretched out his neck, eyes closed, grunting blissfully while Red massaged his muscular hindquarters.

"Do you massage him every day?" Becky edged closer, reassured to see the personal attention the horse received. Ever since she'd learned Chippy wasn't one of Martha's homebreds, she'd had a special empathy for the gelding. She knew what it was like to have no family.

"I always massage them after a race," Red said. "But some horses appreciate it more than others. This guy laps up any sort of attention."

"I have some carrots in the truck. Would it be okay if I gave him a couple after you're finished?"

"Sure. Boss won't mind." Red flexed his fingers and moved further down Chippy's rump. "But I always feed peppermints. He may never have tried a carrot."

"I know what you mean. Last night I gave Echo a carrot and she acted like she'd never seen one before."

Red's forehead wrinkled in disbelief, but his strong hands continued to work on the horse. "I'm pretty sure Echo's had her share of carrots, being bred at Conrad's and all, but if you want to give Chippy a treat, go right ahead. You're the owner."

"Only the owner's rep," she said, but very softly. This was too great a day to worry about semantics.

By asking Becky to come in her place, Martha had given her the best gift ever. From the time she and Dino had returned from the last race, everyone in the shedrow had treated her like a princess. Sure, it helped that Dino had dropped a flat of beer in his office along with chips and tortillas and announced that she'd bought them—all the staff had been delighted to help celebrate Chippy's win.

All but Slim. She glanced over her shoulder to where he slouched against the wall by Echo's stall. He hadn't been at all happy when Dino had ordered him to stay.

At least it had given Echo more time to recover. The filly looked energetic now. Her head poked over the door, hay protruding from her mouth. Her shrill neigh made Slim wince but energized Chippy, who raised his head and answered.

"Don't you mind that filly, Chip," Red said, not interrupting the rhythm of his skillful hands. "You'll have a new best friend tomorrow."

"Do you think Chippy and Echo are friends because they look alike?" she asked.

Red laughed. "No, it's just that horses hook up fast. These two were shipped in the same trailer so that made them good buddies. Echo is herd bound at the best of times." He smiled. "Chippy will get over it. Track relations are always temporary."

"Yeah, guess so," she said, refusing to look in the direction of Dino's office. For three glorious hours at the races, she'd had him all to herself. But it was seven o'clock now and several people had drifted in from other barns.

One girl looked like Stephanie and was probably an exercise rider. The other was taller and spoke with some sort of accent, but they both had throaty laughs and were clearly enthralled with anything Dino said or did. Becky pasted a smile on her face and tried to block their flirtatious giggles.

Shane strolled down the aisle, clipboard in hand, and paused by Chippy's stall. "How's the champ now?"

"Seems to have come back fine," Red said. "Dino wants me to use that new liniment Doc left. I'm almost finished here."

Shane nodded and turned to Becky. "Want a last beer before you and Slim hit the road? A final celebration for your betting success?"

She laughed. "You're the one who taught me how to bet. Thanks for that, Shane. I'm sixty dollars richer because of you."

"Thirty." Dino's lazy drawl sounded behind her. "You still have to pay for the beer and chips."

She checked over his shoulder, relieved to see the fawning girls had vanished. "Be glad to," she said. "It was a great day. No wonder Martha loves this."

"Martha only watches stakes races. Doesn't generally leave her box. And never drinks beer." Dino's smile deepened as he flicked the brim of her hat. "Doubt she owns a ball cap that says 'Hot Fillies' either. But it was a good day, in spite of the scratch." His voice lowered. "Echo is fine to ship now, and Slim's itching to hit the road. But if you're uncomfortable driving with him, I can take you home."

She paused, stunned by his generous offer. She definitely preferred Dino's company, but it was a lot of extra driving and she'd heard him schedule three works for six a.m. tomorrow. It wouldn't be reasonable to ask him to drive her home when he had to be at Lone Star so early. "It's okay," she said. "But thanks. What do you think is bothering Slim?"

Dino's gaze hooded as he glanced at Shane and Red, and he guided her away from Chippy's stall. "Not sure." His voice was low and regretful. "Slim was never a joker. But he used to be good with the horses. Since Malcolm died, he's different. I'm going to suggest to Martha we bring in another barn manager— on a temporary basis of course. Give Slim some time to work out whatever's eating him."

Becky blew out a regretful sigh. She didn't think it would be that easy; Slim was Malcolm's long-time manager, and Martha stuck rigidly to her husband's wishes.

Dino misunderstood her silence. "Slim's not doing his job. And he should never have questioned my decision to scratch the filly. Something's wrong, and I can't let poor judgment hurt the horses."

"Of course," she said slowly. "But sometimes Martha is very stubborn...and loyal. Slim might be just worried about his daughter."

"He's worried about something. Regrettably it's not the horses." Dino's jaw clamped. "And that's my job. So tomorrow I'll be talking to Martha. I also want to use a private shipper instead of having Slim haul. Now do you want a drive home, or what?"

"I'll travel with Slim and the horses," she said. "Slim is always okay with me." Not quite true but she didn't want to admit otherwise, not when Dino looked so angry. Funny though, he didn't scare her. His anger was different from the anger of other men. Controlled, never mean. And he and Shane had been wonderful company. Her voice softened. "Thanks for the great day. It really was fun."

A smile curved his mouth. "Beer does that, Becky."

"I didn't drink that much." She grinned back. "You cut me off at four."

He reached down and again flicked the brim of her cap. "Should have cut you off at three before you started ogling all those jockeys," he drawled. "Come on. We'll wrap that filly and get you on the road."

Slim looked relieved when Dino turned and signaled for Shane to bandage Echo. "It's damn late," Slim said. "Who's wrapping Chippy?"

"Chippy's staying," Dino said, his voice curt.

"But that wasn't the plan. The gelding runs good from Conrad's."

"And he'll run good from here too. So might Echo and all the other horses." Dino's voice hardened, and there was no evidence of any drawl now. His words were clipped and challenging.

Slim's face reddened and for a moment, it looked like he was going to argue.

Becky stepped between them. "I meant to tell you this morning, Slim," she lied. "Martha asked that Chippy stay at Lone Star."

"If that's what she wants, fine." Slim wheeled, not looking at her. "Don't matter to me. I'll get the trailer."

Slim stomped away and she debated the wisdom of asking him to wait so she could collect her carrots. He'd been wanting to leave for hours. Still, Chippy deserved something other than his usual peppermints, and it was her last chance to treat the gelding. She glanced down the aisle.

Shane was still wrapping Echo's legs so she probably had about five minutes to grab the carrot bag from the cab and rush back. If she hurried, she wouldn't delay Slim one bit.

Decision made, she rushed from the barn and jogged after Slim. He must have heard the crunching gravel but didn't slow. Didn't even look back.

"I need to get the carrots Martha sent for Echo," she said, panting from the sprint. "They're locked in the truck. I think Chippy deserves a few, don't you? Won't take but a minute." She knew she was babbling because, despite her assurances to Dino, Slim's presence was rather unnerving. Clearly the man wanted to get home.

Slim raised his hand so quickly she flinched, but he merely pointed the remote. The truck lights flashed, slashing the night with red. Door locks clicked.

"Thanks." She inched her way through the gloom, swung open the passenger door and grabbed the bag of carrots from beneath the seat. "I'll meet you by the shedrow. Promise to be really fast."

She rushed back to the barn, almost tripping in a pothole, but the barn lights were a friendly beacon. Dino, Shane and Red stood in the illuminated aisle beside a bandaged Echo. The filly looked vastly different from the tired animal that had stepped off the trailer. Her head was high, eyes bright and she craned her head, nickering repeatedly at Chippy.

"Where you going with those carrots?" Dino asked, his voice amused.

"I promised Chippy a couple," she said. "I'll go in the stall so the other horses don't see."

"You do that," Dino said. "Maybe he'll stop calling to the filly too."

Chippy looked at her with inquisitive eyes when she entered his stall. She pulled out three carrots, remembering how Lyric had grabbed the bag, almost devouring a piece of plastic. And plastic wouldn't be good for a horse.

She held out a carrot. Chippy sniffed then took such a tentative bite it dropped in the straw. "Hurry up, fellow," she said, bending down and scooping it up. But there was no rushing him—he ate exactly like Echo. Agonizing slow nibbles, so different from the gluttonous Lyric and almost every other horse she knew.

She leaned over the door and nervously scanned the aisle. Echo had disappeared, along with the men. Slim was probably waiting, probably cursing.

"I've got to go, fellow. You're too slow. You'll have to pick those other two off the floor." She snapped the carrots in bite-size pieces, watching as he snuffled at the straw. "Thanks for trying so hard. You'll always be a champ to me." She gave his neck a grateful pat and rushed outside.

Slim and Dino fastened the ramp, and Echo's frantic neigh reverberated throughout the trailer. The men, however, were silent, the air taut. Becky pulled open the door and scrambled into the passenger's seat, eager to escape before Slim and Dino had an irreparable argument.

Dino walked up and when she lowered the window, he dropped a *Racing Form* on her lap. "Give that to Martha," he drawled. "She'll probably want to take a look at Echo's race, even though we didn't run. There's a nice picture of Malcolm on page fourteen. I think she'll like the article."

Becky had already noticed he hid his emotion behind a lazy drawl but his thoughtfulness affected her, so much that she almost drawled herself. "That's very kind, thanks. She keeps a scrapbook of Malcolm and his achievements. I didn't even notice the picture."

Dino nodded, his dark eyes seeming to search her face. He looked past her at Slim and his voice hardened. "We have a few things to discuss, Slim. Eleven a.m." Then he stepped back.

She raised her window and Slim eased the truck and trailer toward the exit. A security guard checked their papers, glanced at Echo and waved them through. Yawning, she slumped against the seat, glad now that Slim wasn't a big talker.

"The old lady isn't going to be happy about Echo not running," Slim said. "You better tell her it was an unnecessary scratch. Don't know what Dino was thinking."

Becky smothered her groan. "It looked to me like Echo wasn't fit to run," she said mildly.

"Nothing wrong with that filly. Did you see how she acted when we left?"

"She looks good now," Becky admitted.

"Fucking Dino is trying to maximize his bonus at the expense of the old lady, me and everyone else."

"What do you mean?"

"He earns a bonus if he keeps the win percentage on homebreds over twenty percent. You watch. He'll enter that filly next week in an easier race. Whenever he wants to make a change in the race schedule, he just calls the old lady and lays on the charm."

Slim's cell buzzed and he jammed it against his ear. "I'm driving," he muttered. Silence. "Don't know. We're taking the filly home now." His voice was slightly more deferential.

Becky closed her eyes and leaned against the seat, trying to pretend she wasn't listening. Whoever was on Slim's phone did most of the talking while Slim only grunted.

Slim gave a last grunt and closed the phone. "You sleeping or are you going to help me stay awake?"

She twisted in surprise, but he seemed to be talking to her. "Help you stay awake, of course," she said quickly although she couldn't imagine what they'd talk about. The only talking Slim wanted to do was on his phone. Maybe it was the same person who'd called him by the rail. Stephanie or Jocelyn maybe?

"I should check on Martha," she said, "but my battery is dead. Could I borrow your phone?"

Slim tossed over his cell as he maneuvered the truck and trailer into the center lane then sped past a line of dawdling vehicles.

She flipped open the phone, pretending confusion with the screen as she checked his list of callers. Five calls today. Three were the same number. She repeated the number until it was seared in her memory then called Martha.

Jocelyn answered on the second ring, sounding rather grumpy and advising that Martha was asleep. Becky cut the connection.

"Did Jocelyn say anything about the scratch?" Slim asked.

"I don't think Jocelyn is very interested in horses," she said.

"That's what you think." He gave a cryptic snort.

CHAPTER FOURTEEN

"Did you see the Thorntons yesterday?" Martha asked as she listened to Becky's stories about the track. "I'm wondering if Chelsea wore her new diamond necklace."

"Didn't see them. We watched from the rail."

Martha shuddered in distaste. "It's so crowded down there. Dino should have taken better care of you."

"Oh, he took great care," Becky said quickly. "Shane did too. It was a lot of fun."

"Malcolm used to like hanging around the rail, but not me. He was so proud when a horse he bred made it to the winner's circle."

"Is there such a difference with homebreds? Malcolm didn't breed Chippy and the race was a claimer, but watching him was still a thrill." Becky gestured over her shoulder. "And he won that nice plaque."

"It's not the same." Martha gave a dismissive sniff. "Malcolm studied bloodlines, matching broodmares with studs, breeding the best to get the best. He wanted to make a name for our stable. Chippy is just an auction horse. Those type come and go. They'll never be part of the Conrad family."

Becky's throat tightened, and she averted her head. *Family.* The word always filled her with longing. For most people, life centered around it. Yet she could hardly remember her parents, only their constant yelling and, more painfully, their obvious relief when she'd been yanked from their care and made a ward of the state. Since then she'd had foster homes, lots of them, but never family. She'd lived with Martha longer than she'd ever lived anywhere—

"Bring over that shoebox in the closet," Martha said. "I'll show you why homebreds are so special."

Glad for the distraction, Becky retrieved the cherished pictures and centered the box on the table in front of Martha.

"These are pictures of Malcolm's favorite foals from the first hour of birth. Aren't they darling?"

Becky admired each picture Martha passed but lingered over one of a black foal with white hair around its muzzle. Such a beautiful, elegant head. "This baby has a head like Lyric," she said slowly.

"That *is* Lyric," Martha said. "Born dark but grayed out at six months. She was Malcolm's first stakes winner. Won over a million dollars."

Becky leaned forward, studying the pictures, smiling as the wobbly-legged foal turned into an elegant filly posed in the winner's circle. "Who's on her?" she asked.

"That's Jill, Slim's daughter." Martha frowned, the grooves in her forehead deepening. "She loved that horse. Can't remember why, but our first call jockey refused to ride so Jill became Lyric's regular rider. Malcolm made all those types of decisions. He was excellent at motivating people."

Becky paused, still holding the picture, remembering Slim's comment. "Does Dino get a bonus based on wins, or is it a bonus paid on earnings?"

"Can't remember. Our accountant looks after it. But the contracts are in Malcolm's desk, and those race pictures should be added to Lyric's file. Malcolm kept everything but the foal pictures there." She fingered an elegant silver necklace, her voice lowering. "Now tell me, what really happened with the scratch yesterday? I had an odd call from Slim. He's questioning Dino's judgment. Doesn't think Hunter should be shipped to Lone Star and didn't agree with the scratch."

"He called you?" Becky stiffened. The doctors had been adamant that Martha not be involved with management problems.

"Don't look so worried. I told him to talk to you or Dino. But for twenty years, Slim was Malcolm's right-hand man. I want to keep him happy."

"Right." Becky took a deep breath. "I don't know much about sick horses but I think Dino was right. And Slim has been acting a little odd."

"But what was wrong with Echo. What did you see?"

"She was lying down. Not interested in anything. Really tired."

"Then Dino was right to scratch. That's not Echo's personality, not at all, although it's inconvenient that Slim and Dino are arguing. You'll have to sort them out, dear. I don't want to lose either of them." She sighed. "Men can be such little boys. Always trying to prove who has the biggest equipment."

Becky's shocked snort changed to a giggle. Sometimes Martha said the most surprising things. Clearly she was feeling better.

"And tell me, what did Dino think of your new dress?" Martha added with a curious gleam in her eyes.

"I didn't have time to change," Becky admitted, still laughing. "But I'll definitely wear it for the next race."

"You should have a haircut too. Change your look. Show off more of that pretty face."

Becky patted Martha's hand, distracting her with a ripe piece of cantaloupe. Lately Martha was always nagging about her appearance, but Becky liked her hair long. She certainly wasn't delusional enough to think a haircut could change her looks.

Later that morning, she drove down to the training barn, full of coffee, cantaloupe and Martha's advice. *Keep Slim happy but remember Dino is the boss. Make them feel appreciated. Men are easier to handle when they're happy.*

She parked the car by Slim's truck, wishing Martha hadn't been quite so adamant about keeping Slim happy. Dino, well he was totally different. She gave a shivery sigh just remembering how *he* made her feel. On impulse, she slipped her hair in a ponytail and grabbed her 'Cold Suds, Hot Fillies' cap. It had been good luck at the track yesterday, and he had constantly tugged at its brim.

And even though she'd overheard him tell Slim they had to be nice to her—and that had definitely hurt—she still enjoyed his company. He made her feel special. Of course, he made a lot of people feel special.

Sobering, she walked into the barn, determined to represent Martha as best she could.

"Good morning," Slim said, glancing up from his clipboard. "Did you talk to the old lady? Did you tell her that filly shouldn't have been scratched?"

She controlled a flash of anger. Two grooms cleaned stalls at the far end of the aisle, too far away to hear, but their presence was comforting. She knew Slim wouldn't be happy with what she had to say.

"Actually, Echo did seem tired yesterday." She kept her voice level. "So I feel Dino's decision to scratch was the right one. And *that's* what I told Martha."

Slim's face twisted, and he tossed the clipboard against a bale of hay. A blue pen rattled, rolling several feet before lodging against the planked wall. She forced herself to focus on his forehead, fought her urge to back up.

"Dino's using you." Slim's sneer turned ugly. "He already has Stephanie eating from his hand—or should I say, from his pants."

"That's enough!" she snapped, surprised by the whip in her voice. "While Mrs. Conrad appreciates your long years of service, Dino is the boss. If you like your job, you need an attitude adjustment. If you want a day off to think about things, go home now. We can reschedule your meeting with Dino for another day."

"So that's the way it's going to be. Typical Conrad loyalty. I should have known." Cursing, he jerked out the door. Seconds later his truck roared down the driveway.

Becky sagged. This hadn't gone well. She wasn't even sure if he'd be back. 'Keep Slim happy,' Martha had said, but he hadn't looked at all happy. She prayed the tossing of his precious clipboard wasn't symbolic.

She picked up the pen and clipboard, swiping off pieces of hay as she scanned the morning sheet. All the horses had been exercised, all except Echo who had been on the hot walker for forty minutes. Maybe that was what you did with a horse following a race, although Echo hadn't actually run.

She flipped through the pages, absently clicking the pen as she scanned previous notations. Everything was organized. No wonder Martha wanted to keep Slim. Each horse's day was noted in detail—how they ate, what they ate, how long they were out of their stall. Even the times she rode Lyric had been recorded, and she was pleasantly surprised to see she now recognized every horse's name.

All except Ebac.

She paused, tapping the name with her pen. That horse she didn't recognize at all. Stephanie hadn't been galloping him. He'd only been exercised on the hot walker so maybe he was coming off an injury or else was very green.

She walked down the aisle, scanning the brass signs at the front of each stall. The registered name was shown first, followed by the barn name, but there was no sign for any horse called Ebac.

She paused by Hunter. His nose was clear now, the rotten smell gone. She slid her finger along Slim's clipboard until she found Hunter's name. Dino had requested the horse be shipped to Lone Star on Monday—not with Slim but with an outside shipper, and the arrangements were clearly noted. If Slim did quit, his records would certainly be invaluable.

She glanced at her watch as a diesel truck roared up the driveway. Must be Dino although he'd said the meeting was at eleven and it was only ten thirty. She dropped the clipboard on the hay bale and walked toward the entrance, trying to control her big smile.

Slim appeared in the doorway. "Sorry," he said. "I was out of line earlier. I will take the day off though. Be back tomorrow." He gathered the clipboard then paused. "Stephanie's not my daughter but she's had her share of men problems. Maybe there should be some rules about that." He tipped his hat and walked out.

Becky stared, swept with relief. Slim was staying. He was even interested enough to worry about Stephanie and suggest new rules. Martha would be delighted.

She collected Lyric's grooming kit, tied the mare in her stall and even hummed as she brushed the horse.

Lyric's coat was spotless and gleaming when a truck sounded in the driveway. Had to be Dino. She adjusted her cap, swiped a piece of hay off the front of her shirt and walked to the front of the stall.

A wave of electricity always accompanied him and she was certain every horse felt it too, at least the mares. They thrust keen heads over their doors, watching Dino stride down the aisle.

"Morning, Becky," he called. "Where's Slim?"

He was definitely in a businesslike mood, and she barely had time to admire how his brown cowboy hat exactly matched his eyes. "He's decided to take the day off," she said.

Dino's eyes narrowed. "Martha's idea? Keep us apart for a bit?"

Becky shrugged and reached for a hoof pick. "She doesn't want to lose Slim. He was handpicked by Malcolm. And basically this entire business is about her husband."

Dino opened the door and pried the pick from her hand. "Lyric's a nasty kicker." His voice softened. "Let me clean her feet."

Becky stepped back, wondering if she'd ever get used to his touch. Yesterday, his hand had been on her hip or elbow a lot, especially in the crowd, but it still made her turn all soft inside. He was naturally chivalrous with women but maybe he liked her—just a bit.

He ran his hand down Lyric's left hind. She flattened her tail, threatening to kick. He swatted her on the rump, and she obediently lifted her leg.

"I don't want to lose Slim either," Dino said, moving around the mare and cleaning the right hind. "But he has to shape up."

"Martha wants to keep him. Even though he's been grumpy lately."

"Grumpy is okay. Incompetence and disrespect are not."

"I think he'll be much better tomorrow."

Dino walked closer and grabbed her hand, sending tingles through her body. His eyes locked on hers, and she couldn't look away. Didn't want to. My God, he was holding her hand.

"I appreciate your efforts and know you worry about Martha." His expression was inscrutable. "But this is a business and everyone is expendable. Everyone."

He released her hand and stepped back, and she saw that he'd merely placed the hoof pick between her fingers. Heat flamed her face and she turned, adjusting Lyric's halter and scolding herself for being naïve. Just because he'd been attentive yesterday, didn't mean a thing. "I think Slim might be a little bothered about your relationship with Stephanie." She cleared her throat. "I think he worries about her."

"Slim said that?" Dino's voice was clipped.

"In a roundabout way."

"All right."

The stall door shut and she heard his steps as he strode down the aisle. His expression had been unreadable. Maybe he wouldn't give up Stephanie but Slim was right. It must be hard on her. How could it not? Sharing Dino would hurt anyone. Most certainly it would affect your work. And Becky was trying very hard to be objective.

Lyric turned and sniffed her chest as though concerned by her stillness. She realized she'd been gripping Lyric's mane for the past two minutes and the mare hadn't even tried to kick. "Good girl," she whispered. "You ready for a paddock ride?"

"How about a trail ride instead?"

She let go of Lyric's neck and jerked around.

Dino leaned over the stall door, his smile wary. "You're right. I just called Slim. He's resentful about Steph. And I apologized for messing with the staff." He reached over the stall door and tugged Becky's cap, his voice gruff. "Steph and I haven't been together for a while. But it won't happen again." He cleared his throat. "So, do you want to ride with me or what?"

Becky stared. She knew Stephanie had been with Dino last week, had heard them talking. But maybe that was 'a while' to a guy like him. Lyric nuzzled her shoulder, jarring her out of her daze, and she managed a quick nod— along with a silent thanks to Slim.

*

Lyric stumbled on the grassy hill yet Becky's shapely butt didn't bounce from the saddle. "Good job," Dino said, slowing Hank to a more sedate walk. "You have a nice seat. Tough to sit straight when a horse trips."

"It's not so hard when we're walking." Becky smiled. "I'd hate to have her stumble at a trot."

"That's why I get rid of stumblers." He studied the mare. Her toes didn't look overly long, and Slim was always meticulous about farrier visits. "Do you know what horse Slim's daughter was riding when she had her accident?"

"Lyric," Becky said, and it was clear her quick brain was whirring beneath the helmet and mop of hair. "Martha said their first-call jockey refused the ride. Isn't that strange? To turn down a horse who's won over a million dollars?"

"It's unusual." He yanked his gaze off her mouth, trying to concentrate on Lyric's feet. He wasn't sure when Becky had turned so attractive but he'd never been as aware of a woman's femininity. A hundred things to do today, and here he was ambling around a field, oddly content. "Lots of horses get lazy at a walk," he added. "Probably that's Lyric's problem."

"Then we should go faster," Becky said.

"Okay." He grinned. "You want to race Hank and I up that hill? Winner gets first pick of the granola bars."

"Do you have any with chocolate?"

"One chocolate and one with oats and bran," he said, not wanting to admit he'd stopped at three gas stations looking for chocolate.

Her eyes narrowed. "Is Hank a racehorse or a pony horse?"

Her competitive instincts made him grin. "Hank raced a long time ago but only in cheap claimers. Now he just escorts other horses. A horse like Lyric should have no problem beating him."

"All right, let's race."

She grinned and charged off, trying to sneak a head start. Hank immediately leaped forward, but Dino checked him, making sure Lyric had a good lead. He didn't want Becky galloping too fast—it was clear she wanted to win. The girl was as competitive as any jockey. She just didn't know it.

Hank pulled at the bit, protesting Dino's hold, but the gelding was used to restraint and soon settled into a slow gallop, still ten feet behind Lyric as they topped the hill. Becky wasn't a race rider and he could have passed her any time. But when he saw her sparkling face, he was glad he'd let her win. She turned Lyric in a triumphant lap, her cheeks flushed with victory.

"We won!" she called. "Now let's see those bars." She scoffed at the first one he held up. "That looks like the health bars Martha eats. Lyric might like it though."

The second granola bar made her smile, and he flipped it to her. "The chocolate is a little melted," he said, "but it should be okay. You can have a beer back at my place and wash away the crumbs." He didn't know where his impulsive invitation came from—he had plenty of work to do back at Lone Star—but when she tugged at her lower lip, it was clear she was gathering some sort of excuse. "I want to enter Echo in an allowance race next weekend," he added quickly. "We can check the condition book."

She tilted her head, still tugging at her lip. "But Martha said Echo was one of her best horses. Doesn't that mean she should run in stakes races?"

"Generally, but the Lone Star meet closes in two weeks. She needs a race now, and this is the only distance that fits."

He didn't know why she looked so skeptical. Malcolm would have understood. It was hard dealing with absentee owners, but his win percentage hovered at nineteen percent and he needed to push it to twenty if he were going to earn his end-of-meet bonus. And, of course, Echo *did* need the race. Frowning, he adjusted his hat. "Are you sure Martha won't meet with me and go over some of these details?"

"Positive. She's not supposed to have any stress. All she said was to keep you and Slim happy and not let either of you quit."

Her glum sigh improved his mood. She was trying hard, learning fast and had helped with Slim. "I see," he said. "Well, it would make me happy if you'd join me for a beer, but I won't quit if you don't."

"You aren't annoyed about Stephanie? Now that she's...out of bounds?" Becky's voice trailed off as though embarrassed, but she was adjusting her reins and it was hard to see her face.

"Stephanie already was out of bounds," he said dryly. "She has a boyfriend. Someone she referred to as having potential for permanence."

Becky lifted her head, her eyes curious. "But isn't that what everyone wants? Permanence? Someone to love?"

"God, no." His legs tightened involuntarily, causing Hank to skitter sideways. "And love isn't permanent. Not like land. Not like this." He gestured at the estate below, much bigger than his tiny ranch, but he'd ridden up here with Malcolm and it was impossible not to share the man's pride of ownership. The blue lake, white fences and immaculate buildings were all connected by a network of roads that led to the top-notch training oval. The first thing he'd do once he bought back his ranch would be to install a training surface with similar footing as Conrad's.

A white van spit dust as it headed past the lake, jarring him from his reverie and onto more pressing problems. "Looks like Martha's surveyors are back," he said grimly.

"What surveyors?"

"Guy said he was surveying for a golf course. Martha didn't say anything?" He studied Becky's face, but she looked genuinely bewildered. And since Martha told Becky everything... He twisted in the saddle, eyes narrowing as he studied the vehicle. "After we put the horses away, we're going to drive over and ask who signed that work order. Then I'm going to coax you into joining me for a beer."

"Thanks for the invitation," she said primly, "but it's way too early to start drinking."

"Not for me," he said.

Becky relaxed in the oversized chair, watching as Dino filled her glass with another cold beer. "That will be my last," she said regretfully. "Martha wakes from her nap at three."

He checked the kitchen clock. "Then you have another two hours."

"I can't show up drunk."

He cocked an amused eyebrow. "Are you drunk?"

"No, not really. Just relaxed." She stretched her legs on the footstool and glanced out the window of his guesthouse. White rails followed the dark oval and the infield resembled a sea of green just beginning to brown beneath the scorching sun. It looked much like Lone Star except it lacked a grandstand. And, of course, it was completely private. "This is really nice. You can watch the horses gallop without even going outside."

"Malcolm used to do that," Dino admitted. "He'd often sit in this room. No one would even know he was watching. A very shrewd man."

Becky cradled her beer glass, wondering if Dino was also very shrewd. She wanted to ask about his contract, but Slim had made it sound dirty. Still, it seemed simple enough to ask about the bonus terms. Dino was always open, always forthright, but maybe the beer gave her false courage.

Besides, Martha had asked her to sort Malcolm's papers, so it might be easier to wait and check Dino's contract on her own. Slim's accusations were probably just the spiteful ramblings of a disgruntled employee. On the other hand, Slim had said Dino would scratch and then enter Echo in an easier race—and that's exactly what he'd done.

She set down her beer, suddenly uneasy. "May I use your bathroom, please?"

"Down the hall." Dino gestured over his shoulder. "Second door on the right."

The bathroom was amazingly clean with fluffy oversized towels, a spotless mirror that she tried to avoid looking at, and four kinds of body lotion. She debated between peppermint hand lotion and aloe. Went with the peppermint and left the bathroom, still rubbing her hands as she sucked in the minty smell.

"Nice bathroom," she said. "Spotless. And you've got some real girly stuff in there." She couldn't stop her teasing grin as she settled back into the chair.

"That stuff was left a while ago." He shrugged. "And someone comes and cleans the place once a week. Slim's guesthouse is the same but his view is of the barn, not the track. He likes to keep an eye on the driveway entrance."

Her grin flattened at his casual reference to old girlfriends, but she worked for Martha and she was supposed to do her job, not brood over a relationship-challenged trainer. She shoved her thoughts back on track. "If Slim had been home, he would have questioned those surveyors," she said. "They probably drove past his house."

Instead the van had vanished by the time they unsaddled. She intended to ask Martha if she'd ordered any survey work. Both Dino and Slim clearly suspected the estate was going on the block, although it seemed more likely that roads were being widened, and Martha had simply forgotten to mention it.

She scooped up the Lone Star condition book. "So Echo will run in the allowance race next Friday?"

"What I recommend," Dino said.

"Is that the best thing? For the horse and for Martha?"

"Absolutely. But this time I'm going to haul Echo myself. I'll stay here Thursday night. You and Slim can travel with me."

Becky blew out a sigh, imagining Slim's resentment when she announced Dino was taking over all the trailering, not just for Hunter.

He reached over and gave her knee a gentle squeeze. "Don't worry. I'll talk to Slim. He's not being rude to my riding buddy, is he?"

His empathy made her breath stall. Or maybe it was his touch which somehow sizzled through the fabric of her jeans, heating her skin and affecting her breathing. But when his eyes settled on her mouth, anticipation rolled over her in waves. This man oozed pheromones.

"Is he?" Dino repeated.

"No." The word came out in a croak. She doubted he even heard, but she didn't want to shake her head and risk jostling his warm hand from her knee. "No," she repeated, with only a slight quaver. "Everything's fine."

He lifted his hand, and her breathing returned to normal. "Good," he said. "Then I'll meet with Slim tomorrow morning and see you both on Thursday night. Want to go for dinner later?"

His touch must have wrecked her hearing because she thought he'd just asked her out. She stared at him, certain he must hear the erratic hammering of her heart.

"Maybe Martha would like to come too," he added.

Her heart steadied. Clearly he was looking for a chance to talk with Martha and gain advantage in his skirmish with Slim.

"Actually we're both busy tonight." She forced a gay note in her voice. "Ted's coming for dinner. It's been planned for a week, and Martha can't avoid him any longer. So that's what we're doing tonight, Ted, Martha, me..." She was babbling and clamped her mouth shut, but he'd already risen and was gathering the beer cans.

"No problem," he said. "Another time."

Clearly no problem for him. It wouldn't take him more than two minutes to find another date. But as she walked to the door, she couldn't help but wish she was free, that she was the lucky one joining him for dinner.

CHAPTER FIFTEEN

Becky tiptoed into the darkened room. "Is Martha still napping?" she whispered to the duty nurse.

Deb closed her paperback, her expression solemn. "Yes. The naps are getting longer. She didn't eat much lunch either. Couple spoonfuls of soup. Her nephew called and wanted to meet alone tonight, but Martha insisted you be there. They were on the phone awhile. I think the conversation sapped her strength."

Becky's guilt surged. Since leaving the guesthouse, she'd been praying Martha wouldn't want her at the family meeting so she'd be free for dinner with Dino. But it was clear Martha needed her now more than ever.

She couldn't let Ted bully his aunt. There was no reason Martha shouldn't remain in her home, if that was her wish. The horses pricked her interest and fulfilling Malcolm's dream was a reason to live. It was thoughtless of Ted to rip that away. She glanced at Martha, whose still form looked vulnerably small in the big bed. Martha had an imperious aura when awake, but asleep she looked almost wasted.

"Call me on my cell when she wakes," Becky whispered as she gathered Lyric's errant pictures. "I'll be in Malcolm's office filing race photos."

She eased from the room, back down the long hall and pushed open the heavy door to Malcolm's study. Paused for a moment, feeling like an intruder. The masculine desk and austere mahogany panels were overpowering, but on the far side of his desk a display of horse pictures decorated the walls, drawing her like a magnet.

Faces beamed from the winner's circle, chronicling Malcolm's passion for racing. Martha was in every picture, but a more robust version, with rosy cheeks and upright shoulders. The caliber of races won increased over the twenty-year period and while most of the pictures on the left side of the office were claiming or allowance, the races above Malcolm's desk were all stakes. Even the frames were more opulent.

She edged closer. Several pictures included people she'd seen at Martha's skybox as well as a relaxed Slim. He held a dark gray horse with a black mane and tail, but the mare's elegant head was unmistakable. The jockey perched on Lyric's back smiled at the camera. 'Jill Barrett and Lyric's Gamble' the caption read.

Becky studied the vibrant young jockey, a girl capable of guiding a twelve-hundred pound horse at blistering speed. There was little resemblance between the jockey and the pasty-faced woman she'd spotted in Slim's creased picture. No wonder the poor man was miserable.

She checked the date. This was probably the last race Jill and Lyric had ever won. The mare had been retired three years ago, just before Becky had come to work for Martha, although there had obviously been one more race—the fateful one that had destroyed Jill's life and sent Lyric into retirement.

A shiver chilled her neck, and she jerked away from the wall. She'd never considered the possibility of accidents but remembered the grim ambulance that followed the riders during each race. Clearly those safety precautions weren't just for show.

She moved to the files, determined to replace Lyric's photos and escape this melancholy room. Martha had said the horse files were kept in the second cabinet, and she pulled open the sliding drawer, relieved to find everything neatly organized. Each horse had a file bulging with bloodline details. Cryptic scrawls in the margins noted weaknesses and strengths, along with comments such as 'more endurance,' 'better bone,' 'too fragile.'

She scanned the notes, interested in spite of her intention to leave. She hadn't realized the breeding business was this complicated or that the family tree was so thoroughly examined. Not only the horse's race record but entire generations were analyzed, along with conformation and attitude. In one instant, Malcolm had banned a stakes-winning mare from the breeding shed because she was prone to stumble.

Understandable. Becky remembered her own fear when Lyric had tripped. Brave, foolhardy jockeys. It would be horrible to go down with a herd of thundering horses hot on your heels. *Like Jill.*

She shook her head and flipped through the folders, hunting for Lyric's file. Checked the names again but found nothing. Maybe retired horses were kept in a different section? But the next cabinet only contained books on equine herbs and vitamins. Nothing about Lyric. Martha had said there was a complete file, packed with pictures and race clippings.

Reluctantly she moved to Malcolm's imposing desk and tugged on the top drawer. It rolled open, revealing an assortment of pens and paperclips, a wrinkled race program and a bag of white peppermints. He'd probably filled his pockets before he drove to the barn. She shoved the heavy drawer shut on a wave of sadness.

The second drawer contained only invoices, all marked 'paid' and initialed JEM. Must be the housekeeper, Jocelyn, who looked after the accounts. Becky shuffled through the papers, even kneeling on the floor and peering behind the drawer, wondering if Lyric's file was stuck in the back.

"What are you doing?"

Becky jumped, slamming her elbow against the desk, startled by the disapproving lady planted in the doorway. "Hi, Jocelyn," she said. "Martha wanted me to replace some horse pictures. I'm trying to find the file."

The housekeeper swung the door open and stalked into the office. "As far as I know, all the horse folders are in the shelves. There may be something in the bottom desk drawer but that's always locked." Disapproval swept her long face. "Martha never gave me the key."

Becky tugged at the brass handle, but the lower drawer didn't budge. "Guess I'll get the key and come back."

"If you take anything, note it on the sheet. Ted asked that nothing be removed unless it's signed out."

Becky's hands curved with resentment. "Well, that's rather presumptuous."

"No, it's good he's looking after things." Jocelyn's mouth tightened. "He's Martha's only relative and with her moving to a retirement home, someone has to take charge."

"But Martha hasn't decided that yet, and she has excellent care here. Who said she was moving?"

"It only makes sense. Don't be so selfish." Jocelyn tilted her head, appraising her for a moment before turning and sweeping from the room.

Becky sank into the soft leather chair. Maybe she was being selfish. Jocelyn had worked here much longer than she had. Maybe Martha would be happier with more chances to socialize. Where she'd be with people her own age, people she could watch television with and sip sweet tea. Perhaps enjoy a game of cards or even Bingo.

No. Becky shuddered at the thought. Martha would absolutely hate it. She was a bit of a snob and preferred to choose her own company. Liked to be queen of the manor, someone who could dispense favors, not receive them. Lately she was happiest talking about Malcolm's horses or simply watching the animals in the fields. No nursing home, however luxurious, could provide that.

Becky's cell buzzed, and she flipped it open.

"Martha's awake now." Deb's voice sounded strained. "And she wants you."

Becky scrambled from Malcolm's chair. "I'll be there in two minutes." She grabbed Lyric's pictures, closed the office door and rushed through the foyer, down the hall and into Martha's bedroom.

"About time." Martha twisted in her chair. "I've been waiting for ages. And I need my hair fixed for dinner." Her frown deepened. "Exactly when are you going to get a proper cut? What's the sense of new clothes if you don't show your face?"

Becky nodded at Deb who smiled with relief and eased from the room. "I've had my hair like this since I was thirteen," Becky said.

"Obviously," Martha said, still glaring at Becky's offending hair. "Don't you remember that Ted's coming?"

"Of course. I heard he called earlier."

"He seems to think you've developed too much sass so your presence at dinner isn't necessary. But I insisted you be there." Martha's lips pursed. "I do enjoy teasing that boy."

"He's not really a boy," Becky said. "He must be at least fifty."

"All men are boys until they get married. Women help them mature. Poor Ted was never interested in anything but making money, although Malcolm said he's a complete failure at that."

"He seems to genuinely think you'd be happier in a retirement home."

"Few things about Ted are genuine." Martha grabbed her hairbrush and passed it to Becky. "And I'm perfectly happy here, especially when you tell me about the horses. How did you make out with Slim and Dino?"

"Neither of them quit. And Dino is entering Echo in a race on Friday."

"Friday?" Martha frowned. "But that can't be a stakes race. They're always on the weekend."

Becky's fingers tightened around the brush. "Dino says she needs the race, and it will put her back on schedule. I thought it sounded fine."

"I suppose it's okay. Malcolm preferred his good horses run in top races, but he always followed his trainer's advice. That's why he only hired the best."

"And Dino's the best?" Becky brushed Martha's thin hair, trying to keep her voice casual, didn't want Martha to know the mere mention of Dino's name made her insides turn buttery.

"He's one of the best in Texas," Martha said. "Had his own racing stable before working for a famous trainer in New York. They won the Derby with Strike A Pose—remember when Malcolm and I went to Louisville? Dino moved back last summer. Malcolm said Dino's ex-wife ended up with his ranch, and he wants it back." She shook her head. "Apparently it was a nasty divorce, but I still think he's a doll."

Becky made a sound deep in her throat. She didn't consider Dino a doll, more as a big hunk of a cowboy—a heartbreaking hunk.

"And no sense pretending you don't agree." Martha twisted, studying Becky's face in the mirror. "I've seen the way you look at him. Just remember, he's fine for starters but definitely not husband material."

"I'm eager to see the main course, if he's only a starter," Becky managed.

Martha's bracelets jangled as she patted Becky's hand. "You know what I mean. It's fine to use Dino for a little fun, but he's a cowboy. No, we want someone different for you, a businessman like Malcolm. But first we have to pull you out of that shell. Help you forget the bad things that make you want to hide."

Becky tried to laugh it off, but Martha squeezed her hand with such understanding her throat thickened. The clock ticked loudly in the abrupt silence.

"Nothing bad happened," she finally managed. "And I'm not hiding. At least, not any more. You've helped me so much." An irritating itch bothered the back of her eyes, and she couldn't stop blinking. Impulsively she leaned forward and kissed Martha's lined cheek. "Gosh, I love you."

"And I love you," Martha said, "but don't cry. I detest crying."

Becky swiped the corners of her eyes. "I'm not crying." But her throat felt tight and her eyes were all prickly and even though she hadn't cried since she was eight, it seemed today she was perilously close. "Look." She grabbed the *Racing Form* Dino had sent. "There's a good picture of Malcolm here, along with a summary of his breed-to-race program. Dino thought you'd like it."

"What a thoughtful man." Martha grabbed the *Form*, slipped on her glasses and studied the page. "Malcolm looks handsome. He would have been thrilled with this coverage. I'll bring it along for our dinner with Ted."

Martha looked so vitalized by the article, it was ludicrous to think she wanted to sell. "Did you hire any surveyors lately?" Becky asked impulsively. "There's a white van doing work on the estate. It drove past the barn today."

Martha didn't look up, still absorbed in the article. "Maybe someone was lost." She jabbed at the page with her finger. "It says here Malcolm had a discerning eye when it came to conformation and was very stringent with bloodlines."

"Yes," Becky said. "I was in Malcolm's office looking for Lyric's file and saw he rejected a nice mare because of a habitual stumble. I didn't even know that kind of problem could be passed on."

Martha's face clouded. "He worried so much about the riders. That tragedy with Slim's daughter was devastating. I remember the race. One minute Lyric and Jill were in front, the next on the ground."

"Did someone else cause the wreck? Or was it Lyric?"

Martha rubbed her forehead. "I can't remember. There was a video—Malcolm watched it over and over—although I've never wanted to see the replay. Maybe you should though, since you're riding Lyric now." A smile softened her face. "It might make you think twice before galloping off and trying to catch Dino."

"Actually we've already raced and I beat him."

"He must not have been trying. Dino is a heck of rider." Martha's voice turned sly. "So he rode with you again?"

"He won't let Lyric and me out of the paddock unless someone is with us." Becky brushed the sparse hair near Martha's forehead. She'd believed she'd won fairly, but maybe he *had* been holding Hank back. How embarrassing. The realization that he hadn't even been trying left her deflated—and eager for a rematch.

Her strokes turned vigorous as she imagined her next race against Dino. But first she needed to improve. Needed to gather tips from someone who knew racing. Someone she trusted. Someone who loved to give advice. "Can you tell me the best way to make a horse run faster?" she asked.

"Trainers have been trying to figure that out for years." Martha winced and reached up, softening Becky's brush hand. "But I certainly have several suggestions."

CHAPTER SIXTEEN

Martha presided over the elegant dinner with gracious assurance. The last time Becky had eaten in the formal dining room, Ted sat at the head and she and Dino had been subjected to his unrelenting boorishness. It wasn't like that tonight. With Martha in fine spirits, Ted was relatively subdued, the conversation almost dull. It would have been nice to have had a fourth dinner guest, one who would have been happy to talk horses—Dino, for example.

She sneaked another peek at her watch, trying to imagine what he was doing now. Probably eating with whomever he'd invited out in her place, although perhaps they'd ordered a pizza and stayed in, and were actually doing…well, whatever he chose to do.

"You look a bit flushed, dear," Martha said. "Are you feeling well?"

"Fine." Becky pushed thoughts of Dino from her head. "This shrimp is delicious."

"Actually it's rather tough." Ted looked down his nose at the plate, the lines around his mouth furrowing in disapproval. "I'll tell Jocelyn to have a word with the cook. Do you work in the kitchen as well, Becky?"

Becky focused on his narrow forehead. She still had trouble looking into his pale eyes, but Martha's forehead trick was effective. He'd made a few disparaging comments earlier, seeming determined to remind Martha that Becky was staff, but it was surprisingly easy to keep him in check simply by following Martha's suggestion.

"No, I'm just a nurse," she said, focusing on the wrinkle below his receding hairline.

"Actually Becky's much more than a nurse," Martha said. "She also oversees the horses for me, and it's been delightful hearing about them from a fresh angle. I'm more optimistic about the race season now than I was two weeks ago."

Ted's displeasure blasted in waves, but Becky kept her gaze riveted on his forehead. Three wrinkles now above eyebrows that deepened when he frowned, and at this moment they resembled crevices.

"So you have experience with horses?" His voice chilled. "I assume your family was in the business?"

"No. My parents turned me over to the State when I was eight," she said. "We didn't have horses." Or a dog or cat or even a hamster, but Ted's expression showed he got the picture.

"Becky was raised in foster homes," Martha said. "Was it five homes, dear?"

"Six." Becky didn't want to look at Ted's boring forehead any longer and took another sip of the lovely white wine which was every bit as tasty as the shrimp.

Martha nodded. "Yes, she made her way with perseverance and bravery. Finished her nursing diploma, worked in a rehab center then found her way here where she's become like a daughter to me."

Becky grabbed her napkin and covered her twitching mouth. Ted glared with open hostility, and she knew if she looked at Martha she wouldn't be able to control her giggle. He never caught on when Martha was playing him. Had spent so little time with his aunt, he wasn't aware of her iron will and somewhat perverse sense of humor. Martha had been manipulative all night, even pulling out the *Daily Racing Form* and pretending she just noticed the glowing praise about Malcolm's breeding program.

"We have a *family* dinner every Sunday," Martha continued in a saccharine tone. "Maybe next month, you'll be able to join Becky and me."

Ouch. Becky peeked across the table, almost feeling sorry for Ted. He simply was no match for Martha when she was in form.

"And maybe we'll have Dino and Slim join us as well," Martha added. "I understand you all got along well the last time you dined here."

Ted's eyebrow rose. "I've only met Dino Anders. Never met Slim."

"Of course." Martha gave a dismissive wave of her hand, but her voice lowered. "Sometimes I forget little details like that." She glanced at Becky and for the first time that evening, looked slightly uncertain.

An hour later, Ted was gone, the wine bottle was empty and they were safely ensconced in Martha's room.

"You were wonderful, Martha."

Martha smirked as she settled against the pillows. "If that young man thinks he can rush me out before I'm ready, he can think again. Did you see his face? I thought he was going to have a heart attack. Better him than me," she added darkly. "I do think his frequent visits are over. Don't know what his hurry is but he'll have to wait until I'm dead before he can waltz in here and take up residence. He's as manipulative as his mother."

"You did lay the family thing on a bit thick. Ted's going to hate me." Becky smiled, her fingers unusually clumsy as she lost count of the pills for the second time. Wine always had that effect.

"He doesn't even notice you." Martha yawned. "But I meant what I said about how I enjoy your company. Malcolm was always the horse authority, and it's nice to be the expert for a change. You're an excellent listener." She fussed with her covers. "Now hurry up with my medicine and let me get some sleep. And tell that night nurse not to stare at me in the dark. She gives me the willies."

Becky tucked the sheet around Martha's shoulders, noting her eyelids had already lowered. Lately she'd been dozing every three or four hours, so this had been a long stretch without a nap. Becky waited until the night nurse arrived then wandered back to her bedroom, restless and too revved to sleep.

The wine left her energized, although it didn't matter if she stayed up late. There was no need to go to the barn early tomorrow. In fact, she was going to make sure she avoided the horses until Dino and Slim finished their meeting. Although then she wouldn't see Dino and possibly catch a glimpse of whatever woman had stayed the night.

Then again, maybe he didn't invite his ladies overnight if he had early-morning meetings. Or maybe they brought their own car and drove themselves home. Or maybe he was actually alone. Her mind flipped through the various scenarios until curiosity propelled her to the closet.

She rifled over hangers until she found a pair of dark pants. Tugged them on, struggling to keep her balance as she hopped on one leg. Perhaps she was a tiny bit tipsy. It was hard to remember how many glasses she'd had; she'd been too entertained by Martha.

She giggled, remembering how Martha had so effectively put Ted in his place. It was unlikely the man would be dropping by anytime soon. He'd pretended interest when Martha said Echo was running Friday—even asked some questions—but it was apparent what he really wanted was for the horses to be sold.

Well, look at that.

She paused, staring at her reflection in the mirror—black sweatshirt and pants, like a mysterious Ninja ready for night maneuvers. It'd be possible to go anywhere unseen, dressed like this. She wasn't curious about Dino and his unknown date, not at all, but she *had* promised Lyric some treats after today's ride. And since she was dressed in black, she could easily wander around without disturbing a soul.

Some nice clover grew very close to Dino's guesthouse, clover Lyric would love. Yes, indeed, she really should take Lyric some of that lush clover.

She scooped up a black scarf and slipped out of the house and into the car. Grinning, she pointed the Mercedes in the direction of the barn. The car was quiet, a perfect spy car; she could barely hear its purring engine. On impulse, she switched off the headlights. What fun, the most she'd had in a long time, the same heady feeling she'd experienced when sneaking out at camp.

She knew where to park so no one could see and eased up to the back door of the barn. It was a longer walk to the guesthouse, but she could cut down the aisle and give some carrots to Lyric. And to Echo as well, although she certainly wasn't going to hold them. Slow eaters like Echo were a bit irritating when you had other things on your mind.

She opened the back door, feeling her way through the darkened corner, to the muted aisle lights around the corner. It seemed ages since her first night visit when Slim had been working with Hunter. Thanks to Martha, she'd learned so much.

A few horses poked hopeful heads over the doors, and she hid the carrots beneath the waistband of her pants, feeling guilty she hadn't brought enough for all.

"No treats, see?" She waved her empty hands.

Lyric wasn't fooled and nickered impatiently. Becky opened the stall door and slipped in, pulling out three carrots and enjoying the mare's eagerness as she gobbled them up. Nothing was ever slow about this horse.

Lyric nuzzled at her chest, wanting more, but Becky gently pushed her head away. "That's all, sweetie. I only have four, and we should save at least one for your buddy."

She fastened the stall door and stepped in with Echo. Pulled out the carrot and held it in her hand, resigned to at least a three-minute wait. The filly opened her mouth, grabbed it, and the carrot vanished.

Crunch, crunch.

Becky blinked. This made no sense. But the carrot was really gone and Echo sniffed for more. Tonight, the filly was an even faster eater than Lyric. But the last time she'd been offered one, she'd been tentative, nibbling like she'd never seen a carrot.

Nibbling like Chippy after his race.

She rubbed her forehead, struggling to separate the two horses. She'd fed Echo in the stall the night before the race but not Chippy who had been on the hot walker. And Chippy had been calling from the dark, like a horse who hated to be alone. Calling like Echo.

She braced against the wall, staggered by suspicions. Slim knew she couldn't tell the two chestnuts apart. Maybe it had been Echo on the hot walker and Chippy in Echo's stall. Forced exercise would explain the filly's exhaustion on race day.

She shook her head, struggling to remember, but the details remained hazy. And even if Slim had switched horses, it still didn't make sense. He'd been the one who was adamant about Echo racing. What an asshole.

Anger swept her, and she rushed from the stall and headed for Slim's house. A few lights glowed so clearly he was awake. Squaring her shoulders, she cut through the dark, stumbling once but walking more evenly as her vision adjusted.

Gravel shifted beneath her feet, a solitary sound in the still night, reminding her that she was very much alone. Her steps dragged as she approached the guesthouse. She wasn't doing anything wrong—shouldn't feel so reluctant. Merely intended to ask a few questions. But she stooped and picked some clover, practicing what she would say, aware she was stalling. Slim could get very belligerent when put on the defensive.

Sucking in a resolute breath, she continued toward his house, uncertain if she should go to the front or the back. The house was the same general layout as Dino's but lacked a porch. Light glowed from a back window, probably the kitchen, but the front lights were off.

She circled toward the back door. Stepped into inky blackness and painfully rammed her knee into the bumper of a car. Not a truck so obviously a visitor's. She groaned, wondering if Slim also slept with someone on staff. Wouldn't that be ironic; Dino, at least, was up front about it.

Obviously it wasn't a good time to knock on Slim's door. Not unless the visitor left soon.

Curious, she placed her palm over the hood. Still warm. The front had a distinctive Mercedes emblem. Her throat went dry. Ted drove a Mercedes.

She inched back, hugging the shadows. Her hands were clammy and she wiped them on her pants. Couldn't be Ted. He didn't even know Slim. If she wasn't such a coward she could find out. Just creep up to the window and look in.

But her heart kicked and tension cramped her stomach. She glanced over her shoulder. The barn was only two hundred yards away, and Dino's house was just beyond it. Out of sight, but not too far.

She drew in a shaky breath, edged to the side of the house and flattened against the wall. No voices. The windows must be shut. She'd have to move a little closer. No big deal.

She wanted to move but her legs refused to leave the sanctuary of the wall, and the fifteen feet between the wall and lighted window stretched like a football field. Her heart pounded and all she could do was hug the wall.

She sensed movement. A door clicked.

"It'll be done," Slim said.

"Make sure."

Ted's voice. Unmistakable. She squeezed her eyes shut, afraid her gaze might draw his attention when he walked to his car.

She kept her eyes clenched shut even as his headlights slashed the darkness, hitting the back of the house. Felt their brightness and cringed as rough wood pricked through her thin shirt. Gravel crunched. She pried her eyes open.

The car was still moving. Hadn't stopped. She sighed with relief as the lights turned along the driveway and down the road. Her top lip tasted salty. She wanted to wipe her damp forehead but knew Slim lingered by the door. Feared he'd sense her movement.

An owl hooted. Something scurried past and she jumped, rattling the gravel, barely able to contain her frightened squeak.

"Thought I heard you out there," Slim said. "Come on."

She squeezed her eyes shut, sucked in a resigned breath and prepared to step out. At least he didn't sound angry.

A plaintive meow sounded. A cat. Slim was talking to his cat. Claws scrambled on the steps, the door slammed and she sagged against the wall, too weak with relief to move.

Dino savored his beer as he studied the form of the speed horse in Echo's race. The fleet California filly, Country Zip, would be her main threat. If the two hooked up on the front end, the pace would be suicidal. Echo could close but preferred to stalk. A lot would depend on post position. God, he hoped she didn't draw the rail.

A knock sounded on the door, too tentative for a horse emergency. He frowned and checked the kitchen clock. Nine-thirty. Stephanie maybe? She often dropped by to watch race video although she was never tentative. He eyed his case of beer. Only three left, and he wanted them all.

He rose from the chair, tossed the *Form* on the table and swung open the door. Took an involuntary step back. Becky in mugger clothes?

"May I come in?" she asked, her voice oddly husky.

She looked like a night pixie, her hair swathed in a voluminous dark scarf. A black shirt was tucked into some sort of pajama pants, and a belt cinched her small waist. Her eyes were brown slashes in a pale face, and her pockets bulged with grass.

He grinned. "Did Martha have a masquerade party?"

Her smile was so brittle, he thought her face would crack. "Come in and sit down," he added quickly. "There's beer or I can make you a cup of coffee. Or maybe you'd prefer tea?"

"Okay," she said.

He guided her to his big chair close to the kitchen. She moved stiffly and he lingered, reluctant to leave her. "What's wrong, honey? Is Martha okay?"

"She's fine."

"Good." He paused then crossed to the kitchen and grabbed his coffee pot. Three hours old, relatively fresh. He remembered she liked milk and checked the fridge. Gave the carton a cautious sniff before splashing some in her cup. He passed her the mug, hooked a chair with his foot, pulled it close and waited.

She sipped the coffee as though unaware of his scrutiny. Her tension seemed to be easing though, until she glanced down the hall. Her face filled with dismay. "Did I interrupt you? I meant to check for another vehicle but forgot."

"I'm alone. You refused my dinner invite, remember?" He smiled but she didn't smile back. Didn't even react. He grabbed her hand, shocked by its coldness. "What's wrong?"

"I think Ted and Slim know each other."

"Okay." It didn't sound like a big deal, and his gaze drifted to her lips. She had such a sexy mouth when she pulled back her hair. Of course, her mouth was always the same, but it was far more noticeable when she tied her hair back. More distracting too.

"Ted said he didn't know Slim. But he was at Slim's house tonight. He must have stopped by after dinner with Martha."

"I see," Dino said, absorbed by the movement of her lips. Her top lip had a fascinating arc. It had looked pale when she first arrived, but now the pink color was returning.

"And I think Slim may have had Echo in the hot walker instead of Chippy." She raised her head, staring at him like she'd just announced a state secret.

"Slim said Echo was in the walker. That's not unusual." He dragged his attention off her mouth. Obviously she was upset about something, although the raw fear he'd sensed earlier had faded.

"But what if Echo was forced to walk around all night?" She wrung her hands in dismay. "Wouldn't that make her too tired to race? Wouldn't that explain why she laid down?"

"Becky, nobody would leave a horse on a walker all night, and Slim wanted that race. He needs the money as badly as I do."

"But there's also that horse, Ebac, the one I don't know, the one who was marked on the clipboard." Her words came out in a rush. "Ebac could stand for Echo Beach and Arctic Chip. That would explain why Slim didn't want me around the barn, even though I couldn't tell them apart."

"I never heard of a horse called Ebac," he said. Her chest heaved, and her shirt tightened over her breasts. He yanked his gaze back to her mouth but then was distracted by the dark smudges on her nose. "Did you put black cream on your nose? Were you spying on Slim?"

"Of course not. I don't spy on anyone." But she averted her head as she struggled to pull off her scarf, and her evasiveness was obvious.

"I'll ask Slim about this tomorrow…now, if you prefer. We'll straighten it out. But please, don't go walking around in the dark."

"Tomorrow's fine," she said. "Thank you." But her tremulous smile tugged at his chest.

He didn't like to see her scared, didn't like that pinched expression. Pieces of grass had fallen from her pocket, and he picked a stalk off the floor. "Were you ignoring the 'Keep Off The Grass' signs," he teased. "Want to go back and pick some more?"

She grabbed his fingers, and he stopped talking. The trusting way she looked at him, the way she clung to his hand sent his thoughts careening back to that kissable mouth. "Or maybe we should just stay here," he said gruffly, sliding his left hand under her chin.

She stared up at him, her mouth slightly parted. Such a sexy little mouth. He tilted her head and lightly kissed her, brushing her soft cheek with his thumb. When she didn't pull away, he slid his tongue in, savoring her sweetness. Her hands crept around his neck. He tugged her closer, cradling her bottom, swinging her around so she straddled him.

God, she was all rounded curves, and he was surprisingly aroused. He deepened the kiss, holding her head still with one hand and pressing her against him with the other. Not that she seemed to want to go anywhere. Her legs were spread over his thighs, her breasts nice and accessible, and her hot mouth made him throb.

He slipped his hand under her shirt, exploring her velvety skin. Sweet, soft and—thank you, God—willing. A quick twist, and he unhooked her bra. Her tongue entwined with his, turning him on with her little gasps, shortening his breath. He slid his hand along her rib cage, sighing with pleasure as he cupped her breast.

Her nipple pebbled between his fingers. God, he wanted two mouths. No way was he moving his lips away from such a hot kisser but her breasts cried for attention. He pried his mouth off hers, shocked by his ragged breathing.

"Take your shirt off, honey," he murmured, keeping his hand filled with the firm roundness of her breast.

She'd stiffened before his mind made the connection something was wrong. A second later she stumbled from the chair, leaving him with a blast of frigid air and a raging hard-on.

He squeezed his eyes shut, didn't want to reveal how badly he wanted her. "What's wrong?" he finally asked, opening his eyes but not moving from the chair.

"You want me to take my clothes off." Her voice was shrill with accusation, and she stared at him like he was a criminal.

"Of course I do," he said. "That's generally what people do when they have sex."

"But I don't want to have sex."

Could have fooled me, he thought, but she looked so distraught, he nodded and straightened in the chair. "Fine, Becky, we won't. It's not a big deal." His gaze drifted ruefully to the bulge in his jeans. "Although for the record, I think it's an excellent idea."

"I didn't sneak down here for sex. I'm not interested in that. It's just...not right." Color flagged her cheeks and she stared at the floor, her mouth trembling so much he thought she might cry.

"Hey, honey." He rose and gently pulled her to him. "It's okay. Don't get all shy on me again. Sex is just sex. It's not a big deal if we do. It's not a big deal if we don't. Nothing's different."

But she felt stiff in his arms, and he sensed something was very different. "Come on back to the chair. Relax and tell me about Slim." He guided her to the chair and pulled her on his lap, determined to restore her balance. "It's all right," he said when she tried to pull away. "I'm just going to rub your back. You're tighter than a drum."

She relaxed under his slow massage and when he finished, she was cuddled against him like a kitten. He redid the clasp of her bra, pleased when she didn't move, didn't stiffen.

"You're finished with the backrub?" she asked with obvious regret.

"For tonight." He kissed the top of her head. "I'm meeting with Slim tomorrow morning at six. I'll ask him about the hot walker and your mystery horse. Okay?"

"Okay," she said. He heard her suck in a deep breath. "And I'm sorry about earlier. I have a thing about taking off my clothes."

"Why's that?"

She shrugged, but her face was tucked into his shoulder and he couldn't read her expression. He slid his hand beneath her hair, using his thumb to massage the base of her neck, sensing she was close to some sort of confidence. "Why's that, honey?"

"I've only had one boyfriend. He...understood things."

"And I wouldn't?"

She raised her head, eyes wide and vulnerable. "We were together a long time. Three years."

He nodded, waiting for more, but she pulled away and scrambled to her feet. "I have to go."

"Okay." He reluctantly rose to his feet. Lifted his arm to hug her but her wary eyes reminded him too much of a deer poised for flight, so he jammed it back to his side, oddly uncertain. "I'll be around." He cleared the gruffness from his throat. "If you need anything. Anything at all."

CHAPTER SEVENTEEN

Becky cracked her eyes open and stared at the clock, fighting a lingering reluctance to wake. Last night's events ran in a relentless replay, and she groaned. Dino, Slim, Ted—none of it good.

She'd knocked on Dino's door, dressed in strange black clothes. He must have guessed she was spying, trying to check out his most recent woman. And she'd pretty much jumped his bones when he kissed her. But gosh he'd been a marvelous kisser. She allowed herself a sinful shiver of pleasure.

Luckily her naked phobia had prevented a disaster. She'd hate to join the ranks of his pillow friends. Knew her pain would be unbearable if she saw him with someone else. It would have made working together achingly hard.

Even now things would be uncomfortable. She squeezed her eyes shut, analyzing every gesture, every comment from last night. He'd assumed she'd come to spy on Slim, so that was some relief.

And the kiss had been a mutual thing. To Dino, sex was like shaking hands, not a big deal. So maybe he didn't know she was infatuated. At least he'd promised to speak to Slim.

But that was a thorny issue too. Accusing Slim of switching horses was a serious charge. Yet she believed he was doing something shady, and her chilling sense of danger when she'd watched from the dark had been bone deep. And very real.

She hoped Dino would be tactful. It was seven-thirty now so their meeting might already be finished. She thrust the covers back and scrambled from the bed. Dino would probably call if Slim admitted anything.

She showered, dressed and hurried to Martha's sitting room.

"Martha is awake and full of energy," Deb said with a yawn. "She's making a list of things to do. Want me hang around?"

"No, I'll be here all morning." Becky gave an involuntary shudder. No way was she going to the barn today, not until she knew what was going on with Slim...and not until she was sure Dino was gone. She slipped into Martha's bedroom.

"Oh, hello, dear." Martha gave a preoccupied smile as she jotted something on a sheet of writing paper. "The hairdresser is coming today. I'm trying out a new girl. Same one Greta used. If there's time, she might be able to squeeze you in."

"No, thanks," Becky said. "The great thing about long hair is that there's no need for regular cuts."

"I see." Martha nodded, scratching another notation on her list. "I also want to drive down to the barn and see Hunter before he's shipped to Lone Star. Tell me though, why is Dino using an outside shipper when we have a perfectly good trailer?"

Because Dino doesn't trust Slim. Becky stared at Martha's bent head, so small, so fragile, and prayed Dino would be able to sort things out. Martha would be devastated if she discovered Slim had been disloyal, would take it as a personal betrayal.

"Slim's probably busy," Becky said slowly, "and Dino wants to ship today so Hunter can train on the track."

"But it's part of Slim's job to ship." Martha frowned over her glasses. "It also gives him some variety. Malcolm always worried about Slim. He doesn't have many friends."

Becky busied herself, straightening the row of medication. "Maybe Slim and Ted are friends?"

"No. Ted has no interest in visiting the barn or the horses. I don't expect to see him soon either. He may phone though, wondering how I'm doing."

Becky's hand tightened over a container, but she kept her tone casual. "Martha, do you remember Ted's phone number?"

"Of course not. I rarely call him. But Jocelyn would have it. She talks to him all the time." Martha's eyes twinkled. "She said you were in Malcolm's study trying to pry open a private drawer.

Was quite indignant about the whole thing. Why didn't you ask me for the key?"

"Didn't know I needed one. Lyric's file wasn't with the others, and the only place I couldn't check was the bottom drawer." Becky gestured over her shoulder. "Lyric's pictures are still in the baby box."

"It's doubtful the missing file is in Malcolm's drawer, but the key is kept in my jewelry box." Martha's voice turned fretful. "I do hope that file isn't lost. It's difficult to obtain replacement papers. The Jockey Club is very strict about that sort of thing."

"I'll check again when you're having your hair done," Becky said.

"We'll see." Martha's voice firmed. "But I would like you with me when the hairdresser comes. She's new and...well, I might not be comfortable."

"I've never seen you uncomfortable with anyone. But I'll stay if you want."

"Very good." Martha nodded with satisfaction. "Now let's have breakfast and then we can drive down to the barn and see Hunter before he leaves. Dino said the shipper was coming at nine."

Becky's head jerked up. "You talked to him?"

"I was busy, but he left a message with Jocelyn."

"What did he say? Did she write it down?" At Martha's narrowed gaze, Becky paused. "I'm just wondering if he entered Echo for Friday," she added weakly.

"Yes. He did enter the filly. He also suggested you come to Lone Star tomorrow and watch Hunter gallop. Of course," Martha added, "you don't *have* to go. Lone Star is a bit of a drive, and I've been asking you to do a lot of work with the horses."

"Oh, no," Becky said quickly. "That's fine. I want to go—" She quit protesting when she caught Martha's knowing smile.

"We have to be back by eleven." Martha stared at the barn as Becky parked the car beside Slim's truck. "I don't want to miss my hair appointment."

Becky nodded and pried her damp hands off the steering wheel, grateful Martha was with her. This would be her first encounter with Slim since Dino had confronted him with questions about hot walkers and the 'horse' called Ebac. It was bound to be awkward.

They headed toward the yawning door. "Slim is probably getting Hunter ready," Martha said, oblivious to Becky's nervousness.

A gray horse emerged from the barn and pranced past them. "Hello ladies," Stephanie called from his back. "Going to ride with me today, Becky?"

"How about Wednesday?"

"Sure. I have more time this week with Chippy gone and Hunter leaving." Stephanie motioned with her head as she guided her horse toward the training track. "Slim's in the barn wrapping Hunter. He's not in a great mood."

"Hunter or Slim?" Becky asked but Stephanie only laughed as if the question was a joke.

They entered the barn, blinking as their eyes adjusted to the light. Martha's grip on Becky's arm loosened, and she straightened and walked unaided toward Hunter's stall. Becky squared her own shoulders, determined to banish her guilt. After all, *she* hadn't done anything wrong.

"Hello, Slim." Martha stared over the stall door to where Hunter was tied to the wall. The colt stood with an air of resignation as Slim wrapped one last hind leg. "How's our boy?"

"Feeling good." But Slim's gaze shot to Becky, and she recoiled at the venom in his eyes. He rose and walked toward them. "I met your nephew last night, Miz Martha. He dropped off some horse papers that belonged to Malcolm."

Becky's breath caught and she stared at the neatly wrapped legs, each one a perfect stovepipe pattern. No doubt about it, Slim was good at bandaging horses. Pretty good at making up stories too.

"How was your meeting with Dino?" She forced herself to speak up, to talk as confidently as Martha always did. "I had a few questions, a few concerns. Was everything cleared up?"

Slim nodded grudgingly and stepped from the stall. "Everything's fine now."

Becky tugged at her lip. Maybe Dino hadn't asked about the hot walker. She would see him tomorrow and could hear all the details then. Best not to say anything else. Best to avoid conflict.

"Did you discuss the horse on the hot walker?" she heard herself ask.

Slim's head shot around. "I told Dino, like I told you, a horse was colicy. And there's no horse here called Ebac. I was checking cheap bedding on eBay, trying to save everyone money. Now, I hear a truck and trailer outside. Miz Martha, do you want to give your colt a treat before he leaves?"

Becky crossed her arms, simmering with frustration as Martha fed Hunter a carrot. Slim's statements were impossible to disprove. And maybe she had been wrong. She watched as the colt devoured the treat in four crunching bites—this was another horse who ate fast. Her breath quickened with fresh optimism. She knew how to prove Echo hadn't been safe in her stall the night before the race.

Tomorrow she'd show Dino the horses' different eating styles. Slim might be able to explain his association with Ted, but he certainly couldn't explain carrots.

"They're here!" Martha hung up the phone, her voice shrill. Becky had never seen her so excited about a routine haircut.

"They? There's more than one stylist?" Becky asked.

Martha stared in the mirror, absorbed with fluffing her thin hair. "I already told you, this is the same lady who cut Greta's hair and she recommended some other services as well. So, of course, there's two of them. Jocelyn is taking them to the yellow room now."

The yellow room, with a nice bathroom and lots of natural light, was a long walk for Martha and not the usual place for her haircut. "Okay," Becky said slowly. "Do you want to walk or take the wheelchair?"

"Wheelchair."

It took ten minutes to navigate the yawning halls and reach the yellow room. Jocelyn stood by the door, her long face creased with curiosity. "Will you be wanting refreshments, Martha?" she asked.

"Sweet tea and sandwiches, please," Martha said. "It's going to be a long day."

Becky pushed the wheelchair into the room, privately doubting Martha's sparse hair would occupy any hairdresser very long. Even her regular perms didn't last more than two hours. She paused, stunned by the appearance of the two waiting ladies, so different from Martha's usual stylist.

The tiny brunette had a lip ring, belly shirt and purple streaks. Her statuesque friend looked like a Swedish playmate, one who'd just rushed from the centerfold of an exotic magazine and hadn't had time to grab all her clothes.

Becky gulped. Martha placed a lot of stock in appearances. She wouldn't be pleased, not one little bit. "Good morning," Becky said politely, scrambling to fill the awkward silence.

"Becky, would you push me back outside for a moment." Martha's voice turned chilly.

Becky pulled the wheelchair back into the corridor and edged around Martha's chair, trying to keep from laughing.

"Those...creatures can't touch me. My heart wouldn't take it. Purple hair!" Martha's voice wobbled with outrage. "But their services have already been paid for, and I don't want to be cheated." She twisted her fingers in agitation.

Becky covered her hand, trying to soothe her. "I'll tell them you're not feeling well. It doesn't matter if they're already paid. Besides, they deserve something for making the house call." And packing all that equipment couldn't have been easy. She'd even spotted a massage table among their extensive supplies.

"Absolutely not," Martha snapped. "People who dress like that don't receive gifts from me. I can't condone paying people for nothing. Charity turns them into beggars."

Her voice rose and Becky flinched, positive the ladies would hear every hurtful word.

"And I'm going back in there to tell them," Martha added.

"Shush, Martha," Becky whispered. "They might look a bit different, but give them a chance. Greta always looked gorgeous, so they're probably good at their job."

"Indeed." Martha leaned forward, her hand swooping over Becky's wrist. "Then you go in for me. Have the services I paid for. Every single one. Otherwise, I insist on stating my mind."

Her voice quivered with emotion, but triumph blazed in those shrewd eyes.

Becky stiffened. "Is this your way of making me have a haircut?"

"I don't know what you're talking about." Martha crossed her arms. "Just go in there. And don't come out until they're finished because they're *not* touching me. Hurry along. Jocelyn can wheel me back."

As if on cue, the door opened and the tall blonde tugged Becky into the room. "We have a lot to do so we can't waste any more time. Sit." She pushed Becky toward a high vinyl chair.

"It's okay," Becky said, slightly intimidated. "I'll make sure you get paid. It doesn't look like you're needed today—"

"Oh, we're definitely needed." She studied Becky with open disapproval, squeezing her nails into Becky's shoulders until she sank into the chair. A bib was locked around her neck amidst a flurry of arms and the smell of citrus and coconut.

Becky leaned forward, gripping the handles of the chair and eying the door.

"Don't you dare move," the blonde snapped, clamping a strong hand around her upper arm. And Becky, overpowered and outmaneuvered, didn't.

Three hours later, Becky opened a cautious eye. "Is this almost over?"

"We're running a bit late." The blonde, who she now knew as Judy, clicked off the hair dryer. Even though Judy's appearance was intimidating, she'd turned out to be the easier of the two.

Becky was certain Pam, the purple-haired girl, enjoyed inflicting pain. Eyebrow plucking, lash tinting, bikini line waxing—Pam had smiled at every one of Becky's involuntary shrieks. At least the facial and manicure had been pleasurable, and the haircut relatively pain-free, although the mound of hair on the floor was frightening.

"Do people really pay for waxing?" Becky asked, tilting her head and trying to see herself in the mirror.

"Sit still." Pam poked at Becky's toes. "The nail polish is wet."

"How long will I smell like this? Because horses won't like it if—"

"Don't talk, Becky," Judy said. "Your head moves every time you speak."

Becky closed her eyes, trying to be patient. But now she knew how Lyric felt when tied to the wall and groomed. Completely and utterly helpless. No wonder the mare lashed out when touched.

Maybe next time she wouldn't tie her. Maybe the mare would behave better if she weren't forced. And on their next ride, she was going to use an English saddle and lean forward, exactly like Martha said the jockeys did. She'd keep contact with Lyric's mouth.

Yes, indeed. Next ride, she intended to find out exactly how fast that horse could run. Stephanie would have some valuable tips too. Dino wouldn't have to hold Hank back again. In fact, he'd be very surprised.

He might be shocked at her smell too, she thought ruefully, as she fought a touch of nausea. Hopefully she wouldn't reek like this when she went to Lone Star. Every product the girls used had a distinctive smell, and the combination was overwhelming.

"Okay, you're done." Pam lifted her arms, gesturing like she'd just completed a major overhaul. "You're allowed to look now."

Becky leaned forward and glanced in the round mirror Judy held. She stared, transfixed by her reflection.

Judy's head dipped closer. "I layered it for a lighter look, but there's still some length in back. And the highlights do wonders for your skin tone."

"Did you put makeup on me too?" Becky's words came out in a disbelieving whisper. She hardly recognized herself. *Wow.* She gulped, still staring.

"No," Pam said. "I only tinted your lashes and shaped your bushy brows. That was one of the things you cried about."

"I didn't cry," Becky said, too enthralled by her makeover to be indignant. "I look different. Almost like you two."

"A little body piercing, some purple in your hair, and you're pretty much there," Pam said with a rare smile.

"So Martha arranged all this?" Becky clung to Judy's hand, not yet ready for the mirror to be taken away. The face staring back at her was familiar but different too; she simply couldn't believe it. She looked—nice.

Judy smiled. "Everything's paid, including a generous tip, so be sure to give Mrs. Conrad our thanks. She certainly knows what she wants."

"She certainly does." Becky swallowed, the words log-jamming in her throat. Dear, wonderful Martha. No one had ever done anything like this for her. She really was the kindest, most thoughtful, stubborn, generous lady.

And very manipulative.

She'd yanked Ted's chain, calling Becky family, knowing it would annoy him. And now she'd coerced Becky into getting new clothes, new haircut, a new look. Not that it was a bad thing; Becky touched her hair, fascinated at how the layers emphasized her features. However, Martha would steamroll anyone, and it was probably best to pretend some annoyance. In a nice way, of course.

She lowered the mirror and grinned—grateful, happy and full of mischief. "Judy, do you have a temporary nose ring I can slip on and some washout highlights? Something in a really flashy color—maybe purple?"

"I hope you didn't mind, dear, but something had to be done." Martha smiled with grim satisfaction. "Come in and let me see. I was right, wasn't I. You look lovely. Good gracious! What did they do to you?" Her satisfaction flipped to horror as Becky stepped further into the room.

"They said body piercing was the new thing. That everyone my age has it." Becky's hand drifted to her nose, checking that the ring still protruded. The lip and tongue studs were tight enough, but the nose ring had dropped off twice, just walking down the hall.

Martha's mouth was still open but her face had turned plum red, displaying much more intense horror than Becky had anticipated. And that probably wasn't healthy. She hastily pulled off the rings and dropped them on the table.

"Actually body piercing isn't my style," she added, relieved when Martha's color faded to a lighter shade of pink. "You might like this tattoo though; it's a very heartfelt one." She rolled her sleeve up.

A reluctant smile brightened Martha's face. She reached up and traced the blue heart and the 'I love Martha' inscription. "I rather appreciate the thought," she said, "but please tell me this tasteless tattoo and purple highlights aren't permanent." However, her smile remained locked on the tattoo.

"No, they'll both wash off." Becky grinned. "We were just having a little fun at the end of my unexpected, but much appreciated, beauty session."

"You're not annoyed?"

"Oh, Martha." Becky wrapped her arms around her. "I never would have done this on my own but I'm so grateful. And strangely enough, not even scared."

"Scared?"

"You know, of drawing attention."

Martha's reassuring squeeze was surprisingly strong. "Don't mumble, dear. Just remember if you look good, you feel good. And if you feel good, there's no limit to what you can do."

"I do feel pretty good." Becky gave a sheepish smile. "I checked every mirror in the hall. Terribly vain of me, but it's amazing what a nice haircut can do."

"Exactly," Martha said. "I've always thought life's more fun when you have a good cut."

CHAPTER EIGHTEEN

"Is it true?" Red asked, brushing Hunter with long, sure strokes. "Did some bastard really stick a sponge up this colt's nose?"

Dino nodded grimly. The meeting with Slim yesterday had been less than satisfactory although Slim had delivered plausible explanations. It hadn't been his actual words that strengthened Dino's suspicions but more the man's evasiveness when he spoke of the hot walker.

At least Hunter was at Lone Star now. No one could get to the colt here, not with a twenty-four hour guard. Now the only homebred left at Conrad's was Echo, the filly that didn't like to sleep in strange stalls—perfectly understandable, Becky would say.

And hadn't *she* been jumping into his head with irritating persistence. It must have been that kiss, the way she'd felt in his arms. But he wasn't what she needed or wanted, and his breath leaked with a sigh of regret.

"You want this guy out after the renovation break?" Red tossed the brush back in the grooming kit, jerking back Dino's attention.

"Yeah, and get Chippy ready too. Becky's coming to watch their gallops." He glanced at his watch, hoping she'd show up early. Maybe stick around for lunch. There was a quiet restaurant around the corner where it would be easier to talk, although he'd have to pry her away from the track.

She definitely enjoyed the horses—unlike his ex-wife.

Laura had complained about every aspect of the job: every owner's dinner, every sick horse, every disappointing race. She'd insisted he take vacations, always at the worst possible times. Trainers didn't have a regular nine-to-five job, but she'd known that before they were married. Training was hard enough without an attention-starved woman. Unfortunately when he couldn't give her what she needed, she'd looked elsewhere.

He didn't want to think about Laura and switched his attention to the five impatient horses pawing in the aisle, groomed, tacked, ready to go. Grooms boosted exercise riders into the saddles, and his first set filed from the barn.

They walked toward the gap, accompanied by squeaking leather and the occasional clink of metal. The sun was warm and optimistic as it poked through the haze, the earthy smells refreshing. Six a.m. He never minded getting out of bed. Not for this. How could Laura possibly have resented this?

"Hey, boss. Saw you at The Corral last week," Speck, an exercise rider, called. "If you get tired of those ladies hanging on your arm, send a few my way."

"They're not horses, Speck." SueAnne, the feisty brunette, snickered. "You wouldn't know what to do with a two-legged female."

Speck grinned and stroked the neck of the gray mare he was riding. "Oh, I know what to do, SueAnne, darling. Same as a mare. Talk soft, ride them gentle, give lots of head."

"That's enough, kids." Dino hid his smile, but he liked his riders relaxed and joking. Horses picked up on moods, and a happy horse was a better horse.

Grooms removed lead shanks and the horses moved along the outside rail, following his earlier instructions. Speck walked the gray on a relaxed rein. The mare was opinionated and liked to look around before going to work. The riders on the two bay colts asked them to trot immediately. The young horses needed action or else they bucked. Just last week one of his riders had been dumped, and the horse had been loose on the track for ten minutes—always a chilling event.

He'd scheduled the other two geldings to jog a lap then gallop a mile, but Shane could look after that and free up more of his time for Becky. Just in case she wanted to eat, look at horses or just talk by the rail.

He checked his watch again; he needed her phone number. Quite likely she wouldn't arrive for another hour, which meant Hunter and Chippy would have to wait. Be nice if she came early though—easier on scheduling. Besides he was looking forward to seeing her.

He stared at the two colts, trying to focus, impatient with how his thoughts kept circling back to women. Both horses were moving well, trotting evenly. The gray mare was still walking, still looking around with her typical bossiness. Speck appeared to be dozing, but he was the most patient rider on the payroll, always willing to give animals plenty of time, unlike some riders who were forever in a rush. Horses sensed stuff like that, just like women.

He rubbed the tightness in his neck. Obviously he'd rushed Becky the other night, but she'd felt so ready. Until she'd leaped away in panic. He couldn't remember the last time he'd so badly misjudged a woman. Of course, after his divorce, he'd always chosen the easy and available, trying to keep his mind off how he and Laura had screwed up their marriage.

Not that he was even thinking of Becky that way. God, no. Too many reasons to keep his distance—Martha being a big one, although she hadn't seemed to mind when Greta and a few other nurses slipped down to his guest house. Still, Martha's relationship with Becky was different, more like Becky was a niece, and he doubted Martha would approve of a horse trainer sleeping with her niece.

No, he preferred a woman like the one Shane drooled over. Curved in all the right places, with the sexiest mouth ever. Just the way it moved made him harden, made him imagine it was Becky with those lips wrapped around—

His hands balled as he stared at that familiar mouth. Goddammit, it was Becky. And she was smiling at him. But she'd cut off her hair and now nothing hid those angelic features. Nothing hid those sexy lips. And she definitely shouldn't be wearing those kinds of clothes—tiny tight jeans, clingy T-shirt, much like the other girls. But somehow on her they were harder to ignore.

No wonder Shane was standing on his head trying to keep her attention. And Shane really should hustle back to the shedrow *now*.

Dino set his jaw and stalked over. "Shane, you better go check on Hunter."

"Sure, boss." But Shane's hopeful gaze didn't leave Becky's face. "Want to go back with me, Becky? Watch Mrs. Conrad's horses get tacked up?"

"She's staying with me." At Dino's snap, they both turned, Shane in confusion and Becky with a questioning smile. "We have some business to discuss," he added. "You can bring over the next set. We'll wait here." His gaze settled on Becky. "I liked your hair when it was long."

Her eyes shadowed.

"But it looks really nice now too," he added quickly, crossing his arms. He just didn't want staff distracted and Shane's mind clearly hadn't been on the horses. Not that it was impossible to work and think of sex at the same time—he did it a lot—but he didn't want Shane similarly occupied. At least not occupied thinking about sex with Becky. My God, the idiot was still standing there. "Got a question, Shane?" he snapped.

"Want me to bring some coffee?" Shane asked.

Dino and Becky both nodded at the same time but it was clear whom Shane was worrying about. "All right," Shane said. "Two coffees, one with milk." He sauntered away, his walk far too cocky for an assistant.

Becky watched Shane leave with obvious interest so Dino snagged her waist and tugged her back to the rail. "See that horse?" he asked.

"Which one?"

Which one, indeed? He scanned the horses, trying to think of something to say, then settled on a bay gelding trotting on the rail. "The one that's winging."

"I see how a front leg swings out. Is that winging?" she asked. "That's not good?"

"If he can run fast and stay sound, it's okay. But he's pigeon-toed so he compensates by winging, especially with the left leg. Might be prone to stumble too."

While she stared at the horse, he had time to admire her new hair, her new face, her new look. He'd never noticed her blond streaks before, but today they glinted under the sun, and when she turned her head he could have sworn he saw glints of purple. Whatever, the overall effect was damn nice. Even dour old Larry from barn twenty-four stared in admiration.

She didn't seem to notice Larry, just looked up at Dino with a conspiratorial smile. "There's a lot to learn, isn't there?"

"Yeah," he said, staring at her mouth. She was going to cause a lot of trouble with that sexy mouth; he'd definitely have to keep her away from Shane. He already knew she was a helluva kisser. Jesus. He twisted uncomfortably, determined to steer his thoughts to neutral ground. "Hunter and Chippy will be here in about fifteen minutes." He checked over his shoulder. Scores of people leaned against the rail, but none too close. "I spoke with Slim about the issues you raised the other night...when you dropped by."

Her cheeks colored. Good, she hadn't forgotten their kiss either. "We better talk about Slim somewhere private," he added. "Maybe go for lunch later?"

"Okay." She'd lowered her voice to match his. "But what did he say about the hot walker?"

Dino tugged her closer, enjoying her freshness, pretending he was worried about other listeners. "He was indignant. Insisted it was a colicy horse."

"Do you believe him?"

"Slim doesn't look me in the eyes at the best of times." He sucked in the floral smell of her hair, the heat of her body, and it was hard to think of Slim. "I'm staying at Conrad's the night before Echo's race. What nights do you work? Maybe we could have dinner?"

"I don't have nursing shifts anymore. Martha wants me free for the horse stuff." She tilted her head, her smile teasing. "She did warn me about you though."

Godammit. He couldn't afford to annoy Martha. "I've taken out some of her nurses before. I'm not an ax murderer." His sulky tone surprised him, and he crossed his arms. "Don't see why she'd start with warnings now."

"*Some* of her nurses?" Becky laughed. "Martha only knows about Greta. And all she said was to have fun but don't get serious."

He realized he'd been holding his breath and slowly exhaled. This should work out all right. "So she wants you to have some fun? Probably wants me to keep away dangerous womanizers like Shane."

She rolled her eyes. "He isn't as dangerous as you."

"Now that's where you're wrong. Shane's a little shifty with women. Blows hot and cold. With me, you know exactly what you're getting."

"And what is that?" She tilted her head, still smiling, but with solemn eyes.

"Someone who will ride with you, listen to you, make you smile. And when you're ready," he stared into her face, hoping she'd feel his sincerity, "make love to you."

"What if I'm never ready?"

"Then that's fine too." He gave her hip a confident squeeze. In his experience, no one who responded as enthusiastically as she did could refrain from sex for very long. He just had to be careful not to scare her.

Speck and the gray mare had stretched into an easy gallop so he gestured at the track. "That's one of our horses coming now. The gray, out for a two-minute lick."

Becky leaned over the rail, her face rapt. "She looks great."

"You love this, don't you? Prefer it to nursing?"

"I'll always want some involvement with nursing. I like rehab work the most but this position with Martha isn't just a job—not anymore. The horses are a wonderful bonus." She shrugged off the subject, her gaze tracking the galloping gray. "There can't be anything more beautiful than a happy, healthy horse."

"Happy and healthy—that's what horses need. Same as people." He shrugged. "I'm trying to decide what to do with Hunter. He may not race until we move to San Antonio. The Retama meet starts in August. Or we could look at something here. The Lone Star Derby didn't take much out of him, considering the sponge stopped him cold."

She nibbled at her lower lip, clearly reluctant. "Is it possible…" she paused, then her words escaped in a rush. "Is it possible Slim stuck that sponge up Hunter?"

"I've been thinking that ever since you told me about the hot walker," he admitted. "I also wonder about the night Lyric got loose." He sighed, hating what he had to do. "So I want to install some surveillance cameras. Think you can swing the expense with Martha?"

"Definitely. I didn't think you were really listening the other night."

"I did have better things on my mind." Her shy blush made him grin.

"Well, hello, Dino," a sultry voice called behind them. "Just the man I want to see. The *Barn Notes* report that your Code Hunter horse shipped in yesterday. Do you have a race in mind?"

Dino's smile slipped as he turned toward the reporter. "Not yet, Danielle."

She pushed closer. "Were you able to find a reason for his disappointing Derby performance? I hear Mrs. Conrad is in serious decline. Barely hanging on. Just hoping to see a homebred win again."

Dino heard Becky's pained breath. So did Danielle who leaned forward, staring curiously. "Are you associated with Conrad Racing Stables too? Perhaps you'd like to comment on Hunter's poor showing. Does it affect the impending sale?"

Dino shifted his shoulder, blocking Danielle's view of Becky. "I'm happy to give an interview later, in private. But if you'll excuse us, we're both busy now."

"You've being evasive." Danielle's moue of disappointment was more threatening than cute. "Perhaps I should write 'trainer had no comment?' Or perhaps Conrad's is considering hiring a new trainer? I really need something."

"Drop by my office around ten." Dino glanced at the gap, where his next string of horses walked onto the track. "I'll make you a coffee," he added, hoping to pacify her, at least enough that she'd leave Becky alone.

"And I'll also make a statement on behalf of Conrad Stables who, by the way, have no intention of selling. Nor do they have any intention of hiring a new trainer," Becky said, her voice so crisp it surprised him.

"Fine. I'll see you both later." Danielle's eyes narrowed at Becky but she stalked away, no doubt searching for other hotbeds of gossip.

He studied Becky's fierce expression, surprised that she'd tried to help. Her arms were crossed, eyes flashing, and she clearly was not one to back away from a fight. "Thanks for having my back," he said quietly. "I don't understand why I never noticed you before."

"You say the most uncomplimentary things. I don't understand why all the women like you."

He grinned. "Maybe you will later."

She rolled her eyes but was silent until Hunter paraded by. "He looks happy. Cocky as ever. Oh, look who's behind him." Her voice rose with such delight, Dino twisted, studying the line of approaching horses.

He should have guessed—not a homebred but a cheap claimer. Chippy pranced, third in line, head bowed, ears pricked. His head abruptly cranked and he jerked to a stop in front of Becky, planting his legs so forcefully even his rider was surprised.

Chippy stuck his nose over the rail, clearly expecting a carrot.

"Keep him moving," Dino said. But Becky's delighted expression made him soften, and he didn't scold the inattentive rider.

"He sure has a good memory." Becky looked guilty but pleased as Chippy swished his tail and continued walking, clearly disappointed he hadn't received a treat. "And I have carrots in the car. I want to show you how he eats, much different from Echo. That's why I think Slim switched those horses."

Shane appeared, three coffees balanced in his hands, and she stopped talking.

Dino's mouth tightened when Shane passed over the coffee, edged past, then sidled in on her other side. Acting way too familiar. Standing much too close. He knew where Shane had slept last night, and it didn't seem right to climb from another woman's bed and then breathe down Becky's neck.

But Shane didn't seem to notice his displeasure. "Hey, boss. Maybe later when I'm finished with the horses, I could take

Becky for breakfast? That would give you more time to look after office stuff."

The guy never quit. It was okay if Shane hit on girls from the other barns, but Becky was sort of with him. A muscle in Dino's jaw twitched. Worse, she seemed to like Shane. It was already clear she considered Dino a pig and obviously didn't realize Shane was an even bigger player. Hell, Shane probably had a different girl every damn week.

His eyes narrowed as he studied Shane, trying to see what Becky saw. The guy was dependable, good with horses, even tolerably good looking if one liked the sissy type. But his hair was too blond, his nose too straight. Even his glittering teeth were too perfect; he looked like a Hollywood cowboy.

Shane yanked his hat lower and shuffled back a step, and Dino realized he'd been glowering.

"Or maybe I'll just do the office work," Shane mumbled, "and you and Becky can go for breakfast."

"That's probably the better plan," Dino said.

CHAPTER NINETEEN

Becky ripped open the plastic bag and brandished a carrot in front of Dino. "This is what I'm talking about. Watch how Chippy eats." She slipped into the horse's stall and held out the carrot. Chippy took a tentative bite, chewing slowly then taking another nibble. It was obvious he hadn't eaten many carrots. She glanced over her shoulder, delighted with the experiment.

Dino only stared, a blank look on his chiseled face.

"Don't you see? It takes three minutes for him to eat one little carrot. He takes polite nibbles. Echo eats like a starving Lab—which shows she wasn't in her own stall the night before her race. It proves she was in the hot walker, and Chippy was in Echo's stall."

"Damning evidence, to be sure," Dino said. A smile curved his mouth but he was staring at her, not even looking at Chippy.

"But carrots tell so much." Her voice rose.

"Carrots tell so much," a feminine voice called. "Is that how Conrad Stables decides which horse to race?" Danielle stopped beside Dino and arched a perfectly shaped eyebrow.

Becky continued stroking Chippy's neck while he chewed the carrot.

"Ten o'clock already?" Dino glanced at his watch, his voice impassive. "Let's move this meeting to my office. Coming, Becky?"

"I'll be along later. I want to finish feeding Chippy." Plus she was developing a strong aversion to the reporter. Dino had warned her that Danielle's paper sought gossip, and it seemed he was correct.

"Hand-feeding spoils horses." Danielle's smug words drifted down the aisle as she and Dino walked away. "It must be *so* annoying when owners do that."

Becky couldn't hear Dino's reply, but he must have made some sort of joke because Danielle's laugh tinkled through the shedrow, and it was hard to shake the notion they were laughing at her. A groom pivoted, eyes wide with appreciation as Danielle sashayed past. Not that Becky blamed him. The woman was jaw-dropping gorgeous.

She turned away, remembering how impressed she'd been at her first sight of Danielle. Even the reticent Slim had been smitten.

Strange that Dino didn't seem particularly enamored, especially odd for a man who so appreciated the opposite sex. Maybe he was accustomed to beautiful people and expected their attention. But it would take more than a haircut for her to even shadow Danielle's gorgeousness—she'd need surgery. Hopelessness welled in her chest.

A gentle nose bumped her shoulder. She turned. Chippy's big eyes were soft and accepting, and when she scratched the itchy spot beneath his jaw, he stretched his neck, grunting in bliss.

"Horses sure like you." Shane paused in front of the stall, jotting a notation on his clipboard. "Red noticed a little swelling in his left leg. Can you hold Chippy while I check?"

"Sure." She snapped on Chippy's lead line and watched with concern. She hadn't noticed anything wrong with his leg. The horse had moved well on the track—at least she thought he had. But Shane frowned as he ran his hand over Chippy's lower leg.

"What's wrong?" Her hands tightened around the lead.

"Some filling around his suspensory. We'll wrap it. Put him on stall rest. Maybe send him back to Conrad's and free this stall up for another horse. Dino will make that call. But it's clear this guy needs to take it easy for a while."

Becky's shoulders slumped. This racing business was heartbreaking. On the positive side, the news wouldn't reach

Martha since she only asked about the homebreds. Never about Chippy.

"He'll be okay," Shane said. "Chippy is playful, always dancing around. Who knows how he did it."

"Does he hurt?"

"No. That's why he needs to stay in the stall. Horses don't understand when you tell them to take it easy." Shane tugged the brim of his hat and gave her one of his wide smiles. "Want me show you how to wrap for this?"

Becky glanced at the office, but the door was now closed. "I was supposed to meet with Dino and that reporter. But they don't seem to miss me."

"I'm sure Dino can handle her." Shane's chuckle was slightly wicked. "Besides I'm much more fun, and you don't have to watch what you say."

"Danielle does seem nosy."

"She's been chasing Dino for a while. Digging for a juicy story. But he's good at juggling, and she hasn't been able to get much from him. Now lean down and see if you feel the swelling."

Becky tried to concentrate on Shane's patient instructions, but her mind kept jumping to Dino. He was out of her league and, by his own admission, dated women only on a casual basis. But he was so easy to be with. She was even able to joke about sex. Had almost told him about Craig.

When Dino looked at her, he made her feel important. Made her want to talk. And if she was ever going to have sex again, it would be nice to have it with someone like him, someone who knew what he was doing...someone who could really kiss.

She quivered in anticipation. Nothing wrong with that. It wasn't as though she'd fall in love. She wasn't that stupid.

"Feel it? A little thickening along the ligament?"

She jerked her attention back to Chippy's leg. Couldn't feel any thickening but definitely felt heat. Chippy flattened his ears when she applied pressure but didn't move. Only turned his head, watching with a trusting eye.

"He sure is a nice horse," she said. "Lyric, the horse I ride at Conrad's, wouldn't be nearly so cooperative. I'm sure she'd kick my head off."

"Yeah. That mare doesn't like many people. Made a ton of money though. Rumor is, Slim owned some breeding rights since his daughter was the only jock who'd ride her."

"But they never bred her?"

Shane shrugged. "Malcolm retired her after Jill's accident. I thought the horse was headed to the broodmare barn."

"How long have you trained the Conrad horses?"

Shane pulled his hat off, swiping his brow with a tanned forearm. "Six years. Started as a groom and worked my way up to assistant trainer. About a year ago, Dino took over the head training job. That guy sure knows horses." He sobered as he studied Becky. "So what's the deal with you and him?"

"Nothing really." But her cheeks felt hot.

"Want to go out for dinner then? If he wouldn't mind, that is."

She smiled. Shane was so sweet and reminded her of a young Brad Pitt. "I don't see why he'd mind," she said.

"Good, let me jot down your phone number."

"Write it down for me too, Shane," Dino drawled, his face expressionless as he stared into the stall.

Becky's heart gave a guilty jump, but Dino didn't seem to mind Shane's interest. He looked distracted, almost bored. "Is Danielle gone?" she asked.

"Yeah. Update me on the leg," he said, his gaze narrowed on Shane.

"Slight filling in the suspensory," Shane said. "Some heat. I put a sweat on along with a magnetic wrap. Ordered stall rest."

"Okay. We'll get the vet in for some x-rays and go from there. Maybe send him back to Conrad's." Dino glanced at Becky, his dark eyes inscrutable. "Sound okay, honey?"

Honey? Her fingers tightened in shock. "Sure," she said but her voice sounded strange and even Chippy flicked his ears, as if surprised at the squeak.

"Good. Now let's get something to eat. We have a lot to talk about." He slipped a hand over her elbow and propelled her down the shedrow so fast she almost had to jog.

She shook his hand off as soon as they stepped from the barn. "Okay. What's going on? *Honey?*"

"Shane's a nice kid but he's a little...fickle. Please don't lead him on. He's too valuable to fire."

"I see," she said, unsure if she was annoyed or happy. She liked the possessive feel of Dino's hand but also liked the idea of having dinner with Shane. He was really more her type anyway. Much more attainable. And Martha always said never burn bridges. She sighed. "Now I understand why you enjoy a variety of dates. It's kind of fun."

"Now you behave or I'll remind Martha the boys here can't be trusted. And she'll keep you on a tight leash back at the distaff mansion." He cupped her chin, stroking the side of her neck with his thumb. She was certain he'd feel the racing of her pulse.

"And I'll be the only man allowed to visit," he went on, his voice gruff. "This is Tuesday. I'll be down Thursday afternoon. I know you have a sexy new haircut and you're feeling your oats—understandably so." His gaze slid over her in warm appreciation. "But could you please behave until then?"

His seductive thumb made every part of her quiver, and her legs felt like noodles. No mistaking his intentions. And she wasn't ready. Not yet. Not for a man like him. Talking with him, riding with him, even stalking him was much safer.

She gulped. "What exactly do you have in mind...for Thursday?"

"You want an itinerary, honey?" But his smile was more gentle than amused. "What I have in mind is a trail ride, dinner and after that we'll see how things progress. We're just following Martha's directions, that you have a little fun. Come on now. Hop in the truck."

She hadn't realized they'd even stopped beside his truck, that he couldn't open the driver's door unless she moved. This wasn't good. Just the stroke of his thumb made her melt. She cocked her head, striving for flippancy. "Maybe it would be a good idea for me to see Shane first. You know, for a little warm-up, just to make sure I'm ready for your...itinerary."

"Now that doesn't seem fair." He pulled open the door. "I have to stay away from other women. Yet you want to come to my barn and run wild. Hop in."

Relief slipped out the corners of her mouth, making her smile. He wasn't seeing anyone else. She climbed in and slid over to the passenger's side, too delighted to ask where they were going.

"I thought we'd eat somewhere else," he said, when they passed the track kitchen and the mouth-watering smell of fried bacon. "There's a spot down the road with more privacy. We can talk about Slim."

"Right." She stiffened, forgot about bacon and eggs, yanked back to reality by their ugly suspicions. Martha wanted to keep Slim on staff, and she didn't want to upset Martha. It was going to be tricky.

She adjusted her seatbelt. "I checked Ted's cell number with the housekeeper. It matches the number Slim called when Echo was scratched, even though he claims to have only met Ted two days ago."

"How do you know who Slim called?"

"Borrowed his phone on the drive home and checked the call history."

"Very good. So either Slim hates me or hates Martha. But I don't understand why he'd jeopardize his job. Not with his daughter to support." He ran a hand over his jaw. "Can you get me a copy of Slim's file? Malcolm sometimes added motivational clauses. In my case, I earn a bonus for a twenty win percentage with his homebreds. Maybe there's something like that in Slim's contract."

"Like if a horse loses, he gets a bonus?" She frowned. "That doesn't make sense. It goes against everything Malcolm wanted."

"Yeah, it's probably something else." Dino kept his gaze on the road as he switched lanes. "Is Ted her sole heir? We both know Martha isn't well?"

"Martha's fine," she said quickly. "Feeling lots better."

Dino made a soothing sound but it didn't help.

"She's feeling lots better," she repeated, her fingers tightening around the edge of the seat.

"I'm sure she is. Just another angle I wanted to check." He bounced the truck into a potholed lot that fronted a square building. A twenty-four hour breakfast sign flashed orange in the window. "This place is better than it looks," he said, "and lucky for you, they have a hungry-horsewoman special."

Becky knew he was trying to make her smile, but her thoughts churned around Martha. The doctors said there had been some damage from her heart attack but that with prudent care, she could live another twenty years. The shock of Malcolm's death had been devastating though, and she had to take it easy. Not get upset.

"Becky?"

Dino's concern stoked her panic. "I better go home." She gripped the metal buckle of her seatbelt. "Martha's probably anxious to hear how Hunter trained this morning. She might be upset if she doesn't hear right away. Yes, I better go home now."

"This place is fast, twenty minutes max. And it's important we discuss the Slim situation." His voice softened. "Maybe you'd like to ask Martha to join us for dinner on Thursday? If she's up to it."

"Okay." She swallowed, moved by his empathy. "Thanks. That would be great. And hopefully Echo will give her a win on Friday. Martha really needs that."

"Yeah. I need the win too." His jaw tightened and all softness vanished. "There's a lot riding on that little filly...a helluva lot."

CHAPTER TWENTY

Dino initialed the farrier's bill, tossed it on the 'approved' pile and tilted in his chair, satisfied with his completed paperwork. Relaxed voices drifted down the barn aisle along with a country singer crooning on a distant radio. Everything was quiet, just the way he liked. Horses did their best running when given a calm environment and set schedule.

Hunter had certainly adapted to track routine. It was more hectic at Lone Star than at Conrad's, but he'd settled like a pro. And he was safe here. A twenty-four hour guard would prevent another sponging or exhausting hike on a walker. Dino was reluctant to accept that Slim was responsible for the sabotage, but someone certainly was.

He dragged a hand over his jaw, cursing the low-life who'd do something like that to a horse. Best not to stress, though. Hunter was fine now. It was too bad Echo couldn't also be transferred from Conrad's, especially with her big race on Friday.

Unfortunately she didn't settle in a new barn. Instead she'd pace and sweat and even try to scramble over the door. She was simply too volatile. He and Malcolm had learned to keep her home until the last hour. Other measures would keep her safe. Besides, it was usually easier to soothe a female than force her from her comfort zone.

Much like Becky. He propped his boots on the scarred desk, brightened by the image of her happy smile. She was more relaxed now—with her job, with life, with him. Difficult to believe she was the awkward and aloof woman who used to mutter in the skybox. Reticent with everyone but Martha.

His gaze drifted to the wall photos, lingering on the smiling faces. Martha looked very different now and had obviously weakened. Her lack of energy was noticeable, and she bore little resemblance to the imperious woman glowing in the winner's circle. Of course, the unexpected loss of her husband had definitely cracked her spirit.

Damn, he hoped she'd rebound. He took a pensive sip of coffee and flipped open the *Racing Form*. Checked his win percentage—twenty-four, top of the trainers' list. But throwing out horses like Chippy, and calculating only with Malcolm's homebreds, it dropped to nineteen, one percent lower than necessary to claim his hundred-grand bonus.

And the last race of the Lone Star meet was in two weeks, two short weeks where success teetered on the backs of fickle horses. He needed more time, time to win almost every race in those two weeks. Or else win with Echo on Friday and then not race any homebred at Lone Star. That would keep him over twenty percent although it wasn't quite the route Malcolm had envisioned. Still, hard times justified hard measures, and he had to look out for his own interests.

He made his decision, squared his shoulders and called his ex-wife. "Laura, there's been a slight delay, but I'll have the down payment in three weeks."

"I've already waited longer than you deserve." Resentment curdled her voice. "Seems like you don't really want this ranch. Maybe you should live at the track, seeing as you spend every minute there. No, I'll only wait one more week."

"But I need three!" He injected what he considered an appropriate amount of panic.

"Two," she said, and the line went dead.

Excellent. He smiled at her predictable response and flipped his phone shut. Two weeks more than what he really needed. He'd only race Echo at Lone Star and once she won on Friday, he'd have his cash. Martha could move to her nursing home, and Ted could do whatever he wanted with the estate. Everyone would be happier without the looming uncertainty that clouded the stable…everyone except Becky.

His mouth flattened. She was blossoming in her new role, dealing with more people and bolstered by the security that came with Martha's affection. However, the operation couldn't continue. She should be okay financially though. When Martha moved to her ritzy nursing home, Becky would find another job. There wouldn't be horses of course, but good nurses were always in demand. She clearly loved her profession. Maybe she'd even find work at a rehab center; that was the area she loved most—lately he tended to remember everything she said.

At least for now, they both wanted the same thing. Keep Martha happy, no emotional upsets, and make sure the filly won on Friday. He'd tighten security with surveillance cameras and a fulltime watch. If he hung around Conrad's and watched Echo like a hawk, nothing could go wrong.

He also intended to stay close to Becky because, contrary to his earlier assumption, she was very much his type of woman.

"Boss?"

His smile lingered as he glanced at Shane hovering in the doorway, clipboard in hand. "You still want a massage and chiro for Hunter?"

"Yeah," Dino said, "as soon as possible."

"Okay. By the way—" Shane edged closer. "If you need me to haul any horses from Conrad's, I'd be glad to help. I could even go down and oversee the gallops."

"Feel like getting away for a day?"

Shane nodded and adjusted his hat, a sure sign he was uncomfortable.

"Got a horse leaving the vet clinic this Friday," Dino said, careful to keep a straight face. "Want to go north and pick him up?"

"North?" Shane's smile faded and he dipped his head, suddenly very interested in his clipboard. "Well, I dunno. Looking at this list, I see we got some races coming up. Maybe it *is* better if I stick around here."

Dino's chair creaked as he leaned back and crossed his arms. "You do remember the rule about not going out with employees?"

Shane raised his palms. "Of course. And I haven't touched any of our girls. Not even SueAnne."

"I'm adding employers to that rule."

"That's not necessary." Shane thrust out his jaw. "You're my only employer and I sure as hell don't want to date you."

"I saw your car at Debbie's this morning," Dino said mildly. "Probably best to finish up with one woman before starting with another." He remembered being given the same warning by Mark when he'd gone a little wild in New York. Remembered his similar resentment. But Shane was young and hadn't yet learned women were like horses. Sure, you admired a good filly and wanted her in your barn, but you damn well didn't put two fillies in the same stall.

"Debbie doesn't care."

But Becky would. Dino's voice hardened. "Leave Becky alone. The downside of dating employers is too big."

However, Shane's scowl only deepened. "Conrad's is your employer, not mine, so this doesn't seem fair."

Thump! Dino's boots slammed to the floor. "Life isn't fair. And I make the rules. Follow them."

A muscle in Shane's jaw twitched and for a brittle moment he held Dino's stare. Finally his shoulders sagged. "Sure, boss," he muttered as he backed into the aisle. "I'll go book that chiro now."

Dino sighed, relieved he'd snuffed that out. Shane wasn't a mean kid but he was a bit of a hound dog. Becky craved security; she didn't need a playboy and the least he could do was look out for her. His own intentions were honest—she knew he wasn't interested in long term. Yet Shane came across as a bashful, 'aw shucks' type of cowboy, and those kind of guys were tricky. Martha wanted her nurse to have a little fun, not have her heart broken.

It was also important to keep things cool at Conrad's. No excitement, no emotional upsets, keep both ladies happy. He sighed with approval. Yes, it was obvious he was the best man for Becky.

CHAPTER TWENTY-ONE

"Think I'll have a little nap while you ride." Martha pushed aside her untouched bowl of strawberries. "And you haven't told me anything about Hunter. Has he settled well?"

"Don't you remember?" Becky stopped, swallowing her words. She'd already updated Martha twice yesterday—once when she returned from Lone Star and then again in the evening, but Martha was too listless to remember. "He's doing great," Becky said. "Eating well. Comfortable galloping over the track. Strange but he's more laid back at Lone Star. Didn't even nip yesterday."

"Does Dino have him in a stall next to that big chestnut, Rocky? Horse with the Roman nose?"

Becky nodded, picturing the big red horse. Shane said he was a six-year-old who ran in low-level claimers, but his real value was in settling the colts. Rocky had stared over Becky's head as though she were beneath his notice, and she hadn't dared approach him. The horse didn't look like he wanted new friends.

"Tell me about Rocky?" Becky asked, reaching for any subject that might interest Martha. "How does he settle the colts?"

"It's a boy thing. Rocky's an older, tougher stallion. Hunter's not ready to challenge him for mares, attention or even food. Often that translates into a more tractable racehorse. Makes them quieter so they can save energy and focus on running." A sparkle animated her face, reminding Becky of how she'd looked when Malcolm was alive. "Surely you've noticed that sort of thing, dear," Martha added with a knowing smile. "Young men try to impress a pretty girl but when a truly dynamic man walks into the room, they turn meek and back off." Her voice turned wistful. "Malcolm had that effect, even before he made his fortune."

Becky nodded, picturing Dino when he entered the skybox, the men shrinking, the women fluttering. "I know exactly what you mean," she said.

Becky eased the car past the training track. Stephanie was still riding, spraying dirt as she galloped a bay horse along the inner rail. Clearly there would be plenty of time to groom Lyric and still be ready for their trail ride.

She parked by Stephanie's bright compact car. Slim slouched by the barn door. Becky squared her shoulders before walking toward him, determined not to let his animosity sour the morning.

"Lyric's in her stall." He studied his clipboard, not looking at her. "I hear you and Stephanie are going for a ride."

"Yes. Dino said it was okay to leave the paddock if someone was with me."

"Be careful," he said. "That mare isn't always obliging, and the old lady would be a mite upset if you got hurt."

"I'll be careful, thanks." The tightness in her chest eased a notch. Slim didn't seem to hold a grudge. He wouldn't meet her eyes but at least he was talking, even worrying about her safety.

She continued down the aisle. Lyric poked her head over the stall door, nickering a greeting and lifting her spirits higher. A barn, a horse, a sunny Texas morning. Life was perfect.

She entered the stall, grooming kit in hand, and pulled a peppermint from her back pocket. Despite the controversy surrounding Slim, he had provided several useful tips. Peppermints *were* easier to feed, especially when you were riding and didn't have room for apples or carrots.

She buckled Lyric's halter and slipped the lead through the ring in the wall. The mare instantly flattened her ears, reminding Becky of her own helpless feeling when she'd been wrangled into the esthetic chair. Maybe the horse would be more cooperative if she wasn't tied. Maybe she'd be so happy, she wouldn't kick.

Becky unsnapped the lead. The mare didn't sidle away. In fact, she even tilted her head, encouraging Becky to brush between her ears.

"Okay, girl," she murmured, spending extra time on the horse's itchy spots. So far, so good. Lyric usually pinned her ears and fidgeted, but now she was nothing but a sweetheart. Becky scooped up a hoof pick and picked the debris out of her front feet, eying Lyric's back legs with healthy respect.

The mare always tried to jerk away from Slim and Dino and gave a nasty kick if touched on the flank. Plus she was loose, so she'd be able to put her head down, turn and slam with both feet and really do damage.

Just imagining that kind of kick made Becky's body ache— she'd be a fool to risk it. She leaned over the stall guard and checked the aisle for Slim. A stable hand rushed past with a wheelbarrow but didn't slow, obviously hurrying to finish his chores. Lyric tracked his progress with curious eyes but still didn't move.

Becky tugged at her lower lip. So far, the mare hadn't done anything wrong, and Lyric did seem to like her. Maybe she should give her a chance. She took a deep breath, ran a hand along Lyric's back and down her left hind.

"Up," she said, trying to sound like the request was perfectly reasonable.

Lyric obligingly lifted her leg.

Becky was so shocked she dropped the hoof pick in the straw. After a moment of fumbling, she cleaned the hoof and placed Lyric's foot back down.

Wow. That was easy.

Hiding her shock, she rounded the mare and asked her to lift the right hind. Lyric lifted it, docile as any lesson pony. And then they were finished.

Becky tossed the hoof pick back into the grooming kit and gratefully patted the mare's neck. "You're not really a bitch at all," she whispered.

She grabbed her English saddle and pad, hoping to be tacked up by the time Stephanie finished galloping. A sweaty horse clopped down the aisle, led by a groom, and followed by a bouncing Stephanie.

"Hey, girl!" Stephanie paused. "Love your sexy haircut. I'll just throw my saddle on Hank and join you outside. One minute."

And it would only be one minute. It was incomprehensible how Dino and Stephanie tacked up so quickly. It took her at least triple the time. But she wanted to be on Lyric's back before Stephanie came out with Hank. Didn't want her new riding buddy to see her awkward mount using baler twine.

Stephanie followed her rueful glance and pulled a red jackknife from her pocket. "You won't need that baler twine anymore. Let me cut it off. Dino arranged for a fancy mounting block."

Becky nodded, relieved she could get rid of the twine dangling from her stirrup, a sure mark of a greenhorn. "That was nice of him," she said.

"Yes, but he is nice. To everyone, if you know what I mean." Stephanie expertly sliced the twine. She refolded her knife, her gaze sharpening on Becky's face. "Look, I don't want to be out of line here, but you should know he has a lot of female friends."

"I know that." Becky turned her head and fiddled with her stirrup, avoiding Stephanie's probing blue eyes.

"It's just that you're really sweet. Those other nurses from the big house wouldn't even talk to me. Not one of the six—"

"Six?" Becky's head shot up. "That many?"

"Yeah," Stephanie gave a dismissive shrug, "but not at the same time. Dino believes in spreading his love. Thinks that way he won't get hooked again. Look, I'm not really a gossip," she said. "Just thought you should know. Here, take this." She pressed her jackknife into Becky's hand. "Every horseperson should have a knife."

Becky squeezed the small knife, moved by the empathy in Stephanie's eyes. She'd always considered the gallop girl too cool to be hurt, and her jealousy when Stephanie flirted with Dino now left her ashamed. She hadn't wanted Dino sleeping with Stephanie but had given no thought to how the new rules might hurt this girl.

"But what about you?" Becky's voice thickened with regret. "Do you still want to...see him?"

"Nah. I tried to change him and couldn't. My new guy is way easier." Her smile turned mischievous. "Just remember, there are some horses you buy, and some horses you only ride. Now let's get going before it's too hot. I'll grab Hank."

Becky led Lyric from the barn, unsettled by Stephanie's blunt words. No doubt about it, if she did decide to sleep with Dino, he had plenty of experience. And on the positive side, he seemed to leave everyone happy. Old girlfriends, new girlfriends, even Martha—they all loved him.

"I'll open the gate." Slim's voice cut into her thoughts. "There's a new mounting block in the ring. You girls riding far?"

"Don't know." Becky checked her watch. Nine-forty. "Guess it depends on the heat." She led Lyric toward the big red block.

The mare snorted and planted her feet.

"Dino warned she might be scared. Race riders always get legged up. They don't use an old woman mounting block." Slim scowled at Lyric. "And that bitch mare is never helpful about anything."

Lyric's nostrils flared pink as she stared at the strange plastic steps in the middle of the ring.

"Guess it looks a little odd," Becky said, disappointed the mare didn't trust her enough to move closer. "But it beats scrambling up on a piece of rope."

"Most jocks vault up, although it's not great for the horse's back." Slim jabbed his thumb at Stephanie as she led her horse from the barn. "Watch her."

Stephanie grabbed a piece of Hank's mane and lithely swung into the tiny exercise saddle. Becky shook her head in awe. "Don't worry. I'll teach you to mount." Stephanie shrugged. "There's lots of time."

Maybe, Becky thought, but vaulting up looked like a demanding maneuver, and she'd never considered herself particularly athletic. Probably she'd always be stuck using the old woman steps.

She sighed and coaxed Lyric a few inches closer to the mounting block, fervently wishing she'd mounted before Slim and Stephanie were around to watch.

Lyric edged closer to the block, every muscle in her sleek body taut.

"She looks spooky. Want me hold her?" Slim asked.

"It's okay," Becky said. "I have a way to make her stand." She dropped three peppermints on the ground, stepped up on the block and scrambled into the saddle while Lyric gobbled up the mints. "I'm not sure if that's in any training manual," she added sheepishly.

A ghost of a smile tugged at Slim's mouth. "Actually Jill used that trick when she was little. Guess whatever works. Listen." He scraped his boot in the dirt. "Don't ride too fast today, Becky. Take it easy."

"Come on," Stephanie called with a hint of impatience. "That sun is getting hot."

Becky nodded at Slim but knew she didn't intend to take it easy. "Which way?" she asked, following Stephanie.

"Dino told me to stick to the hillside." Stephanie gestured. "And not let you go too fast."

There it was again. Another warning. Everyone considered her incompetent—someone who needed special mounting steps—and her determination to learn swelled. "Dino just doesn't want me to beat him." She forced a nonchalant smile, wishing it really *were* possible to beat him. That would prove she could actually ride. It might even impress him.

"Well, you should be able to beat him if you're on Lyric," Stephanie said. "But she's used to riders crouching over her withers. Shorten your stirrups and get your ass out of the saddle so she knows what you want."

Becky tucked her knees higher, imitating Stephanie's position. "Like this?"

Lyric definitely perked up when she cranked her legs. Now there was a bounce in the mare's walk along with an arch in her neck. But it felt awkward, like she was leaning too far forward. She missed being able to grip Lyric's sides with her legs.

Stephanie sighed. "Good try, but you look funny. Those English saddles suck for hardcore galloping."

Becky looked dubiously at Stephanie's exercise saddle. It was tiny, probably only seven pounds, although race saddles were even smaller. And 'hardcore galloping' seemed a little faster than she wanted to go. Still, she'd never be able to beat Dino unless she shook off her fear. "Could I try your saddle?" she asked impulsively.

"Wow, you want to step on the gas? Can't say I blame you," Stephanie said. "But first, practice in that saddle."

Becky stared over Lyric's pricked ears, concentrating on feeling her horse's rhythm. With her legs pulled up, balance was more important, not grip. Clearly jockeys were superb athletes to gallop at breakneck speed, surrounded by a bunch of racing horses.

"That's better," Stephanie said after another twenty minutes. "Later we can trot to the bottom of the hill, switch saddles and we'll gallop up the ridge."

"You may not be able to keep up," Becky teased. "Not if I have your wicked fast saddle."

Stephanie snorted and Becky took a second to admire her supple grace. "You're a beautiful rider," she said.

Stephanie flashed a big smile. "Imagine getting paid to do something that's this much fun. My money problems disappear when I'm riding. Now watch my hands, and make sure you don't jerk Lyric in the mouth. You can't use my saddle until you're totally balanced."

After a little more practice, Stephanie finally pronounced her ready. Both horses stood quietly while they changed tack. Stephanie vaulted up, but Becky's stomach squirmed. Now that they'd switched saddles, Lyric's back looked foreign—the saddle too tiny, the seat too little, the stirrups way too short.

Stephanie spotted her hesitation. "You can lengthen the stirrups, like an old woman." She snickered. "Or I could dismount and boost your ass into the saddle."

"I was starting to like you," Becky said, leading Lyric to the side of a jagged rock and searching in her pocket for another mint.

Lyric sidled away, then stopped and sniffed. Becky edged closer and stepped onto the rock. Now she could reach the stirrup, but what she really wanted was to learn Stephanie's vaulting move. She visualized the mane grab, the graceful hop, the leg hook over the horse's back. Dino might not notice she was galloping more aggressively, but vaulting onto a horse's back would have to impress him.

She dropped two peppermints on the ground, sucked in a resolute breath, grabbed mane and swung up. Her face slammed into Lyric's shoulder. The pain burned her nose as she tumbled to the ground and scraped the side of the rock. "Shit," she muttered.

"Actually that wasn't a bad first attempt. I'm surprised you tried." Stephanie wasn't even laughing. "Try again. You might need a run-on."

But Lyric finished the peppermints and sidled away from the rock, her eye flashing with a streak of perverseness. Becky resolutely wiped her sore nose then backed Lyric alongside the rock. If she dropped the reins, used her last remaining peppermint and took three running steps, she might be okay. But Lyric would have to stand perfectly still and the stubborn glint in her eye indicated trouble.

It would be fun to try though. Especially with someone around to help. She could feel Steph's encouragement rolling over her like waves.

Becky stepped back, dropped the peppermint, and took a running leap. Lyric stepped sideways just as she flung a leg over her back. *Oh, God.* This was bad. Her heart pounded and she stared down at the flashing ground. If she let go of Lyric's mane, she'd be down between the horse's feet—her deadly kicking feet and the unyielding rock. She tried to pull herself up but her knee bumped Lyric's ribs, and the mare lurched further to the right.

Something hard pressed against her ribs, and she heard Stephanie's calm voice. "We got you, girl." Stephanie grabbed Lyric's rein with one hand and yanked Becky into the saddle with another. Hank stayed beside Lyric, a warm, solid presence—a horse who clearly was used to flailing riders.

"You almost did it." Stephanie grinned. "And that's a tough maneuver. I'm surprised you had the guts to try."

"But I didn't do it." Becky sighed and placed her toes in the short stirrups. "If Hank wasn't here, I would have hit the ground."

"Still, you tried. Even Slim can't mount like that. And Lyric isn't the most cooperative horse in the barn."

"Hank sure is though." Becky studied the bay with fresh interest. "Why doesn't Dino let me ride him?"

"He's a good horse." Stephanie gave the gelding an affectionate pat. "He knows his job, and the outriders love him. Saved a lot of riders. Horses too. On the other hand, he turns too fast and will dump a green rider. No, you're better on Lyric. She only goes one direction. Now get going before I ask why you're so keen to learn. Or why you suddenly care about your looks."

Becky pushed Lyric into a canter, anxious to escape Stephanie's astute eyes. It took a moment to balance in the smaller saddle, but the difference was apparent. The exercise saddle, although smaller, helped her keep a forward position and Lyric loved it. The mare moved more rhythmically—straight, forward and true.

The fresh breeze cooled her throbbing nose. Stephanie had moved alongside so she loosened her reins a notch, and Lyric's stride extended. Gosh, this mare could motor. And it felt like she had several more gears.

Both girls grinned as they crested the hill and pulled their horses up.

"Not bad for a beginner," Stephanie said. "We usually eat up here. Did you bring any food?"

"Oh, I'm sorry," Becky said, instantly contrite. Stephanie was probably starving. She'd been at the barn since six and was taking personal time to accompany her. It had been a long time since Becky had enjoyed the company of a woman her own age, and it was almost as much fun as riding with Dino. Almost. "I'll bring a bunch of granola bars next time," she said.

"Fill your pockets with mints too," Stephanie said, "and we'll have you mounting like Zorro in no time. But I have to pick my daughter up now. Sitter charges double if I'm late. We can ride again tomorrow. This was fun."

Fun? Someone like Stephanie thought she was fun. Becky's heart gave a happy skip. No one but Martha had ever said that. Her parents had pawned her off, her only boyfriend had dumped her, and Craig the Creep had her jumping at shadows. Well, nobody could hurt her now. Lyric made her feel strong. Invincible. "Let's gallop one more time," she coaxed.

Stephanie checked her watch. "Okay but we have to be quick. Means I'm not holding Hank back."

They broke off together. Both horses burst forward, ready to run. Hank was faster at the start, but Lyric quickly caught up and soon they pounded over the ground in tandem. Stephanie clucked at Hank while Becky pushed her hands against Lyric's neck, asking for more speed.

Lyric dug in. The wind whipped mane against Becky's face but the sting, the speed, the exultant feeling were glorious, and she forgot about her sore nose. She was holding her own with a real jockey. She shot Stephanie a grateful grin. Felt like she was soaring.

Saw it happen.

Stephanie's eyes widened, a split second of shock, then her slim body vanished beneath Hank's hooves.

Becky rose in the stirrups, sawing desperately at Lyric's mouth. The mare protested, but raw fear gave Becky the strength to slow down and yank her around.

Hank had already circled back to Stephanie, trotting sideways, trying to avoid a dragging stirrup. Lyric, however, snorted and refused to approach the crumpled figure.

Becky leaped off with an impatient curse and charged past Hank, who lowered his head and sniffed at Stephanie's helmet.

"Fuck!" Stephanie said.

Becky sagged with relief, dropping to the ground on boneless legs. "Don't move," she said, pulling out her cell.

"It's not my neck. It's my goddamn arm. You're a nurse. Can't you splint it or something?"

Becky gulped at the sight of Stephanie's distorted arm. "I'm calling for help." Not Martha, God, not Martha. Slim would know what to do. He wouldn't get upset and have a heart attack.

He answered on the first ring.

"We need a four-wheel-drive truck on the south hill, by the trees," Becky said, "and an ambulance waiting at the barn."

"You got it." Slim cut the connection, and for once Becky appreciated his brevity.

"Fuck," Stephanie said again. "Please stop Hank from bumping my arm."

The gelding's concern was obvious, and Becky backed him up. Lyric remained thirty feet away, oblivious to the drama, intent on taking advantage of the opportunity to graze.

"Slim's coming," Becky said. "I'm going to see if I can rig a splint. An ambulance can't get up here so we'll get you out in his truck."

Stephanie forced a smile through bloodless lips. "Just remember, I was in the lead when my stirrup broke."

"It broke?" Becky's gaze drifted to Hank's saddle. The right stirrup dangled in two strips, and the iron hung uselessly by the horse's knee. The broken leather might be of some use though. She rose and pulled it from the stirrup bar. Hank stood like a rock, and Becky's appreciation for a good pony horse swelled.

"Is the bone sticking out?" Stephanie asked.

"No, nothing's protruding. It looks good." Becky forced her voice to remain calm as she gathered some sticks and wrapped the leather around Stephanie's arm. Stephanie didn't make a sound. God, she was tough. "Have you broken bones before?"

"Collar bone three times. Ribs twice, nose once, pelvis once."

"Jesus."

"But this is the stupidest yet." Stephanie gave a weak smile. "Not even on the track. This was a quiet trail ride."

"I'm sorry." Becky's voice caught. "If I hadn't asked you to gallop that last time, it wouldn't have happened."

"Lucky it was me. I know how to fall, and Hank won't kick a rider's head off. Who knows what Lyric might have done." She stared at her arm. "I think Hank clipped me with a hind foot though. Did you see me fall?"

"No, I'd passed by the time you hit the ground."

"Sure. Rub it in." Stephanie made a face. "Where the hell is Slim?"

Hank lifted his head, ears pricked. A blue diesel truck rumbled through the trees and up the hill. Water dripped from the truck's muddy fender. Slim had obviously taken the shortcut over the riverbed.

He leaped out, his eyes anxious. "Where are you hurt, Becky?"

"It's not me. It's Stephanie."

Slim recoiled, and the stunned look on his face would have been humorous in any other situation.

"Just my arm," Stephanie said. "Help me up. The Rangeland Hospital is closest." Her face blanched as Becky and Slim helped her rise, but the splint kept her arm relatively immobile.

"Can you lead these horses back?" Slim asked Becky as he slammed the passenger door. "I'll call from the hospital."

Becky nodded, stepping closer to Hank, fortified by the gelding's steady presence. Hank seemed to share her misery and watched the truck rumble away before taking a half-hearted nibble of grass. Lyric, however, munched with a complete lack of interest in events.

Becky rubbed the back of her neck, uncertain how cooperative the mare would be. It might be easier to ride the gelding and lead Lyric, but Hank's saddle only had one stirrup. The escort riders at the track made ponying look easy but the actual mechanics of it were daunting. Of course, that was assuming she could even catch Lyric.

She led Hank closer to the mare, pretending they were only joining to graze. Lyric raised a suspicious head but decided they were no threat, and Becky snagged the reins before the mare guessed her intentions.

Good thing too. She wasn't in a mood to chase after the willful mare, especially with the prospect of a two-mile hike and the temperature rising. She organized the horses—Lyric on her right, Hank on her left—and began the trek.

Luckily they were subdued from their gallop, and if they thought it odd she was walking, they didn't show it. However, she did feel silly, leading two saddled horses. The phone chirped, jarring her rhythm, and she juggled Lyric's reins, managing to jam the phone to her ear by the fourth beep.

"Hi, Becky," Deb said. "Martha wonders if you're joining her for lunch." The nurse's voice lowered. "She's fine but as usual wants only you."

Lyric took advantage of the stop to grab some grass, and Becky struggled to balance the phone and keep the mare from stepping on the drooping rein.

"I'm hurrying." She untangled the rein from Lyric's left leg. "Be there in about an hour." She closed the phone but Hank, puzzled by the delay turned and now faced both Becky and Lyric. *Click!* Lyric's teeth snapped as she lunged forward and bit Hank.

The gelding wheeled, desperate to escape her teeth, and yanked the reins from Becky's hand.

Becky froze but the obliging gelding only walked a few steps then stopped and stared as though awaiting further instructions. He seemed the type who wanted to help, unlike Lyric, who made everything difficult. Unfortunately, Lyric had the saddle with two intact stirrups, and it would be impossible to switch saddles with Hank, who was clearly afraid of the bossy mare.

Becky's nose and feet hurt. She was hot, worried about Stephanie, and Martha wanted her. She wasn't a good enough rider to pony Hank from Lyric's back but if she removed Hank's bridle, at least he wouldn't step on the reins and hurt his mouth. And he'd already proven he'd stay with Lyric and Becky.

She slipped off his bridle with only a slight qualm, hung it over her shoulder and stepped up to Lyric's side. Keep eating, girl, she willed, as she took a running start, made a desperate leap and vaulted onto the horse's back.

It wasn't pretty, and she had to pull herself up the last couple of inches, but she was in the saddle. She'd done it.

Lyric still hadn't moved, chomping at the grass like it was her last meal. Becky pulled Lyric's head up and pointed the mare in the direction of the barn while the ever-patient Hank trailed behind. Now they could make better time. Twice he came too close, but Lyric simply swished her tail and Hank was content to remain a length back.

They crossed the rolling green pasture, past the bluebonnets and goldenrod. Even when they entered the manicured drive flanked with clover, Hank kept his respectful position. Lately the Conrad grooms had been more attentive, and Cody rushed from the barn with a halter and lead line.

"Heard Stephanie fell off this old guy." He shook his head in disbelief and haltered Hank.

"She didn't fall off," Becky said. "Her stirrup leather broke." Actually it was Becky's stirrup that had snapped, and her own guilt rubbed raw. She was the one who'd asked to switch saddles; she was the one who'd pleaded for another gallop. She dismounted and pulled out her phone. "Did you hear from Slim yet?"

"No, they'll be awhile. It's always a wait at Rangelands. Poor Steph." Cody buckled the halter and coiled Hank's lead. "More medical bills, and now no paycheck."

"No pay? Why not?"

"Can't ride, don't get paid. Them's the breaks." Cody grinned at his wit and turned Hank toward the barn.

Becky pulled Lyric away from the long grass by the barn and rushed after the groom. "But that's not fair," she said.

"The horse industry isn't fair." He shrugged with total acceptance. "Money's scarce, workers aren't."

Her feet dragged as she led Lyric into her stall. Surely Martha and Malcolm had some sort of insurance. She looked after her own coverage but her policy had been in place when she accepted the nursing job, and Malcolm had topped off her salary to compensate.

She couldn't remember what he'd said about the standard Conrad plan, although nothing appeared standard with Malcolm. Still, she was positive Martha would want to look after Stephanie. In fact, Martha would be very upset when she heard about the accident.

If she heard.

Becky slipped off Lyric's bridle, her mind churning as she wiped grass off the snaffle. Maybe she shouldn't tell. But Martha often watched the horses during their morning gallops; she'd notice a new rider. And perhaps there was no need to worry about Stephanie's finances. Cody could be wrong, and it was possible Malcolm had insurance for his staff.

Shouldn't be hard to find out.

Her movements quickened as she unbuckled the girth. It was definitely time for another visit to Malcolm's grim office.

CHAPTER TWENTY-TWO

"He's the family lawyer, Ted. He won't mind coming out to amend a few clauses. There's no need for you to bring the documents." Martha closed the phone, shaking her head at Becky. "So rude. That boy has his mother's personality but got his bad manners from his father. That side never had any breeding." Her frown deepened. "Still glum, dear? You must understand people are hurt all the time. Riding is a gamble."

"But I can't believe there's no insurance."

"I said there *probably* isn't any. Workers move around so they're usually hired as casual labor." A hint of defensiveness crept into Martha's voice. "Stephanie did float from track to track. She only settled down after she had a baby."

"But that's more reason to look after her," Becky said. "And what about Jill?"

"Jill? That was a while ago. And Malcolm handled it. Gave Slim a promotion as well as a house to live in. People nowadays want everything for free." Her back stiffened.

Becky forced a soothing nod. No need to upset Martha before they knew all the facts. It'd be easy enough to get the key from the jewelry box and check Malcolm's desk. "Slim said Stephanie had a clean break and should be back riding in six to eight weeks," she added.

"Did Slim call Dino yet?" Martha asked, her posture still tight. "He'll need a new rider for tomorrow, especially with Echo racing on Friday."

"Not sure if he did." Becky tugged out her cell. Slim had sounded frazzled on the phone. Besides, it had been a full day since she'd seen Dino; she'd be happy to call. More than happy.

She fumbled with the directory, fingers over-eager and awkward.

"You look a little flushed, dear," Martha said wryly.

Becky pressed the phone against her ear and edged away.

"Dino Anders."

His sudden voice sucked away her oxygen. "Hi," she managed, ignoring Martha's knowing smirk.

"Becky? Are the horses okay?"

"Yes, they're fine. But Stephanie broke her arm this morning. Slim took her to the hospital."

"Who was she riding?"

"Hank."

He was silent for so long, she thought he'd hung up. "Hank," he finally said. The disbelief in his voice spoke volumes.

"We were on a trail ride. Her stirrup leather broke." A fresh ball of misery lodged in Becky's throat. If only she hadn't asked Stephanie to gallop one last time.

"Did she gallop Echo first?"

"Pardon?"

"Did she gallop Echo before your ride?"

Becky's fingers tightened around the phone, appalled that his biggest concern was whether Echo had been exercised. And he wasn't only Stephanie's boss; he'd slept with her. Everyone talked about how expendable workers were, but the reality made her stomach heave.

"Becky? Did Echo gallop today?"

"Yes." Resentment hardened her voice. "Stephanie did every bit of her work before going on the trail ride."

"All right," he said. "I'll bring a replacement rider when I come tomorrow. Where's Slim now?"

"Probably driving from the hospital."

"Okay," he said. "See you."

The line disconnected and he was gone.

She closed her phone, unable to look at Martha. "He'll arrange for a new rider," she muttered. "We didn't have time to talk about insurance." She didn't want to admit he'd hung up, that he'd rushed off to find Stephanie's replacement. It all seemed too callous.

Slim, at least, was worried. His face had been gray when he'd helped Stephanie into the truck, and when he called from the hospital, his voice had cracked. Obviously Stephanie and Slim were close.

But Stephanie and Dino had shared a bed. Shouldn't Dino show some concern too? Clearly he'd meant it when he said sex was just sex. Her chest twisted—she'd even considered sleeping with him. With a man who had sex as casually as he shook hands.

Poor Steph.

Well, she at least wasn't going to desert her new friend. Her troubled gaze drifted to Martha's jewelry box.

"Horses come first." Martha gave a smug sniff. "That's why needy women should avoid trainers."

"Stephanie's not needy."

"She is now," Martha said. "And I wasn't talking about her. Go ahead. Take the key and check the files. I hope Malcolm has insurance set up. And while you're in his study, don't forget to look for Lyric's papers."

Becky pocketed her phone and slowly opened the yawning mahogany box. The vast jewelry collection always amazed her yet Martha knew and treasured each piece.

"Key's on the right," Martha said. "Beside the pearls."

The key was small, almost hidden beneath the necklace and somewhat incongruous against the luxurious contents of the box. Becky glanced over her shoulder, aware Martha probably wanted her company.

"Don't rush." Martha fluttered a hand in dismissal. "Stephanie's my responsibility now, and this needs to be sorted out. Perhaps I haven't thought about the staff as much as I should. And it's best you sift through Malcolm's papers, not Jocelyn or Ted."

Becky's sneeze cut the silence of the room. She brushed away a spiral of dust and pulled the last file from Malcolm's drawer, adding it to the stack already piled on the thick carpet. Most of the workers' names were unfamiliar, and clearly Martha was correct—stable hands didn't stick around for long. No wonder they were hired as casual labor.

Still, the lack of benefits sucked for Stephanie.

Her mouth tightened when she picked up the contracts for the racing and barn manager. These agreements were vastly different. Dino had negotiated a wide range of health benefits as well as a huge bonus if he achieved a win rate of twenty percent. He really was a clever guy. But his incentive only applied to homebreds; other wins didn't count.

She shook her head, exasperated that horses like Chippy were discounted, and turned to Slim's contract. This one was much shorter than Dino's, only two pages, and the legal paper was stained with brown. Life insurance was the same as Dino's, but there were no health benefits or bonuses. However, a clause had been scrawled at the bottom in blue ink: *In consideration of Jill Barrett's jockey services, it is agreed that half ownership of Lyric will be transferred to Jill and Slim Barrett if and when Lyric is retired as a broodmare. Said retirement subject to vet check and Malcolm Conrad's final stock approval.*

She sank down on the carpet, absorbing the words. It seemed odd yet straightforward and a fabulous deal for Slim and Jill. No wonder Slim had compromised on his contract. Part ownership of a horse like Lyric was better than any race bonus.

She reread the handwritten clause. *If and when Lyric is retired as a broodmare.* But Lyric hadn't been bred. She was retired, but her stall was in the race barn. So who owned Lyric? And did that mean Slim had life insurance but nothing else?

She scrambled to her feet. Malcolm's copier whirred as she made duplicates of Slim's file. She carefully folded the copies then dumped out the contents of a bulging brown envelope labeled 'Lyric's Gamble.' A disc, legal correspondence, a memo from Malcolm and finally Lyric's wayward papers. The certificate appeared to be the unaltered original issued by The Jockey Club, the central registry for Thoroughbreds. Conrad Racing Stable was listed as the sole owner.

Malcolm's memo was attached to the papers. She unfolded it and flattened the sheet against her knee. The witnessed statement was short, concise and irreversible. *The mare Lyric's Gamble, No.*

9926160, is deemed unsuitable for breeding because of the offset in her right ankle and ensuing propensity to stumble.

Becky stared at the memo, her fingers reflexively creasing the paper. Clearly Slim and his daughter had gambled on Lyric—gambled and lost—although Jill had lost much more than a share in a stakes horse. Her life was shattered that fateful day at the track.

The disc was innocuously labeled 'Lyric, Race Seven.' She tried to remember what she'd heard about Lyric's last start. Someone had said the accident wasn't the mare's fault, but why had the other jockeys refused to ride her? It seemed only Jill had piloted Lyric—Jill, who had a vested interest in her success.

She didn't want to linger in Malcolm's bleak office, but it was better to watch the race here rather than subject Martha to a potentially upsetting replay. She slipped the disc in the machine and clicked on the huge wall screen TV.

Lone Star Park. The landscaped paddock set against the distinctive Spanish-style clubhouse was unmistakable. A sunny-afternoon crowd clustered around the rail while grooms led their horses around the spacious walking ring. A familiar gray horse filled the screen——Lyric—darker but with the same elegant head. Her ears were pricked, head arched, sleek muscles fit and toned.

She'd always thought Lyric beautiful, certainly not fat, but there was a world of difference in this conditioned racehorse and the mare she now rode. Lyric's muscles rippled when she walked and her belly was tucked—the screen abruptly switched from Lyric to the next horse.

Becky kept her gaze pinned to the screen, searching for familiar faces in the confusion of onlookers. The announcers seemed to be talking but she couldn't get any sound, even after jabbing buttons on the remote. And now the horses filed onto the track. She caught another glimpse of Lyric with a jaunty jockey perched on her back, wearing Conrad's yellow silks with the black diamond.

'Jockey Jill Barrett,' the caption on the television said. Jill flicked her whip, flashing a white smile as she saluted someone at the rail. And there was Slim, looking proud as his daughter guided the beautiful gray mare, number three, onto the track.

Becky pressed her damp palms against her jeans as the horses paraded across the screen. Nine fillies and mares, seven furlongs, two hundred thousand dollars in purse money. A big day at Lone Star.

She wanted to snap the television off—leave now—but stayed rooted, caught in a weird mixture of fascination and fear. A bugler's cheeks swelled when he blew a shiny horn. Spectators smiled and cheered when the line of vibrant horses paraded past the grandstand.

Still no sound.

A commercial break. She swallowed and set the remote on the table. Trucks and a beer commercial. She shivered and rubbed her prickling arms.

And then the horses reappeared, almost at the starting gate now, and Lyric's colors shone brightest of all. A summary of the horses lit the bottom of the screen, flashed their betting odds. Jill, still smiling. Lyric's odds five to two.

An assistant starter reached up and led Lyric toward the gate. *Don't go in.* But of course she walked in. Lyric, poised and professional, Jill's face now set with concentration.

The remaining horses disappeared, one by one into the gate. Doors slammed behind their muscled haunches. No way out except forward. One horse left to load. The blazed chestnut in the nine hole balked, and a flurry of attendants surrounded the horse, pushing until the door closed. All in now.

Malcolm's office was very still. Tomblike. Not even the chirp of birds passed through the windows. He liked his privacy, Becky remembered as she stared at the TV screen. She felt alone in this wing of the house, alone in this foreign room.

The starting gate burst open, and nine colorful horses spread across the screen.

She'd moved too close to the TV and stepped back, away from the mass of horses charging from the gate, away from their wide eyes and flailing hooves, away from the silent vibration of their bodies that choked her chest.

Lyric's distinctive color made her easy to spot. Becky watched the familiar gray head as she grabbed position behind the frontrunner. Her nose was shoved in the tail of the number five horse, a little bay with a white bridle, gaily leading the way into the first turn with the pack of remaining horses galloping in hot pursuit.

Jill crouched on Lyric's back, riding easy, not pushing her horse, keeping her comfortably in second. The chestnut with a blaze moved up on Lyric's outside, boxing them in against the gleaming white rail.

Becky realized she was rocking on stiff legs but was unable to tear her eyes from the screen. Fear warred with optimism. This might not be *the* race. It looked benign, no need to be tense. Just nine horses galloping around the track, riders and horses doing what they were supposed to be doing.

But dread snaked down her back and she wanted to look away, away from the brave, vibrant girl paired with the talented gray filly.

The horses entered the turn and the chestnut swung wide. Jill grabbed the chance to escape, deftly moving Lyric out from the rail. Now she was at the leader's hip with nothing blocking her way, and Becky breathed again.

The white-bridled bay seemed to be tiring. Lyric relentlessly closed the gap, her stride strong and even. As the horses entered the homestretch, the two horses were shoulder to shoulder. Lyric appeared to be galloping for fun. Her ears flicked at the crowd but Jill pushed on her neck, seeming to draw out another gear, and they left the bay laboring on the rail.

Two horses surged from the back, but it was clear they couldn't catch the streaking Lyric. The chestnut was still running second, far on the outside as two closers fought for second and third. Becky blew out a sigh of relief. This wasn't the race.

Lyric buckled, her hindquarters flipping over her head, and a splash of yellow colored the ground.

The two closing horses tried to clear the sudden obstacle. One leaped to the left, caught a front leg on Lyric's shoulder and somersaulted onto the patch of yellow. The other horse seemed clear, but a thrashing leg hooked her hind end and she stumbled, nose furrowing the ground until both rider and animal joined the melee.

Becky clenched her arms in anguish as a bewildered Lyric scrambled to her feet and slowly cantered after the pack of horses. The second horse thrashed on the ground, struggling to rise. A front leg hung at an odd angle and every time the filly moved, yellow silks gleamed beneath her. The third horse was pinned beneath the inner rail. She tried twice to find her feet, pushing awkwardly on her front legs, then stopped struggling and stared into the crowd with stoic acceptance.

A rider in red silks tried to calm the flailing horse on top of Jill, while the third downed jockey twitched an arm. And then an ambulance charged up, a white screen blocked the view, and the silent scene was replaced with a commercial featuring a lean cowboy, his rugged truck and a blue merle dog.

The commercial switched to a shiny airplane with drinks being served by a beaming attendant.

Becky's breath came in horrified gasps. She grabbed the remote and snapped off the television. The screen turned black.

No wonder Malcolm had refused to breed Lyric despite her obvious speed. Slim had been there that day. Had seen his daughter in the carnage. And now he'd just driven Stephanie to the hospital. Naturally he was upset.

Sucking in a shaky breath, she left Malcolm's office and hurried out the side door. No doubt Stephanie's accident had stirred up horrible memories. Dino wasn't the type to worry about people but Slim had sounded distraught on the phone—and someone needed to check on him.

CHAPTER TWENTY-THREE

Rap, rap. Becky knocked at Slim's door while a scruffy gray cat circled her ankles. Probably the same one that had darted out when Ted had visited Slim. Now though, Slim was clearly alone, his truck slanted across the driveway as though parked in a hurry.

She rapped a third time.

The impatient cat mewled, clearly wondering why she didn't open the door. "Slim," she called. "It's Becky. I just want to hear about Steph."

A grunt. Heavy steps and the door opened. Slim's face appeared and the cat darted through his legs. "Come in," he said, not smiling but not frowning either. He thumped into the kitchen. Dropped onto a hard-backed chair and picked up a glass half-filled with amber liquid. "Join me."

She pulled out a chair and sat, trying to ignore the reek of stale air and sweaty socks. "No, thanks. I just wondered how Stephanie's doing. How you're doing...if there's anything I, or Martha, can do to help."

He didn't speak. Just lifted the glass to his mouth and swallowed. She glanced at the counter. No mix, no ice. Only a bottle of rum on the vinyl-topped table.

She turned back to Slim. "Does Stephanie need surgery?"

"Yup." Slim grabbed the bottle and splashed more rum into his glass. He'd stopped staring at her, and there was a definite glassiness in his eyes.

"Will she be able to go home soon?" she asked.

"Yup."

The cat wandered under Becky's chair. She reached down and stroked its back, worrying about Slim. Lines bracketed his mouth, and it looked like he'd aged ten years. Clearly he was hurting.

"Maybe I'll have a little drink with you," she said.

He rose and clumsily grabbed a glass, splashed in some rum, then shoved it across the table. "To Stephanie." He raised his glass.

Two words—an improvement, she thought, as they shared a toast. She tried not to wrinkle her nose, but straight rum was not her usual drink. She cradled the glass between her hands, mirroring Slim, hoping he wouldn't notice she'd barely wet her lips.

"I didn't think you girls would ride so fast," he muttered.

"Told you not to."

"It wasn't your fault. She was teaching me to gallop."

"I didn't want anyone to be hurt, not like my Jill. That's gotta get to the old lady."

"It's okay. Martha's not upset. She knows Stephanie will be back." Becky took a sip of the strong rum.

His mouth twisted into a caricature of a smile. "Malcolm was quite a man, you know. Was going to give me half of his next good mare."

Becky's hands tightened around her glass. "To make up for Lyric?" she asked softly.

Slim stared at some point above her head as a ticking clock marked the time. She glanced around; there were some beautiful pencil sketches of horses on the fridge, but nothing else to account for his long silence.

"He wanted to be fair," Slim finally said. "Was waiting for a good horse to replace Lyric. We were thinking of Echo but the old lady don't know nothing about it. When I asked her, she brushed me off." His throat moved convulsively. "I gotta look out for Jilly…you understand that, don't you?"

Becky nodded.

"Not many jobs around but I got life insurance." Slim's glass jerked in his hand, dangerously close to spilling. "I can look after her without any scumbag's help." He slammed his glass on the table with such force, drops splattered the air.

Becky's palms were slick with sweat, and she gripped the sides of her chair. Slim had a wild look, and the tiny hairs on her arms stood straight up. "I have to go now," she said, "but I wonder if you'd give me Stephanie's phone number?"

"You can't leave yet."

"I can't?" Her voice gave an annoying squeak.

"Not until you finish your drink. I get pissed when people waste my good rum."

She picked up her glass. "Understandable," she said.

Dino shifted the bags of groceries to his left arm and tilted an empty flower pot, extracting Stephanie's door key. Slim said she needed surgery but would be home tomorrow. If all went well, the cast would be off in six weeks. Six long weeks.

He walked into the kitchen, set the groceries on the table and unpacked the bags. He'd only been to her apartment once before, wasn't familiar with her cupboards but guessed she'd be in a tight spot. He encouraged his riders to carry insurance. Often though, there wasn't enough cash at the end of a paycheck. Even with a policy, it took months to receive compensation.

He set the milk in the fridge, heavy with worry about employees and horses and ex-lovers. The deadline on the ranch loomed, and Echo simply had to win on Friday. The race wouldn't be a walkover, but there were only two runners he was afraid of, and with a little racing luck...

He left some cash in an envelope by Stephanie's phone, locked the door on the way out and checked his watch. Conrad's was only thirty minutes away, and surveillance cameras were scheduled to be installed that afternoon—thanks to Becky for Martha's speedy approval.

Becky had proven more of an ally than a pain, and he definitely enjoyed her company, her conversation, her smile. He was still ambivalent about the haircut though. Guys were sniffing around and he didn't like it. Shane wasn't helping matters either. She was just starting to gain some confidence, and the last thing she needed was a guy screwing her up.

It wouldn't hurt to drop by Conrad's and see how she was doing. She'd sounded upset about Stephanie's fall although Slim had said she'd made a pretty awesome splint. He shook his head in bewilderment. Weird that it was Stephanie who'd been hurt. He was guiltily relieved it wasn't Becky though—that would have knocked Martha off stride. She'd probably never have let Becky ride again.

He turned his truck and headed for Conrad's estate. Drove into the back entrance, automatically checking the broodmare pasture where horses swished their tails and dozed contentedly beneath the trees. Parked by his guesthouse and walked to the barn. The hot walker was motionless, but an unfamiliar Ford truck was parked by the entrance. Fortunately, Slim's vehicle wasn't in sight.

He strode down the aisle and nodded at the man on the stepladder. "I'm Dino," he said. "You putting a camera at each end?"

A second man patted a work order jutting from the pocket of his brown coveralls. "Yup, but I wanted to ask about the third camera—the covert one."

"I want it covering stall nine." Dino pointed at Echo's stall.

"Sure. We'll put the nanny cam right here. It'll cover a couple stalls and have a separate feed to your computer. Is it okay to run that now? The order states we might have to come back and install another time."

"No, this is perfect timing." Dino glanced over his shoulder. Mid-afternoon, no one around except the mute horses. But a bad taste lingered in his mouth. Monitoring a man like Slim. Damn sad.

The technician on the ladder fiddled with a smoke detector. Plenty of people used monitors. But Slim would be livid, and understandably so, if he discovered its presence. Dino walked back to the man on the stepladder. "You can hide that thing pretty good, right?"

"No one will know unless you tell them," the man said.

Dino nodded and wandered back to the front of the barn. Slim might look out his window and wonder about the strange truck. "How much longer?" he called.

"Twenty minutes."

He grabbed a condition book and headed toward Slim's house. Best to keep the man occupied rather than risk him walking over.

He rapped at the door and pushed it open, calling for Slim.

"In here," Slim said.

Dino walked into the kitchen and paused, shocked to see Becky, even more shocked when she leaped from her chair and rushed to his side.

"Hi," she said, her voice breathless.

"Hello, Becky." He didn't know why she grabbed his hand, but he certainly appreciated the warm reception. He glanced over her head, saw the bottle and two glasses and laughed. "You two drink like this every afternoon?"

Slim said nothing, so he hooked a chair with his boot and joined them at the table. Becky sank back down but hauled her chair so close her shoulder brushed his side. He draped his arm over the back of her chair and gave her shoulder a reassuring squeeze.

"Stephanie's going to be fine," he said. "You and Slim took great care of her."

She looked at him with big eyes then glanced warily at Slim who examined his hands.

Dino chuckled. "This must be your second bottle." Slim's eyes were glassy. Becky looked normal but was certainly much friendlier than usual. Not that he was complaining. He shifted his arm off the back of her chair and laid it over her shoulders. Slim didn't seem inclined to pour him a drink, so he picked up Becky's glass and raised a questioning eyebrow. "May I?" he asked.

"Go ahead," she said, peeking at Slim. "Good rum shouldn't be wasted."

The man was oblivious. Neither hostile nor friendly but definitely pickled. Clearly, there was little danger he'd notice the workmen in the barn. Dino relaxed, leaned back in his chair, and sipped Becky's rum. Pretty good rum actually. "Think I'll get my own glass."

He rose from the table and opened a cupboard. Coffee, sugar, flour. Second cupboard was full of canned beans and cat food. The third cupboard contained a stack of mismatched glasses. He poured himself a generous shot, sat down and stretched his arm back over Becky's shoulders.

"Let's go for a ride," she said, eying the back door with obvious longing.

"If you really want to, but haven't you ridden enough for one day?" Besides, he liked her attention, her warm curves, the way she pressed into his side. "Be good if we stayed here a bit longer," he added, thinking of the nanny cam. "I brought some race entries to review with Slim."

"She doesn't like my rum." Slim finally spoke, his voice slurred. "She's too good to have a little drink with me."

From the looks of Slim, he'd had more than a little drink, but Dino's shoulders stiffened. She never liked to hurt anyone's feelings. "I think she prefers wine, don't you, Becky?"

"Yes." She nodded quickly. "But this rum is good too." She looked at Slim with such an anxious expression, Dino's heart kicked. Obviously Steph's fall had been tough on all of them. It was nice to have a little drink together. Christ, he hated when people got hurt.

He stroked her cheek with a finger. "Don't worry. Stephanie's going to be fine. Be riding again by mid-summer. There's some wine at my place. Want me go get it?"

"I got wine. Bottom cupboard." Slim tilted his glass and took another long swig. Wiped his mouth with the back of his hand. "Ted left it."

Dino stiffened and his eyes met Becky's. He slowly rose, found a half bottle of Claret and poured her a glass. "You drink with Ted now, Slim?" he asked, careful to keep his voice casual.

"Never again." Slim burped. "But a man has to do right by his daughter."

Dino glanced back at Becky, who shrugged and took a fortifying sip of wine. No wonder she'd been glad when he'd walked through the door. Slim reeked of rum and resentment and something else, something darker. Plus, the asshole had lied. "Thought you didn't know Ted?" Dino leaned forward, carefully studying Slim's expression.

"Won't be seeing him anymore. Enough is enough." Slim yanked his hat lower. "When I saw Stephanie..."

"Maybe you better tell me about the accident, Becky," Dino said, keeping his gaze pinned on Slim.

"Stephanie was teaching me to gallop," she said. "I wanted to use her exercise saddle so we switched. Everything was going great. Lyric was really moving."

Dino glanced sideways, temporarily distracted by the way her mouth curved. God, she was sweet. Relaxed too, no longer poised for flight as she spoke about riding.

She caught his grin and smiled back. "I plan to beat you next time we ride."

"I may have my own plans," he said softly.

She rolled her eyes and glanced across the table at Slim. "Then the stirrup broke and Stephanie fell. Slim came with the truck, and I took the horses home. That was it."

"The stirrup leather broke?" He frowned. Slim hadn't said that, hadn't mentioned it. Conrad tack was top quality and always well maintained. Grooms cleaned it every day. Were taught to watch for leather wear. "Where is it now?"

"I used it to support Stephanie's arm," Becky said. "It's probably at the hospital."

"I'll pick it up," Slim said.

"No," Dino snapped. "I'll do that." He swallowed, sickened by his suspicions, and any guilt about a hidden camera disappeared. "Let's get out of here, Becky," he said, shoving his chair back. "I'll supervise the night feeding, Slim. Sober up. We'll continue this conversation tomorrow."

Becky rose, placed their glasses in the sink and walked to the back door.

Dino didn't speak until they were twenty yards from the house. "How long were you in there?" He glanced at the barn. The service truck was gone, the parking lot deserted. "And where's your car?"

"It's parked behind the barn. I was only with Slim half an hour, but it seemed like an eternity." She looked up at him, her eyes candid. "I was very glad to see you today."

"I'm always glad to see you." He slipped his arm around her hip.

She paused for a long moment, clearly preoccupied. "I'd just watched Jill's last race," she said, "and it was horrible. I wanted to find out about Stephanie, but he asked me to have a drink with him. He seemed...really upset."

Dino steered her to his guesthouse, his voice hardening. "I want to know everything Slim said." He'd call the hospital and make sure he personally examined that piece of leather. It was inconceivable Slim would want to hurt Becky, but she and Steph had switched saddles. A vein throbbed in his forehead as he swung open the door. "You stay away from Slim," he added gruffly. "And I don't want you riding anymore unless I'm with you."

She stepped into the house and paused, her eyes widening. "I know what you're thinking. But I can't believe Slim hates me that much."

He closed the door with a decisive click. "I don't think he hates you either. But something's going on. And despite Martha's loyalty, I can't let him work here any longer. I'll look after both places," he added. "Come in the afternoon, sleep here. Race days will be tough but I don't want Slim around you. Or the horses."

"I'm not sure how he'll react." She squeezed her eyes shut for a moment, her dark lashes fanning her cheeks. "Losing his job. His house. And he has Jill to look after. Did you know Malcolm planned to give him half of Lyric? But she wasn't accepted for breeding so the deal fell through. They were considering Echo as the replacement, but Malcolm died before it happened."

"That's *his* story." Dino shrugged. By all accounts, Malcolm was a generous man but to give up half of a valuable mare seemed ludicrous.

"No, it's true. At least the part about Lyric. I saw papers in the study. Malcolm thought she tripped too much and then that race...I'm going to show Malcolm's note to Martha. Ask her to make it right." Becky's voice quavered. "I never thought about how dangerous it was to be a jockey. Jill smiled when she got on Lyric. Then she went down, and nothing was ever the same again. It wasn't the fall. It was the horses behind her. I'm glad you're a trainer, not a rider."

Her lips trembled and he impulsively dipped his head, soothing her with his mouth. She tasted of rum and sweetness, and he tugged her closer. Her curves fit him perfectly, and he immediately hardened.

He slid his hand beneath her shirt and cupped her breast, thumbing her nipple beneath the bra. Christ, he wanted her. No need for either of them to think about Slim right now. He edged her bra up, pushing it out of the way, exploring her soft breasts.

He loved the feel of her, ripe with the promise of hot sex— much like before, when she'd jerked away in panic. What was it that had set her off?

He wished she'd tell him. He'd have to work around it, but damn, she was worth the wait. He lifted her up and carried her to the sofa.

"Don't take your clothes off." He dragged his mouth gently over her neck but kept a possessive hand on her breast. "Not until we get to know one another better."

Her arms stiffened around his neck.

"For instance," he said, "does this tickle? Or does it feel good?" His mouth skimmed a warm path behind her earlobe. She arched into his chest.

"Kind of both. It's...nice." Her voice was throaty.

"What about this?" He thumbed her nipple, watching her face. Her eyes were closed as though to shut out reality. But her mouth parted, and he couldn't resist covering her mouth with another hungry kiss.

He pushed her shirt higher, exposing her flat belly and twisted bra, her lovely breasts on full display. She lay beneath him, eyes still closed. He lowered his mouth over her nipple, swirling it gently, enjoying her involuntary moan.

She didn't seem gun-shy at this point and he was more than ready, but he didn't want to scare her again either. Best to get her accustomed to his hands and mouth, erase any of that previous jumpiness. And he liked her breasts, her pink nipples all hard and puckered from his touch. He also liked the way she curled so trustingly against him. Could spend all day kissing her.

Her eyes flickered open at his satisfied sigh. "Doesn't seem fair that my shirt is half off," she said, "and you're still dressed."

"We're not taking any clothes off today." He possessively palmed her breast, watching her face.

"Really?" She arched an eyebrow. "My shirt is pretty much off."

"Not technically. Only lifted." He leaned down and sucked her left nipple, spending even more time with a detailed exploration of her chest. "Why don't you tell me about it?" he finally whispered, raising his head and skimming her neck with reassuring kisses.

"Tell you what?"

"What happened? Why you're scared." He reached back and unhooked her bra. "Why you're not allowed to take your clothes off."

"Is this your usual strategy?" She smiled, clearly unaware he'd undid her bra. "A little reverse psychology?"

He hadn't intended to unhook her bra. Force of habit. But at least her chest was bare, and she seemed comfortable with that. Heck, she was even smiling, her lower lip thick and sexy. However, it was clear she was trying to trivialize an event in her past and suddenly it was important she trust him. He cupped her breast, stroking her with his thumb, alert for any sign of panic.

"Aggressive boyfriend maybe?" he asked.

"No, not that. It was the home..." She stopped talking.

He moved his hand to her neck and kneaded the tightness. Silent but waiting.

"There was a man there," she finally said, peeking up at him. "Creepy Craig we called him, but of course never to his face. If you were a girl, a certain age, he pretended to be nice. But after a while he'd make you strip. He'd take pictures."

Her voice turned so low, he had to lean closer.

"Guess he sold them on the Internet," she said. "I tried to hide but he'd corner you in the basement—he had a camera set up. He noticed me when I was thirteen. He was big and...strong."

Dino's jaw flexed. "Where's the fucker live?"

She shook her head. "It's okay. They're not allowed to foster any more. Not after the police incident."

His arms tightened, and he forced them to loosen, aware he was squeezing her much too tightly.

She didn't seem to notice. Just continued speaking in a flat voice. "There was a new girl, Olivia. She had the prettiest hair, always wore a pink ribbon. She was crying, calling for help. I couldn't stand it. Whacked Craig in the head with a pot. He was in the hospital for a while and after that...well, not many foster homes would take me."

His arms tightened again, and he realized his hands had fisted. But he couldn't seem to speak. "Wish I had been there. To help," he finally managed, his voice hoarse.

He adjusted her shirt, his emotions churning. Her long hair, her oversize clothes. No wonder she'd been hiding. And the thought of her going after the creep with nothing but a pot. He swallowed, hard. "Those foster homes missed out on one brave little girl."

He tucked her head under his chin, his hand wrapped around her hair, and neither of them spoke for a long time.

She was the first to move away, tilting her wrist and discretely checking her watch.

"It's only four," he said, glancing at the clock in the kitchen, oddly loath to move. "Why don't you hang around here? Go for dinner later?"

"I thought we were all going for dinner tomorrow?"

"That's right. We are." He stroked her hair, staring over her head at the second guesthouse. He couldn't protect her from the past, but he could sure as hell protect her from Slim. Make sure she wasn't alone until things were sorted out. Besides, he wanted to see her. "Do you eat with Martha every night?"

"Usually. She likes to hear about the horses over dinner, although lately she doesn't eat much. A few spoonfuls of soup."

"But you have to eat," he said. "How about I'll pick up some Chinese food. If you're hungry later, drop back down." He watched her face but she didn't look enthused. Maybe she didn't like Chinese food. "Or I can order pizza," he added quickly. "And I can show you how the new surveillance works."

"It's already installed?" She twisted in his arms. "Does Slim know?"

"I'll tell him about the two cameras on the entrance but not the one on Echo's stall." He dropped an apologetic kiss on her forehead. "That's why we couldn't leave Slim's place right away—they were installing the nanny cam. Once I program the computer, we'll have a live feed of Echo and the stall on the left."

"Then we'll be able to watch Lyric too. See if she tries to escape." She wiggled in his arms, her voice rising with excitement. "What time will you have it working?"

He smiled. Food hadn't been the draw but Lyric was. "Drop back around eight, and it should be set up."

"Okay. And I'll bring a copy of Slim's file for you." She edged from his arms, struggling to refasten her bra.

"Here. Let me." He reached around and attached the clasp, stoically returning his hands to his side.

"Thank you. You're really understanding about all this." Her smile wavered but she kept her steady gaze on his face. "Or are you feeling grossed out that my pictures might be on the Internet?"

"I'm feeling a lot of things," he said, "but grossed out is definitely not one of them."

Martha's face was pale, her hand clammy and cold, and Becky's concern spiked. "Here's a smaller fork. Try the shrimp. They're delicious. Jocelyn said they're from Canada."

"Yes," Martha said. "Coldwater shrimp are always tastier than our bigger shrimp."

"Cold water? Is that what makes them so good?" Becky pretended interest in the plate, but her despair rose in waves. Martha was barely eating and despite the small size of the truly delicious shrimp, she only toyed with her food. "Echo races in two days," Becky added brightly.

"How exciting." Martha's mouth curled in a wan imitation of a smile, and she didn't look at all excited.

It wouldn't matter now if Slim were fired, Becky thought, balling her napkin. Didn't appear Martha would even care. Probably Dino would fire him tomorrow—definitely not tonight when Slim was obviously plastered. She only hoped his contract provided for some sort of severance, for Jill's sake.

"I like the blouse you're wearing. And the earrings." Martha's gaze lingered on Becky's face, and her eyes sparked with a hint of approval. "You're really quite lovely when you take some care with your appearance. Always remember that clothes make a woman."

Becky tried to work the lump from her throat. She couldn't imagine life without Martha—without her opinions, her advice, her affection. "Tomorrow night," she said, "Dino wants to take us for dinner. Said you should pick the restaurant. That you know all the best places."

"Oh, no, I couldn't stand the drive. But you go. Relax with Dino. Stop taking things so seriously."

Becky's cheeks warmed, and she refolded her napkin. "I'm not," she said. She hadn't felt one bit serious when his mouth had roamed over her breasts. Not one whiff of embarrassment. Or fear. Middle of the afternoon and she'd literally bared her chest.

"It's time you live a little." Martha leaned forward and there was no missing the interest in her eyes. "What happened before is in the past. Everyone needs some fun, and Dino is excellent at making women feel good."

Becky's face flamed and she dropped any pretense of eating. She considered pressing her cold glass against her cheeks, but Martha's smile was too knowing. Still, this topic had definitely injected Martha with some vitality and if talking about sex helped, then Becky was all for it. If only she could control her self-consciousness.

She forced her head up, keeping her voice light, pretending it really wasn't a big decision. "You think I should sleep with Dino?"

"My dear," Martha said dryly, "judging by the way he looks at you, there won't be much sleeping."

Becky almost dropped her glass. "Really," she squeaked.

Martha's smile widened as she picked up her fork and speared a pink shrimp. "Just because I'm old doesn't mean I can't see. And I love talking about sex. Why Malcolm and I, the things we did..."

And now Becky did press the glass against her face. "But that's different," she said, firmly blocking any visuals. "You loved each other."

"Well, I certainly had my share of men before Malcolm. How else does one know how a husband ranks as a lover?"

She sounded so adamant, Becky leaned forward, embarrassment tempered with curiosity. "Really? Don't you think it's important that the man cares for you first?"

Martha gave an unladylike snort. "Of course they care for you. But men are like stallions. At breeding time, the mare standing in front of them is the most important thing in the world."

"I guess," Becky said. "But Dino has a lot of women in front of him."

"I haven't seen any lately."

"No, but—"

"Don't make things complicated. Before I die, I need to know you're ready to live."

Becky jerked back. This was the first time Martha had actually talked about dying, and her calm acceptance ripped at her. "Well I'm not ready," she said, her voice cracking, "so you'll have to stick around for years and years. A man took pictures of me naked, and I don't want sex, and I don't want Dino. I just want you."

Martha's smile turned smug. "Pictures. So that's what it was. I always wondered why you hated attention. But now look at you." She opened her arms. "Come here and give an old woman a hug."

Becky leaned over, swept with a fierce protectiveness, wanting to squeeze Martha and keep her safe forever. Her tiny body felt so brittle, it only made her throat convulse. And Martha never hugged, had never been demonstrative—even with Malcolm.

"Don't worry. I'm not saying goodbye," Martha said dryly, as if reading her thoughts. "Some legal items need to be finalized first, and I want to hear all about your transition sex with Dino."

Transition sex? Becky's tears mingled with laughter as Martha gently freed herself from the embrace and edged to the front of her chair. "Good God, Martha. Okay. If it happens, I'll let you know." She wiped her eyes before reaching down to help Martha up, not sure if the tears were from laughter or sorrow. "And there's also Echo's race and then Hunter runs."

"Oh? Well, that sounds good." Martha tilted her head. "When exactly is Hunter's race?"

"In two weeks, maybe, or when the meets move south. Sometime soon anyway," Becky said, noting Martha's reaction. Tonight she'd ask Dino to enter Hunter in a race. Any race. And if sex stories would stoke Martha's interest, she'd provide details, even if she had to make every one of them up.

CHAPTER TWENTY-FOUR

Stars dotted the sky, and a bold yellow moon lit Dino's driveway. A beautiful night for lovers. Or even just sex. A rush of nerves jolted Becky, and she jammed the car to a stop and stepped out. Slim's file felt awkward in her hand, and she realized her fingers shook.

Steps crunched and she whirled, slamming her elbow painfully on the door.

"Heard your car," Dino said, his voice calm and slow and assured. "I was checking the horses. Want to walk back over before we go inside?"

"Sure," she said, rubbing her elbow, not sure if he sensed she was nervous or because the stall check wasn't finished. He probably knew she was nervous. He was always so savvy, so confident, so...experienced.

"The sky's pretty tonight, isn't it?" He looked up, seemed in no hurry to return to the barn.

She nodded then realized he couldn't see her head. "That's a nice bright star beneath the moon."

He slipped his arm around her. "Not a star, honey. That's a planet."

"Oh." And she didn't feel stupid, only reassured by the natural way he tucked her against him. "What planet?" she asked.

"Venus."

His deep voice rumbled, his breath fanning her hair, as he pointed out constellations, mentioning several names she'd heard of but had never really noted. She nodded, interested in the sky but mainly thinking how nice he was.

He must have felt her sigh because he chuckled and turned her around. "Am I boring you?"

"Not at all," she said.

He stared for a moment. Then his head dipped, covering her mouth with his, and she forgot about the planets and stars and constellations. She arched forward, seeking the feel of his mouth, the hardness of his body, his hot maleness. The kiss deepened

When he finally lifted his head, she was breathing hard and couldn't squash her gasp of regret.

"Come on," he said thickly, "before you drive me nuts."

He stuck the file under his arm and tugged her toward the barn. She followed, a glow warming the center of her chest. She drove him nuts? Dino, the man who could have his pick of so many beautiful women.

"I want to show you the cameras." He looped his arm around her waist when they entered the barn.

"Have you seen Slim again today?" she asked, barely recognizing her voice and its odd sultry sound.

"Nope. I'll let the asshole sober up first."

The muscles in his arm tightened and he dropped his hand. She immediately regretted mentioning Slim. "Who can see the monitors?" she asked, peering at the ceiling.

"The entrances and aisle can be seen on the computer in the barn office, my computer, and eventually in the house Slim's living in. The third can only be monitored from my laptop." He stopped her in the center of the aisle. "The last camera is hidden but look around. Tell me if you see it."

She studied the ceiling around the lights and smoke detector but saw nothing, only the two silver cams at the ends of the aisle. Lyric poked her head over the stall and she absently scratched the mare's jaw, still checking the ceiling, the sides of the walls, any place a camera could be hidden. "I don't see a thing," she finally said.

"Good. Then it's well hidden." His eyes narrowed on Lyric. "That mare sure likes you. Able to clean her feet yet?"

"Yes," she said, with a ring of pride. "And I don't have to tie her up either."

"That's my girl," he said, his easy familiarity making her heart skip. He stared at her for a moment and his voice roughened. "Let's go home."

He grabbed her hand and guided her from the barn, clearly in a hurry to reach his house. It wasn't a dark night but even so, she stumbled. He immediately shortened his steps to match hers, but his urgency pulsed in waves.

The back door stuck. He pushed it back with his boot and tossed Slim's file on the side table, without releasing her hand. "Are you hungry? I have pizza and Chinese food."

"Both?"

"I didn't know what you wanted," he admitted with a boyish grin. He passed the bootjack and helped tug off her boots. "You're turning into a real cowgirl. When we first met, you wore white running shoes with really thick soles."

"Nurse's shoes." She smiled, secretly shocked he remembered. "And I still have those. They're quiet in Martha's house."

"Is quiet what she needs?"

"No." Becky sighed. "Actually she needs something to make her care. And the horses are all I can think of. That's why it's important Echo wins on Friday."

"It's important to me too. A win there and my bonus kicks in."

Becky tossed her boots aside, uncomfortable with his candor. He made no secret he was racing for himself. Not Conrad Stables. Not Martha. "I guess we both want the same thing then," she said slowly.

He didn't notice her hesitation. Had already crossed the room. "Want to see Lyric on the cam?"

He motioned her over and flipped open his laptop. Touched some keys. The barn aisle appeared with Echo, pulling at her hay net, and Lyric, nosing her door. "We can see Echo, along with the stalls on each side," he said. "It's all taped too, so everything's on record."

Lyric quit trying to open her door and leaned over, stealing a bite of Echo's hay. Movement flashed at the bottom of the screen, and a mouse scurried along the floor then disappeared in the crack beneath Lyric's door. "That's so cute." She laughed. "The picture is clear too."

"Clear and uneventful. Exactly what we want." He touched her shoulder. "I'll heat up the food."

"Did I tell you what I wanted?" she asked, still studying the aisle, hoping the little mouse would reappear.

"I'm hoping everything."

The husky undertone in his voice pulled her around. He'd paused in front of the kitchen island, looking so damn gorgeous, she could only gulp. "I want pizza," she said, unable to look away. "And I thought...maybe I'd stay the night."

He crossed the room in three long strides. "Then we'll eat after." He scooped her up with easy strength and carried her into his bedroom.

She clung to his shoulders, slightly awkward. She'd already decided to do this, but it would be easier if he'd turn out the light. The brightness didn't seem to bother him though and he laid her on the bed, eyes dark with purpose as he slowly unbuttoned her shirt.

"Please turn out the light," she whispered.

He studied her for a moment, then without a word, rose and snapped it off. Darkness cloaked the room, pitch black except for two stars twinkling through the window. The bed moved when he rejoined her. He'd seemed in a hurry earlier so she was surprised when he wrapped her in his arms and gently kissed her forehead.

"There's nobody in here taking pictures, honey. It's just you and me." He rubbed the knot at the base of her neck.

Slowly she relaxed, savoring his familiar smell, her sense of security whenever he was around. She felt the release of her bra, then the pressure of his fingers as he massaged her back. She arched into him, liking his touch. His arousal was obvious but it seemed so right, so natural, her self-consciousness eased.

His hands moved to her breasts, molding them to his palms, and when he stroked her nipples she quivered with awareness, wrapped her arms around his neck and pressed closer. And it didn't matter anymore that he might forget her in a month, a week, a day.

She'd expected her relationship with her boyfriend to last, but that had burst when Jared left, along with her lifelong dream for a real family. Dino, at least, was honest. When she was with him, he made her feel like she was the only girl in the world. And that was enough. Transition sex was a wonderful thing.

She quit thinking as his tongue explored her mouth, sending tingles along her spine. He undid the last of her buttons, and then his clever fingers were everywhere. She slid her hand beneath his shirt, feeling his heat, his ridges, and a contented sound escaped from deep in her throat.

He eased her back as his mouth closed over her nipple. Ripples of pleasure shot to her toes. He tugged off his shirt but continued sucking, until the throbbing between her legs ached. She heard the clink of his belt, the unzipping of her pants, a lift and a tug, then air chilled her bare skin. He could be a nurse, she thought inanely, with his obvious skill at clothes removal. She automatically closed her legs, but he didn't seem concerned. His warm mouth rasped over her chest, honing again on her nipples, pleasure and pain at the same time, and she didn't want it to stop.

She'd never known her breasts were so sensitive, so connected to the ache pooling between her legs. An insistent knee pushed her thighs apart. She tensed but his hand slipped lower, sweeping her with startling pleasure and her legs parted as though possessing a mind of their own.

Her groan startled her, raw, impatient, needy. This was definitely not the kind of foreplay she'd had with Jared. This hit a whole new level. She pulled at his shoulders, not wanting him to move his head from her breasts, but his hand was driving her crazy and she wanted more. Much more.

She writhed against him, realized her breath was coming in pants. He lifted his head, covering her mouth in a deep kiss that seemed to stroke her soul.

She felt his hardness and rose against him, welcoming the intrusion. But he was big and she hadn't had sex in five years and couldn't help but stiffen. His mouth returned to her nipple and his bold hand stroked her until she yanked at his shoulders, urging him closer.

Slowly he pushed in, filling her with his maleness. He lifted her legs, hooked them around his hips and drove deeper, heating her body with long, even strokes. She gripped his back, eyes clenched. God, it was incredibly good. She didn't care now if lights were on, didn't even care if cameras flashed. Obviously he was a professional lover and if having lots of girlfriends resulted in this brain-blowing sex, she didn't begrudge him the practice.

"Don't ever stop," she whispered fiercely, stupidly. Of course he'd have to stop sometime, but rising waves of pleasure overrode rational thought.

His strokes grew harder, faster. She buried her head in his shoulder, crying out as her body spasmed around him. He gave a final thrust, his grip tightening and his big body relaxed.

He rolled to the side, pulling her to him. "You okay?" he murmured.

Okay? She pressed against his damp chest, glad it was too dark to see. She was way more than okay. And now it was clear why all the women chased him. It wasn't his looks at all. Not his good humor. Not his kindness.

She didn't have a lot of experience with sex but if she were to rank her two men, Jared would be a two and Dino a ten. Actually she had better drop Jared to a one and Dino to a nine and a half. Martha said it was always wise to leave room for improvement.

Her ragged breathing threaded with unease. Maybe he ranked his lovers too? Maybe he'd just given her a one.

"You okay?" he repeated. There was no mistaking the concern in his voice.

"Wonderful," she said quickly.

"You are wonderful." His hand slid beneath her hair, stroking the base of her neck. The gruffness in his tone chased away her insecurities. He sounded sincere. And of course, Martha was right. Sex was never bad for a guy. Yes, he was the perfect man to help with her naked phobia. Shouldn't take more than a month or so.

He moved. *Click.*

Light flooded the room and she flailed in panic, yanking the sheet to her neck. "Turn it off," she yelped.

"It's just us, honey. No worries." He disposed of his condom then calmly wrapped the sheet around them both and pulled her to him, holding her close, saying nothing. Just being there.

Slowly her heart stopped its panicked hammering.

His hand traced her cheek. "How many times did that cockroach take pictures?"

"Whenever his wife was gone, he'd grab his camera and look for someone. We'd try to hide. Make ourselves invisible." Her voice sounded rusty. "But when he locked the basement door and brightened the lights, we were terrified." She shrugged helplessly. "I'm sorry."

He tilted her chin, his face calm and reassuring. "It's okay. He's been out of your life awhile. Come on. I know what you need." He scooped her up, ignoring her protests, totally relaxed with nakedness. And no wonder. He was beautiful. Dark hair shadowed his chest, running in a line down his muscled stomach. She tried to peek lower, but her head was tucked too close to his shoulder.

She gave a little squeal but even to her, the protest sounded feeble. After all, it was just the two of them. And she felt safe, liked the feel of his rough palms on her skin, his easy assurance as he carried her effortlessly down the hall and into the bathroom.

"In you go." He deposited her in the shower and slid the door shut. Turned on the water, adjusted the shower head and picked up a bar of soap.

His confident hands on her back, combined with the warm soapy water, soothed her lingering inhibitions. It was quite lovely. The pulsing water, the perfect temperature, the tang of masculine soap. Her shoulders lowered, and she closed her eyes in trust.

"Turn around, honey," he said. So she did. His hands slid over her slick breasts, then returned to linger and the rasp of his calloused palm made her nipples tingle all over again. She cracked open her eyes, staring at him beneath the sluicing water. He looked like a Greek god, a slightly disreputable one, his eyes dark and heavy lidded as he admired her body. And she didn't feel a bit dirty. She felt beautiful. Bold and beautiful.

"Let me." She slid the soap from his hand. Dragged the bar over the front of his rippled chest, along his flat stomach, following the trail of dark hair. Heard his sharp intake of breath as she moved lower. Exploring. Lingering.

The soap slid from her hand as she cupped him. She watched, fascinated, when he thickened in her hand. She kneeled and tentatively ran her tongue over the bulbous tip. He was fresh and clean and wonderful. Slowly she took him in her mouth.

The muscles in his thighs strained under her hand. He reached out and flattened his palms against the wall but otherwise didn't move, didn't push or force her mouth deeper, not like Jared had done. Simply waited as she explored him beneath the pulsing water.

And now he was so huge he really did look like a Greek god. She looked up, unable to hide a mischievous grin.

He abruptly turned, jammed open the shower door and fumbled in a drawer. Ripped open a condom and rolled it on. She wasn't sure how he was going to manage sex in the slippery shower, but clearly he was comfortable with the procedure. And then he picked her up, braced her against the wall and it wasn't difficult at all.

Her legs wrapped around his hips and he entered her fast and hard, making her gasp from the intrusion. He slowed but only to yank her legs higher.

"Sorry," he muttered, his voice hoarse. "Next time I'll make it better for you."

The cords in his neck bulged, his eyes half closed, but he found her breast and when his urgent mouth closed around her nipple, waves of pleasure jolted her. She jerked in response but couldn't move, her back pressed against the wall, legs spread wide as he drove deeper, and it was all so primal she whimpered with need.

She clenched the straining muscles in his back, wanting more, needing more, but when his teeth skimmed over her nipple, coiling waves swept her. She jerked against him, her muscles quivering from the unexpected climax.

He shuddered over her in a last powerful thrust, his body shaking. It was surprising he had enough strength to stand. She was boneless, limp to her toes, yet he was still buried. She should have felt vulnerable, her legs splayed around his back, no clothes in sight, but the only thing she felt was damn good.

And he'd said he would make the next time better. *Oh, wow.* She kissed his shoulder in complete gratitude.

"Wow, indeed," he said and she realized she'd spoken out loud. He was looking at her, his face relaxed, almost boyish, and it was then she realized how much stress he carried. He tilted her chin and kissed her. "You're wonderful, sweetie."

He slid out, lowering her feet to the shower floor. She abruptly felt bereft. He'd already turned to adjust the shower head, already moved on to the washing procedure with quick, efficient strokes. The water sprayed over them, washing away the smell of passion and sex. Washing away the intimacy.

Her throat tightened; she blinked away the tightness behind her eyes. It shouldn't bother her that he was used to showering with company, that he kept a supply of condoms in the bathroom. After all, she was using him to get over a few tiny issues of her own.

She'd already made considerable progress too—standing naked in the shower, lights on, not a bit uptight. She hadn't even thought about Craig, although she probably needed a lot more practice, needed to ensure this new comfort level was totally ingrained.

Dino slid open the shower door, grabbed an oversized blue towel and wrapped it around her. "Need anything else?"

"No. I think I was well provided for."

He smiled and slid a kiss across her mouth. "I mean shampoo, conditioner. There's stuff beneath the sink."

She managed to keep smiling even thought that pesky lump filled her throat. He had lots of women—she knew that—but now a traitorous jealousy gnawed at her insides, an emotion it would be folly to reveal.

"Thanks. I'll just be a couple more minutes." She turned away, pretending to adjust the towel.

She waited until the bathroom door shut then stepped from the shower and peeked beneath the sink. Her heart sank. It was worse than expected. Fancy containers jammed the storage space—high-end stuff too, not many drug store products. She scanned the labels: conditioners, shampoo, three types of tampons, two hair dryers, and a wrinkled magazine featuring a tanned Jennifer Aniston on the cover. January issue.

Greta had been here in January. Maybe some of this stuff was hers. Some might be Stephanie's, although maybe a container or two belonged to that dark-haired girl who'd mauled Dino at the kitchen. Or some could belong to the beautiful but bitchy reporter.

Or it could be any number of unknown women.

She quietly closed the cupboard door. She didn't care. After all, she wanted the same thing. This relationship was about sex, and that was perfect. Absolutely perfect.

She clamped her mouth and toweled herself dry, then wrapped it around her chest, sarong style. Generally she used moisturizer after a shower, but tonight she'd skip that step. She glared at the cupboard. No way was she going to use any of that stuff. Who even knew what kind of order it was in? It wouldn't do to mix January's with June.

Impulsively, she bent back down and rearranged the containers in alphabetical order. She even hummed when she emerged from the bathroom.

Dino's lingering appraisal made her heart thump. "Pizza or Chinese?" he asked. "I heated both."

He appeared naked behind the counter, and it was hard to drag her eyes off his impressive chest. However, she made a concerted effort to study the pizza. Looked pretty good. Lots of cheese. Her gaze darted back. He had a small scar on the side of his ribs that she hadn't noticed earlier. She craned over the counter, trying to see if he really was naked, or if he had a towel wrapped around those lean hips.

"Pizza?"

"Um, yes, please." She dragged her gaze back to the pizza.

"You look hungry." He tossed two slices on a plate and slid it across the counter. "Beer, wine?"

A case of beer sat on the counter. On the far side of the kitchen, a compact wine rack squatted next to the liquor cabinet. Only fifteen feet away, and there was an unobstructed view.

"Red wine, please," she said primly.

He walked toward the wine rack, and she blew out her disappointment. He wore sweat pants. Gray, low on his hips, although he definitely had a beautiful back. She'd felt it, of course, but seeing the hard contours, the ripples, even the contrasting color of his skin, made her insides melt.

"Okay?" He was holding up a bottle and obviously had asked a question. She nodded blankly but he walked around the counter, wine and corkscrew in his hand, his concerned eyes on her face. "You comfortable, honey? You seem distracted. Want a bathrobe?"

She smiled, relieved he had no idea how much she enjoyed looking at him, thought she was worried about clothes. Yet oddly, she was comfortable wearing the towel, at least around him. And it almost reached her knees, probably covered as much as a bathrobe. Besides his robe would be so big, she'd trip in it.

Unless he had others.

Her smile faded. "Do you have one that would fit?"

"There's some in the spare bedroom," he said. "They'd fit."

She pretended absorption in the corkscrew as he deftly opened the bottle. "Girls sure leave a lot of stuff here," she said, keeping her voice casual.

"A lot of it was here when I came," he said, his attention on the wine. "Comes in handy though. There's a pair of leather riding boots in the closet you can try." He passed her the wine glass and checked her bare feet. "Size six, right?"

She nodded, glad her toenails gleamed from the recent pedicure, but reluctant to borrow an old girlfriend's boots. If they were left by a past trainer, that was different. She didn't know why it mattered—after all, she was just using him for sex—but it did.

She twirled the stem of her glass, trying to imagine his social life. "How long were you married?" she blurted.

"Eight years. Two were happy." He pulled up a chair and grabbed a piece of pizza, totally at ease. "It wasn't all Laura's fault. Training is demanding, and it made her miserable. I'll never marry again."

"Don't you want children?" She nibbled on a slice of pizza, pretending to concentrate on the cheese as it stretched in a thin line. "I mean, not now, but sometime down the road?"

"Never felt the urge. Horses fill that hole."

He didn't return her questions. She'd already noticed that if he didn't care, he didn't ask. A relief, really. His face would have blanched if she admitted she wanted a husband, three kids, and a yellow Lab to chase sticks in their backyard.

But of course, she didn't want that now. And as Martha had said, she needed to get out, have fun, gain a little confidence. He was only a stepping stone. The fact that she was so comfortable with him was a bonus. In fact, she realized, adjusting the knot in her towel, she was as comfortable with him as she was with Martha.

"Another slice?" His voice was husky, his eyes lowering to watch her hands.

"No, thanks. I'm full."

"I, on the other hand," he stepped closer, "can't seem to get enough." He tilted her head with a finger. His warm lips skimmed over her collarbone. She steadied her hand on the counter, trying not to move as that slow mouth drifted along her shoulder, leaving her breathless.

He wasn't even touching her, except with his mouth, but already she swayed on the stool. And now he toyed with an earlobe.

She slid off the stool and leaned into him. A flick of his finger and the towel dropped to the floor, settling over her pink toes.

"We're doing pretty good working on this clothes hang-up." His thumb brushed the bottom of her breast. "But there's a couple more things I should show you."

"Is this something best shown in the bedroom?" she murmured, standing on her tiptoes and pressing her lips against his cheek.

"Absolutely."

"Good," she said.

CHAPTER TWENTY-FIVE

Dino pried his eyes open and checked the bedside clock, surprised it was already five a.m. Years of waking at four had left him with an ingrained habit. He never overslept. Except today. He raised his arms and stretched, not tired, just completely and utterly satisfied.

Rarely had he had a better lover. Or a more generous one. Becky certainly didn't worry about hiding that sexy body anymore. He reached over, feeling for her, but already sensed he was alone. He rose, pulled on a pair of jeans and padded from the bedroom.

Light filtered from the living room. She was curled in the armchair, staring intently at his computer screen. Unfortunately, she was dressed.

He touched her shoulder. She reached back and squeezed his hand. "They're feeding breakfast," she said. "Gosh, Lyric's a fast eater. She's already finished her grain."

"We're supposed to be watching Echo," he said dryly. "The filly that's racing tomorrow."

Her laugh was quick and infectious, but she kept her attention on the screen. "I'm watching them both. But Lyric is much more entertaining."

He didn't realize he still held her hand until she tugged it away and pointed at the screen. "Look at her trying to sneak out the door when the groom checks the water."

"Fascinating," he drawled, watching Becky's face. She hadn't really looked at him yet, had given no hint they'd just shared a very special night. Maybe she didn't realize how good it had been. He was positive he'd made her come three or four times. In fact, he was getting hard just remembering her throaty whimpers.

"Are you leaving for the track now?" She finally turned and glanced up. Her lower lip was slightly swollen, hair rumpled, not a trace of makeup. She looked beautiful.

"I'm not sure." He dragged a hand over his jaw. He'd intended to drive up to Lone Star but was now reluctant to rush off. "It's kind of late. Shane can probably handle it. What time does Martha wake?"

"About seven."

"So we have a few hours. I don't have much breakfast food, but I can make coffee." Picking up his phone, he moved into the kitchen and called Shane. "You're in charge today. I'm staying at Conrad's."

"Sure, boss." Shane sounded surprised but delighted.

"Remember to put blinkers on the Barkeeper colt," Dino said as he one-handed the coffee tin from the cupboard, "and the new filly needs a shadow roll. She should jog three laps."

"Okay," Shane said. "And that hot-assed reporter called again. Wanted some news on the Conrad filly. Said you promised her an update. She sounded pissed."

"I'll look after her."

"And if you see Becky, say hi," Shane added. "Is she coming to the races tomorrow?"

Dino stiffened, his gaze drifting to Becky. He had the juvenile urge to tell Shane she was right beside him, fresh from his bed. "Yes. She'll be driving down with me when I bring Echo. And driving back with me as well," he added, his voice clipped.

"Slim's not hauling?"

"Nope." Dino tossed a spoon in the sink, mentally ticking off his morning. Feed Becky, oversee new exercise rider, pick up broken leather, fire Slim. Find his replacement as quickly as possible. It was unfortunate Stephanie was gone. She knew the animals, and Slim wouldn't be as missed if she were around.

Or maybe Shane could move to Conrad's and help out for a few weeks. He'd be the ideal person since he already knew the horses. But the thought made him scowl. "I'll call you at noon." He cut the connection and walked back into the living room.

Becky was still watching the screen, smiling at something Lyric did. He bent over and gave her a possessive kiss. Usually women were the ones who wanted to talk relationships, but she hadn't said a word last night, not even when she cuddled in his arms, sweet and sated.

He'd been relieved; he didn't do relationships and that direction of talk generally made him sweat. But the sex had been damn good. Too good for them not to continue for a while.

"So we're still on for dinner tonight, right?" He stared at the computer screen, pretending interest as one of the stable hands plunked a blue wheelbarrow in front of Lyric's stall.

She glanced up in surprise. "You're going to stay here? Until we haul out tomorrow?"

It did sound odd, and he crossed his arms, slightly defensive. "Echo's race is important. I have to win for my bonus to kick in. So I *have* to stick around."

"Right." She nodded and looked back at the screen. "Of course, the race is important to Martha too."

"Of course." He shrugged. "Anyway I need to stay here. I got a new girl coming by to fill in for Stephanie. She's ridden for me before but unfortunately never galloped Echo. So I'll need to watch her. Got a bunch of other stuff to do here too."

"You sound busy so I'll clear out now." She smiled but didn't look away from the computer screen. "I appreciate how you helped me, you know, be more…comfortable. It was a lot of fun."

"Fun?" He stared at the top of her head, thoughts of Slim and Echo sliding right out of his mind. She thought their lovemaking had been fun? Of course, she'd only slept with one other guy before. Maybe she didn't realize how good the sex was. "I'm not sure if *fun* is the best description," he said cautiously.

"Well, I thought it was." She unfolded her legs and rose from the chair. "You were most impressive and certainly justify all the shampoo. Thanks for everything." She stood on her tiptoes, brushed his cheek with a cool kiss and headed toward the door.

The reference to shampoo was confusing but it was clear she intended to leave, and since he had a lot to do, that was probably a good thing. But he didn't want her to go, not yet. The knowledge left him irritated. "But I just made a pot of coffee. Stay and help me drink it."

She smiled over her shoulder. "But you don't have any food."

"I have pizza. It's delicious cold. And Chinese food, which I can heat."

She wrinkled her nose, gave a little wave, and walked out. Probably in a hurry to see Martha. Understandable, of course, but he didn't like to be abandoned. He scooped his boots off the mat and rushed after her.

The sun hadn't poked over the ridge yet, the vehicles were only a dark shape in the gloom, but a car door clicked. Christ, she was fast. He'd only hauled one boot on, and she was pretty much gone.

He stopped hopping on one leg, yanked the boot off and tossed it aside with a clunk. "If you want to go on a trail ride," he yelled, "be at the barn by ten."

"You have time to ride with me?" He caught an indistinct blur of movement as she called out the window, and the delight in her voice was obvious.

"Of course I do." He grinned foolishly.

And then the car crunched over the gravel. Headlights panned the driveway as it wheeled around and whipped down the road. He propped his hip against the door, watching until it disappeared. She drove faster now, with more confidence. Yes, indeed. Quite a bit had changed about Martha's meek little nurse.

He closed the door, determined to concentrate on more pressing issues. Echo, Hunter, Slim. Plus call Laura and assure her he'd have the money. He'd hang around Conrad's for the next twenty-four hours. Ensure nothing went wrong. His ranch was only one win away, and the filly was primed to run.

He grabbed a steaming cup of coffee, considering the competition. Seven furlongs. The horses would start in the chute, a long backstretch run, one turn and then gallop home. The speed horse from California, Country Zip, had drawn the four hole and would no doubt lead the way. Echo liked to stalk and would break from the six hole—perfect for her since she'd have the speed on her inside. She was tractable. Brad could ride a smart race, keeping Country Zip in his sights until it was time to move.

Should be a relatively easy win. Still…he took a quick gulp of coffee, almost burning his mouth. Races were never easy, horses never predictable. On paper it looked like Echo towered over her rivals. She was a stakes winner; this was an allowance race and two horses were still maidens.

If Malcolm were alive, he wouldn't be thrilled about dropping Echo in class. A loss at this level could erode her breeding value. But the horse needed a race, and a win by a homebred would deliver his bonus. Besides, Echo couldn't lose—she was training perfectly. Even Stephanie said the filly never felt better. A win at any cost was what Martha needed. A win would keep her interested. No need to second guess.

Besides, he didn't need to justify his decisions. Echo needed the race, he needed the money, and he was going to make sure that horse crossed the wire first.

CHAPTER TWENTY-SIX

Martha's eyes twinkled, the mischief in her voice reassuring. "I don't like Ted calling me every day, urging me to move. And pretending I was changing my will was the only way to make him shut up. Now show me the entries for Echo's race."

Becky smoothed the crumpled sheet on the table, delighted to see the return of Martha's gumption. Thanks to Echo's race, this was definitely going to be a good week.

"Echo will be the favorite. Country Zip is the second favorite." She leaned forward and adjusted the patio umbrella, shielding Martha's head from the morning sun. Eight-thirty and already it was warm. She wondered if Echo had finished her gallop yet, wondered if Slim had sobered up, wondered if the new rider would flirt with Dino.

She grabbed a metal chair, dragging it over the patio tiles closer to Martha. Of course the new girl would flirt with Dino. And of course he'd respond. She knew that. Expected it even. She'd seen the shampoo bottles, knew he liked variety, and that knowledge didn't bother her. Not a bit.

"Goodness." Martha winced. "Don't grate the chair like that. It's a horrible noise. Very unladylike."

"Sorry. I wasn't thinking." Becky picked up the chair and dropped it next to Martha.

"I disagree." Martha gave her hand a comforting squeeze. "Obviously you're thinking of something. Horses or men?"

"Horses," Becky said. "Dino wants to win tomorrow. He can buy his ranch from his ex if he earns that bonus." She swallowed but Martha's gaze was empathetic. "What was she like?"

"Laura? Never met her. They were divorced long before Dino came to work for us. But rumor is she craved a lot of male attention and that they were both unhappy." Martha patted her hand. "Sounds like you're really thinking of a man. I heard your car early this morning. Did you have a fun evening?"

Becky studied the garden. A monarch butterfly landed on some white azaleas then fluttered away in search of brighter flowers. "Sure. Dino was very nice but it's a new day now." She kept her gaze on the flowers. "Unfortunately it's hard to pretend not to care."

"But you don't want a trainer. Someone who gets up early every morning, won't take vacations and probably will never be rich." Martha's voice filled with repugnance. "You'd be stuck living in a rundown ranch, throwing feed for chickens while Dino gallivants at the track."

"He wants to stay single anyway." Becky's eyes burned, but she blinked away the itch.

Martha made a dismissive noise in her throat. "All men think that. Just remember, he's a trainer."

Becky sneaked a quick eye rub then checked Martha's face. Her color and energy were good, but her words didn't make sense. "Well, of course I remember he's a trainer. I can't imagine him being anything else."

Martha gave a knowing smile. "I've never met a trainer who wasn't intensely competitive."

"Yes, he wants to win every time he runs."

"Well, if you want Dino, think of it like a race. My Malcolm told me he didn't want to get married too. Always had a different girl hanging on his arm."

"Really?" Becky leaned forward, forgetting about hiding her watery eyes. "But he was so in love with you."

"Of course he was. But he didn't know it. And the most important thing was for me to decide I loved him."

Becky's shoulders drooped. Martha liked to give advice, but it wasn't wise to accept everything she said. Perhaps it was best to be content with simple progress. Two months ago, she wouldn't have believed Dino would even want to share a coffee with her. Now they'd had some great sex and she hadn't even been self-conscious; in fact she'd been surprisingly bold. She should be happy with that. He was just so damn nice—

"Are you listening?"

Becky gave a guilty jerk.

"So if you remember life is one big horse race," Martha continued, "you'll have all the men you want. Now, for my bets. Fifty dollars on Echo to win, throw in a twenty-dollar exacta with the other favorite and any longshot you like in the paddock. Give all my winnings to Stephanie. When can you visit her?"

"Monday." Becky grabbed a pen, relieved Martha hadn't forgotten Stephanie's plight, and jotted down her instructions. It was hard keeping exotic bets straight but if Shane were around, she'd ask for help. He'd already taught her a lot about watching horses in the paddock. "Think this will be an easy race?"

"I certainly hope so. Echo's plummeted in class, and Malcolm would roll in his grave if she lost. But trainers make the decisions, and Malcolm always trusted Dino." Martha yawned. "What about Slim? Is he going to the track with you tomorrow?"

"I'm not sure." Becky doodled on the paper, reluctant to look at Martha. "Dino hasn't been happy with Slim lately."

"I've gathered," Martha said dryly. "But Slim was Malcolm's first manager. They've been through a lot together, including that terrible accident with Jill." Her voice firmed. "I don't believe in coddling but even if Slim leaves, he's welcome to stay in the guesthouse. Remain on salary until he finds another job. Promise you'll work that out with Dino?"

Becky nodded. She'd been agonizing about Slim and Jill, so it was a relief Martha felt an increasing degree of responsibility. No need to upset her with ugly suspicions. Slim had already been handed a huge chunk of grief. The image of Jill's body bouncing like a rag doll made her sick. Who knew how it had affected him?

The patio door opened and Jocelyn emerged, balancing glasses and a water pitcher on a small tray. "Nine o'clock. Time for your medication, Mrs. Conrad. And you have a visitor this morning. Should I bring a pot of tea?"

"Depends on the visitor," Martha said. Her voice trailed off as a smiling Ted appeared in the doorway. His gaze settled on Becky and his smile slipped.

"Hello, Martha." He strolled over and brushed her cheek with his mouth. "Jocelyn didn't tell me your nurse was here."

"I keep telling you, Becky's much more than a nurse," Martha said. "And she's indispensable with the horses."

"She certainly hasn't helped them run any faster," he said. "Or made your operation any safer. It's a good thing Malcolm isn't here. I heard another of your riders was hurt yesterday. Such a shame."

Martha frowned. "What jockey was hurt?"

"Exercise rider," Becky said. "Stephanie. It's just her arm though."

"Just her arm." Ted's mouth curled. "You wouldn't be so dismissive if it happened to you. And it could have been a spine or head injury, just like that other girl. Damaged for life. Horses are dangerous, even on a trail ride."

"Ted's right." Martha turned toward Becky, the color leaching from her face. "Maybe you shouldn't ride."

Becky shot a disgusted look at Ted. No wonder Martha avoided his visits. His barbs were unnecessary and he was a selfish, inconsiderate prick. "Ted," she leaned forward, "for someone who doesn't like horses, you have an avid interest in what's going on. How did you find out about Stephanie? It only happened yesterday."

He was pouring a glass of water but lifted his head, and the resentment on his face shoved her backwards. She straightened in the chair but refused to look away, focusing on the three deep scowl lines on his forehead.

"Jocelyn told me," Ted finally said. "After all, I'm Martha's only blood relative." His voice sounded defensive and Becky calmly picked up her glass. Ted was just another bully, another Craig, and she could handle him.

Martha still looked worried though. She stared at Becky, her eyes thoughtful. "I want to give you Lyric," she said. "But first the mare should be sent away for training. Make her into a safer riding horse—"

Ted jerked upright, hissing with displeasure. "Give a nurse a horse! That's nuts. Isn't Lyric the animal that won so much money?"

"She's retired now and Malcolm didn't want her bred," Martha said. "Becky likes her."

"I can't afford to keep a horse." Becky's words came out in a rush and she didn't dare look at Ted. "I do appreciate the thought, really I do, but you know I can't accept her."

"Of course she can't." Ted paced around the table, shaking his head. "This kind of talk is ridiculous. Makes me question your mental facilities."

"My facilities are fine," Martha snapped.

"Doesn't sound like it," Ted said. "Giving away an expensive horse. And I think most people—most doctors—would agree with me."

"I won't tolerate that sort of rudeness, even from you." Martha's voice could have chipped ice. "You may leave now."

"I didn't mean—"

"Go away, Ted," Martha said. "You can call later and apologize."

Ted crossed his arms. "Now, listen. You must realize the value of the stable, the horses, is falling every week. The time to sell is now. I know someone who will give us a very good price. But he won't wait much longer."

"It's not the value of the horses I'm concerned about," Martha said. "It's the reputation. Malcolm wanted to leave something of value. And Dino's doing a good job, in spite of a run of bad luck. I'll re-evaluate at the end of the Lone Star meet. But for now, nothing changes." She leaned back in her chair, a smile curving her lips. "Except, perhaps, the ownership of Lyric."

Becky peeked at Ted, wondering if he realized his aunt was goading. But his eyes had narrowed, and he obviously found little humor in her words.

Martha, however, was just starting to have fun. She leaned forward, fluttering a solicitous hand at the pitcher of water. "Would you like some more water, Becky dearest?"

Ted's face turned an unflattering shade of red. He stared at Becky then wheeled and stalked away. The patio door slammed behind him.

Martha shrugged. "I shouldn't tease. But he's always been the most irritating little boy. Reminds me of my sister. So easy to push her buttons."

Becky's troubled gaze remained on the door, where the blinds still shuddered from the force of Ted's exit. Martha might consider him a harmless boy, but the comment he'd made about her mental state wasn't just irritating—it had sounded like a threat.

CHAPTER TWENTY-SEVEN

The groom slowed a dripping Echo in front of Becky. "I don't know where anybody is. Mr. Anders and the new exercise rider might be in the office. Slim was here earlier but didn't even check Echo." Cody shrugged, appearing slightly bewildered.

"Thanks," Becky said, following his gaze to Slim's house. From this angle, it was impossible to see if Slim's truck was still parked in the driveway; maybe Dino had already handed him a pink slip. She'd have to tell Slim it wasn't necessary to move out until he found another job, although Dino wouldn't be happy about having him around, even with a security cam.

At least Echo's race was tomorrow. Only twenty-four hours to keep her safe. The filly looked healthy, fresh from a bath and impatient at being restrained outside the barn. Her muscles rippled as she pawed at the dirt, and a whiff of lavender soap freshened the air.

Becky patted her slick neck. "How'd she gallop today?"

"Real eager. Tried to run off with the new rider. Tracey isn't as strong as Stephanie, and Mr. Anders yelled a bit."

"He yelled? That's too bad." But a relieved smile tilted her mouth. It didn't sound like the new rider and Dino had hit it off. Probably a good thing since there really wasn't room for any more shampoo in his bathroom.

She slipped her hands in her pockets, forcing a casual stance despite the butterflies churning in her stomach. It had only been five hours since she'd left Dino's bed but it seemed like weeks, and her insecurities mushroomed. She didn't regret the sex. She only regretted having to see him so soon after the event. Didn't know the etiquette.

She glanced down the shadowed aisle, reluctant to move. It was ten o'clock, but maybe Dino was busy in his office. Maybe he didn't have time to go for a ride. Maybe she could put off their first meeting until tonight. She'd be more composed then, more prepared.

But if he didn't have time, that would be a bad sign. Probably meant he didn't want to go out with her again. Maybe even wanted to cancel their dinner tonight. Or possibly he was charmed by the new rider, and of course she was prepared for that too; it didn't bother her overly much.

She pulled her hands out of her pockets and gripped her stomach, then rechecked her watch. Three minutes after ten. Having sex with someone you worked with created a rash of complications. Martha made it sound easy, but Becky knew she wasn't as tough as Dino's other women. Definitely not as tough as Stephanie.

Cody was still holding Echo, and she glanced longingly past him at her car. She could leave a message. Go now, make it easier. Dino didn't want any entanglements and, of course, neither did she. Her feelings wouldn't be bruised just because he didn't have time for a trail ride on the morning after.

"Mr. Anders asked me to groom and saddle Hank, but I didn't get Lyric ready," Cody said. "He thought you'd want to do that yourself."

She swung around, propelled by such relief she couldn't stop beaming. He still wanted to ride.

"He asked me to clean Lyric's feet for you though," Cody added. "She's touchy about her hind end. Pushy around the door too."

"Oh, that's okay," Becky said, still smiling. "I don't need any help."

"You sure? I'd be glad to help." Cody's gaze drifted over her chest and she edged back a step. The new T-shirt dipped lower than usual, but Martha had assured her it was perfect. Still, she wasn't comfortable with form-fitting clothes and the way men looked at her. Except for Dino. She was quite comfortable with all the ways he looked.

"No, thanks. I'm fine." She smiled and headed into the barn, eager to brush Lyric. It was ironic that earlier the grooms had been indifferent, but now when she didn't need any help, they were attentive. All because of a haircut and some new clothes— another thing about which Martha had been absolutely correct.

"Well, I'll be close by," Cody called. "Holler if you need me."

She waved and bounced down the aisle. Tried not to look at the security cam but wondered if Dino watched and fought a rush of self-consciousness. Of course, there was always the chance he was busy with the new rider—going over schedules, signing waivers and employment contracts. Or maybe they were just enjoying a chat and coffee, getting to know each other. Maybe they were getting really close.

Stop it. She shoved open Lyric's stall door. Obviously she couldn't worry about every single girl. She wouldn't have worried yesterday, before she slept with him, before she had expectations. Besides, she'd already noticed that most of the time it was the girls who flirted with him. He was merely nice to everyone, just like he'd been nice to her, back when she'd been invisible.

God, she must have been a pain. It was uncomfortable when Slim didn't talk or smile, and that was exactly how she'd been. No wonder people hadn't been friendly.

She was so preoccupied, Lyric almost escaped, pinning her ears when Becky pulled the door shut.

"Oh, stop." Becky slapped Lyric's chest, forcing the mare back. "I know you're bluffing." She picked up the hoof pick, determined to banish Dino from her thoughts, at least for five minutes. Besides, Lyric wasn't the type of horse one should daydream around. It was doubtful she'd kick without reason, but she did have a spiteful streak along with an extremely sensitive spot on her belly.

Lyric's soulful eyes darkened with reproach but she lifted both front feet, standing stock-still even though she wasn't tied.

Becky moved to her hindquarters, careful not to touch her flank, and the mare obediently lifted her hind leg. "You're a good girl," Becky said softly before moving around her rump and cleaning the remaining foot.

The mare blew out a resigned sigh, ears flicking back and forth, but otherwise remained motionless while Becky brushed her sleek coat. Obviously she preferred not to be tied, or maybe it was Slim's kicking that had made her belly so sensitive. Or maybe she just didn't like men.

Footsteps sounded. Becky moved to the front of Lyric's stall and glanced over the door. Must be Tracey. The dark-haired woman was tiny, attractive and walked with athletic grace. Friendly too. She nodded and smiled at Becky. The whip sticking from her back pocket gave a jaunty air. Becky's heart sank as Tracey sauntered down the aisle and disappeared into the sunlight.

Lyric gave Becky an impatient nudge, obviously not as impressed with the new rider.

"You're right. I can't worry about every one of them, past, present and future," Becky muttered, resuming her brushing.

"If you're talking to me, you're going to have to speak up," a familiar voice drawled.

She wheeled, heart thumping. Dino leaned over the stall door, eyes enigmatic. Obviously he'd shaved; the rakish morning stubble was gone although his skin was still dark with its perpetual tan. His mouth curved in a sexy smile, and his jaw hinted of aftershave.

She licked her lips.

His eyes darkened and he opened the door. Swooped in and covered her mouth with a hungry kiss. He tasted of coffee and aroused male and when he finally raised his head, his breathing was ragged. "Damn, I got it bad." He buried his face in her hair before checking the aisle and reluctantly backing away. "We're still on for dinner tonight, right?"

She nodded, unable to speak, her body still humming from the intensity of his greeting. And she felt foolish for worrying. He wasn't the type to fake it. When he didn't want her, she'd know.

His hot gaze skimmed her body. "Leave Lyric's halter on beneath the bridle. We might find a quiet spot to dismount and...rest the horses."

Dino shook his head and relaxed in the saddle, shrugging off Becky's repeated challenge to race. Stephanie had obviously given some riding tips, but there was no way she could beat him. Even though Lyric was faster than Hank, Becky didn't have that killer instinct. Couldn't crouch over her horse's neck and ride for her life.

"No, I don't want to race," he repeated, tightening the reins, keeping Hank at a sedate walk. "Don't want you in a bad mood for tonight," he added, liking how she blushed.

"Losing won't put me in a bad mood." Her eyes widened as though shocked at the suggestion. "I'm not at all competitive."

He grinned at the absurd statement. Or maybe he hadn't stopped grinning since he'd seen her this morning. She was so damn sweet, so refreshing. The sex was damn good too, and no doubt that was the reason he couldn't stop smiling.

Or maybe it was other things, like her mouth. He loved the way she slid it over him, the feel of her beneath his hand, how she really listened when he spoke. And unlike his ex-wife, she was incapable of guile, incapable of tricks—except she erroneously thought she wasn't competitive. Everyone wanted to win.

"Honey," he said, "you don't stand a chance of beating me. And it's not fair to Hank to always hold him back."

"So you *were* holding him back that day." Her voice rose and Lyric tossed her head, as if sharing Becky's indignation.

"I've been riding all my life," he said. "Hard riding. I can get a hundred percent from a horse. You're maybe working with sixty."

"Okay, so I'm a hack rider." But her mouth set in a stubborn line as she studied Hank. "But what percentage would Lyric need to beat him?"

"This isn't math." He chuckled but she looked so serious, he sobered. "At least eighty percent. Hank has a bit of run, for a short distance. But we're not racing. In fact, we're going to tie the horses under that big oak tree and relax. I have food in the saddlebags and some cold beer."

And hopefully they'd relax more than a bit. Tonight seemed a long way off; he was already semi-erect remembering how her legs wrapped around his hips, the sweetness of her breasts beneath his mouth, her throaty moans.

She raised her chin. "I think you're scared to lose. Maybe we should just go back and have a slow walk around the paddock."

"Aw, honey." He dragged his wistful gaze off the trees. Her nose was still stuck in the air, and her expression had definitely turned mutinous. "I don't want to race. There are so many other fun things we could be doing."

"But I've been practicing." Her nose tilted higher. "And you don't think I'm worthy enough to race. If I was one of your other women, you'd race in a minute."

Oh, Christ. He straightened, staring stiffly through Hank's black-tipped ears. Why did they always steer the conversation around to other women? "But you're not a jockey or an exercise rider," he said carefully. "I don't want you to get hurt. And I'm not in the mood for a fake race, not today."

"It won't be a fake race. Just a gallop to that stream over there."

"We can't run there. It's full of rocks. Hard to slow down. Dangerous for the horses."

"All right." She pounced on the opening. "We'll just run to the big oak tree."

Which was exactly where he wanted to end up. "Okay."

"But we don't dismount unless you win," she added.

"Sure," he repeated, hiding his smile. He'd make sure he won, just by a length or two, anything to keep her happy. It would be cooler under the trees, and he'd have her all to himself. He'd even turned off his phone.

"And if I win, you get rid of all that shampoo in your bathroom."

He blinked. "What are you talking about?"

She wouldn't look at him, seemingly intent on straightening Lyric's mane. "I really thought your other women wouldn't bother me." Her voice was so low he could scarcely hear. "But it does. I don't care who you have at your Lone Star apartment, but I care what you do here."

A bead of sweat tickled his forehead, and he lifted his Stetson and wiped it off. She seemed to have an inflated opinion of his social life. He wasn't such an ass that he would drag another woman home, although it appeared that kind of behavior at his apartment was okay. And that didn't make sense. Either she minded or she didn't.

"No women at Conrad's place?" He forced a careless chuckle. "That's a wasted bet. There won't be any other women. Not while I'm seeing you."

"But what's your definition of seeing someone?"

Definition? Christ. Why did women have to dissect something that was supposed to be fun? Pain throbbed behind his temple, and a tight smile cut his face. A mockingbird sang, emphasizing the quiet. He had the urge to kick Hank into a lope and escape over the hill.

But she was staring at him, taut as a bird dog on a trail. "I don't have definitions," he said. "I only know I'm not getting married again and I'm not looking for a permanent relationship. If that's enough for a woman, we go from there."

"But where is there to go? How can you not want a home? Someone to love?"

She looked so puzzled, the pounding in his head slowed. Of course, he wanted a home, and after Echo won tomorrow, he'd buy back his ranch. But someone to love wasn't critical. Laura's cheating had left him soured, and racing had enough challenges to keep him occupied.

He yanked his hat lower and flicked his reins to the other side of Hank's neck. She still stared, her eyes wide and curious. He didn't want to disappoint her, didn't want her to expect something he couldn't give, but it wouldn't hurt to open up a bit. Generally he avoided talk about his busted marriage, but she had a concrete core of loyalty that he appreciated.

"Seeing my wife unhappy hurt like hell," he said, "but I couldn't give up training. That's my job and I love it. She kept bugging me to quit. I couldn't provide what she wanted so she found it with another man...a few other men." His jaw tightened but he kept talking. "Some trainers are big enough to balance family and job. Big enough to make sacrifices. I'm not one of them."

"Maybe your marriage would have worked if you two lived closer to the track."

"We tried. Didn't matter." His mouth lifted in a wry smile. Many nights he'd dropped over to the barn to check on a sick horse or just to share a beer with the boys. Laura had often gone to bed livid. And then she'd just gone to someone else's bed.

He shrugged. "When my parents retired, we bought their ranch hoping it would help. Laura was a barrel racer, and I thought she'd enjoy riding again. We had a few quarter horses but by then, she'd lost all interest. Preferred city life. She's still living at the ranch though, waiting for me to buy her out."

"I'm sorry," Becky said.

"Well, I'm not." He yanked his hat lower. "Horses are easier. And it helps knowing I'm going to own the place soon. It's a distance from Lone Star but I'll make it work. Pick up a nice mare or two. I've got a breeding right to Hunter after he's retired."

"So Malcolm *did* make side deals on breeding?" Becky's voice rose. "Do you have it in writing? Because Slim didn't, and I think he and Jill were supposed to get a broodmare."

Dino relaxed, settling deeper in the saddle. Anything was better than talk of relationships and the number of shampoo bottles beneath the sink. He hadn't looked under there in ages, didn't realize women noticed stuff like that. He'd thought it weird they all left their junk in his bathroom, but it simply hadn't mattered. "I don't know much about Slim's side deals with Malcolm," he said, "but unfortunately if Slim didn't get it in writing, there's not much you can do about it."

"I might show the file to Martha though." Becky's voice turned thoughtful. "It's pretty clear Malcolm intended to give Slim a share of Lyric but was so upset about Jill's accident, he didn't want the mare bred. According to Slim, Malcolm was going to substitute Echo."

There it was again, her complete generosity of spirit. He hid his skepticism but considered Slim an idiot for not having the clause added to his contract, and he'd never ever met Jill. Unlike Becky, he didn't get all warm and fuzzy over strangers, no matter how sad their life story. And Slim's claim to Lyric seemed a mite shaky.

He sighed. Of course, Slim might be telling the truth or at least believed it to be the truth. Malcolm had been in vigorous health, his heart attack totally unexpected. Slim would have trusted him completely. Probably thought they had plenty of time to flesh out a deal.

But life had changed on a dime. Now Martha's health was in a tailspin and the very existence of Conrad Stable in jeopardy.

Which was the pits for Becky. She was devoted to Martha and obviously considered the estate her home—her desire for security no doubt the result of a rocky childhood.

"You should start thinking of yourself instead of worrying about Slim," he said. "And I doubt Ted is going to like anyone chipping away at his inheritance. Echo's worth millions—only a drop in the Conrad bucket, but he won't want to give her away."

Becky's expression shadowed, and he regretted mentioning Ted. The man was an asshole, circling like a vulture, and his association with Slim was worrisome.

"No," she said, "Ted definitely isn't happy when Martha talks about giving away horses. But it's not fair that Slim gets nothing, especially with a high-needs daughter. By the way—" her words came in a rush, "Martha asked that Slim be able to stay in his house until he finds another job."

"Absolutely not. I don't trust Slim near the horses. Or with you. He's already fired. I told him to be out by the weekend."

"But she wants him to stay. Slim was Malcolm's most loyal employee."

"Maybe. But we both know Slim isn't loyal to her." Dino kept his voice level. "If you explain the situation, she'll understand that he has to go."

"But I can't tell her that. She'd be shattered."

Dino swallowed his frustration. News of Slim's treachery certainly wouldn't improve Martha's health, but the truth was the truth. "I don't want him around here. I can't prove it, not yet, but there's something rotten going on."

"But you have the surveillance. Echo runs tomorrow, and all the other good horses are stabled at Lone Star. There's really not much he can do. Not anymore. Please, Dino. I don't want Martha upset. I couldn't stand it if something happened to her."

A fat tear rolled down her cheek. *Fuck!* He leaned over Hank's shoulder and wiped it away but another took its place. "Goddammit, don't cry."

"I'm not crying." She twisted from his touch, swiping at her face. "I only wish you'd consider people for a change. Not just your precious ranch."

He jerked upright, feeling like he'd been sucker punched. It was always that way with women. Open up a bit, tell them something personal and they'd throw it in your face. She didn't understand how much he wanted his ranch, had probably never lived anywhere longer than a few years.

The silence between them turned brittle, accentuated by the horses' steady breathing.

"I'm sorry. I didn't mean it that way," she finally said. "Of course you want your ranch, but I want Martha to live another twenty years. And I'm worried about her reaction. She's accepted that you don't want Slim as a foreman but she wants him to stay here until he finds another job. I think she feels a little guilty...and maybe for good reason."

Dino dragged a hand over his jaw. If only Slim had come clean today. He'd badgered him this morning, trying to make him admit he'd cut the stirrup leather, that he'd sponged Hunter, even let Lyric loose, but the man had remained stubbornly silent. His expression though, when pushed about his relationship with Ted, was chilling. Since neither of the two men would benefit from the plummeting value of Martha's horses, it seemed any sabotage was purely vindictive. In his book that was even worse.

"Becky," he said, using his most reasonable tone, "it's not safe to let Slim stay. And it's not my job to think beyond that. I'm not here to worry about Martha's reaction." She shot him such a reproachful look, he flinched. "I didn't mean it like that. Of course I worry about her. Just not the way you do."

Hank pranced and jigged, acting like he wanted to run, and it took a moment to settle him back to a walk. Dino blew out a sigh, trying to relax his body, trying to hide his frustration from both her and the horse. But Becky's back was now ramrod stiff and it looked like someone had shoved a pole up her ass. Any hope of a recreational pit stop now seemed wildly optimistic.

Lyric was happy though, prancing beside Hank. Becky's breasts bounced with each of the mare's steps, and her jeans accentuated her shapely rear. It was a simple matter to mentally strip her. However, she shot him a glower as though sensing what he was doing, and he averted his head.

"We're still on for dinner?" he asked, his voice slightly husky.

"I don't know," she said. "Once I tell Martha you kicked Slim out, she'll probably need my company. No, I expect to be busy tonight."

"That's not playing fair." He pulled his hat off and swiped his forehead with the back of his arm. It wouldn't kill him not to see her tonight. A day. A week. He could wait. Goddammit though, he wanted her now.

He adjusted himself in the saddle, annoyed at his erection, hoping she wouldn't notice. Wished she wanted him as much as he wanted her. Next time he'd have to do better. Damn but he hoped there was a next time.

He shoved his hat back on, adjusted it to the correct angle, and glanced longingly at the oak tree. Drew in a big breath. "Guess I can get a watchman. It's Martha's money. Maybe Slim can stay for a week or two."

"Until he finds a new job."

"A new job then." He sighed. "But I liked it better when you didn't have quite so much to say." However, the grateful way she looked at him made his chest swell.

"That is so nice of you, Dino."

"Against my better judgment though. And you're not playing fair." He tried to look pissed but he liked making her happy. "You really want Slim around?" he asked. "Might be months before he can find another job. I'm damn well not giving him a reference."

"Martha will, though. And Slim's a good horseman. He must have some connections."

Dino gave a grudging nod. Slim would pop up somewhere; he just hoped it was far away from Conrad's. Far away from Becky.

"So," she continued brightly, "do you want to race to the tree? Go with our original bet?"

"Sure," he said quickly. "But make sure you don't veer to the stream. Horses tend to want to run the easiest route—" He stopped. "What are you doing?"

"Shortening my stirrups to proper race length."

He watched in consternation as she cranked her stirrups then crouched over Lyric's neck. She flashed him a challenging smile. "Ready to run, cowboy?"

He shook his head, secretly impressed at how quickly she'd adjusted her tack. "No, that's too dangerous. I'm not racing if you ride like that."

"Ready, set, go!" she said.

Lyric catapulted forward.

"Goddammit, stop."

Hank charged after them, unwilling to be left behind, and Dino, still cursing, gave the gelding his head. Becky and Lyric were already ten lengths in front, her little butt waving in his face. She really was race riding and if he didn't get Hank moving, she was going to kick his ass. Unbelievable. He shook the reins and whistled at Hank.

She shouldn't be riding so damn fast, he thought, even as he urged Hank for more speed. Martha would be livid, and horses could stumble. *Jesus.* Fear swept him. He abruptly sat back, hauling Hank into a lope as he remembered the details he'd dug up about Lyric.

Stumblekins, they'd called her. A jockey death trap. He barely breathed until the streaking pair safely reached the crest, his heart continuing its painful jackhammer even when she slowed Lyric and triumphantly circled the oak tree.

He trotted Hank the remaining distance, tightlipped and tense, unable to shake his churning fear. Nothing had happened. Lyric hadn't stumbled. Becky was okay.

She waved her arm, grinning in jubilation. "I've been practicing. Both Martha and Stephanie gave me tips and I really wanted to show—"

"Goddammit!" he hollered, still twenty feet away. "That was fucking stupid. What the hell were you thinking?"

Her smile faded, the color draining from her cheeks.

"If you're going to race like an idiot, you'll have to stay in the ring," he snapped. "Now get off and lead that mare back. She's hot and winded and doesn't deserve such an irresponsible rider."

He yanked Hank around and headed back to the ranch, still smoldering. Goddammit. Stumblekins. Well, he'd make sure she never rode Lyric again now that she fancied herself a jockey.

That mare wasn't safe for fast work. Stephanie should have known better. And Becky.

She'd watched the video of Jill's final race. What would have prompted her to run like that? She'd mentioned she'd been practicing but he'd pictured a half-assed canter, had never imagined she'd have the guts to go that fast. Lyric was an experienced racehorse and wouldn't need much encouragement.

With Becky's shortened stirrups and forward seat, no wonder the mare had flattened out and beaten Hank. And they had beaten him, fair and square. He and Hank never would have caught the smoking pair.

He shot a reluctant glance over his shoulder. Becky had a mutinous look on her face, although Lyric looked pleased with the turn of events. The sun was hot, and the horse was happy to be riderless with a chance to grab bites of grass.

What a fuck-up. He squared his shoulders and cursed.

The best thing about leading, instead of riding, was that it gave plenty of time to observe one's horse. Lyric's gray cheek was right next to Becky's shoulder, and she could watch the mare's expressive eye, her long ears as they flicked at a darting rabbit. Yes, it was much better to stare at Lyric than at the asshole in front of her.

Her eyes stung, and she shot another glare at Dino's stiff back as he rode down the hill. He hadn't looked back, not once, his broad shoulders set in a rigid line. A lump climbed her throat. She swallowed, forcing it down, unwilling to admit how much his anger hurt.

All she'd wanted was to show him how much she'd improved. She'd never intended to put Lyric at risk; in fact, the mare was barely winded. She flattened the back of her hand against Lyric's chest—not even hot. There was no reason she had to walk home, leading her horse like a chastised kid.

She'd never seen him so angry. Martha had said all trainers were intensely competitive, but she hadn't cheated or anything. Maybe she had grabbed a tiny head start, miniscule really, but the count had been fair. Maybe he couldn't stand to be beaten. Or perhaps he didn't want to lose the bet they'd made and thereby limit his range of women.

The bet. That must be it—the only thing that could have caused such a reaction. She stumbled over the uneven grass, trying to ignore the painful rubbing of her heels, the sweat beading on her neck, the crack in her heart.

Dino abruptly turned Hank and faced her, his expression shaded beneath his cowboy hat. She squared her shoulders, trying not to limp although she definitely would have worn thicker socks if she'd known there'd be a three-mile hike.

"Feet sore?"

"No." She patted Lyric's neck, comforted by the mare's presence.

"It's getting hot." He leaned down and took Lyric's reins. "Come on up on Hank."

"No, thanks." She ignored his extended hand. "I'm happy to walk. Wouldn't want to be an irresponsible rider."

"Look, I shouldn't have lost my temper. I'm sorry."

Sorry? He was sorry. Her head swiveled. In her experience, men rarely apologized. He even looked sorry, although he still had that stern look, which was rather disconcerting when directed at her. Like it was now.

"Lyric doesn't seem hot," she said. "Why don't I just get back on?"

"No!"

His vehemence startled her, and she stepped back. Even Lyric jumped, her eyes flashing a worried white.

"That mare isn't safe, not for galloping." His voice gentled. "I don't want you riding her again. You can ride back with me."

She gaped. Realized her mouth was open and forced it shut. So that's what this was about. He wasn't resentful about the bet at all, just worried. Weird but kind of neat, and now her throat filled with an entirely different kind of lump.

He mistook her silence. "All right then. You can still ride Lyric but only in the paddock. I'll find you another horse to gallop on the trails. You saw Jill's fall. You must have some sense."

His voice roughened but this time it didn't bother her, not a bit. She even let him take her hand and swing her behind his saddle and onto Hank's back. "Hold tight," he said, switching Lyric's reins and leading the mare with one hand.

Even though she didn't need to hold on, not at Hank's ambulatory walk, she looped both hands around Dino's waist. This was better anyway. She pressed her cheek against his back, absorbing his familiar smell. "We did beat you though," she whispered.

"Yeah," he said. "You won."

And then it was quiet, except for the thud of horses' hooves, the rhythmic motion of Hank's hindquarters and the occasional swish of Lyric's tail. A hawk circled lazily but other than that, they were utterly alone. Odd, how five minutes ago she was deep in despair and now felt buoyant, perfectly at peace.

Her hands drifted along the ridge of his flat stomach. She slid her fingers between the buttonholes, feeling his warm skin, the smattering of crisp hair.

"I was so fucking scared, honey," he whispered, squeezing her hand.

"But Lyric feels surefooted when she gallops. I didn't really think something like that could happen to me." He immediately tensed and she soothingly stroked his hard abs.

"There's a good reason Malcolm wouldn't breed that mare," he said, "but I shouldn't have lost my temper...a little lower please." He tugged her hand downward.

"I thought you were angry because of our bet." She obligingly stroked the bulge in his jeans. "That you'd be bored without your usual variety of women."

He shook his head. "Clearly that isn't going to be a problem."

"Doesn't feel like it," she said.

"Put ten dollars to win on Echo," Stephanie said, her voice barely audible. "If I had more money, I'd bet more. And thanks for the flowers. The card said from Martha, but I sensed your influence."

"Does your arm hurt a lot?" Becky switched the phone to her other ear, straining to hear Stephanie's reply.

"Not bad. I sleep a lot. Drop by on Monday. And then you can tell me about Echo's race." Her voice strengthened, and for a moment she sounded like the old Stephanie. "Who galloped her today?"

"Someone called Tracey. Dark hair, nice smile. But I didn't meet her."

"She's okay, but Hunter would make mincemeat out of her. That girl needs to pump weights. I hope Slim used a ring bit."

"Dino looked after the gallop."

"Where was Slim?"

"Guess he was busy somewhere." Becky's voice trailed off. Right after their ride, Dino had headed to Slim's house. By now, Slim would know he didn't have to move. Thanks to Martha's largesse, he'd have ample time to job search.

But obviously Slim couldn't be trusted. When she'd left the barn, a watchful groom had been camped in a chair beside Echo's stall. It was a relief the filly had a twenty-four hour guard—Dino was taking no chances. She was grateful it was him, not her, who had to confront Slim.

"Yeah, maybe he was at the hospital." Stephanie's voice turned increasingly drowsy. "Jocelyn called. Wanted to know where the stirrup leather was from the splint. Guess Slim was picking it up."

Becky's phone suddenly weighed ten pounds. Dino had told Slim he'd get the leather. "What did you tell her?"

"I gave the hospital permission for release. It'll cost more to repair than replace, but that's Slim's decision. By the way, did you practice on Lyric today?"

"Dino and I raced," Becky said absently, still thinking of Slim. "Thanks to you, I won."

"Wow, girl. You're a fast learner. Dino must have been shocked."

"I wouldn't say shocked," Becky said. "More like mad."

"He should have been impressed, not mad. What aren't you telling me?"

"He thought Lyric might stumble."

"Well, shit. I've galloped Lyric. He never worried then." Stephanie snorted. "Still, you beat him in a race, so you must have got his attention. Have you had sex with him yet?"

Becky forced a chuckle, but Stephanie's casual question stung. *Sex.* It sounded so trivial, so mundane, and did nothing to describe the wonderful way he made her feel. The way she soared when they touched. Riding double, being able to wrap her arms around him—she hadn't wanted the ride to end. And his possessive kiss, right before he left to tell Slim it wasn't necessary to move, had left her breathless.

She shook her head, trying to ward off a rush of heat, but her heart was already skipping. Tonight she'd see him again. Dinner at a nice restaurant. And she had the perfect dress, compliments of generous Martha—

"I asked if you had sex yet?" Stephanie repeated, softening her question with a slight laugh. "Stacey is wondering because Dino left the bar alone again this week, even though some reporter was all over him like a tick on a dog. She figures he has a hot chick stashed somewhere."

"Who's Stacey?" Becky asked, grabbing the diversion.

"Another trainer. She has a thing for him, but so far he hasn't taken advantage. She's a bit of a snob, and Dino doesn't like people like that." Stephanie's voice lifted with a hint of smugness.

Becky made an agreeable sound hoping to keep Stephanie talking, while she scanned her memory for any image of Stacey. Could have been any one of a number of women standing at the rail—she really didn't remember, although she definitely remembered the reporter, Danielle. Beautiful, aggressive, determined.

"But you're okay with all this, right?" Becky asked, her fingers squeezing the tiny phone. "You don't mind if Dino and I hook up?"

"Go for it. All we've done for the last few months is watch race video."

"Video? You mean you go to his place at night and watch races?"

"Of course. That's part of my job. Besides, Dino is fun but not the keeping kind. Girl, I'm not a complete fool."

Becky paced a circle around her bedroom. There it was again—someone to have fun with, the same thing Martha kept saying, and the well-meaning warnings were tiresome. She didn't intend to fall for Dino but it was only natural she didn't want to share him. And since she'd won the race today, he'd have to follow the terms of the bet and not see anyone else while at Conrad's.

A month would be more than enough to get him out of her system. To make sure she was comfortable with sex and nakedness and hot men. Then she'd be ready to look for what Martha and Stephanie called the 'keeping kind,' someone open to settling down and starting a family.

She propped the phone against her ear and relaxed against the window sill, enjoying the sweeping view. It was always comforting to have a plan.

CHAPTER TWENTY-EIGHT

"Goddammit, Slim." Dino glanced over his shoulder at the gaping groom, then grabbed Slim's arm and propelled him along the driveway, away from gossiping tongues. "Lay off the liquor. It'll be impossible to find another job if people think you're a drunk." He angled his head, avoiding the reek of the man's breath. "Come on. I'll make a pot of coffee, and you can explain why you went to the hospital this morning."

"I don't have to tell you why I go anywhere." Slim belched but leaned on Dino's arm as he staggered toward his house. "At least not anymore."

"I'm guessing you picked up the stirrup leather. I want to know why."

"Jocelyn told me to go. And I didn't mean for all this to happen." Slim's words slurred. "Need the money."

"Let's talk about it." Dino pushed open Slim's door and followed him into the dark coolness. "I might make a few calls if you come clean. Got a friend with a broodmare facility who needs a good man. But you have to 'fess up."

Slim sank in a chair, almost falling off the side before lowering his head into his hands. "I can't leave Jilly. I asked her to ride that day. Fucking bitch. I oughta shoot her."

"Lyric?"

"Fucking horse bitch." Slim groaned. "And now my baby girl barely knows me." He looked at Dino with bloodshot eyes. "Don't you see? You'd be tempted too. Anyone would. Just a few races. To own half a mare like that." A ball of spittle hung on the corner of his mouth. "The other jockeys knew she wasn't safe, but my brave little Jilly rode, just for me. Such a good rider too. Beauty bucked her off every day but she never cared. Loves horses. Still does. Wonder where that old pony is. Might do her good to see Beauty."

Dino rubbed his temple then rose and yanked open the cupboards. Coffee. The man might make more sense after coffee. But based on his ramblings, Becky was right—Jill and Slim had been promised part ownership of Lyric. What a mess.

He added water to the machine and walked across the room to grab a mug, almost tripping over a meowing cat.

Slim raised his head, displaying a drunk's sudden belligerence. "She's the only horse I ever let loose. Never would have done that to any of the others."

Dino's hands fisted. He stalked closer, realizing Slim was no longer talking about a long-lost pony named Beauty.

"Wanna hit me? Come on. I deserve it." Slim waved at his face but the gesture left him unbalanced, and he knocked the table instead. He looked at Dino, seemed to absorb his disgust, and his aggression faded as quickly as it had arisen. "I ain't proud of all this. Worked hard, made my name, going to keep that at least."

"Aw, fuck, Slim. You need a lawyer." Dino paced around the kitchen, his movements jerky. He'd suspected Slim had left Lyric's stall open, but having it confirmed shocked him. The man was a horseman, for chrissakes. He shook his head in disbelief. "You hate the mare that much?"

Slim groaned and covered his face.

Dino flung open the cupboard. Clearly Slim was contrite, but he would have to get his head straightened before he was allowed near horses again, and Dino was too revolted to even look at him. "Got any more liquor?" He banged open the cupboards, checking every shelf, searching for a hidden stash.

"Ain't going to drink anymore," Slim said. "Too late for that."

"When I come back tomorrow night, I want you sober. We have to find you a place to live, somewhere to work, a doctor." Dino squeezed his eyes shut. Martha's insistence that Slim be allowed to stay on the grounds was now even more troubling. He wanted the man gone today.

"I'm sorry, Dino." Slim's hands muffled his voice. "You're a good man. Just in the wrong place."

Dino poured a cup of black coffee and slammed it on the table, but Slim's head lolled forward, his eyelids lowering.

"I'll talk to you after the race tomorrow," Dino snapped. "Stay out of the barn. Away from the horses. Away from people. And sober up. You're lucky if the police don't get involved." He checked one last cupboard but found no more rum, dumped some food in the dish for the yowling cat and stomped out the door.

He stalked back to the barn, shaking his head at Slim's ramblings about shooting Lyric. One thing was clear. Whether the mare's faults were real or imagined, no way was anyone riding her again. If Becky was hurt, he'd never forgive himself.

Some of his concern eased when he saw Cody camped in front of Echo's stall, which meant Lyric, stabled in the adjoining stall, was also protected.

"Want a little break?" he asked

"Sure, boss." Cody reached under his folding chair and pulled out a greasy brown bag. "I want to heat up some leftover pork for supper."

"Okay. Do it now. And grab anything else you want from the kitchen. I don't want you leaving this spot again tonight."

"Sure." Cody gave a good-natured grin. "Don't know what I'm watching for though. Only people around were you and Slim."

"Slim? How long was he here?"

"Only a minute," Cody said. "He was in the office. Paid back the ten bucks he owed me. Told me I was a good groom. I know you said he doesn't work here anymore…"

"The barn's off limits. He knows that." Dino checked Echo's stall. The filly looked back, eyes bright and eager. "She looks fine though," he added, his tension easing.

"He didn't do anything. I swear it, boss. Just wanted to pay me back my money."

"Okay. Heat up your supper. I'll watch her for a bit."

"Sure thing." Cody walked down the aisle, shaking his head as Lyric stretched over her door, threatening to bite. "That mare is damn saucy," he called over his shoulder.

"She doesn't like many people," Dino said. Only Becky. Lyric had liked her from the very first day. Maybe the mare had sensed her depth. But what person would have guessed such an appealing woman hid behind that prickly surface? He rubbed his jaw, trying to remember when they'd first met.

He hoped she hadn't been around when he'd been sleeping with Greta. He wasn't sure why that made him uneasy but he felt vaguely stupid, like when he overlooked a promising filly in the sale ring. Not that any rival trainer was about to waltz in and scoop up Becky. She didn't get off the property much, and her time was devoted to Martha. And Lyric. And him.

A smile creased his face. Not a bad setup really. He had her to himself, safely kept, and it didn't seem like they'd tire of each other any time soon. He scratched Echo beneath her jaw and blew out a sigh, liking the fact that Becky was far removed from the casual alliances that often sullied track life. Of course, that hadn't stopped Laura.

The chime of his cell phone startled Echo, and he stepped back and dug in his pocket. "Yeah."

"Big day tomorrow?" Laura's saccharine-sweet voice filled the phone.

"Well, speak of the devil. I was just thinking of you. How soon can you and lover boy move out?"

Her voice rose. "If you had stayed home a little, it wouldn't have happened."

"I know," he said.

"I just wanted to make you jealous." She stopped. "What did you say?"

"Sorry I couldn't make you happy. How soon can you move out?"

She was silent for a moment. "Two weeks after I have my money," she said. "And this is the absolute last extension. I'm sick of living in the boonies."

You didn't have to live there. But he clamped his mouth shut knowing they'd each slung enough mud. Too many times. "I'll call after the race," he said.

"What is this big race tomorrow? The one you're sure you'll win?"

"It doesn't matter," he said, suddenly superstitious. "I'll call you in the evening." But he couldn't keep the longing from his voice. "Christ, it'll be nice to get home."

"Maybe not so nice. The barn roof is leaking, and the north fence blew down. Place is falling apart."

He chuckled but didn't bother to reply. Finally, it seemed, her barbs no longer hurt. "Talk to you tomorrow, Laura, and...thanks." He closed the phone.

Cody ambled down the aisle, wiping his mouth with the back of one hand and carrying a Coke in the other. A fresh grease stain marked the center of his shirt. He dropped into the chair with a grunt. "Man, those porkers are delicious. Got a few more ribs if you want to try some. Left over from my sister's wedding."

"Thanks but I'm going out for dinner." Dino tilted his watch. Just enough time to shower and change. "I'll check back before Becky and I leave, and again at midnight."

"So Becky will be with you? Is she coming by the barn?" Cody rubbed vigorously at his shirt, suddenly worried about the grease stain.

Dino's eyes narrowed. Cody was about Becky's age; it made sense that the two were friends. Cody always seemed to be hanging around when she groomed Lyric too. He'd noticed them talking when he'd completed Tracey's paperwork. The camera in the office was actually rather convenient. "You married, Cody?" he asked abruptly.

"Not yet. Looking though."

"You *want* to get married?" Dino couldn't keep the incredulity from his voice.

"Sure, if I can find a nice girl. Someone who likes football and horses. Big tits wouldn't hurt either." He reached in his pocket, unwrapped a stick of gum and shoved it in his mouth.

Dino didn't think Becky liked football, but he didn't want to take any chances either. He folded his arms and stepped forward, pasting on his gravest expression. "Did Slim tell you about the new dating rules we implemented last week?"

CHAPTER TWENTY-NINE

The tie was too much. Dino tossed it over the chair then rifled through his closet, looking for a sports jacket. Becky probably didn't own a cocktail dress, and he didn't want her to feel uncomfortable. Quite possibly she'd show up in jeans, although lately her clothes had changed. Tighter, colorful, sexy. Maybe she'd wear those tight black jeans and white shirt that dipped really low.

His hand stilled over a hanger. Sometimes he wished she'd return to her baggy clothes. It had always meant trouble when Laura dressed up. Not that he was going to open himself up to a woman again. God, no. He liked to make them happy, not turn them all sour like he'd done with his wife.

He just wanted to give Becky a nice night. Her face had glowed when she spoke of Martha's favorite restaurant. But maybe he'd better dress down too. Jeans, white shirt, jacket. He could leave the jacket in the truck if she wore casual clothes. The restaurant might not like it but the hell with them.

A car purred outside and he crossed to the window. Distinctive Mercedes headlights. One driver, no passengers. Good. Becky had said Martha wasn't planning to come, but he hadn't been sure. While he hoped she was feeling okay, he preferred Becky to himself.

He slipped his phone and wallet in his pocket, tossed the jacket over his shoulder and stepped outside. She waved and he waved back, unable to contain his foolish grin. She was unaffected and sweet. And if the restaurant wouldn't let them in with jeans, they'd find another spot. Didn't matter—

The smile slid from his face as she stepped out.

Oh, Christ, a princess. That's what she was, a golden princess. The sleek dress molded to her curves, making it impossible to see where the material stopped and her skin started—somewhere on her chest, just below a magnificent pearl necklace that set off the dress to perfection. He dragged his eyes off the swell of her breasts and checked out the generous length of leg.

Gulped. Couldn't stop staring.

The dress wasn't really short, slightly above her knees, but her legs had stretched, especially with those strappy, sparkly shoes. The type of fuck-me shoes Laura had always worn when she went out—dressed, perfumed and primed to flirt with anyone in pants.

He'd never noticed before but Becky looked an awful lot like his ex-wife.

She paused by the fender of the car. "What's wrong?"

"Not a thing." He yanked on his jacket, his movements jerky. "But I have to stop by the barn. Probably have to come back early and check on Echo. Going to be a long night."

Hurt blanched her face, and he closed his mouth. Didn't want to be a jerk, but Christ, he could see it now. She looked exactly like Laura—Laura who'd wanted to dine and dance, stay up late every night—the hell with horses, racing and working. The hell with wedding vows.

"You look nice," he added stiffly. "Maybe we'll have time to squeeze in a few dances after dinner."

"I'm not much of a dancer."

"Neither am I." The tightness in his jaw loosened a notch, and he pulled open his truck door. Grimaced when he saw the horse brush, the sweaty riding helmet, the hair on the leather seat. Laura had always hated his truck. "Maybe we should take your fancy car instead." He couldn't quite hide the edge in his voice.

"It's not my car. It's Martha's. And hair wipes off." She waited, seemed unfazed by the condition of his truck, merely puzzled as she waited for him to step back so she could climb in.

"Just a sec," he said. "I have a blanket in the back, brand new. Won it last week."

She smiled and suddenly looked kissable, but Laura had never liked her makeup messed, so he grabbed the blanket and folded it over the seat. "There. Hop in." He helped her up, circled to the driver's seat and turned the ignition. The diesel engine roared to life, overly loud in the still night—something else that had always bothered Laura. She'd hated going out in the truck, had always wanted a sleek car.

He glanced sideways, waiting for a comment, but Becky didn't say a word. She's not Laura, he reminded himself. They didn't even look that similar, not really, although when Becky was dressed up she looked high-maintenance, exactly the kind of woman he'd sworn to avoid.

And here he was, taking her out for a formal dinner when he should be thinking of Echo—watching race video, checking weather forecasts, calculating the speed on the inside and figuring out jock instructions. And he should have reminded Shane to double bed the stall for Echo tomorrow, and they really should switch the stall-walking gelding with Chippy. Echo would be calmer if she were beside a confident horse like Chippy.

But no, on the eve of the most important race of his career, he was driving to a restaurant forty miles away and sliding into a relationship he didn't need or want. Making the same damn mistakes all over again, with someone who would be impossible to avoid. Someone he needed to get along with. He must be nuts.

"I'm going to be really busy tomorrow," he said, "and over the next few weeks." He switched from CD to radio, hoping to catch a weather forecast. "Be moving to my place soon." He glanced sideways, checking her reaction, but she seemed unfazed by his announcement. "Depending on when Slim moves, we'll probably put the new manager in my guesthouse," he added.

"Makes sense," she said.

Obviously she didn't understand what he was saying, and he snapped off the twanging radio, irritated with the singer and the song. "You could always come out to my ranch and visit once in a while, but I know you want to stay close to Martha."

"Yes, it would be inconvenient."

Inconvenient. His knuckles whitened around the steering wheel. "It's not that far," he said perversely. "A couple hundred miles."

"You're pretty sure you'll get your ranch back?"

"The way Echo looked this morning, she'll win if I can just get her to the starting gate." And he'd be pocketing his bonus four days later. Malcolm had set up an excellent accounting system, and Conrad employees were always promptly paid.

"I really hope you get it," her voice softened with concern, "but racing is so unpredictable."

He impulsively reached over and squeezed her hand. "She'll win. Trainers know these things." Plus, it helped that the filly's speed figures were the highest, that she had a veteran jockey, an excellent post position and was training like a tiger. Lately she'd been super aggressive. Almost pulled Tracey's arms off this morning. Even the track handicapper had her tagged at even money.

But it had been a long time since someone had genuinely cared on his account; he liked the feeling. He also liked the feel of her hand in his, so soft and trusting. Reminded him of Laura when they first met, when she'd seemed so sweetly interested in racing, so supportive of his job.

Women often pretended.

He released her hand and punched another station on the radio. Different song, same irritation. Christ, he hoped Becky didn't want to stay out late. It was probably just the big race tomorrow, but he was feeling itchy and the prospect of driving forty minutes to sit in a snotty restaurant suddenly had no appeal.

He glanced sideways as they whipped past the brightly illuminated barn. "Damn!" He jerked the truck to a stop.

"What's wrong?" She twisted in her seat.

"Should only be the night lights on. Echo needs her sleep." He clicked open his door. "I'll be right back. Cody doesn't know the routine like Slim."

He stepped from the truck and walked down the aisle, automatically checking each horse. Echo's eyes were wide and welcoming, but the watchman's chair by her stall was conspicuously vacant—empty except for a greasy bag and a crinkled Playboy magazine.

"Goddammit, Cody!" he hollered.

A muffled noise leaked from the back, and he stalked down the aisle and around the corner. Paused in front of the washroom.

"In here, boss." Cody's voice was weak and plaintive.

The door was slightly ajar. Cody was down on his knees, hands splayed around the bowl, head jammed over the toilet. "Got the flu or something," he said, leaning forward and puking.

Dino averted his head and backed up several steps. "When did it start?"

"About an hour ago," Cody managed between groans. "Feels like a knife slicing my gut."

"Maybe it's those ribs. How old were they?"

"Three, four days," Cody said. "Never eating meat again. I want to die."

Dino blew out a sigh. "Guess we should go to the hospital."

"No, I'll be okay." Cody leaned further over the bowl, his voice muffled. "Just give me this fucking toilet."

"Oh, Cody." Becky's soft voice swept them. "I'll get you some water."

Cody glanced up, his eyes wet. "You're an angel. Look like one too," he added before twisting and tightening his grip around the bowl.

Dino squeezed the bridge of his nose as Becky and her beautiful dress disappeared into the kitchen. She didn't look annoyed, didn't seem worried a piece of hay might stick to her clothes. Laura would never enter a barn when she was gussied up, had always been pissed when plans were disrupted by horses.

Becky reappeared, carrying a bottle of water and a blanket. Crouched over Cody and checked his vitals. Rose and whispered to Dino, "Looks like food poisoning. If it gets any worse, we better take him to the hospital."

Dino dragged a hand over his jaw. "The problem is—" He stared at the door to the aisle, not wanting to see her annoyance when he cancelled dinner. "I can't leave Echo alone, not before the big race. Not while Slim is around."

"Of course you can't."

She sounded so matter of fact, he jerked around, searching for signs of sarcasm, but she brushed past, intent on looking after Cody. Didn't seem annoyed, frustrated or even disappointed that their night was a bust. She wrapped a blanket around Cody's shivering shoulders and twisted the cap off a water bottle. Something she said made Cody laugh. A weak chuckle, but nevertheless the kid now seemed to think he might live.

She closed both doors and rejoined Dino. "He just wants to be alone," she whispered.

"Maybe we can go out tomorrow night." He forced some enthusiasm as they walked around the corner and back toward the stalls. Tomorrow would be hectic. He had to haul Echo home, meet with Slim and find a new manager. And there were thirty other horses at Lone Star that he hadn't watched gallop today. Shane had assured him everything was fine, but he liked to see his horses on the track, not compensate with a phone report.

"Doesn't matter." She fingered her pearl necklace, noticed his gaze and gave a wan smile. "I can't stop touching this. Martha gave it to me. Promises it will bring us luck tomorrow."

His eyes narrowed. The necklace looked identical to the one Martha often wore to the races. Malcolm had once told him it cost more than a stakes horse. "Loaned it, you mean?" He propped his hip against the wall, his voice casual.

"No, she insists I keep it. It's her copy of the original." Her face flickered with regret. "She's trying to give me a lot of things. Seems to be organizing everything. Like she's getting ready, you know..." Becky shrugged and averted her head.

"Hey, don't worry. There's nothing you can do." He squeezed her shoulder. "Martha has always known exactly what she wants. The Lone Star season is over soon, and if she's ready to check out—"

"Check out!" Becky jerked from his touch. "How callous. Life isn't just about racing. It's not just about your bonus."

"I meant check into a retirement home. Not check out permanently." He shoved his hands in his pocket, trying to choose his words more carefully. "But she doesn't have any reason to stay in that huge house. Her goal was always Malcolm's—to leave some sort of legacy. For him. If Echo wins tomorrow, the filly remains undefeated. The race isn't a graded stakes, but it's still a win. And it's clear Martha lost her bounce when Malcolm died. She likes people around, likes to have them look up to her. She'd have all that in a retirement home, without the stress."

Becky jammed her hands on her hips. "But she *has* people around. And she loves her horses. She's excited about the race, even talking about a victory dinner with Slim and Stephanie and everyone."

"Stephanie's in a lot of pain, and Slim won't be around."

"What do you mean?" she asked. "Slim's allowed to live here. Didn't I tell you what Martha wants?"

Dino blew out a sigh. "Slim was drunk again this afternoon. Made some nasty confessions. He's bitter about Jill. I don't want to upset Martha, but I'll get all the facts tomorrow once he's sober. We may have to notify the police."

"I know he's unstable, but can't we have a guard and let him stay?" She sank down on a bale of hay. "Martha wants him to have that choice."

The quaver in her voice wrenched at his chest but he stepped back, folding his arms. "He let Lyric loose, sponged Hunter, walked Echo into the ground, and almost killed Steph." His anger hardened as he thought of Slim's rambling admissions. "All because of some misguided resentment. You think he deserves a break?"

"I guess we all make sacrifices when we love someone," she said. "But you wouldn't know that. It's always about you and the horses."

Oh yeah, here it comes. Another dig about horses, just like Laura, all over again. He spun around and stalked back down the aisle, around the corner and banged on the bathroom door. "How you doing in there, Cody?" He cracked the door open and glanced in. "Any better?"

"Nothing left to throw up." Cody's voice was slightly stronger. "But I don't want to move."

"You don't have to. I'll have a security guard by tomorrow."

"Looks like I'll be hugging the toilet all night, boss. Sorry to screw up your night."

"No problem. I can go out any night." But not with Becky. Once he moved home, she wouldn't be convenient. And he liked convenient. Besides, he wouldn't be able to make her happy. She craved security, not a long-distance relationship.

He walked back down the aisle, watching as she scratched Lyric's jaw. Weird how the mare didn't try to nip, never even put her ears back when Becky was around. The two made an attractive pair; Lyric had the most elegant head and Becky was simply stunning. Stunning and probably starving.

"Sorry." He pulled out his phone, his voice more curt than he intended. "But I have to cancel our dinner reservation. What about tomorrow night instead?"

"Not a good time." She didn't look up, her attention on Lyric. "I'll want to celebrate Echo's win with Martha, the win you're pretty much guaranteeing."

He ignored her tone and punched in the restaurant's number. "All right. How about Sunday then?"

"Carol's on vacation so I'll be busy the whole week."

"The whole week? You can't get one night off?" He snapped the phone shut, surprised by his dismay. "What about some morning then? I'll find a quiet gelding and we can go for a ride."

"It's not dinner though." She shrugged and his gaze was pulled to her chest. Always a mystery how those low-cut dresses stayed in place. They seemed unstable, as if a sudden laugh or cough might send breasts tumbling. He'd never actually seen that happen, but it was always a possibility, a dream actually. He blew out a wistful sigh.

"Don't pretend to be disappointed," she said. "I'm just not used to getting dressed up and going out. It's no big deal."

"I'm disappointed too," he said quickly but his groin felt heavy, and he didn't want to admit he'd been thinking of breasts. "But we'll go for dinner sometime down the road."

She smiled but looked skeptical, as though she guessed it wouldn't happen, and he figured she was probably right. However, he couldn't drum up much disappointment about food, not when his brain kept streaming images of that dress peeled to her waist.

"Here, sit down." His voice was husky. "We can make the most of the night. I'll grab another chair."

He strode to the office fridge, pulled out two beers and a chunk of cheese, rummaged further until he found a glass and a box of crackers. Switched the music from country to classical, turned off the video and dimmed the lights. Walked back down the aisle, balancing the food, drinks and chair.

She smiled as he poured. "I've had more beer this month than in my entire life."

"That's right. You like wine."

"Only because Martha served it whenever she had a dinner guest, and usually that guest was Ted. Those dinners were horrible." She wrinkled her nose, carefully arranging cheese on a cracker. "He's not much fun." Her voice lowered as though she shared a little-known fact, and he smiled in sympathy.

"Ted's coming to the races tomorrow, so you better stop grinning," she added. "You'll have to deal with him too."

"Only for a couple minutes though," he said, cutting more cheese, feeling a pang of guilt as she eagerly picked up another slice. Small substitute for a fancy dinner, yet she hadn't complained. "You can hang out with me on the backside," he said. "Ted won't be able to get past security. He doesn't have an owner's pass—not yet anyway."

"And he doesn't want one. He plans to sell the property and every horse on it once Martha moves."

"What will you do?"

"Find another nursing job close to Martha, maybe in a rehab center. But I'm hoping she stays in her home." She smoothed her dress over her thighs, avoiding his gaze. "What about you?" she asked.

"Find another big owner." He topped her glass with the rest of the beer, surprised at how fast she was drinking. "And buy a couple broodmares, breed some runners of my own. The bonus tomorrow is a kick start."

She rose and walked to the front of Lyric's stall, her bare shoulders gleaming under the muted lights. The dress was really quite tiny. He could see the graceful sweep of her backbone, her slight shiver. Damn, she was cold. He rose, intending to give her his jacket, but she swung around. "So you're already making other plans?"

"Well, yeah, I'm looking at a few offers."

Her face blanched. "You'd just leave Martha. Even though she no longer has Slim. Ted would use that—" Her voice broke and she turned away.

He stepped forward and gently turned her around. "Hey. I won't live here any longer but I'm not leaving Martha, so long as she has horses to race. I promised Malcolm to deliver winners."

"Really? You won't leave her?" Her lips trembled as she searched his face. "That's good. I worry about her."

"I know." He leaned down and kissed her, surprised she looked so skeptical. Malcolm had always been fair, and he certainly wouldn't desert the man's widow. Of course, he'd be living at his own ranch, wouldn't need the Conrad guesthouse, but he'd still train—if Martha had any horses left to train.

He'd intended only a quick kiss, something to reassure her, but she wrapped her arms around his neck and pressed closer, and he stopped thinking about Martha and horses and driving distances. She tasted good, her skin so soft, dress so silky. And with just the right touch he could free those breasts.

He flicked the top of her dress with a finger, exhaling with pleasure as her bare breast filled his hand. He lowered his head and wrapped his mouth around her nipple. She arched against him with a groan, her leg curving around his calf, and he swelled with desire.

His hands splayed around her rear, pressing her against his throbbing erection. "I'd like to spread you on the office desk," he said, raising his head in frustration and checking for Cody. "Tomorrow we'll—"

"Okay," she said, reaching between his legs.

Goddammit. Sweat broke out on his neck as she stroked him. Groaning, he slid his hand under her dress and beneath her panties. Dragged his finger over her until she was creamy wet and quivering. "You going to complain to the manager," he muttered, "if I fuck you in the stall?"

"You are the manager," she breathed, her eyes half-lidded. "I have to do...whatever you want...where ever you want."

She was full of surprises. "Exactly," he growled. He scooped her over his shoulder, unlatched Echo's stall and booted the door open. Swung it shut and pushed past the surprised filly. Propped Becky against the back wall and yanked down his zipper. Her breasts were bare, her dress rolled to her waist, and she stared at him with dark eyes and lips that were slightly swollen.

"You drive me crazy, honey." He fumbled with a condom then slid his hand between her legs, not even pausing to remove her panties, just yanking them aside, making room for his needy cock as it bee-lined into her silky warmth.

He yanked her legs over his hips, angling her against the wall. Pushed deeper. Her head tilted back, throat long and exposed, breasts bared. All his. His senses filled with her scent, her earthy groans, the way she clenched around him, and nothing existed but her loving warmth.

"Jesus, Becky," he groaned when she convulsed around him. One last thrust and he joined her, gripping her as they slumped against the wall.

Slowly their breathing steadied. Straw rustled and something tickled his neck.

"We have an audience," she whispered as Echo nuzzled the back of his head.

"She doesn't seem too shocked." He gave the filly a pat before pushing her head away and easing Becky's legs back down. He carefully adjusted the top of her dress but kept an arm looped around her waist, reluctant to let go.

"The horses have probably seen this type of activity before," she said quietly.

"Maybe. But not from me." He stroked her bare shoulder. "You surprise me, honey. Weren't you worried about the cam?"

"I know you'd delete it…if it was even on." And the trusting smile she gave him made his chest puff. God, she made him feel good. Maybe four hundred miles wasn't all that far. "And Martha said I should have more fun," she added, her voice slightly muffled as she adjusted her dress. "So I'm trying everything, everywhere."

The warm feeling in his chest disappeared, and he stared at her bent head, fighting his indignation. Really, he should be delighted. The evening had provided the perfect result. No need for a time-consuming drive and expensive dinner, just good sex with a woman he liked. Yet as he adjusted his jeans, he felt oddly pissed. "So that's all you want? Love on the rail?"

She glanced up, cheeks still rosy from a post-coital flush. "What do you mean?"

"Just an expression. You're walking back from the clubhouse, it's dark and you're drinking. Maybe even celebrating a win. The rail is the perfect height."

Her eyes widened, but she didn't look dismayed, jealous or even surprised. She just glanced back at the wall and grinned. "So that's where you perfected your technique."

"Jesus, Becky. I don't find this a bit funny." His voice sharpened and he glanced over the stall door, checking for Cody. "You shouldn't do everything Martha says. Going wild, trying to catch up on life by banging the first interested guy."

"It's not like that." She crossed her arms, her face pinched.

He couldn't seem to shut up. "You deserve more than that wall. More than this stall. Christ, I didn't even buy you dinner. We could have ruined your dress," he added lamely.

She rolled her eyes. "I'm going to check on Cody." She flounced past him, opened the door and swept down the aisle. Didn't even look back to make sure Echo didn't escape.

He pushed the filly back and closed the door.

Lyric stuck her head over the adjoining stall, no doubt disappointed she hadn't been offered the same opportunity. Good thing. She would have barged through an open door and galloped for the highway. Would have kicked their heads off if they'd had ten-minute sex in the back of her stall.

Goddammit, what had he done? He dragged a hand over his jaw and walked down the aisle. Turned the monitors back on, listening to Becky's low murmur as she spoke with Cody. Some sort of apology was in order, but he didn't know exactly what he wanted to apologize for. He'd never thought much about double standards, but hell, she was taking advice from an old lady and she could land in a lot of trouble listening to Martha.

He grabbed his dinner jacket and arranged it over her chair. It wasn't that late, but the air had chilled and she was probably cold. He'd warm her up and feed her properly. Should have thought of ordering something, the least he could do.

He called the local diner, ordered enough food for four, and even cajoled the lady on the phone until she promised to include a bottle of wine and send the food by taxi.

He closed his phone, eying Becky warily as she walked back down the aisle.

"Cody's feeling better," she said, "but isn't ready to leave the bathroom."

"That's okay. We can watch the horses." He reached down and picked up his jacket. "Here, put this on. I ordered some food. Should be here soon."

"No, thanks. I've had enough. Gotta go."

He jerked in surprise. He'd assumed she'd stick around, talk at little, at least for a couple of hours. After all, they had a date so she must be free. But maybe it was better if she went home. It would give him time to check Echo's wraps, figure out tomorrow's schedule, think about who he'd hire to replace Slim.

Still, he was surprised she wanted to leave. Christ, they'd just had sex. Usually women liked to talk and cuddle and talk some more. He was always the one edging out the door. He gave her what he considered his most persuasive smile. "Okay. But wait a bit. Once Cody is up, I can walk you to your car."

"That's okay. Just concentrate on Echo. Like you explained earlier, you're very busy this week."

She blew an airy kiss but didn't slow, didn't look back. Her shapely legs disappeared out the end door—leaving him feeling lonely, aggrieved and abandoned.

CHAPTER THIRTY

Becky swiveled on the truck seat, taut with anticipation. She loved hauling a horse to the track, relished those hours before a race when it was still a mystery who'd win. The sun hadn't risen yet, but she could make out Cody's cheerful grin as he waved goodbye. Clearly his food poisoning bout had passed.

"There's coffee in the thermos. Doughnuts too," Dino said as he edged the truck and trailer past Slim's darkened windows.

"Wow, and I was thinking it couldn't get any better." She grabbed two cups and carefully poured the steaming liquid.

"You like getting up at four?"

She heard the skepticism in his voice and laughed. "I was awake at three. Couldn't sleep. Kept worrying how Echo would run." And the prospect of driving with Dino had made her heart thump. Even though Martha called Dino her interim guy, she still thrilled to his smile, his voice, his touch.

She couldn't imagine that the next guy—her keeper guy— would make her feel the same way. Maybe she was wrecked for other men. She tugged pensively at her lower lip.

Dino's gaze lingered on her mouth. "You should have stayed longer last night, instead of leaving me alone with Cody."

He still wanted her even though she'd gone a little wild last night. Relief warmed her, and she stopped biting her lip. It didn't matter how long this thing lasted, she was going to enjoy every minute. Didn't matter what they did or where they did it. Being with him made her come alive. And he may have spoiled her for other men, but at least she was over her naked hang-up.

"Were you lonely?" she asked, remembering how he'd tossed her over his shoulder and made her feel like she was the most desirable woman on Earth.

"Sure was. Why'd you leave so quickly?" He scowled. "I didn't like it."

She sipped her coffee, stalling for time. It would be foolhardy to admit she'd wanted to tuck into his big chest and stay forever. Those old cravings for family and security always heightened after their love making—sex, she corrected, which to him was all it was.

She forced a smile. "I thought we were finished, you know, after the stall thing."

"Stall thing!" His voice rose along with the truck's speed. "Well, we're definitely not finished. And just so you know, this exclusiveness works both ways." He scowled at her for a long moment and the truck clipped along the highway. "You can't be running around the track, going crazy, trying new things with other men."

"Of course not," she said, aghast.

"You want to try something new, you come to me."

His scowl made her heart kick, but she gave a cool nod as though his possessiveness was not in the least surprising. She stared out the side window, pretending an interest in a red minivan, trying to hide her smile. Martha claimed men were like horses. Maybe Martha was right.

She sneaked a sideways peek. He was still frowning, looking like a sulky but gorgeous sex god. A sex god who wanted exclusivity.

He glanced over at her, his scowl deepening. "And be careful with Shane or he might get ideas."

She blinked, momentarily startled. Dino sounded almost jealous. "I'm not really his type," she said.

"He doesn't agree with that," Dino said, not looking at her. "He's a good guy but young and...a bit of a player."

She couldn't contain a snort. "Gosh, that's rich, coming from a guy whose bathroom is stocked with ten brands of shampoo."

"What's the big deal about that?" He gave a dismissive shrug. "None of it's mine. I don't use that stuff. Look, when I'm not around, I just want you to be careful."

He totally missed the point. Despair welled deep in her chest, and she pressed her arms together, trying to contain the ache. He didn't even look at things the same way. It was crazy to hope he'd ever want her as anyone other than a pillow friend.

Martha's words came back to haunt. *Have fun but save your heart for the marrying kind.* Unfortunately, dear Martha hadn't provided instructions on how to protect the heart.

"I've arranged for a gelding to be shipped in tomorrow," he went on, oblivious to her despair. "Nice little quarter horse, great on the trails. Never stumbles and won't kick or bite. I know you like Lyric, but you'll be a lot safer with this fellow. And then maybe I won't worry so much."

He shot her a rueful smile that made her eyes burn. He did care, just not enough, and it didn't matter. He'd walk away, but the ride was worth it. She'd had more fun this past month than in her entire life. Could deal with the backlash later.

"A new gelding is coming?" Her voice cracked. "That's nice. Is he off the track?"

"No. Belongs to my ex-wife. Laura doesn't want him anymore, and he deserves a good home."

Becky's heart lurched in dismay, and the smile she'd been forcing faded.

"What's wrong?" Dino looked genuinely puzzled. "Old Smoke's a nice horse. I think a lot of him. So did Laura."

He just didn't get it. She pressed her hands together, trying to soothe her hopelessness. His wife's horse. At least he was loyal. Maybe not to people, but to his animals. He did seem concerned about her riding Lyric. All in all, it was a thoughtful gesture, but she couldn't imagine tying that horse and making love to Dino beneath the oak tree. It would seem wrong to do that with Laura's horse watching.

Chirp. Dino lifted a hand off the wheel, jabbed a button on his speaker phone and a crisp voice filled the cab.

"Dino, Jim Sapp here. Just a reminder your purchase option expires next week."

"Yeah, no problem. Got everything lined up now."

"Yeah?" The caller sounded skeptical. "I could request more time, but it's doubtful we'd get another extension. We don't want to let this slip by. I know how badly you want that property."

"The money will be no problem," Dino repeated. "Guaranteed. I'll call you after the race." He cut the connection and made a face at Becky. "Lawyers. Too bad we need them. So, are you ready for your win picture?"

She forced a smile, wishing she shared his confidence. It seemed Martha's homebreds were fated to lose and the more she knew about horses, the more she appreciated how many things could go wrong. She plucked a piece of straw off her jeans and rolled it between her fingers. "I brought some nice clothes to change into closer to the race. I'm also wearing Martha's good-luck necklace."

"Is it the same necklace you wore last night?"

Last night. Heat warmed her cheeks, and she fingered the outline of the necklace beneath her shirt. "Yes. She says the pearls are lucky and not to take them off."

The pearls had stayed on last night too. Hadn't moved, although her panties certainly had. Her pulse kicked reminding her how he'd propped her against the wall, lifted her dress and made her body sing. And afterwards she'd felt so exposed, so vulnerable, terrified he would guess the depth of her emotions. Surely he must know she wouldn't have sex in a stall with just anyone.

He glanced sideways, giving her one of his heart-melting smiles. "I'm staying at the guesthouse tonight. Please tell me Martha has a night nurse so you don't have to run off again."

She nodded, reassured he had no idea why she'd fled last night. But for her, sex and love were intertwined. It was impossible to keep those feelings separate. "You must be tired," she said, keen to change the subject. "Did Cody relieve you at all?"

"For a few hours. I never sleep much before a big race so it doesn't matter if I'm in a chair or a bed. And sex is a great way to relax."

"Oh, yes. It's ah...great for relaxing." She forced a painful smile and averted her head, trying once again to change the topic. "So from now on, a security guard will be in the barn?"

"As long as Slim's around, yes."

Thoughts of Slim pushed aside her own worries, and she straightened in the seat. "I understand he has to go. I just don't want Martha too upset."

Dino edged the truck and trailer past a noisy transport truck. "My job is to worry about the horses, not Martha."

"And my job is to worry about Martha," she said. "She's everything to me. Just like your ranch is to you."

"At least you're remembering that it's only a job. And jobs can vanish in a flash. That's why you have to make money when you can."

"Of course, like your bonus."

"A bonus isn't a dirty word, Becky. It's a condition I negotiated. Something I've worked hard for so I can move home."

Home. Where she'd never get to see him. Yet, he was happy about it, eager in fact, and she knew she should be happy for him too. But maybe Echo wouldn't win today. "Nothing's for sure in racing," she said almost wistfully.

"This race is as sure as they come." His smile was quick and confident. "Echo outclasses the other fillies and is feeling amazingly good. She's muscled up and aggressive. I'm hoping a win will please Martha and her lovable little nurse."

He reached over and squeezed her hand, making her heart stutter. She knew he didn't mean 'lovable' in anything but the most superficial way, but her heart still flipped despite her despair.

They turned into the Lone Star entrance, rumbled through the security gate and along the tree-lined drive. Stopped when a goat trotted in front of them, chased by a teary-eyed boy.

Dino lowered his window. "That's a wild-looking goat. Need any help?"

"No, thank you, señor." The boy swiped his eyes. "I'm supposed to rope him. But he keeps running away."

Dino nodded soberly. "Goats are tricky. Try dropping this." He tossed the boy a doughnut, calling out helpful encouragement while the kid scattered pieces on the ground. The goat circled back, tempted despite the threat of capture.

Dino turned toward her, pausing when he saw her expression. "Hey, why the sad face? Did you want that doughnut?"

She shook her head, but couldn't stop thinking how nice he was, how he made time for everyone. Probably would make a great dad.

"Please stop worrying about Martha," he said gently. "A win today will energize her."

She nodded, checking over her shoulder and hiding her expression. The goat was chewing pieces of doughnut, head up and standing still. The boy's arm windmilled. The rope coiled through the air and settled haphazardly over the goat's head, and the boy leaped with relief.

"Oh, look!" she said. "He caught him."

Dino just stared at her, his eyes oddly intent. "You really like it here? The people? The horses?"

"Of course. How could I not?" But her voice quavered. He still held her hand, and it was dangerously easy to pretend he cared.

"You were a little reluctant before," he said. "You never looked happy in the clubhouse."

"Guess it's not scary anymore. It's actually intoxicating."

"I guess 'intoxicating' is a good description, although it's not a word Laura ever used." He stuck his arm out the window and saluted the jubilant boy.

He was still smiling and no longer looked like he was sucking lemons when he spoke of his ex. "Guess you're friends with her again," she asked, "taking her horse and all that?"

"Hardly friends. But we were young and both trying to make each other into something we weren't. Our marriage flop was as much my fault as hers." He stared at Becky, as if settling something with himself. "You're not like her at all."

Becky's fingers curved convulsively into her palms. She wasn't sure if it was a good or bad thing, to be compared to an ex, although Dino looked completely satisfied as he backed into the area adjoining his barn. He even surprised her by stretching his hard arm across her lap and pushing open the door. "Please don't go running off with any cowboys, even if they promise a hot breakfast."

She started to laugh, but he tilted her head, covering her mouth in a possessive kiss.

"Hey, you want me drop the ramp...oh, sorry, boss—" Shane's voice stopped abruptly. Dino lifted his head. "You'll have breakfast later. With me. Okay?"

"I'm not at all hungry," she managed, staring into his intent eyes, not even embarrassed that Shane hovered by the door. She just wanted the kiss to continue. And the way Dino was looking, he seemed to want that too.

He traced a finger over her top lip, his voice husky. "Gotta unload the filly." He grabbed his keys and disappeared.

She gathered her composure and slid from the truck, slightly surprised that her legs didn't buckle. It wasn't just the kiss but the way he'd looked at her...full of wanting.

"Wow, she looks way better than last time," Shane said.

Becky flushed but Shane wasn't looking at her. He stared at Echo. And the filly did look good. Head high, eyes bright, tugging at the lead line as she danced around.

"Put her beside Chippy," Dino said. "He'll keep her calm. She definitely won't be napping today."

"Stall's all ready, boss." Shane turned Echo and led her to the barn. "Good morning, Becky," he called over his shoulder.

"Hi, Shane," Becky said but clearly he wasn't expecting a reply. After the kiss he'd witnessed, his interest was now polite and perfunctory...and Dino's expression, extremely satisfied.

CHAPTER THIRTY-ONE

Dino watched Red lead an aggressive Echo around the paddock. The filly pranced with eagerness, a sharp contrast to her last trip to the track, when she'd been too tired to stand. *That fucking Slim.* Well, Slim couldn't sabotage her anymore, and the filly looked like a winner now that she hadn't been hung out to dry on a hot walker.

Her main challenge would be from the four horse, the speedy filly from California. But if the race unfolded the way he expected and the fractions were sensible, Echo would run third or fourth and then gallop past them in the stretch. The one horse was a closer and would be around at the wire but shouldn't pose too big a threat.

"Our horse is looking good, boss," Shane said.

Dino nodded but instinctively tugged Becky a step closer. Shane had been staring at her with wistful eyes, and it was important that a man mark his territory. He'd never realized Shane was so persistent.

Or that he could feel so possessive.

Sighing, he lowered his arm. Becky wasn't like Laura. She'd been friendly to Shane, but definitely not flirtatious. And it wasn't her fault she was so damn pretty. Shane wasn't the only guy looking.

She'd changed from her jeans and T-shirt and now wore a silky sky-blue dress that dipped a bit too low over her breasts. He rubbed his jaw, still undecided about that detail. Maybe it wasn't all that low, but he knew what was underneath so his imagination was working overtime.

It could be the necklace and not the dress at all. Martha's pearls looked vastly different on Becky, so sexy, especially when her dress was pushed down and her beautiful breasts bared. Like last night. Jesus, he stiffened just thinking about last night.

"Think the four horse will run under twenty-three?" Shane asked.

Dino jerked sideways, trying to corral his thoughts. Generally he could think of sex and horses at the same time, but today he was a little tired, a little confused. Couldn't figure out why his arm kept reaching for Becky's waist. It must be that fucking Shane.

"Yeah, should go about twenty-three," he finally said.

Shane nodded. "That'll be good for our filly then. She's a different horse today. What do you think was wrong with her last time?"

Dino felt Becky's tension and gave her hand a reassuring squeeze. She always agonized about how bad news might knock Martha into a tailspin, and if remaining mute about Slim kept her happy, then he was committed to keeping his mouth shut.

"Guess we'll never know," he said.

His eyes met hers, and she gave a grateful smile. She wore lipstick, some pinkish shiny stuff, and her mouth looked soft, sexy, delicious—

"Guess we'll tell Brad to sit third or fourth?"

Dino pulled his attention back to the paddock and the colorful riders filing from the jocks' room. "Yeah. Tell him to sit close if they run that first quarter in twenty-three. If the California horse shoots off much faster, he'll have to rate our filly."

"You want *me* to give Brad the instructions?"

"Sure."

Shane grinned, tilting his hat at Becky before stepping forward.

"That was nice of you," she whispered.

"I just wanted him to leave us alone," Dino admitted.

Her brow furrowed. "Aren't we going to bet?"

"You told me once you never bet," he teased. "Now you've devised your own betting theory. Which one are you using today?"

"The dress-up angle," she said. "The four horse looks nice but so do the people around the one horse. I'm betting Echo and the four horse for my exacta, and I'm using the one horse in the trifecta."

He pretended to shake his head, but she'd chosen the exact same horses he'd picked, after an hour of detailed analysis. Maybe her theory had some validity. She'd definitely learned a lot since that day in the clubhouse when she'd averted her head and mumbled that she didn't bet.

"You've chosen good ones," he said. "Just remember to leave Echo on top. She's going to win."

"All right." She pulled some crisp bills from her purse. "I was going to box them but that will raise the payoff, and Stephanie needs the money. Everyone seems to have forgotten her."

There was an accusatory note in her voice that he didn't understand, but Brad was nodding as he listened to Shane, and the paddock judge yelled 'Riders up!' It was time.

Red held a prancing Echo, and Shane boosted Brad into the saddle. Brad slipped his toes in the irons and Shane followed the filly, looking so proud Dino was glad he'd let him handle the saddling. Shane was smart and dependable, and more responsibility would keep him from breaking off and starting his own stable.

It would also give Dino more time with Becky—although soon, he'd be living at his ranch and racing closer to San Antonio, and Martha would probably be in some retirement home, and who the hell knew where Becky would be.

"Why are you frowning?" she asked. "Is something wrong with Echo?"

Her eyes had widened with such concern he squeezed her hand, grabbing any excuse to touch her. "No. Echo looks fine. Things are going to work out great." *But maybe not so great for Becky.*

The Lone Star meet was closing soon, and a win today would be good for Conrad Stables. And for him. It'd be an excellent time for Martha to sell. Hunter had posted a bullet work and was back in form, and Conrad horses had been receiving positive press. Becky, however, would be stripped of the job she loved.

There probably weren't many nursing positions that included racehorses.

"Let's find a spot at the rail," he said, shaking off his melancholy. "Unless you want to watch from Martha's box."

"I prefer the rail," she said. "Besides, I don't want to see Ted."

Amen to that. They threaded through the crowd and joined the lineup at the betting windows. She rattled off her wagering instructions to a solemn pari-mutuel attendant then stuffed the tickets in her purse.

"You sound like a pro," he said, "and you bet a helluva lot too."

Her eyes sparkled with anticipation. "I bet for Martha and Stephanie, and I wanted to put money on Echo too, seeing as how her trainer is unusually confident." Her face turned serious and she touched his arm. "I really pray you earn your bonus today. You work hard and deserve every good thing."

Her generosity shocked him. She wasn't thinking about her own job or what Echo's win might mean but truly placed other people first. Probably why she was a nurse.

And maybe that explained why he wanted to forget the race and simply enjoy her company. "Guess as long as the horse and rider come back safe, that'll be enough." His voice was gruff. "Just pray for that, honey."

"Hey, Anders! You're the guy I want to see."

A wiry man limped from the crowd, clumsily transferring a shiny cane to his left hand so he could extend his arm.

"Jimmy," Dino said, shaking his hand. "How's rehab going?"

"Super. Couldn't be better. Just need to climb on some horses and get the old leg working again. Be back in the jock room soon."

"Glad to hear it." Dino nodded, uncomfortable with Jimmy's forced enthusiasm and the unmistakable tint of desperation.

"That's why I wanted to see you. I really need something to gallop." Jimmy's throat rippled convulsively. "Quiet ones, nothing fancy. I'll even do it free."

Dino stared in dismay. Nine months ago, Jimmy Jones had been a top jock on the Texas circuit. One unlucky fall and he was propped on a crutch, begging for rides. Worse, the man looked beaten. Definitely not in any shape to gallop a finely tuned Thoroughbred.

He paused, searching for an excuse, knowing he couldn't live with his guilt if Jimmy suffered another accident. "Don't really have anything. Maybe a pony horse."

"Yeah, anything," Jimmy said but his shoulders drooped. No jock wanted to be relegated to a tractable pony horse, especially a rider of his status. "I just need to get back on the track. Miss the horses…it's tough, you know."

"What about Chippy?" Becky asked softly.

"Chippy? Yeah, Chip." Dino brightened, relieved he could help after all. The gelding would be perfect. The vet had prescribed long trots for his injured leg and Chippy was ever-obliging, always looking after his rider. Jimmy wouldn't be over-mounted yet could keep his dignity. "When can you start?" Dino asked. "Got a horse in rehab. Needs a light rider. No one has hands quite like you."

"Tomorrow morning. I'll come by at six." Jimmy's voice broke and he blinked rapidly. "Sure appreciate this. Man, I appreciate this." He pumped Dino's hand and hobbled away, swinging his cane with renewed vigor.

"I'm sorry," Becky said. "I know you need Chippy's stall and he was going back to Martha's, but Chippy can help that jockey."

"No, everything's good," Dino said. "I should have thought of Chippy." He followed her gaze as Jimmy weaved through the crowd, his limp almost jaunty. It would be a little costly—Chip taking up a race stall—but hell, it was the right thing to do. And Malcolm would have approved. He'd always worried about the riders as much as the horses. The race industry truly missed a man like Malcolm.

"One minute to post," the announcer's voice blared, jolting him from his reverie.

"Let's go." He grabbed Becky's hand, hustled her through the surging spectators, and joined Red and Shane by the rail.

Shane gestured at Echo, circling behind the starting gate. "She looks like dynamite, boss. Never saw her so composed, yet so on the muscle."

Dino glanced at Becky but she wasn't looking at Shane, wasn't posing or giggling or flashing her eyes. She watched Echo with rapt attention, content to be at the track, content to be with him. And when she gave him her beautiful smile, something kicked in his chest, and he gratefully kissed her cheek.

An assistant starter guided Echo into the gate, and Becky tightened her grip on Dino's hand. Both Dino and Shane thought the California horse would lead the way but also believed Echo would have no problem running her down in the stretch. Still, racing was unpredictable. She fingered Martha's necklace with her other hand, trying not to chew her nails.

Martha always said 'pace makes the race' but it seemed that if a horse was faster, it was more likely to win. And clearly the California horse was fast. Dino said Country Zip could run an opening quarter in just over twenty-two seconds but that Echo had a stronger closing kick.

So, she'd bet Echo to win, Zip to place, and the one horse, Rocky Atlantic, to come third. If the horses finished in that order, Stephanie's rent would be covered for three months— even longer because Martha had said she'd also give her winnings to Stephanie.

Becky glanced at Dino. She used to think he was always composed before a race but now that he was touching her, she noticed the tenseness in his body.

And he was holding her hand! Never in her wildest dreams had she imagined a moment like this. She wanted to pinch herself. Best of all, he didn't look at other women, not even the pink-shirted blonde who'd literally bumped his hip trying to snag his attention.

He caught her gaze. "Give that lucky necklace a rub," he said. "Horses are ready to go."

"They're in," the announcer called.

She edged further between Shane and Dino, straining to see the chute. Heads jostled in the starting gate, and jockeys' silks flashed. She concentrated on Brad's distinctive yellow, praying for a clean break.

The gates snapped open. "They're off!" the announcer blared.

Turquoise silks flashed as Country Zip burst to the lead. A clump of horses followed, but she couldn't see Echo. She twisted, staring first at the big screen then at the live action on the track, not sure which was the best view.

Beside her, Dino stood rock steady, his gaze on the horses. "Wait, Brad," he murmured.

"Opening quarter in twenty-two seconds flat," the announcer said, and the crowd gasped.

"Looking good," Shane said.

"That's good, right?" Becky gripped Dino's arm and tried to stop bouncing.

"Good for Echo," Dino said, "but you need the California horse to hang on for second. Might be hard for her at that speed. Although the one horse should be able to close for third."

Becky gulped. It was impossible to watch and cheer for three horses. Hard enough to find Echo. She stretched on her toes, spotting Brad's yellow silks moving fluidly in fourth. Tight on the rail.

"Move her out, Brad," Dino muttered.

The horses swept around the turn with California Zip showing the way, five lengths clear of the pack and Echo comfortable in fourth. Becky had no idea where the one horse was, but she couldn't stop jumping as Brad edged Echo wide and took dead aim on the leader.

Echo's ears flicked forward. Brad seemed to melt into her neck. Her stride lengthened and slowly, oh so slowly, she inched up to Country Zip. The California horse was all heart and struggled gamely, but Echo was too strong. The filly flattened her ears and streamed past, leaving Zip galloping vainly in her wake. Two lengths. Three—Becky gasped in awe as Echo crossed the wire four lengths in front.

Country Zip staggered across in second, and a bay horse closed on the outside for third.

Shane hollered and thrust his fist in the air.

Becky was lifted off her feet. "It's done!" Dino said, his eyes glinting with satisfaction as he whirled her around. "And you cashed in big too."

"What horse came third?"

He grinned and set her back on the ground. "Rocky Atlantic. You got the trifecta, honey. Echo, Zip and the longshot. Should be a nice payout."

She squeezed her purse and studied the tote board. She hadn't known the one horse had got up for third, had been concentrating on Echo. But she'd done it. She was cashing in on a trifecta—one of the hardest bets to make.

"Just remember who taught you to bet, Miss Becky," Shane said.

Becky grinned, couldn't remember being happier. Martha finally had a win, Stephanie too, and Echo had just earned Dino his bonus—and his ranch. Which meant he'd be leaving soon.

Her face tightened and suddenly her smile hurt.

"Come on, honey," Dino said. "Let's get a picture."

A security guard congratulated them, opening the gate so they could enter the winner's circle. Red proudly led Echo and a grinning Brad into their midst. Dino patted Echo then reached up and shook Brad's hand. The photographer gestured.

"A happy moment."

Ted's voice. Becky locked her expression before turning to greet him. She'd forgotten about Ted but this was perfect. He couldn't criticize the Conrad horses today—Echo had shown both courage and ability.

However, Ted looked genuinely happy about the win. Even smiled. "An excellent result. Wish Martha could have seen this." His gaze drifted to her throat, and his smile disappeared. "What are *you* doing with that necklace? That belongs to my aunt."

"She loaned it to me." Becky's hands swept to the pearls. "It's just a copy. For luck."

"Doesn't look like a copy," Ted snapped. "And it's not ethical to wheedle into her affections."

"Hey, Ted. Come join the picture," Dino called. He walked up, tugging her closer to Echo. He felt so solid, so normal and she pressed closer to his side. Ted turned on his heels and stalked from the enclosure.

"Why's he leaving?" Dino asked.

"Look this way," the photographer called. *Click.*

Payouts flashed on the screen behind them, and the crowd roared. A three hundred and eighty-four dollar trifecta! Becky stared at the numbers, trying to calculate Stephanie's winnings, but the sum was too big and she was still off balance from Ted's accusation.

Echo tossed her head and spun, almost bumping the confident lady who breezed past the guard and into the winner's circle. Danielle always looked so assured, so gorgeous, so perfect. Becky swallowed, forgetting about the race, about the winnings. Forgetting even about Ted, as Danielle rose on her toes and boldly kissed Dino's cheek.

"That was an amazing race," Danielle purred. "Those fractions were impressive. A track record. I'd like to run a feature on your training methods. Dinner this week?"

Dino gestured at Shane and Red who were high-fiving beside Echo. "Probably you should talk to those boys, Slim and Stephanie too. It was a team effort."

Danielle laid a possessive hand on Dino's arm. "Of course. But I was thinking of a quiet dinner, just the two of us."

Becky stepped back, an awkward smile plastered on her face. Shane, Red and Echo were already leaving. Should she go with them or wait for Dino? Good media was critical, and Dino would have to play nice with Danielle, even if he didn't want to. But maybe he did. She backed another uncertain step.

Dino pulled her back to his side. "Wait for me, honey. We need to figure out how many pictures we want." He thought for a second then looked over Danielle's head and called to the photographer. "Eight copies please, Jack."

Danielle looked at Becky, a slight frown marring her perfect skin. "I understand if you're working tonight but what evening are you free? This would be a full feature."

"Great. Drop by the office tomorrow," Dino said. "Around ten. We can all talk then." He winked at Becky. "You'll have to get up early though."

"What about Wednesday or Thursday night? I'd like a candid interview, just the two of us." Danielle gave Becky a contemptuous once-over. "You don't mind sharing him one night, do you?"

Becky's face turned warm, and she wished she'd left with Echo. She could feel Dino's gaze but didn't want to look at him.

Wasn't sure what to say. That she'd won his fidelity in a horse race?

"I hope she doesn't want to share," Dino drawled, "because I surely don't want to."

And then Becky did look at him. He always spoke slowly when he was thinking, tended to hide his emotion behind a lazy drawl. And he stared now with such intensity, not paying a drop of attention to Danielle, that she was swept with gratitude and a sense of belonging.

Danielle's heels clicked and slowly faded, but Becky couldn't drag her gaze from Dino. Her heart seemed to be pounding out of her chest. "I can never tell if you're serious or just being nice," she finally managed.

"Guess that means I'll have to try harder. Come on. Let's join our horse." He guided her along the pathway toward the backside. "Echo's probably at the test barn. Can't leave until she passes her urine."

She walked beside him, still slightly stunned. But she'd witnessed it. He'd turned down the gorgeous Danielle Whitlock. And they weren't even on Conrad property. "How do they take urine from a horse?" she asked, surprised she could even formulate a sensible question.

"A pee catcher, a little cup on a stick. Aren't you forgetting something?" He waved his cell phone. "Better call Martha. She'll be anxious for the results."

Oh, God, she'd forgotten about Martha. She grabbed his phone and pressed in the number. "Echo won!" Becky said. "Won easy."

Martha gave a delighted squeal. "Malcolm would be so pleased. I'll have Jocelyn chill the champagne. Be sure to bring Dino and Slim with you." She gave a girlish giggle. "And give Dino a kiss for me. I'm sure you won't mind that."

Becky closed the phone and looked at Dino. He'd obviously heard because he grinned and opened his arms. It took her less than two seconds to leap into them.

CHAPTER THIRTY-TWO

"And then Echo flattened her ears and started running. Watch her in the stretch, Martha." Dino raised the volume on his laptop; the crowd's cheers filled the living room.

Martha stared at the screen, watching the replay as Echo blasted past Country Zip. "Those California horses can't hold their speed," she said. "Malcolm always bred for distance. Play it again, please."

Becky sipped her champagne while Dino replayed the race for the fifth time. He was wonderfully patient, and Martha glowed with a sense of achievement. Echo had tied a track record, and the phone hadn't stopped ringing. Dino had said it would be a good time to start dispersing the two-year-olds, as the value of Conrad stock had escalated with Echo's convincing win. But of course, he was satisfied. Soon he'd be in southern Texas, at his ranch—he had what he wanted.

"Oh, this is such a perfect day." Martha clapped her hands, pulling back Becky's attention. "But where's Slim? He should be celebrating with us."

Dino sighed and crossed his arms.

He's going to tell her. "Slim's around." Becky scrambled to her feet. "Just couldn't come tonight."

"He should be here," Martha said. "He worked hard. This is as much his victory as Malcolm's."

Dino's face hardened but Becky gave him a pleading smile. He turned and silently replaced the laptop in its case.

"You must take my winnings to Stephanie," Martha said to Becky. "And a win picture. This is an historical day. Oh, the heck with water. Pour me some champagne."

Dino lifted the bottle from the silver wine chiller. "One glass won't hurt," he said, looking over Martha's head at Becky.

Fine for him, she thought, tugging at her lower lip. Martha didn't matter so much, not now. She clenched her hands, wishing she could recapture her earlier euphoria. Wished she had more time—with the horses, with Martha, with Dino. A band tightened around her chest.

Ring. The doorbell chimed from the entry. Seconds later, Jocelyn jerked into the room, taut and white-faced, followed by a policeman with nervous eyes and a hat clenched in his hands.

"I'm very sorry." His gaze darted to the right, and his bald head gleamed under the chandelier. "I'm sorry," he repeated, "but there's been a traffic fatality. David Barrett was killed."

David Barrett? Becky stared blankly.

"Oh, no! Slim!" Martha's face blanched, her mouth still wrapped around Slim's name. The glass slid from her fingers and shattered on the unforgiving marble floor. Dino grabbed her slumping body before she joined the shards glittering at her feet.

The rest of the evening was a blur. The frantic drive to the hospital with Martha had blended into a numbing wait and now even the doctor's face seemed smudged. Becky blinked, trying to absorb his words.

"She's resting comfortably," the doctor said. "We'll know more later. The first twelve hours are crucial." He nodded gravely and disappeared through a door marked 'restricted.'

Becky rubbed her itchy eyes. "I have to call Ted."

"I already called him," Dino said. "He'll come by tomorrow."

"Tomorrow? But did you tell him she had a heart attack? Just like Malcolm. That they don't know—" Her voice broke as Dino pulled her to his chest, his comforting hand slipping beneath her hair to rub her neck. She sucked in a choky breath. "I knew she couldn't take any upsets. I shouldn't have let you fire Slim. Maybe should have stopped the policeman from telling her."

"It's not your fault. Martha doesn't want to live in a vacuum." Dino's reassuring voice rumbled against her ear. "She wouldn't want a life like that."

"But I want that. If it helps her live longer." She drew in his familiar smell, his calmness. He was always so focused. Didn't worry about people coming and going...dying. "What exactly did you say to Slim? Do you think he drove into the ditch on purpose? Was he upset?"

"I fired him, Becky. No doubt he was a bit upset."

"Couldn't you have waited?" She twisted from his arms. "Made sure he was sober?"

"Now I wish I'd waited, of course. But at the time it seemed important to keep him away from the horses. To make sure Echo had a good race."

"Because you wanted your bonus." Her voice rose. "And now Slim is dead and Jill is alone and Martha—"

"You need to calm down, honey. Let's get some coffee."

"I don't want coffee." A man with a bandaged elbow shot her a curious glance, but she didn't care. "And I'm calm. I just want to be alone."

"Really?"

"Yes, really. I'll stay with Martha."

"You sure?"

His remote expression showed he was already beyond the hospital, no doubt making barn notes. He never worried about people like he did about horses. Probably one of the reasons he was such a good trainer. He probably wanted to go. It was early morning and, like her, he was exhausted. No reason for him to hang around too. But a voice in the back of her head wouldn't shut up. *Please stay, please stay, please stay.*

"Yes, you go," she said evenly.

He stared at her for a long moment then nodded. "All right. I'll drop back later. Let me know how she's doing."

He kissed her cheek and walked toward the swinging doors, past two nurses who both smiled prettily. Then the door shut and she was alone.

*

"So an animal may have caused the accident." Dino loosened his grip on the phone, his aching guilt easing as he spoke to the police officer. There had been no note, no evidence to show Slim had deliberately driven off the road. There was also no evidence of alcohol so his insurance would be valid. "Yes, that's right," Dino added. "I've never known him to use drugs. Guess something made him swerve. Thanks for the update."

He closed his phone and gestured at Cody who hovered in the barn aisle. "You're in charge today," he said. "Make sure Echo is walked and wrapped. Call if you have questions."

"Sure. Don't worry about a thing." Cody tucked the clipboard under his arm and shook his head. "Damn shame about Slim. Did someone go to that place where his daughter lives? Don't think he had any other family."

Dino dragged a hand over his jaw. Of course, Jill. And Stephanie also should be told in person—she'd known Slim for years. "Does Jill live in that big gray building on the way to Lone Star?" he asked. "*Helping Hands* something?"

"That's the place." Cody grimaced. "Looks like a jail."

"Okay. I'll stop by on the way to the track." Dino cast a longing look at the training oval, wishing he could stay. The new exercise rider was okay and probably could follow instructions, but Cody was a groom and knew little about conditioning.

At least Echo had bounced back from her race in good shape. Her legs were tight and cool, and Cody could look after things. He didn't want Becky stuck with all the fallout from Slim's death—she was centered on Martha, and rightly so. It wouldn't be a big deal to take some of the load off her shoulders.

He fortified himself with a deep breath, stopped at his house to pick up Slim's employee file and headed to the interstate.

The *Helping Hands Living Center* was easy to find and only forty-five minutes from Conrad's. Proximity had probably been important; Slim hadn't picked the place for its aesthetic appeal.

He lingered in the parking lot and flipped through the file, glad Becky had made a copy. Slim's wife had died of cancer eleven years ago, and it appeared Jill was the only living relative. He shook his head at the sparse information. Damn shame. Both Jill and Slim had been dealt an excessive amount of bad luck.

He found what he was looking for and tossed the file on the seat with a relieved grunt. Finally, a break for the Barrett family. Slim's insurance policy included a hefty death payout. And none of the exclusions applied.

He swung open the door of his pickup, pausing to study the bleak building. He disliked hospitals, avoided institutions of any type—the smell, the confinement, the despair. Tainted air seemed to seep into his skin and always made him want to bolt.

He trudged into the foyer. The receptionist was young, perky and delighted to have a visitor. Full of smiles, she seated him in a cramped office with a motley assortment of pictures and an oversized desk tag that read, John C. Chisholm.

Two minutes later, a solemn-faced man strode behind the desk. "Yes," he said after shaking Dino's hand. "We heard a rumor of the accident. Mr. Barrett visited Jill almost every day." He cleared his throat, suddenly very interested in the tip of his pen. "Will someone else be looking after the monthly payments? Our facility has a waiting list and naturally we're a bit concerned."

"No problem." Dino shifted, uncomfortable in the hard seat. "It will take time but insurance will cover all Jill's costs. Give me your card, and I'll have the insurance company contact you."

"Very good." The man smiled, happy again, and passed over a white business card. "Jill's outside with the others. Please don't say anything about her father. We'll have a psychiatrist break the news. It's difficult to know what she understands."

"Oh, I don't need to see her," Dino said, but John C. Chisholm had already risen with an air of expectancy and opened the door.

Dino squared his shoulders and followed the man down a long corridor. They took a sharp right through a wide double door, down a ramp and into a fenced courtyard.

"That's Jill, the one in the wheelchair. She likes to sit close to the grass. Thanks for dropping by." Chisholm nodded and turned away.

Dino headed toward Jill who was propped in the chair. A kind-eyed nurse adjusted a pink blanket and gave him an encouraging smile before edging away.

Jill's hair was short, almost shaved, her eyes blank, and a thin notebook lay on her wasted legs. *Jesus.*

"Hello, Jill. My name's Dino." He knelt in front of her. She seemed to be watching some swooping swallows, and he fervently wished Becky was with him. She'd know how to handle this. Was always generous with her time and love. In fact, he resolved to bring her here as soon as Martha improved.

The birds disappeared, and he drew in a deep breath. "I dropped in to say hi. Check if you need anything." He paused, not sure if she could even understand him. "I'll drop by again. Maybe next week."

"Orse."

"Pardon." He leaned closer, watching her lips. She'd definitely said something, and her attention was now focused on his chest.

"Orse."

He looked down and noted the small Polo crest on his shirt.

Her eyes flashed with interest, the blank expression gone. "Orse," she repeated and then she smiled, a big, beautiful grin that ripped at his chest.

His mouth opened but he could only nod as he tried to work words around the lump welling in his throat. "Yes, Jill," he finally managed. "It's a horse."

"She loves horses." The hovering nurse placed a gentle hand on Jill's shoulder. "She's a great artist too. Show him your drawings, Jill."

Jill slowly opened her notebook, still distracted by his shirt.

"She's always been able to draw," the nurse said proudly. "Sometimes she sketches for hours."

Dino's eyes widened as Lyric filled the pages. "I know that horse. She's a mare Jill used to ride."

"She draws that particular one a lot, although she sketches birds and trees and round roads too. But she especially likes to draw horses. She's very talented. And it makes her happy."

Jill's pencil skimmed over the page, her attention fixed on his shirt. Already he could see the image of the tiny Polo horse as she recreated it on the blank page. She laid her pencil down, awkwardly ripped out the page and passed it to him. "Orse."

The nurse laughed. "She must like you. She doesn't usually give away her pictures."

Dino scanned the remarkable replica of the Polo logo and immediately saw the road the nurse mentioned—not a round road but an oval track. He swallowed again, buffeted by emotions impossible to contain.

Everyone spoke about how hard it was to give up the track, to give up the horses. Clearly Jill hadn't been able to give them up either. The love she felt for Lyric, for the horses, was evident in her shining eyes and the lovingly drawn pictures.

He clasped the paper to his chest. "Thank you, Jill," he said. "Thank you very much."

Dino leaned back on Stephanie's couch and downed a badly needed coffee.

"I can't believe Slim's dead." Stephanie shook her head in sorrow. "Thanks for dropping by. But what'll happen to Jill?"

"She'll be okay once the insurance is settled. You should see her, Steph. She's quite a little artist. She remembered every detail of Lyric, right down to the cowlick on that mare's forehead. She came alive when she was drawing."

"Horses get in your blood, a natural high. Imagine how thrilled she'd be to get out in the country and see some real ones. I've only been stuck inside for a week and already I'm depressed."

Dino glanced around the tiny room, uncomfortably fingering his cup, knowing he'd go stark-raving mad confined to an apartment. Unable to find solace with horses. Or even worse, stuck in an institution.

He abruptly rose. "When's your cast off?"

"Another four weeks."

"Well, hurry up. We need you back galloping." He checked his watch. It had been a depressing day, and obviously he wasn't going to make it to Lone Star until noon. He'd already spent too much time at Stephanie's, but it would have been callous to rush off after hitting her with news of Slim's accident. He reached for his wallet. "I'm going to leave you some cash. Back payment for all those videos you analyzed with me."

"No, I'm good. And you don't have to buy any more groceries either. Becky texted me the results of Echo's race and her genius betting. She made me a pile of money—hit the trifecta—and apparently Martha is tossing in her profits too. Man, I love that girl."

"Martha?"

Stephanie rolled her eyes. "No, Becky. Best nurse ever. I'm sure she won't have trouble finding another job."

He set his mug in the sink, the clink loud as it rattled against several dirty dishes. Of course Becky would have to find another job. Rather quickly too, if Martha didn't return to her mansion. He was moving anyway, so it was irrelevant where she went; any job would be too far from his isolated ranch. Too far for any meaningful relationship.

He stepped over some toy horses scattered on the carpet and walked toward the door. "Gotta go. But drop by Conrad's and visit whenever you need space." He gave a wry smile. "I promise not to make you work."

"Really." Her face lit up. "I'd love to come and enjoy the place. Not much I can do though, except give advice to your new gallop girl."

"Advice is always appreciated." He glanced around the tiny apartment. Not bad if only used for sleeping, but anything more and it would turn cramped in a hurry. "Guess you and your daughter could always move into Slim's place," he said thoughtfully. "Be temporary, but free. If Ted has any say, he'll sell out damn quick, but you should get at least six months there. And you could do some of Slim's job, help Cody with the horses until they're disbursed."

"Really? Oh, Dino!" She squealed with delight—obviously forgetting her kid was napping—and flung her arms around his neck. "You really are the kindest man. I'd love to convalesce at Conrad's. And I'll organize Slim's things. Do my share to help."

He gave her shoulder an affectionate pat, careful to avoid the arm with the cast. "All right. I'll tell Martha when I go to the hospital. And maybe you can look after Slim's cat. Now I really gotta go."

"In a rush to get back to the hospital? And probably not just to see Martha." She grinned. "Be careful. Your playboy reputation is slipping."

He rolled his eyes but her knowing laugh followed him to his truck, lingered as he rumbled back onto the highway.

Jill's drawing fluttered on the seat. He eased his foot off the accelerator, thinking of Slim as he slowed the pickup to just over the limit. Probably the man had been speeding and swerved to avoid an animal. Maybe even a loose horse.

Slim definitely would have tried to avoid a horse. Most horses. Maybe not Lyric. It must have been bittersweet to see Jill draw pictures of the mare that had derailed her life. Ironically, that seemed to be the only horse she remembered.

He shook his head, trying to banish useless, sentimental thoughts. Some things simply couldn't be changed. No sense brooding. Best to keep it simple. Set goals, go after them, have a little fun along the way.

Although he'd have to remember to snap some pictures of Lyric. Maybe Becky would help with that. Groom Lyric for a photo. Come with him to visit Jill. Maybe move down south with him.

Whoa. Where did that come from? He blew out an exasperated breath. She wouldn't like his ranch anyway; it was much too isolated. She'd want a nursing job close by so she could visit Martha in her fancy retirement home. Martha was definitely more than an employer, and Becky would be ripped in two if she were far away. Her face would turn all pinched and sad, and he couldn't go through that again. No way.

It wouldn't be smart to piss off Martha either—he hoped to keep her best horses in training, at least until they were sold. Although all the politics and second guessing didn't really matter anymore.

He'd done it. He had his ranch, his own slice of heaven. Godammit, he'd done it. But he stared through the windshield at the gray stretch of highway, wondering why the accomplishment felt so hollow.

CHAPTER THIRTY-THREE

Three tractors harrowed the oval by the time Dino reached Lone Star. High noon and not a horse in sight, not even on the hot walkers. Once training hours were over, the bustling backside slowed to a crawl. He eased his pickup to a stop, relieved Shane's vehicle was still on the grounds. Tomorrow he'd come for the gallops although that meant he'd have to stay at his apartment and not at Conrad's. Damn he hoped Becky was doing okay.

He walked toward his shedrow, texting her a message: *Hope Martha's okay. Will bring supper tonight.* Entered the shedrow. Horses eyed him curiously. Hunter stuck his head over the door then dismissed him and returned to his hay net.

The colt looked good. Legs wrapped, coat sleek. He'd even put on a few pounds following his nasal infection. *Goddamn, Slim.* Dino rubbed his forehead. The man had been mixed-up and bitter about Jill, but Dino couldn't quite forgive him for sponging Hunter. Couldn't understand it either. Now he never would.

Becky wanted to hide Slim's treachery from Martha, but Dino didn't believe in coddling. The truth was the truth.

"Afternoon, boss," Shane called. "I wasn't sure if you were going to make it today. How's my favorite girl?"

Dino blew out a sigh. So what if Shane was half in love with his woman. Becky didn't look at Shane the way she looked at him, and she had a lot more depth than Laura. Maybe they could even make this thing work. Four hundred miles wasn't that far. He had a good truck and, besides, he'd never needed much sleep.

"She sore anywhere?"

Dino stared at Shane, eyes narrowing. This was getting a little too personal.

Shane backed up a step. "Just wondered how she moved today. Quite an effort, you know, fast time."

Echo, of course. What the hell was wrong with him? He nodded quickly. "She's perfect, legs nice and tight, sound as a dollar."

"Thanks for letting me saddle yesterday. A real honor. And she made us all a chunk of money."

Especially me. That filly earned me my bonus. Dino gestured at his office. "Let's grab a coffee and go over our plans for San Antonio. You'll be looking at more responsibility there. And more pay." His words came out, slowly at first then in a rush. "I'll be moving around a bit, between my ranch, San Antonio…and Conrad's."

"What about Mrs. Conrad's horses? A bloodstock agent dropped by, interested in Hunter and a few others. Left his card."

"I expect she'll sell over the next few months. Have everything dispersed by the fall. Unfortunately Slim's death hit her hard."

Shane blew out a ragged sigh. "I told the staff, like you asked. Hard to believe he was walking around here yesterday, right as rain."

"Slim was here? At Lone Star?"

"Yeah. Looked worn out. Wouldn't surprise me if he fell asleep at the wheel."

What time of day was that?" Dino asked.

"I don't know. Just before night feed. I assumed he came to watch the race."

"Was he near Hunter?" Dino's voice sharpened.

"No, boss. You know we watch the horses close. No one's allowed to feed or go in their stalls."

Dino nodded, his tension easing. "Was he drinking?"

"No. Just grabbed a Coke from the fridge, talked a little and left. Looked exhausted though. Eyes all baggy."

So Slim really *had* fallen asleep. No need for him—for anyone—to feel guilty.

Gravel rattled, and a Jeep with orange roof lights pulled up to the door, stopping too fast, parking too close. He scowled as exhaust drifted down the aisle. Horses needed good air, and this wasn't even a vet or farrier, only a security vehicle. Those people never thought about the horses, too preoccupied with rules and regulations.

A second vehicle rammed beside the first, and three grim-faced men trooped into the barn.

"Dino Anders?" the short one asked.

"Right here." Sighing, he walked toward them. Some saddles had been stolen from barn fourteen, and one of his grooms had been charged with theft. This was probably follow-up but it was bad timing. He wanted to hurry back to Becky. Seemed the shit never stopped.

"We're here to inspect your office and feed room," the short security guard said.

Dino gestured at his office. "Go ahead. Door's open. Saddles are around the corner although they're all legit." He glanced back at Shane, dismissing the guards. "We'll work Hunter five furlongs tomorrow. Call Brad's agent and see if he can ride next week."

Voices rose, intrusive and oddly triumphant. "Mr. Anders? Are these your needles?"

He spun around in disbelief. "Fuck, no! Where'd you find them?"

"In the fridge, behind the milk. I'm afraid we have to report this as possession."

They dropped some vials and needles into a plastic bag. Dino stared, stunned to silence. Shane's face was white and he looked just as shocked.

"As the trainer on record, you're responsible for these drugs," the tall officer said.

Dino squeezed his eyes shut. A muscle ticked in his left jaw. When he opened his eyes, the solemn men were still standing in the aisle, still holding the needles, still staring in accusation. "I know the rules," he said, his voice rusty. "How long's the suspension?"

"Medication infraction—first offence, thirty days."

Jesus. Thirty fucking days. He felt like a criminal.

"And we're bringing a vet to pull blood from your horses."

"Please do," he snapped. "Test every single one. And I'll be fighting this at the damn hearing."

"No need to swear, Mr. Anders."

His phone chirped and he scanned the display. Shot a warning scowl at the listening officers, turned and took the call.

"You look tired, dear."

Becky opened her eyes and scrambled from the hard hospital chair. "Oh, Martha, I was so worried."

"Was it my heart again?"

Becky nodded, her fingers automatically reaching for Martha's hand. "Not bad though. They don't think there's any damage. The paramedics were wonderful."

Martha's face blanched in memory. "I can't believe Slim is dead. What happened?" Sorrow cracked her voice.

Becky hesitated. The doctors wanted to keep her calm.

"Tell me." Martha's voice rose.

"It was a highway accident," Becky said. "No one else was involved. He wasn't wearing a seatbelt. Died instantly."

Martha closed her eyes, but moisture seeped from the corners. "We'll make sure he has a nice funeral," she finally said. "Ask Jocelyn to help. She's good with funerals. Organized two for Ted. Don't know what to do about Jill though." Her fingers twisted at the edge of the sheet.

"I'll check into that," Becky said. "You rest, and I'll be here when you wake up."

"You're a good girl." Her gaze drifted to Becky's neck, and her mouth curved in a weak smile. "Glad you're wearing those pearls. I want you to have my diamonds too. But you need some makeup. You look pale, and your hair needs washing. Never let your looks go." She made a disapproving sound then closed her eyes.

Becky almost choked with relief. Doctors had been cautiously optimistic, but the fact that Martha already worrying about her nurse's appearance was far more reassuring than any medical report. She turned away, jerking in shock at the figure framed in the doorway.

"Satisfied?" Ted's sneer was low and nasty, and she edged back a step.

"What do you mean?"

"Trying to weasel into her affections. First pearls, then diamonds. Well, it won't work. The will is made, and she doesn't look healthy."

"Shut up, Ted." Anger propelled her forward, and she grabbed his arm. "If you're going to talk like this," she hissed, "at least have the decency to take it outside."

His arm was hard and sinewy and revolting. Everything about him was revolting. But she tugged him out the door, turned and shut it behind them. "I resent your nasty insinuations," she added in a more level voice. "Your aunt's wellbeing has always been my biggest concern. If you're going to make negative comments, I'll insist you're banned from her room. Because contrary to what you think, she has plenty of life left."

"Plenty of life left." His mouth thinned. "One can only hope. And I do apologize but I've been worried. Now please advise me of *my* aunt's condition."

"She had another heart attack, mild though. Not as bad as the first." Becky crossed her arms. "There doesn't seem to be much damage. They're still running tests."

"But clearly it's time she moves. She needs more support, more of a buffer. I assume selfishness about your job won't affect your professional opinion?" He raised an eyebrow.

She numbly shook her head.

"Good," he said. "Living in a large house, owning a stable of racehorses, simply has too many inherent risks. She can't deal with much shock, and it's best she move. I'm glad we agree on that. I'll talk to Mr. Anders or that other man, Slim, about the fastest way to dispose of the animals."

"Slim's dead," Becky said dully. "And we're not doing anything until Martha makes the decision. After the doctors' input."

"Dead? What are you talking about?"

"I'm sorry." She softened her voice, surprised by Ted's reaction. "He died in a highway accident yesterday."

"When? After the races?"

"I'm not sure. The fact is, he died unnecessarily and people who cared for him, people like your aunt, are upset."

"Yes. Yes, of course. But why didn't someone tell me? And who's going to manage the place?" He pivoted and walked slowly down the corridor.

She pressed a hand against the wall, confused and exhausted. Ted seemed genuinely upset about Slim but less concerned about his aunt. A chill snaked down her back and she resolved never to leave him alone with Martha. It would be a simple matter to arrange for a cot. All she needed was to gather a few clothes. She'd call Jocelyn and have her pack a bag.

She pulled out her phone, spirits lifting when she saw Dino's text message: Hope Martha's okay. Will bring supper tonight.

He really was thoughtful, and it had been unfair to blame him for Slim's accident. He'd only been doing his job and had promoted Conrad Stables exactly as Martha and Malcolm had wished.

And bought his ranch in the process.

She shoved away that niggling thought, didn't want to let his bonus bother her. He'd never made a secret about his reasons for winning, and that single-minded determination was one of the reasons she loved him.

She loved him.

Despair swept her. That wasn't supposed to happen. Martha had warned he wasn't good husband material. And it was no secret he didn't want to get married again, that racing was the most important thing in his life.

He had changed though. Didn't flirt or look at other women. He'd been genuinely concerned about Martha too, was leaving Lone Star and driving back to the hospital tonight. Maybe he'd pick up her bag of clothes on the way.

Her despair mingled with optimism. She hoped he was here the next time Ted popped by—Dino was tough. He'd put Ted in his place. And she wanted to discuss Ted's odd reaction to the news of Slim's death. She pulled out her phone and pressed Dino's number, eager to hear his voice.

"Hello, Becky."

His voice was tight, so guarded she knew instantly something was wrong. Darn. She shouldn't have called him at the track where he was always busy. Should have sent a text message. Flustered, her words came in a rush. "Are you dropping by the hospital tonight?"

The taut silence made her heart crash. "Doesn't matter," she added, "but if you come, can you bring some clothes? Jocelyn will have a bag ready."

"Becky, I don't think—"

"It's okay. I know you're busy." Her knuckles whitened around the phone. This was her fault and she obviously was expecting more than he could give. "I'll find someone else. Good luck with the horses. Hope Echo is okay."

"This is a really bad time. There's some track officials here with me."

"No problem. See you later," she said brightly, determined to keep her dignity, desperate to cut the connection before he heard the crack in her voice.

CHAPTER THIRTY-FOUR

"Her biggest problem is apathy." The doctor paused, consulting Martha's chart before glancing at Becky. "She's only seventy-four. We just need something to keep her going. Any grandchildren expecting babies?"

Becky shook her head. "She only has one nephew, and he's not married."

"That won't work then." The doctor smiled boyishly, looking so young it was hard to believe he was in charge of Martha's wellbeing. "But anything that cranks her interest, makes her feel needed, would be beneficial. I'll talk to the family tonight."

He walked down the aisle, his head swiveling as Stephanie bounced past with an oversized shoulder bag and a graffiti-colored cast on her arm. Her perkiness drew a smile from the doctor and a disapproving frown from a slit-eyed nurse.

"Hey, girl. I have everything you need," Stephanie hollered, patting the overnight bag. "The housekeeper had it ready. She sent along some sandwiches too, just in case the food here sucks, which I already know it does."

"Great." Becky rushed toward Stephanie, relieved to see a familiar face. "And thanks for driving to Conrad's."

"No problem. I had to go there anyway and box up Slim's stuff. I'm moving in next week."

"What do you mean?"

Stephanie shrugged. "I thought Dino would have told you. He's letting me live there until the place is sold. Also paying me to oversee the gallops. All I have to do is look after Slim's cat."

Becky's stomach gave an odd kick. Dino hadn't forgotten Stephanie after all. And the arrangements made perfect sense. Slim's house was empty. Cody needed help. It would be foolish to hire someone to replace Slim when Conrad Racing was headed for the block. And it wasn't like Dino was sleeping with Stephanie, not any more. Still, he had time to do all the horse-related stuff, cat stuff too, but couldn't give her more than thirty seconds on the phone—

"What's wrong?" Stephanie tilted her head, staring with concerned eyes. "Did Martha take a bad turn?"

"Oh, no. She's stable. Just doesn't care about anything. The horses are the only thing that keeps her interest, but everyone says racing is too stressful. A catch twenty-two. I don't even know what's best anymore." Becky's lower lip quivered, and she clamped her mouth shut.

"Aw, sweetie." Stephanie thumped the bag on the floor and wrapped her in a hug. "There's nothing else you can do. Jocelyn and Ted already told me the place would be sold, along with all the horses. That Martha's giving up her home."

Stephanie's hug felt good and Becky didn't want to move but something nagged at her, and she stepped back, cocking her head. "When were you talking to Ted?"

"About an hour ago," Stephanie said. "He was in Slim's guesthouse when I arrived. Dropped by to pick up some horse papers." She scooped the bag up with her good arm, linking her other around Becky. "Now can I visit Martha? I'll tell her some horse stories from when Malcolm was racing, and you can relax and have a glass of Beaujolais. I always thought that housekeeper was kind of cold, but she did send some great wine."

"Morning, honey."

Becky squeezed her eyes shut, didn't want her dream to end. Dino's arms, his smell, his voice all seemed so real, and in the dream he didn't like Stephanie, the reporter, or any other woman. He only loved her.

"I love you too," she whispered, snuggling closer.

His arms stiffened, and the hospital cot suddenly turned confining. She jerked her eyes open. Dino's face, his real face, was only inches away, unreadable in the dark. Martha's shallow breathing huffed from the bed, muted chatter sounded from the hallway, but he was completely still.

"Oh, hi. I was dreaming of Martha," she whispered, happy he'd somehow shown up but afraid he'd heard her whispered confession. "What time is it?"

"Almost four. I have to go back to the track," he said. "You and Martha were both sleeping when I arrived. Sorry I was so late. I brought some food. The nurses offered to keep it in their private fridge."

"What time did you come?"

"Just after midnight. Got busy with a couple of unexpected...issues. What are the doctors saying?"

Becky checked Martha's sleeping form, keeping her voice low. "She shouldn't have much stress, but she needs to stay interested. People around, goals, things like that. Anything that makes her feel like she's contributing."

"Racing is too stressful?"

Becky nodded.

"What she really wants is to establish Malcolm's name," he said. "Bit of a dilemma."

She nodded again, lightened by his presence. Everything would be okay now. Martha always perked up with Dino; she still wore full makeup when he was around. Becky snuggled into his chest, absorbing the calm beat of his heart, her sense of security. He'd know what to do; he always fixed everything.

"I'm going to be busy at Lone Star," he said, "but call if you need me. Any time. And give Martha my best. We've already had some bloodstock agents express interest in her horses, so they shouldn't be hard to sell."

Her breath caught as she absorbed his blunt words. That was his fix? Put the horses on the market? Now that he'd earned his bonus, he was leaving? And while removing stressors was a good thing, it effectively stripped Martha of her sole interest in living.

Her breathing sounded loud, ragged even. But he'd already risen from the cot and was now only a dark silhouette. He was leaving without seeing Martha, without any mention of a return. But horses didn't exercise in the afternoon. Surely he'd find some time?

Although maybe she'd scared him with her declaration of love. Not fair. He'd caught her groggy with sleep when feelings always ran a little rampant. And she'd drank a lot of wine with Stephanie.

"See you later." He stooped over the bed, brushing her cheek with a chaste kiss.

"When?" *Shit.* Somehow that needy word just popped out. "Because Martha will have instructions for you soon," she added quickly. "You know, about the horses."

"All right." He tousled her hair and left.

"Asshole," she muttered, realizing he'd evaded her question.

"I heard that." Martha's voice was cranky with sleep. "And ladies shouldn't swear."

"Guess I'm not much of a lady."

"You seem to be enough for him."

"What do you mean?" Becky peered through the dark, in the direction of the prone form on the bed.

"He said you could call anytime." Martha's huff was definitely indignant. "He doesn't even let *me* call during training hours. Now go back to sleep. And tell your young man I don't appreciate being wakened at four in the morning. The next time he visits, it had better be daylight."

Becky shifted to the warm spot Dino had left, feeling slightly better. Martha was right. He had said she could call him anytime. That had to mean something.

God, she prayed it meant something.

"Those kind of flowers make me sneeze." Martha fluttered a dismissive hand at Ted. "You should know that. Your mother had the same allergy. Give them to the lady in the next room, the nice one with the scarf over her head."

"Okay," Ted said, his face turning so red Becky almost felt sorry for him.

He placed the flowers on the chair and clicked open his briefcase. "But first you need to sign some papers. I found a legitimate buyer for the estate. And we can instruct Mr. Anders to start immediate dispersal of the animals."

"Those *animals* are horses," Martha said, her tone petulant. "And my lawyer should be here. There are a few changes I need made to my will."

"Oh?" Ted looked at Martha, his lips tight. "I have a copy of the will you and Malcolm drew up last year. Seems up to date...what Uncle wanted."

"What Malcolm wanted was to be remembered as a horseman so perhaps I should keep racing, regardless of my health." Martha harrumphed. "It's difficult to decide."

"We'll lose this buyer if you keep waffling. Please think about it." Ted closed his briefcase, his frustrated gaze turning to Becky. "I seem to be the only one worrying about her long-term health." Grabbing the flowers, he stalked from the room.

"I know what Ted and the doctors think." Martha's voice turned pensive. "But I really don't know what to do."

Becky dragged her chair closer to the bed. "You don't have to decide today."

"I want to keep racing, but Dino will be far away and hiring two new managers is daunting. I simply don't have the energy." She squeezed her eyes shut, her words a faint whisper. "I'm sorry to disappoint you, Malcolm."

Becky's throat thickened. If only Dino could be more helpful. "Malcolm only wanted you happy," she said. "He wouldn't want you racing if it wasn't healthy."

"Probably not." Martha gave a glimmer of a smile. "But he was a man. And men crave recognition. It's a rare one who will step back from the limelight."

Malcolm is dead. His ego doesn't matter. But she didn't want to burst Martha's bubble of interest so she sat beside her in companionable silence, holding her thin hand.

Dino scowled, snapped his phone shut and looked at Shane. "Bill Taylor's moving his horses to another trainer. He heard about the steroids. Says he'll be back after the dust settles."

"Doesn't seem fair, boss." Shane stepped closer to the desk, his face troubled. "Anyone could have stuck those steroids in our fridge."

Not anyone. Slim. Dino dragged a hand over his jaw. "But I'm the trainer on record. And that's the way this business works. Shit has to stop somewhere."

Dino shoved a pile of invoices aside. It'd be good to get away and race in South Texas. He could train some horses at his ranch, cut down on costs, buy a few claimers. Reduce his dependency on fickle owners who yanked their horses at the very worst time.

Even dealing with Martha—one of the best owners in the business—was frustrating. One day she talked of selling, the next she wanted to finish the season. Enough to give a man ulcers. At least she'd helped him earn his ranch, and for that he'd always be grateful. And for meeting Becky, that was another good thing.

"Hey, Dino." Jimmy Jones paused in the doorway, twirling his aluminum cane. "Just wanted to thank you again. That Chippy is a real nice horse. Feeling good too. Even bucked a bit this morning."

"Jesus, Jimmy." Dino jerked forward. The last thing he wanted was for the jock to hurt himself. "You're only supposed to be trotting. Your leg—"

"Is perfect." Jimmy gestured with shades of his former cockiness. "Hell, I'm soon ready to win races again. Body is strengthening. Just getting out in the fresh air with the horses is good."

Jimmy did look well. He no longer leaned on his cane but instead waved it in the air as he regaled Shane and Dino with Chippy's latest antics. "Yeah, well, thanks again," he said as he pumped Dino's hand. "I was dying cut off from the track. The worst thing about getting hurt is giving up the horse life."

He limped from the room and yelled a ribald comment to someone in the aisle.

Shane waited a moment then glanced at Dino. "Kinda puts a warm, fuzzy feeling in your gut, don't it, boss? Like a long drink of good whisky."

"Yeah, it kinda does." Dino smiled, feeling more content than he had in days. "Gotta thank Becky for that one. I wouldn't even have thought of Chippy."

"Some folks are good about thinking of other people," Shane said.

"Yeah." Dino shifted uncomfortably. He hadn't called her today, but she hadn't called him either. Hadn't even sent a text.

"She moving to your ranch?"

His head shot up. "Who? Becky?"

"That's who we're talking about, isn't it?" Shane gave a crooked grin. "Just want you to know I'd be happy if she doesn't. After the Conrad horses are gone, guess there's no reason I can't call her. Providing that's okay with you, of course."

"Don't push it," Dino said.

Shane just adjusted his hat and sauntered from the office.

Cocky sonofabitch. Dino scowled at the empty doorway then at his silent phone. Maybe he *could* mention his ranch. See what she thought about living a stone's throw from the Mexican border. Hell, all she could do was say no. He didn't know if she'd leave Martha, but for damn sure he didn't want her leaving him.

The phone buzzed and he smiled. Must be Becky. No one else would dare call him in the morning. But it wasn't Becky; the display showed the Lone Star Race Office.

He answered with a sense of resignation. A call from a steward was generally a pain in the ass but they were vital for enforcing Racing Commission rules.

"Dino Anders?" a vaguely familiar voice said.

"Yeah."

"This is Brandon Emeneau." The man cleared his throat. "I'm calling to advise of a drug violation. Echo Beach tested positive for Winstrol. She'll be disqualified from her most recent win. We're also handing down a twenty-five-hundred dollar fine and a six-month suspension. You have the right to file an appeal within three days."

Dino rose so fast his chair slammed the wall. "You're fucking kidding!"

"Sorry," the steward said. "I'm not."

"That slop is appalling." Martha knocked the spoon away, spilling chicken soup over Becky's wrist. "I'm not hungry anyway."

The nurse checked the gauge, frowning. "Mrs. Conrad, your blood pressure is very high. Try to relax."

"If I relaxed any more, I'd be dead. For goodness sakes, I just want to go home."

"Your nephew is here," the nurse's tone turned soothing, "talking to the doctor about that very thing. Meanwhile, I'll try to find a different meal." She gave Becky a tight smile and swept from the room.

"Where's the food your young man left?" Martha asked. "I bet those nurses ate it. Dino said it was in their fridge."

Yes. But he'd brought chicken fried steak. Hardly the best food for Martha. "I'll check out the restaurant across the street," Becky said soothingly. "What would you like?"

"Never mind." Martha shook her head in irritation. "Call Dino and tell him to bring me some fresh peaches. Ripe ones. I don't like them hard."

"I'll get them for you," Becky said. "No need to call him."

"He's my trainer. Call him now."

Becky crossed her arms. Buying peaches was hardly in Dino's job description and besides, he hadn't called her all day. Obviously she'd spooked him with her rash admission of love. "I don't want to call him," she said.

Martha settled against her pillow, scowling. "You two need to sort this out, and I prefer it happen while I'm still breathing."

"Sort what out?"

"Just because a room is dark doesn't mean I can't hear. Besides, I warned you not to fall in love." Martha sniffed. "He obviously cares for you, but can you be happy with a man who puts his career first?"

Becky crossed the room and stared blindly out the window as honking traffic bottlenecked at the busy intersection below. *Maybe.*

"You wouldn't, dear," Martha went on, as though reading her mind. "You have so much love to give. You deserve it in return."

"Doesn't matter." Becky's knuckles whitened around the window sill. "He's moving anyway."

"What about you? It's not much of a life, stuck in a lonely house with a cranky old woman. But I like people around, and I'm too selfish to give you up."

"Oh, Martha." Becky circled the bed and kissed her lined cheek. "I'm not leaving you."

"Promise?"

"I promise."

"Maybe I'll try to live to a bit longer then," Martha said.

They both turned at the sound of measured footsteps. The doctor entered, followed by a solemn-faced Ted.

"Well, Mrs. Conrad," the doctor said, "I hear you own many exciting racehorses."

"That's correct. My husband bred them."

"Not the usual hobby for my patients. What about knitting? That's excellent for arthritic fingers."

Ted's head bobbed in agreement, but Becky crossed her arms. "She doesn't knit, and she doesn't watch races either, Doctor. So the excitement can be kept to a manageable level."

"Oh, so it's not stressful then? I thought it was." He frowned at Ted. "Fine. Well, a calm environment is what you need. And of course, anything you enjoy is beneficial. There are several excellent retirement homes that could be considered. In the meantime, we'll get your blood pressure down to an acceptable level."

"When can I go home?" Martha asked.

"If all goes well, by the end of the week."

Wonderful, Becky thought. This doctor was sensible. A calm environment with horses. They could do that. She peeked at Ted, knowing he'd be displeased. However, his expression surprised her. Not anger or frustration but something very much like satisfaction.

Ted politely pulled out a chair in the hospital cafeteria, waiting for Becky to sit. *Maybe I've misjudged him?* She lowered herself on the seat. He was arrogant, selfish and unpleasant, but today he seemed to care about Martha's health. Seemed content with the doctor's suggestions.

It was ridiculous to harbor an aversion. Even though his eyes were the same color as Creepy Craig's, she'd never had the sense that he viewed her as a woman. He was almost asexual—unlike Dino, who exuded such raw masculinity it made her reel.

Dino would be happy to hear the news. He'd be able to race Hunter and Echo on the circuit, so would have two good stakes horses. Even though his ranch was in the south, he'd have to call and report race results, maybe visit every six weeks when he picked up horses.

Every six weeks. Her heart cracked.

"As long as there's no stress," Ted said.

She forced her thoughts off Dino, trying to concentrate on the conversation. "That's right," she said. "As long as Martha doesn't attend the races, there's not much associated stress. She really wants to continue for Malcolm."

"Yes, good old Malcolm." Ted's voice hardened. "This is entirely his fault."

"What do you mean?"

Ted gave a negligible shrug, but his expression hardened. "As her executor, I wonder if Martha's signed a living will. Perhaps that's why she's making noises about seeing her lawyer."

Becky inched her chair back, suddenly needing more breathing room. "Martha doesn't 'make noises.' Her lawyer is coming on Thursday."

"That's quick." His nostrils flared.

"You're the one who keeps reminding her she's fragile. Guess she wants to make sure everything is finalized."

"Do you know what changes she's making?" He studied her over steepled fingers. "I'm confident you're too ethical to accept a horse. It wouldn't be appropriate."

Becky nodded. Much as she would love to keep Lyric, she couldn't afford to own the cantankerous mare. Lyric was a high-maintenance horse and not the safest animal to handle. Still, you couldn't choose the horses you fell in love with—much like men.

"And of course Martha should respect Malcolm's wishes," Ted added. "After all, *he* never wanted to give you a horse."

Becky squeezed her eyes shut, gathering her patience. Now she realized what this meeting was about. Ted hated losing a few bucks from a billion dollar estate. It must have been Martha's little joke about giving away Lyric that had spurred this private conversation. What an ass.

"And of course you'll return the necklace," Ted went on.

Her hand swept to her bare neck. The necklace was in her suitcase, but she wanted to keep it, along with the memories. "It's just a copy, Ted," she said wearily. "The real one is in Martha's jewelry box. I'll pay you for the cost if that makes you happy."

"It's not a copy. I asked Jocelyn for all the bills over the last three months. Martha never had a copy made. And someone like you shouldn't waltz away with a family heirloom."

Becky gulped. She'd been wearing Martha's prized necklace in the barn? Frolicking in the hay? At the track? She might have lost it. The clasp could have broken; someone could have ripped it off her neck. Her pulse pounded so furiously the wave of dizziness left her unbalanced.

Ted mistook her silence. "If you refuse, I'll have Martha declared incompetent."

"She's not incompetent!"

"But she'd hate the scandal. The stress alone might kill her. And we don't want that, do we?" He patted her hand and rose. "Don't worry. I know you'll do the right thing."

Becky jerked back, revolted by his touch, but he'd already turned away and headed for the door. Greed. The man was consumed with it. He had a wonderful aunt to share his life with, yet chose to count down her days on a calendar. How sick.

Well, she'd certainly return the necklace, but she was also going to make sure Martha lived another decade. No stress, no troubles, only love and smiles. And if Ted made Martha's blood pressure leap, she'd keep him away too.

She rummaged through her purse, searching for her phone. She needed someone to talk to and despite Dino's preoccupation with his own affairs, he was always the voice of reason.

Ring, ring, ring. She checked her watch. Two p.m. He could be at his apartment, could be at Conrad's. Could be anywhere. She hadn't talked to him today, not since he left the hospital room early this morning...not since she'd admitted she loved him.

"Yeah," he finally answered after seven rings.

"Hi." Her relief was so great, her voice cracked. "It's Becky."

"I know."

Of course he knew. Her number would be displayed, but she'd hoped for a warmer reception. He sounded gruff, grumpy, slurred.

"When are you coming?" She glanced around the cafeteria as people streamed in and out, pushing trays and looking solemn. She wished he were here now.

"I'm not."

She paused. "You're not coming to the hospital today?"

"How's Martha?" he asked abruptly.

"She's doing well. And there's some good news. Looks like she'll keep all the horses, at least until the fall. So you'll have the stakes horses to race at Retama. Isn't that great!"

He was silent for so long, her fingers twisted, digging her nails painfully into her palm. Silence wasn't the reaction she'd expected.

"Have to see her...explain."

"Explain what?" she asked.

"We'll talk tomorrow." The phone went dead.

She blinked in disbelief. Had he hung up? Yes, it was definitely dead air. She closed her phone, dropped it in her purse, and struggled to act normal. But something pricked at the back of her eyes and rapid swallowing didn't stop the convulsive tightening of her throat.

What had she done? Obviously he was spooked. Wasn't even visiting the hospital. And there was so much to tell—about Martha, about Ted, about the horses.

She dropped her head in her hands, regretting those impulsive words whispered in the dark. Wished she could pull them back, wished he wasn't quite so selfish, but most of all wished she didn't feel so achingly alone.

CHAPTER THIRTY-FIVE

Dino pried his eyes open, squinting at the harsh sun slanting through the window. Goddammit. He was lying on the clammy kitchen floor. His head hurt and his boots were still on. He shuffled to his feet, groaning, and averted his gaze from the two empty whiskey bottles.

Didn't want to think about yesterday. *Fuck, fuck, fuck.* Disqualified for steroids. No win, no bonus, no ranch. Couldn't even train with a six-month suspension.

He'd appeal. Had to try. If he could prove Slim had been a disgruntled employee, the Racing Commission might reverse the ruling. There'd already been a sponging incident. Any idiot should know a trainer wouldn't sponge his own horse. Unfortunately the legal process was lengthy, and there was no way Laura would wait for him to raise the money. His home was history.

He shuffled to the shower, still cursing. Stood under hot, pulsing water until his head marginally cleared and coherent thought returned. Slim had to have been responsible but why? Maybe Becky would have some insight. She was observant and smart. Loyal as hell.

Plenty of witnesses would testify Slim had been acting weird. No solid proof of sabotage—eating carrots slowly wouldn't count, but surely there was enough for a workable defense. It wouldn't help get his ranch though. He flexed his knuckles, fighting the urge to drive his fist through the wall. Dammit.

He yanked on some clean clothes and powered up his laptop. Scanned the recent rulings, stewards' decisions and appeal process. Fucking depressing that they could strip away his livelihood, bang, just like that. And the repercussions to employees, to staff, to owners.

Aw shit, Martha. He squeezed his eyes shut then checked his watch. Seven a.m. He'd have to break the news to her. Call Shane. Explain to his staff. Hopefully Stephanie was in the barn. If not, he'd call on the way to the hospital. He rubbed his forehead, feeling a rush of shame and wishing his brain were clearer.

Considering Martha's fragile state, it might be best to follow Becky's need-to-know policy and keep the drug charge secret. Save her some heartache. Best to talk to Becky first. She'd know what was best.

He exited the Racing Commission website with its onerous list of sanctions, penalties and fines and flipped to the surveillance cam. Stephanie wasn't in the aisle, and the only activity was Lyric nosing at her stall lock, trying to figure a way to escape. He didn't want to wait for Stephanie. His career was crashing and the only person he needed to see—the only person he wanted—was Becky.

"You look tired this morning. I should send you home for a good night's sleep, but it's nice to have you here. Besides, I've always been rather selfish."

Becky forced a smile, cutting the peach into bite-sized pieces. Dino was the selfish one, and her despair welled. If only she didn't love him, if only she hadn't told him she loved him…if only he cared. She glanced at Martha, guiltily realizing she hadn't been listening.

"I never really worried about people, not like Malcolm. At least I helped cement his legacy. Do you think that's enough?" Martha's voice turned pensive, and her gaze settled on her bible.

"Oh, Martha. You're a wonderful lady. You don't have to suddenly worry about pleasing God."

"Easy for you to say. You're young and healthy." Martha's eyes narrowed. "You're not going to run off with Dino and leave me, are you? Remember your promise?"

"He doesn't want me anyway." Becky's voice sounded oddly tight.

"I'm sorry, dear. Very sorry."

"Nothing to be sorry about. He only worries about himself." Becky firmed her voice. "He's a good trainer but definitely not someone I could ever love."

"Definitely not," Martha said dryly.

"I mean it. He's good with the horses. But that's it."

"Yes, of course," Martha said. "Although a handsome trainer is preferable to an ugly one. The win pictures are much nicer."

Becky choked on a blend of amusement and despair.

"And Dino did what he was hired for," Martha went on. "Echo tied a track record. The race world will remember Malcolm Conrad."

"Indeed they will." Ted's voice sounded behind them, his steps forceful.

Becky swung around, instinctively moving in front of the bed, not trusting his aggressive walk or the way he brandished a sheet of paper.

"It's too early for visitors," she said. "Martha hasn't finished breakfast yet."

"She seems to have time for racing news though," he said. "And this is an online version, hot off the press. But perhaps you'd like to see it first, Nurse Becky." He shoved the paper in her hand, standing so close his stale coffee breath fanned her face.

An excerpt from *Racing Daily*. She stared uncomprehendingly at the article: "The Miracle of Steroids" by Danielle Whitlock. Danielle's face was grainy, but the words below her picture were clear.

> *When a trainer consistently achieves a high win percentage, racing fans take notice. But after Echo Beach, trained by Dino Anders, scored a scintillating victory at Lone Star Park, stewards also noticed. The result—a positive test for steroids, which results in disqualification of the horse, trainer suspension and a punitive fine.*
>
> *Insiders whisper that Anders has mastered the art of chemical warfare and relies extensively on illegal drugs to propel his horses to the front of the pack. Conrad Racing Stables, the owner of Echo Beach, is*

*his latest partner in crime and it's understandable now why Conrad
horses improved significantly under Anders' tutelage. Unfortunately,
honest trainers have little chance of beating an injected horse, and this
most recent violation corrodes the integrity of American racing.*

*Despite the steroid ban and stringent testing, some people crave a
win at any cost, which casts a blight on the race world. Fortunately for
horse lovers, this time the cheaters were caught.*

The paper slipped from Becky's stiff fingers. Ted bent and
scooped it off the floor. "No problem," he said. "I'll read it
aloud."

"No!" But her protest emerged as a cracked whisper.

"What is it?" Martha propped her arm on the pillow, staring
first at Becky, then at Ted.

"Only that your overpaid trainer spends more time trying to
beat a drug test than he does with honest methods. And he was
caught." Ted's mouth tightened. "The Conrad name has been
dragged through the mud. So much for Uncle Malcolm's legacy.
What do you suppose this will do for our prices?"

Martha stared at the paper in Ted's hand, her color fading to
a sickly white. A trolley squeaked down the hall and a nurse
giggled, but there was no sound in the room.

Becky couldn't move. Tried to speak but no words came out.
And there was nothing to say. *Dino had failed a drug test.* He'd said
he'd do anything to win, do anything to buy back his ranch, but
she'd never imagined he'd cheat. Never imagined he'd jeopardize
Martha's health, smearing her horses and stable in the process.

But she remembered how easily Echo had trounced the
competition, remembered his unusual confidence. She should
have suspected something was wrong. Her stomach twisted.
They'd even celebrated afterwards—celebrated Echo's win,
Conrad success, Dino's bonus. Now in a single stroke, he'd
shattered everything. "How could he?"

She didn't realize she'd voiced her anguish until Ted turned,
his voice bitter. "You never know what lengths people will go.
But the stewards will punish Mr. Anders. His career is finished.
No reputable owners will send horses to him. I know this is
upsetting but racing has too many variables for someone in
fragile health to be involved." He glanced from Becky to Martha

and back to Becky. "I'm sure you agree the horses and estate should be sold, and Martha moved to a more controlled environment."

His voice faded to an incomprehensible drone. Becky could see his face, his moving mouth, but was incapable of coherent thought. This couldn't be blamed on Slim. Echo had been under a tight watch. But maybe, just maybe, Dino hadn't known. Maybe he had an excuse. "Has...the trainer seen this?" she asked, clinging to a kernel of hope.

"Of course. The stewards give notice before publication."

She swallowed convulsively but couldn't seem to get enough air. *He'd known yesterday.* That's why he'd stayed away. They had to find out through a sleazy paper from a sleazy article written by a sleazy reporter.

Part of her wanted to punch Danielle. The woman was jealous, vindictive and obviously didn't take rejection well. Becky even understood some of the woman's pain. This last betrayal shredded her own heart and oh God, she should be worrying about Martha right now.

She rushed to her side.

"It's over then." Martha's voice wobbled. "I don't have the time or energy to fight a steroid scandal."

"Of course not." Ted inched closer to the bed.

Becky glared, refusing to step back. He might be acting solicitous now, but he should have known better than to blindside her with such devastating news. It was lucky Martha hadn't suffered another heart attack. What a prick. She wanted to boot him out the door.

"I'm very tired." Martha squeezed her eyes shut, her face a mask of despair. "I want to talk to Dino at some point. And, Ted, call that real estate agent. But right now I want to be alone. Please, I just want to sleep." Her eyes closed.

Becky frantically grabbed her wrist. "Pulse is f-fine." She glanced at Ted, her words tripping in relief.

Ted exhaled and walked across the room, motioning her to follow. He waited by the door, his expression grave. "We have to safeguard her health. Best we don't bother her with many details. The horses will be sold, and I have a buyer for the property. Pick out a few things from her room that she'd want transferred to the new facility. I think a month's severance will give you plenty of time to find another job."

She just stared, unable to speak, unable to fathom life without Martha. Not seeing her every day, not hearing her suggestions, her criticism, her advice. She knew this day would come, thought she was prepared, but the reality was staggering.

Ted shoved a set of keys into her hand. "I arranged for one of Martha's cars to be delivered to the hospital. You can drive over to Autumn Acres and check out her apartment. Tomorrow you can take care of your own packing. Jocelyn has given me a detailed inventory of Martha's valuables, so I know everything will remain intact." His gaze flickered over her neck. "Including the pearls. You must return the necklace. It's only ethical."

Becky stared mutely.

"Martha should decide that." Dino's deep voice sounded behind them. "It's only *ethical*."

She twisted. Dino propped a big arm against the wall above her head. Didn't look at her but instead stared so coldly at Ted, he looked almost unfamiliar.

"That's rich." Ted's sneer remained but he edged back a step. "You're not in any position to be talking ethics. Did you think the steroids wouldn't be discovered?"

Dino dismissed Ted, his expression shuttering as he turned to Becky. "I'm sorry. I'd hoped to tell you myself."

She could feel his shame but was shocked at his words. As if announcing it himself would make everything all right. "How could you d-do that?" she asked. "How could you crush everything she ever worked for?"

"Becky, I'm not responsible for this." He crossed his arms. "And it doesn't only impact Martha. My career is crushed too."

"It's always about you, isn't it. Your career. You hurt Martha so badly." Her own eyes itched and she swiped them, annoyed to feel hot tears. She needed to escape, needed to go somewhere and cry. Away from Dino, away from the hospital, away from the world.

Ted cupped her elbow and urged her down the hallway and for once she was grateful for his presence. "Come with me," he said, almost gently. "I'll show you where the car is parked."

Dino stared at his office wall, ignoring the insistent vibrating of his phone. The lawyer again, and there wasn't a damn thing left to say. Echo's disqualification stripped him of his win, his bonus, his ranch. Worse, he felt like scum. The way Becky had looked at him, the hurt and betrayal in her eyes, had cut him far worse than Laura's cheating ever had.

He reached for the coffee mug, surprised to see his hand shook. But hell, she must know he'd never do that. He cared for her, dammit, wanted to make her happy. And now she'd just lost her job, her home and Martha. Everything she'd ever loved—and blamed him.

Unfortunately he had nothing to offer in their place. Just another unemployed trainer with piss-poor prospects.

"Hey, boss." Stephanie poked her head around the door, her eyes grave. "Shane called. That Kentucky agent firmed his offer on a couple horses. Can have a trailer come by in the morning."

Dino sighed and leaned back in his chair. Already the news was flying. "Which horses?"

"Hunter and Lyric."

Lyric. Ted wanted the animals disbursed quickly but dammit, he needed to get some pictures of Lyric for Jill, and Becky probably wanted a last ride. He dragged a hand over his jaw, remembering her smile when she was around Lyric. The mare was cranky and opinionated, probably too intelligent for her own good, but she made Becky happy.

"We'll hold off on Lyric," he said. "Hunter can go if the price is right."

"Really?" Stephanie tilted her head. "That doesn't make sense. I thought you'd try to keep Hunter, not Lyric, a mare that doesn't even race. Aren't you going to fight the suspension?"

"No grounds. Echo was in my care, and Slim is dead. Trainer is always responsible."

"Well that sucks," she said.

"Just tell Shane that Martha's nephew wants the horses gone within the next thirty days. But I'm keeping Lyric around until the end."

Stephanie dropped into a chair, scratching absently at the skin beneath her cast. "Where will you go?"

"Guess my apartment by Lone Star."

"But you won't be able to go to any public track. Not for six months. You can't train. Can't even talk to Shane." She paused, hit with the significance of the ban. "Are you going to be okay?"

"Sure." But the word sounded rusty. He cleared his throat. "Don't worry. I'll try to find jobs for you and Cody and the rest. By the time your wrist is healed, I'll have something for you."

"But what about *you*? And your reputation? It'll be hard to get good horses, hard to find owners—" She must have seen the despair in his face and snapped her mouth shut. "You'll find something," she said quickly. "And I'm glad Martha is okay. Can't imagine her in a seniors' home, but I'm sure it'll be fancy with top-notch care." Her eyes widened. "Oh, hell! What about Becky? She won't have a job, and Martha means the world to her. She must be devastated."

Dino gripped his coffee mug, fighting another rush of pain. "Probably she's a little upset," he drawled. "Just like everyone else."

"Don't pretend you don't care. I know you better than that."

Liquid sloshed the side of the cup, splashing his desk. "She thinks I'm selfish." He blotted at the spill. "That I used steroids. Forced Martha to a nursing home. I'm not one of her favorite people. Not now."

"Don't be ridiculous," Stephanie said. "This is Becky we're talking about, not your ex-wife. Becky's as loyal as they come. She might be a little upset, but she still cares. My God, look how she feels about that battle-ax Martha."

"I could never make her happy."

"What a cop-out. Women always love you. Your ego doesn't need stroking." She rolled her eyes and stood up. "Becky's solid. I'm going over to watch the new gallop girl. It's been weeks since I've been around a horse and I miss them. Thanks for the cat food."

"Wait. Did she ever talk to you?" But Stephanie strode out the door.

He rubbed his temple. No time to brood anyway. He had plenty to do. Evaluate Martha's horses, figure a way to keep his business afloat, tell Laura the deal was dead. But he wished he'd talked to Becky about moving south—should have brought it up days ago—back when he thought he might own a ranch.

Now he had nothing. And now she thought him a scumbag.

But only yesterday morning she'd said she loved him. Yesterday morning when he'd pretended not to hear. He should have jumped on it then, but he'd been stunned. Hadn't been ready. Like when someone drops an unexpected gift in your hands, and you can only stare.

And how could she still love him if she thought him so selfish? Of course, Martha was selfish too, and she still loved Martha.

Martha hadn't been caught doping horses.

Goddammit, this was stupid. He shook his head and yanked open his drawer. Everything he'd ever worked for was at risk, and there was no time to agonize over a woman. He grabbed his cumbersome stack of Stewards' rulings and Racing Commission announcements. Laboratory tests were sometimes wrong. Maybe he could hire an independent lab and prove Echo's sample was contaminated.

A manila envelope slipped to the floor.

He scooped it up. His name was scrawled in black ink. Slim's writing. He ripped it open.

Can't do this any longer, Dino. The life insurance will look after Jilly better than I ever could. Didn't mean to hurt the horses, only wanted to scare Martha. Tell her I'm sorry. Echo was the only horse I ever injected. You always were fair, but Jilly's my daughter. I owe her.

He stared for a long moment, swallowed and lowered the letter. So it hadn't been an accident. Slim *had* committed suicide. Was responsible for the positive test, the sabotage, everything. A disgruntled ex-employee and the reason didn't even matter. Not anymore. Because now he had proof.

The stewards would review the evidence. If mitigating circumstances could be proven, he'd be back in business. No harm done. And if Echo's win was reinstated, he'd earn his bonus and be able to buy back the ranch.

He whooped and scrambled to his feet, pulling out his phone.

Call the lawyer first. Clinch the deal before Laura sold elsewhere—then ask Becky how she'd feel about moving. File an appeal before the end of the day and celebrate. Life was good again.

But not so good for Jill.

Aw, dammit. Comprehension struck, and he sank slowly back in his chair. Slim's insurance policy mirrored his, and one of the clauses exempted benefits for suicide. If the letter were made public, Jill would get nothing. Either Slim hadn't read the fine print or had trusted him to keep it secret.

Hell, Slim. You're asking way too much. He reached again for the phone, squeezing his eyes shut, blocking the image of Jill's trusting smile when she'd gifted him with the sketch of a lovingly drawn horse.

CHAPTER THIRTY-SIX

"I'm not hungry." Martha knocked Becky's hand away. "I wonder if the food is any better at the old people's home."

"It's not an old people's home," Ted said. "It's a very posh residence for seniors. Becky has checked out the property and agrees that it's very nice."

Becky silently removed the spoon and plate. The apartment was beautiful, the facility was beautiful, but it didn't have the things that gave Martha pleasure—the estate, horses, her nurse.

"There's a whirlpool and solarium as well as planned activities," Ted went on, "and without the stress of racing, you could live to be a hundred."

"God, I hope not," Martha said.

Becky wished Ted would just shut up. Reminding Martha she had to find new interests only made her grumpier and already her expression shuttered. She clearly wasn't listening to a word Ted was saying; in fact, she appeared deep in thought.

"You'll probably be able to move in by the end of the week."

"Oh, do stop prattling, Ted," Martha said. "I need to talk to Dino again. And I still haven't seen my lawyer."

"That's not necessary," Ted said. "I'll take care of everything for you."

"Did you talk to Dino this morning?" Becky asked. She knew Martha and Dino had talked several times on the phone—was surprised, in fact, that Martha wasn't more angry.

"Yes," Martha said. "He was here while you and Ted were visiting my new home. He left you flowers."

"You mean he left *you* flowers," Becky said.

"I mean he left us both flowers, carnations and roses." Martha gestured with a touch of impatience. "Are you deaf?"

Becky's traitorous heart leaped. She couldn't quite forgive Dino, wasn't yet ready to talk—but she couldn't stop loving him either. She bolted across the room and scanned the beautiful bouquets. He'd been selfish, disloyal, committed a crime *and* was moving out of her life, but she'd never received flowers before and if this was a goodbye gesture, it was only natural to take a closer look. Only natural to check the card.

"Yours are the red roses beside my carnations," Martha said, her voice surprisingly strong.

Ted still droned on about lawyers but Becky could only stare at the card. 'Love, Dino.'

Love? Heat warmed her chest at the sight of his bold writing. Of course, she knew it was just an expression, a common phrase. Didn't mean a thing. He probably wrote that whenever he sent flowers to women, but still, it was a nice gesture.

She checked Martha's colorful carnations—curious about the wording—but couldn't see a card.

"Dino said your phone's been turned off," Martha said, totally ignoring Ted. "He wants to talk to you."

Becky nodded. She wanted to talk to him too, eventually. Part of her even understood how passion for his ranch could push him to such desperate measures, but the toll it had taken on Martha was still too fresh. "When does he move to his ranch?" she asked, running a finger over a velvet rose petal.

"He won't." Martha sniffed with impatience. "Don't you understand what happens when a horse tests? Echo was disqualified. There's no winnings, no bonus, nothing."

"What?" She jerked around, forgetting the flowers and their confusing card.

"That's the way it is," Martha said. "Some trainers never rebound from the stigma. He'll be suspended too. Won't be able to train for at least six months."

"But that's horrible. Training is his life, all he cares about."

"He should have considered that before he drugged the horse," Ted said. "Before he dragged the Conrad name through the mud."

"Yes, he certainly didn't help Malcolm in that regard," Martha said but her voice was surprisingly level.

Becky stared, confused by her calm acceptance. Dino had lost his job, his ranch, his career, and thrust Conrad Stables into a steroid scandal. One mistake, one bad decision, but the consequences had been disastrous. Yet Martha didn't seem upset; in fact she looked almost smug, so different than yesterday when she'd been crushed.

Becky rounded the foot of the bed and checked the patient chart. Medications were unchanged. Nothing new prescribed. "You had a nice visit with Dino today?" she asked, studying Martha's face.

"Very nice." Martha's smile resembled that of a cat that had just licked a bowl of cream.

"I hope he left a list of horses," Ted said, seemingly oblivious to his aunt's bizarre mood. "We want to get top prices. Heard there was already an offer on two of them."

"That would be Lyric and Hunter," Martha said. "But I've decided to give all the horses to Becky."

"What!" Becky's and Ted's voices rose in unison. The chart dropped from her stunned fingers, clanking against the steel bed frame.

Not just Lyric but all the horses? Impossible. She'd love to keep Lyric but board was so high, and in a short month she wouldn't even have a job. Of course Hunter and others could win races and maybe make money, but then she'd need a trainer. And Dino was the only trainer she ever wanted.

Martha seemed to read her thoughts. "Dino won't be able to train for you, dear, but Shane will do a good job. He knows the animals and is already making plans to race at San Antonio. Lyric can stay where she is. She won't have to leave her stall."

"N-now wait a moment!" Ted was so shocked he could barely speak. "This is ridiculous. The property is being sold, and livestock is part of the property. Those animals aren't pets. Besides," he glanced pointedly at Becky, "your *nurse* is far too ethical to accept such a gift."

"Oh, it's not a gift." Martha's chest puffed, the way it always did before a big announcement. "Becky will be working with the Malcolm Conrad Rehab Center. If she wants to, of course."

"What the hell?"

Becky heard Ted swearing but couldn't look at him. Her legs wobbled, and she shuffled sideways and sunk into the nearest chair.

"Don't worry, Ted," Martha said dryly. "There's oodles of money left, and I've made provisions for you as well. You'll make an excellent administrator and can leave that hospital job you so despise. Of course, we'll need to find different horses, steady animals, to help with rehab. Horses like Chippy. Dino told me all about what it's done for Jimmy Jones.

"Yes, there'll be a place for everybody." Her face glowed as she propped herself higher in the bed, eyes sparkling with largesse, the true lady of the manor once more. "Bungalows will be built, and part of the house converted for high-need residents." She turned toward Becky, eyes sparkling. "Jill Barrett will be able to return to the horses she loves. Slim would like that, don't you think?"

Becky gripped the side of the chair, still trying to absorb Martha's vision. "But what about you?" she finally managed. "Will you like so many people around?"

"My dear, I'll never be lonely again. I can watch everyone progress and have permanent access to an onsite health team. Imagine. Injured riders will have a place to heal, a place in the country with fresh air and medical support, a place that will help them climb back into the saddle. We'll even install some of those sauna and infrared things." Her voice turned smug. "The race world will definitely remember Malcolm now."

"But..." Ted's face strobed with red.

"I know. It leaves me speechless too." Martha's eyes actually twinkled. "But it's not entirely my idea. Dino was instrumental. He spoke about Jill and Stephanie and Jimmy. How injured riders are stripped of a way of life when they most need the boost that horses can provide." She gestured at the table. "He left a picture Jill drew. It's clear she would thrive in a horse setting and since some other details came to light, I decided to help the people in this industry. Because I should. And because I can.

"My lawyer will help with legalities," she went on. "I don't know why Malcolm and I didn't think of this before. God knows we have way too much money."

Ted jerked out of the room.

Becky turned back to Martha, her heart drumming a staccato of hope. "So you're really not moving?"

"That's right, dear. I'm not moving. I'm going do something unselfish for a change. You can concentrate on which of your horses will stay at Conrad's and which ones will race. Do as little or as much nursing as you want."

Becky's mouth trembled. "I can't accept this."

"Nonsense." Martha waved a hand. "You're like my daughter. I'm only taking measures to ensure you stay. In fact, I'm going to build a house at the west end of the track so you'll never leave."

Becky could feel her shivers, heard her breath escaping in gasps. She was going to be able to stay with Martha. Have a real home and never move again. A place that would always need a nurse. A place with horses of all types, even grumpy gray ones. "So Shane will be the new trainer?" she managed.

"Only until Dino's suspension is over."

"You'd hire him again? After...after what he did?"

"After a positive test? Yes, of course. Always go for the best. And some other information has come up." She scowled. "But I don't want him stealing you away. Probably just as well he didn't get his ranch. He can't ask you to move away with him now."

Becky forced a weak smile. No need for Martha to worry about that. Dino preferred the single life, preferred to look after himself. He'd risked everything to buy his ranch, even Martha's reputation. "I'm surprised you'd take him back," she said slowly. "I'm still angry with him even though I—"

"Love him?" Martha interrupted.

She rose and walked to the window, pretending not to hear Martha's question. "Wow," she said, "we have a lot to do. Not even sure where to start."

"Dino will help. He can't set foot on a public track, not for six months."

Becky battled with mixed emotions. At least there'd be more time to enjoy his company, more time to enjoy his attention. She only prayed he wasn't completely crushed. Her mouth wobbled at the thought of him banned from the career he loved. He'd be miserable. And he'd wanted his ranch so badly. "Six months seems harsh. On top of the disqualification. Isn't there something we can do? I know he deserves it, still..." Her voice cracked.

"He doesn't deserve it at all," Martha said. "In fact, he's showing incredible selflessness. It was Slim who gave the steroids to Echo. Slim who planted them in the fridge."

Becky whirled from the window. "Slim *had* been acting odd. Dino wanted him gone but I didn't want you upset... Oh, no." She squeezed her eyes shut, swept with regret.

"It seems Slim had some twisted idea of revenge," Martha said. "He may have blamed Malcolm for Jill's accident. And he had access to all the horses."

"Then the steroids were my fault." Becky's voice dropped to a horrified whisper. "Dino wanted Slim off the property. Now he has nothing. And I blamed him. God, he must hate me."

"He doesn't hate you. Quite the opposite. In fact, he made his priorities clear. I remember when I first met Malcolm and the things he did for me—"

"What do you mean, made his priorities clear?"

Martha gestured for Becky to close the door. Her voice lowered. "Slim left a note admitting responsibility. If Dino showed it to the stewards, the charges against him would most certainly be dropped."

Becky thrust her fist in the air. "Then that's perfect!"

"But Slim's life insurance would be revoked."

"Oh, no." Becky's voice hushed, matching Martha's. "It was suicide? Everything Slim did was for Jill?"

"I didn't know he was so desperate. He didn't ask for help, and I never took the time to offer." Martha picked up a tissue and dabbed at her eyes. "I don't want Slim to carry the stain of suicide. And no one will ever know about the...other things. So Dino and I agreed to remain silent. And the note was destroyed."

"But that's not fair." Becky sagged against the bed. She could understand Martha feeling guilty but not Dino. "You can't ask him to give it all up—his ranch, training, reputation."

"It was his suggestion. Besides, everyone loves him. No one thinks he was responsible. They'll welcome him back with open arms. But right now other things are more important. He's very determined, much like Malcolm. Persuasive too." Martha sniffed. "Guess he's fine as your keeper man so long as you promise to stay close."

Becky's head pounded so hard she could barely hear, let alone think. She flattened both hands on the bed, trying to steady herself and her chaotic emotions. "I'm not sure he wants to be my keeper man," she finally managed. "He disappeared when I said I loved him. I called him selfish and wouldn't answer his calls. I let Slim stay. He probably hates me."

"Oh, I don't think he hates you. In fact, I seem to have a rival for your affections. He even asked your brand of shampoo. Luckily I remember things like that. The hair stylist with the tattoo sold—"

But Becky couldn't wait. She grabbed her purse and bolted toward the door. "I need to see him," she called over her shoulder. "Excuse me, Martha, but I really need to see him now."

"All right, dear." Martha's amused voice followed her down the hall. "But don't speed."

CHAPTER THIRTY-SEVEN

Gravel rattled beneath the Mercedes as Becky jerked the car to a disappointed halt. Dino's truck wasn't in the driveway, and his house squatted in the night, dark, silent and deserted.

She rushed up the steps and turned the handle. Unlocked. Pushed the door open and flipped on a light. His computer was gone but the phone was in the charger, and her breath oozed in relief. His cell was his lifeline. If he planned to sleep at his Lone Star apartment, he definitely would have taken his phone.

Remembering Martha's comment, she hurried down the hall to the bathroom. Opened the cupboard door and dropped to her knees, stunned at the sight. Familiar gold caps crowned every bottle of shampoo. *Her shampoo.* No other brands in sight. No magazines, no conditioners, no hair dryers. Not a remnant of another woman.

She stared through a blur of tears. Even if he couldn't speak the words, it was clear he was trying to say something. And this was more than enough.

Oh, God, Dino. You wonderful, generous, misjudged man.

Swiping her cheeks, she bounced into the living room. Circled in front of the darkened window, humming with happiness. Eager to hug him, to thank him, to apologize.

He probably hadn't gone far, maybe for something to eat. Or maybe he was at the house. She called Jocelyn.

The housekeeper answered on the first ring.

"Hi, Jocelyn," Becky said, breathless. "I'm looking for Dino. Is he there by any chance?"

"He was," Jocelyn said. "Where are you?"

"At his house. His phone is here so I knew he hadn't gone far."

"No, not far at all. Just a minute." Jocelyn's voice faded, her footsteps sounding as she walked down the hall. Muted conversation. Becky thought she heard Dino's voice and her heart did a funny dance of anticipation.

"He'll meet you at the barn," Jocelyn said abruptly.

"Okay, great," Becky said, hurrying to the door. "And thanks for sending that wine earlier. It was very thoughtful." But the housekeeper had already hung up.

She shrugged—Jocelyn was never one for small talk—jumped in her car and sped to the stable.

Not surprisingly, the parking lot was empty. It was hours past feeding time, and the barn was always deserted this time of night, a watchman no longer necessary after Slim's death.

She tapped her fingers on the steering wheel, studying Slim's guesthouse and the single porch light. Maybe Stephanie had already moved in. She could pop over and say hi but she wanted to be alone when she saw Dino. And she hadn't visited Lyric in almost a week.

She rummaged through her purse, searching for peppermints. Loose change, wallet, cell phone—nothing that would make a horse happy. She tossed her purse on the seat and headed into the barn. Lyric would just have to accept her empty handed.

Horses peered over doors, contentedly chewing hay, but Lyric stopped eating and swept to the front of her stall, surprising Becky with an affectionate nicker.

"Did you miss me, girl, or just hoping for mints?" She scratched Lyric's jaw, unable to believe this horse was really hers. *My horse.* So much had happened today but two things were clear: Dino cared for her and she owned a number of fine racehorses.

This was her first visit since turning into a genuine owner, and Lyric seemed to sense the gravity of the occasion. She pressed her head against Becky's chest before nuzzling at her pockets, still optimistic they weren't really empty.

"You're mine now, girl," Becky whispered. "And we can stay here forever. Thanks to dear old Martha." *And Dino.* She stepped into the stall and hugged Lyric's neck, overcome with gratitude. This was incredible. Dino was incredible.

She doubted she'd be gallant enough to make a similar sacrifice. The knowledge was humbling, leaving her with an aching need to apologize. She'd tried to convince herself he didn't care for people when in reality he was the nicest person she'd ever met—just as Martha had always said.

Something sounded outside, definitely not a diesel engine. She peered down the aisle but the dark entrance was empty, so she stepped back to Lyric's neck. Her mane was tangled and she ran her hands through the long hairs, concentrating on removing a stubborn knot.

"You're going to have such a good life, girl." Lyric's ear flicked as she stood rock still, listening to Becky's voice, seeming to enjoy the impromptu grooming. "Jill will feed you peppermints too and draw your picture. It's going to be so much fun." *As long as Dino stays around.* Oh, God, she prayed he'd stick around.

The mare suddenly jerked away, tossing her head and re-tangling the entire section of mane. Becky grimaced. Lyric would never be an easy horse. She stepped closer, trying once again to unravel the knot, but Lyric snaked her head and the rim of her eye flared a warning white.

Maybe she *was* a little dangerous; she certainly had strong opinions. Probably best to cut the tangles out, especially as Lyric no longer seemed tolerant of the grooming. Becky slipped her hand in her pocket, turned and jumped in shock.

Ted stared over the stall door, tall, silent, impassive.

"Hi, Ted. You scared me."

He didn't say a word, only looked at her with expressionless eyes.

"Did you come to see the horses?" She hated how her voice squeaked, but the way he stared was so weird. "This is Lyric, and Echo is in the next stall. Echo's the filly that was disqualified for steroids but she's fine now. No ill effects." She was babbling but couldn't shut up. Her legs and hands were stiff, and the only thing that seemed to work was her mouth. "Do you want to see Dino?" she squeaked, unable to look away from his eyes. "He'll be here in a minute."

"No, he won't. Jocelyn sent him to the hospital to meet you. Now come out of the stall."

Her nails dug into her palms. Tonight, more than ever, Ted reminded her of Craig—the amoral glitter of pale eyes, the cruel set of his mouth, the utter sense of ruthlessness.

"I n-need to finish grooming Lyric."

"Millions of dollars in horseflesh, and she gives it to you." His lips barely moved, taut with bottled rage. "You ruined everything. My plans. My life."

She swallowed, but her words came out scratchy. "Martha wants you to work here. Said she'd make provisions."

"Provisions! I'm sick of working." He shook his head so emphatically spittle flew threw the air. "This was supposed to be mine. I had a buyer. Surveys taken. Now it's going to the *cripples*. She'd never have conceived such a stupid idea without you."

Actually, it had been Dino. Generous, kind, compassionate Dino, whom she'd so badly misjudged. But it didn't seem a good time to debate the subject. Ted was in a foul mood, and her heart was pounding so hard she could barely breathe.

"And Slim. What a waste of money." Ted shook his head, seemed to be talking to himself.

Becky's entire body trembled now and she clung to Lyric's neck. *Please don't tell me this.* She opened and closed her mouth but nothing came out. "Let's go up to the house," she finally managed, "and join Jocelyn. We can talk there."

Ted's lip curled. "*She* wanted to do Martha first, not Malcolm. Should have listened." He reached in his pocket, held a needle and vial to the light and poured a clear liquid. "Potassium chloride. No one ever questions a heart attack. How much do you weigh?" He tilted his head, surveying her thoughtfully. "Cat got your tongue? Don't worry. It's painful but quick. And I promise to stay until it's over."

Terror crashed over her. Her legs would have buckled if she wasn't clinging to Lyric. "P-people will know. They'll tie you to Slim."

"Doubtful. I already checked his house. Nothing to link us. Now come on out." His voice turned high, almost singsong. "Or perhaps you'd rather I come in. That's all right too. Everything will work out just fine."

"But Martha—"

"Won't be a problem." He pushed open the door and stepped into the stall. "She'll be distraught by your death, of course. I expect she'll lose that newfound energy and kick off on her own. But if she doesn't..."

He laughed, an ugly, chilling laugh that made her gut spasm. She pressed against Lyric's side. The mare swished her tail, humping in protest.

Ted paused. "I hate horses."

Becky's breath came in painful gasps but she deliberately pressed Lyric's ticklish spot until the mare swung at the wooden wall with her hind foot. "Lyric doesn't like you either," she squeaked. "Better stay back."

Ted edged forward. "I don't like horses. Doesn't mean I don't know them. They're not dogs. They won't protect you."

A whimper caught in Becky's throat, and she pressed into Lyric's solid bulk. God, she wished Lyric *were* a dog. Dogs were loyal. Tough too. They'd fight when cornered, not cower like she always did.

"Come now." Ted smiled. "Jocelyn's waiting for me. We promise to take good care of Martha."

Becky twitched in horror. Martha wouldn't have a chance. She might be suspicious of Ted but never of Jocelyn. No one had even questioned Malcolm's death. Her hands fisted and she jerked forward, propelled by raw fear. "You bastards. Don't hurt her!" She kicked at his arm but he leaped sideways, the loaded needle safe in his hand.

He scowled, glancing around for a spot to place the needle. A sob caught in her throat. Soon he'd have two hands free. She wanted to rush past but her legs wobbled, and he was much too close to the door.

A couple feet. If only he'd move a couple feet. She squeezed her fists, trying to control her shaking. Maybe she'd be able to get him talking. Maybe even surprise him like she had Craig that day. *God, please help me.*

"How did you inject Malcolm?" Her voice was surprisingly steady considering her entire body trembled with an adrenaline shock.

"He was napping. Jocelyn let me in the back door." Ted shrugged, eying the narrow ledge by Lyric's bucket. "Had to do it that way. He was a tough man. He wouldn't have gone easy."

No, he wouldn't. And neither would she.

She slipped her hand in her pocket, fingering the knife Stephanie had given her, the tiny jackknife barely sharp enough to cut mane. It was so little. Ted was so tall. She stifled a sob, knowing there'd only be one chance, knowing she was fighting for her life—for Martha's life.

She backed against Lyric's flank, trying to control her trembles. Felt cold, awkward. It was hard to imagine fighting when she could barely stand. Lyric flattened her ears, and her breath leaked out in a ragged groan. The cranky horse beside her wasn't any help.

She slid the knife from her pocket, opening it with stiff fingers, trying not to fumble, trying to control her terror as Ted balanced the needle on the ledge.

It's not wide enough. The needle will fall in the straw. Please, God, make it fall. I don't want to die. I haven't apologized to Dino yet.

But the needle didn't fall.

He turned to her, eyes grim. She rushed around Lyric's rump, past the mare's irritated tail swish, racing for the door. He lunged like a snake, his cruel fingers biting her arm.

She stuck him with her knife.

"Bitch!" He stepped back against the wall, staring at the prick of red on his hand.

Lyric's ears shot forward, eyeing the open door. Becky's hope flared. She'd vaulted on Lyric's back once before. Maybe, just maybe, she could do it again.

Gulping for air, she charged forward, grabbed mane and tried to scramble onto the mare's back. Nearly made it but her right leg couldn't quite swing over. Shit. She wasn't going to make it. Lyric was simply too big.

God, please.

She clung to Lyric's side, consumed with despair. For her, for Martha, for Dino, her legs thumping futilely against the mare's flank.

Ted chuckled.

Thump! Lyric kicked out with both feet, cutting off his laugh. Her abrupt kick thrust Becky forward and onto her neck. She hesitated, giving Becky time to straddle her back then bolted through the open door.

Lyric's hooves clacked as she charged down the aisle, past wide-eyed horses staring from their stalls. She slipped once on the concrete, but gamely kept her feet. And then crisp night air slammed Becky's face.

Lyric swerved, heading toward the dark field. Becky squealed and slid sideways. She grabbed another hunk of blowing mane, not daring to look back. She couldn't fall off. Ted would be following, would hear the hooves and know their direction.

But Lyric's back was slippery—she bit back another cry as the mare leaped a ditch and then she simply blanked her mind and concentrated on riding.

Slowly she adapted to the horse's rhythm and Lyric's gallop didn't feel quite so frenzied, or the night so black. Maybe her eyes were accustomed to the dark. *Please stay dark. Please, so he can't see us.* But they were in an open field. Lyric was a beacon of white and already her arms and legs ached. If Lyric bucked or shied, she'd be on the ground. A sitting target.

"Good girl," she muttered, but wind pushed the words in her face. If Lyric would run up the hill, they could hide in the trees. And it would be easier to stay on going up the hill. Yes, they could do that. She stared at the dark ridge, willing Lyric to gallop in that direction.

But Lyric, ever perverse, veered to the right. Toward open ground and the rocky river. Oh, God, she'd never stay on over rough ground.

"No," she pleaded.

A vehicle roared behind her, and she whimpered in panic. She had to get the horse to change direction. She unwrapped a hand from her death grip on the mane and flashed it past Lyric's right eye, trying to flag her to the left. But Becky's balance was too precarious, and she slipped and had to grab mane again.

All right then. She set her jaw, staring through Lyric's pointed ears. Her only chance was to stay on the horse and make it past the river. Dino had said the riverbed was rocky. If it were too rough for a horse, surely it would be impassable for Ted's car?

We'll be okay, she thought, drawing comfort from the powerful horse beneath her. At least a renegade like Lyric wouldn't swing back to the barn. She actually seemed to be enjoying this unorthodox gallop. Her stride had steadied too, making it easier to balance, although Becky had no illusions about her riding ability. If the mare stumbled...

But Lyric wasn't going to stumble. She blocked any more thought of tripping, desperate to believe. Lyric hadn't faltered once since that slip in the aisle. She even seemed to be taking special care, and they were almost to the river. Almost safe.

Headlights cut the night, slashing the ground in front of them. She whimpered with fresh fear. Lyric's stride shortened, jerking her forward, and Becky's face smashed against the top of the horse's head. Pain ripped through her nose, and her breathing turned ragged.

They hit the rocky riverbed with a clatter of hooves. The water sprayed, numbingly cold. She slipped sideways but clung to Lyric's mane, desperately wrapping her legs around the mare's wet barrel. Lyric scrambled over a rock, leaped from the river to the opposite shore.

Becky's fragile grip snapped. She slammed into rock-hard ground.

Impossible to breathe. Her chest was on fire, mouth open, throat banded tight. Someone whimpered and she realized it was her. Then her breath returned in quick, aching gasps.

Oh, Christ. The engine had stopped, too close, lights blinding. She tried to crawl but there were no trees. Nowhere to go. She pressed into the grass, praying Ted wouldn't see her.

He was running. Feet pounded as he moved closer. *Splash!* Must be crossing the water now. Moving fast, very fast. She groped frantically for a rock but her nails only dug into dirt. Maybe he wouldn't see her. Or maybe she could blind him and then scratch his face. Do enough, at least, that Martha would suspect.

Warm breath snuffled against the back of her neck and she flinched. Shit. Lyric! White Lyric, marking her spot.

Becky muffled her frustrated sob as Lyric's muzzle pressed against her neck. Damn, crazy mare. Of all the nights for Lyric to demonstrate loyalty.

"Becky!"

Dino? Oh, God, it was Dino. Relief slammed her and she slumped against the ground, limp as a noodle. His frantic hands were on her. But he cursed and let go way too soon.

"Easy, Lyric," he said. "It's okay."

Typical, he was already checking the mare. But that was good. She could wait. Besides, Lyric deserved it. She swiped her nose, trying to see Dino, trying to see past Lyric's white bulk, but the mare wouldn't stand still.

"You okay, Becky?"

"Fine." But her voice cracked and she wanted him close. He'd dropped his arms so fast, almost as though he couldn't stand her touch. Clearly he hadn't forgiven her for the unfair accusations. She propped herself up on a painful elbow. "I'm so sorry about what I said. The things I thought. Martha told me about your idea for a rehab center."

She swiped at her nose again but couldn't see through the gloom. He seemed to be on the opposite side of Lyric but wasn't speaking. At least he'd come. But maybe he didn't even know about Ted? Maybe Ted was out there now, watching, sneaking around with that horrible needle. She twisted, frantically scanning the darkness.

"We have to look out for T-Ted. And Jocelyn. He tried to kill me. The way they k-killed Malcolm." She thought she was calm, but her voice shook and she crossed her arms, trying to control her shivers. "It was scary."

But Dino didn't move any closer, just continued circling on the other side of Lyric. Didn't rush to offer comfort. Even though she'd almost been killed.

She hiccupped, drawing her arms tighter around her chest while her breath leaked in a sob. "Lyric's fine. She helped me get away. I think she kicked Ted."

Becky stared at the shuffling pair. Dino didn't usually take *that* long to check a horse. Clearly, he wasn't going to help her stand. All right then. She'd do it herself. She cautiously stretched her arms, her legs.

"Don't move!" His voice was strangely hoarse.

He did sound worried, and she knew she shouldn't be jealous over a horse. He would always have his priorities, but she accepted that. She loved him anyway. "Lyric galloped over the rocks pretty fast but didn't stumble once," she said with a burst of pride. "She really helped me, even though it was by accident. I fell off on my own."

Dino grunted. She pushed herself to one knee, trying to stop her teeth from chattering. Even if he no longer cared, it would be nice if he'd wrap her in his arms, let her absorb some of his wonderful warmth. Maybe even lend his jacket. She peered hopefully through the gloom, trying to see if he even wore a jacket, but he remained on the other side of Lyric, even though they'd now shuffled a complete circle.

It seemed like ages since he'd driven up, yet he still hadn't bothered to come close. She thought he'd be a teensy bit worried, especially since he'd filled his bathroom with her shampoo. It had to mean he liked her a little. *And* she'd almost been killed. The memory of Ted's expression as he held the syringe tore a sob from her throat. She struggled to her feet, glanced over her shoulder, unable to control her convulsive shivers.

"Wait, Becky! Don't move. "

"I'm okay. Just c-cold."

"Goddammit, Lyric! I'm not going to hurt her." Dino's voice thickened with frustration and an emotion Becky couldn't place.

She balanced on shaky legs and understanding dawned. Lyric was keeping Dino away, ears flattened as she circled protectively around her fallen rider. "Wow," she whispered. "That is very cool."

"Maybe try walking toward me, honey. She already bit me twice."

"She bit you?" Becky couldn't flatten her smile. She'd seen mares protect their foals but had never expected behavior like this. Not from Lyric, not from the horse everyone called a bitch.

"Control your horse please, honey." Dino's voice thickened with frustration.

Still stunned, she grabbed a handful of grass and clucked. Lyric swung around, snatched the grass from her hand, and finally Dino's warm arms wrapped around her. She could feel his pounding heart, inhale his smell—savor his cocoon of warmness. Oh, God, she really was safe.

His sure hands moved over her, calmly, gently, in stark contrast to his rough voice. "Did that fucker hurt you?"

"No, we got away in time." She jerked in horror. "But we have to hurry. He might go after Martha. And Jocelyn is helping him."

"I know, honey. They're not going anywhere. I had my...moment with him. He said you stabbed him and a horse broke his ribs." Dino's voice hardened as he inspected his knuckles. "He was quite cooperative when I finished. The police are picking them up."

"He had a needle—"

"I know. Jocelyn said you wanted to meet me at the hospital. But I checked the nanny cam. Figured he'd been paying Slim. Came as fast as I could."

"He's crazy. He killed Malcolm." Shivering, she buried her head in Dino's shirt. God, he felt so warm. She never wanted to move, ever.

"Don't know how you got away—" His voice caught. "But thank God you did. Jesus, honey." He dipped his head in her hair, his arms so tight they hurt.

"I was afraid I wouldn't see you again," she whispered. "Wouldn't have a chance to apologize. I heard what you did for Slim. For Jill. And I'm sorry you won't get your ranch back. You're not selfish at all. I was just telling myself that so I wouldn't love you."

His big body stiffened as he studied her face. "And how did that work?" he drawled, his lazy voice at odds with the tension in his arms.

"Not very well," she admitted.

His smile started in his eyes then swept across his face and then she couldn't see any more because his mouth covered hers, kissing her like she'd never been kissed before, spilling out his emotion, his heart, his soul. He finally raised his head a notch. "I love you too, sweetheart."

Joy sputtered through her chest. She could only stare as emotion clogged her throat.

"And I intend to spend a lifetime proving it," he added, his voice husky. "Of course, I realize I'll have to share you with two others, but that's all right."

She tilted her head, studying his face, stripped of words. Martha and Dino were more than enough for any woman, and it was hard to comprehend this wonderful gift of love. A home, two people to love, so much more than she'd ever dreamed. More than she deserved. But share with *two* others?

Warm breath tickled the back of her neck, and she glanced over her shoulder. Understood then, the reason for his wry chuckle. Despite being free, Lyric hadn't wandered. Hadn't even tried to graze. She remained less than a foot away, a white sentry in the night, eyes wide and luminous as she watched over Becky.

***

Read Chapter One of BEV PETTERSEN's Next Novel

THOROUGHBREDS AND TRAILER TRASH

It wasn't really stealing. But Jenna fought a stab of guilt as she grabbed a bag of vitamins along with some horse dewormer. Wally had given permission—and a tiny pony didn't need much—but her compensation package was growing increasingly murky.

Her phone buzzed, a familiar Philadelphia number, and she silenced her conscience, loaded the precious supplements into her backpack and flipped open the phone. "Hi, Em," she said. "How are classes?"

"Great," Emily said. "Other than biology, the spring semester should be a cinch. But I need more money. When are you getting paid?"

"Today, I hope." Jenna kept her voice level, careful to hide her worry. "I'll transfer it as soon as I can."

"Thanks, sis. How's Peanut?"

"His hair is still falling out but good vitamins help." Jenna dropped a guilty glance on her backpack. "You should have seen him trot—"

"That's great. Give him a pat for me." Laughter bubbled in the background and Emily's words drifted. "Gotta go."

"Wait. When are you coming home?" But a harsh beep replaced her sister's voice, and Jenna closed her phone with a sigh. Be nice if Em would visit some weekend, although college courses were understandably consuming.

Wally Turner, manager of Three Brooks Equine Center, poked his balding head into the feed room, drawing back her attention. His voice lowered to a conspiratorial whisper. "Take some of that hoof supplement too. Consider it Sunday's pay. And drop by my office. You can pick up the rest of your overtime in cash."

She nodded with relief. Working for horse products was great, but with an ailing pony and Em away at school, cash was critical. "I'll be right along," she said. "This room is overdue for a cleaning."

"No worries. It's another week before they take over." But his smile looked strained, and it was clear he *was* worried. Little wonder. The Center had just gone through a messy buyout, and incoming owners had a history of ruthlessly culling management.

She swept the concrete floor, dumped the spoiled grain and debris into an overflowing trash bin, then detoured to pick up her pay. Thank God for Wally.

His door was closed when she arrived, his voice droning unintelligibly through the thin office wall. A shut door signaled stay out—Wally was anal about that—so she dropped her bulging pack on the floor and flexed her stiff shoulder.

Other than a hang-up about privacy, Wally was generally easy-going and it would be no problem to leave work early, send Em the money and still have time to massage Peanut. Of course, that was assuming her shoulder held up. Massage was physical work, doubly hard since she was trying to learn a more traditional technique. She'd borrowed a new library book on equine therapy, but was stuck on page thirty-eight and so far hadn't learned much. Her mom had taught her far more than anything ever printed in a book.

The aisle door slammed and a workman stalked in, dented hard hat clamped under his arm. The construction crew had been working non-stop, rushing to build a storage shed for the new owners, and occasionally they ducked into the air-conditioned Center to grab a drink from the pop machine. But this man didn't stop for a drink.

His stride was long and forceful. Metal-toed boots pounded the concrete then quieted on the rubber mats. Sweat-stained shirt, eyes as dark as his hair, and heading this way. She straightened, ready to defend her spot in line.

"Wally Turner in there?" Impatience roughened his words, and he barely looked at her. A bit of a surprise. Men were usually a sucker for long legs and blond hair, and often just a smile was enough to extricate her from a tight spot. A smile wasn't going to work with this man though. Clearly he liked to bulldoze.

"Yes." She squared her shoulders. "But I'm also waiting—"

His scowl jerked from Wally's door to her face, cutting off her words with the force of his displeasure. The female exercise riders had been detouring past the construction site all week, smiling and flirting with the crew, but it was doubtful they'd sent many jokes this guy's way. There was something hard about him, the same ruthless element that had emanated from her father's cellmates.

He dismissed her as though inconsequential, the muscles in his arm bunching as he reached for the door. However, she was accustomed to fighting for every little scrap and had certainly faced tougher men.

Lifting her chin, she squeezed between him and the door. "Sorry. You'll have to wait your turn."

The scowl deepened as he loomed above her, his annoyance mixed with the smell of freshly cut lumber, something piney that was actually quite pleasant. She was tall but he was taller and for an instant she was distracted by his big workman's body. Damn, she hated when that happened. She snapped her attention back to his face.

He frowned for a moment then something lightened and his lip twitched, a tiny movement, almost imperceptible, but enough to crack that ruthless expression. "Of course." He inclined his dark head and stepped back. "It wasn't my intention to butt in."

Sure it was. However, that glimmer of a smile made her soften. If he ever cut loose and actually grinned, he'd be devastatingly handsome. "I won't be long," she said.

"You hurt yourself on the job?"

He hadn't appeared to look at her earlier and she blinked at his question; no one had asked about her health since her mom died. "I'm fine. Sort of a chronic thing." She straightened her shoulder, hiding the discomfort. "And I won't be long with Wally. Just picking something up before I go."

"Leaving early?" He glanced at his watch, his flattened mouth wiping away any hint of previous amusement.

"Yes, but Wally doesn't mind."

"Nice of him."

His tone was definitely disapproving, and she crossed her arms. "Not much sense hanging around if the work's done."

"If it's done." He glanced at a wheelbarrow abandoned in the aisle, still brimming with manure. A blue pitchfork rested haphazardly against the wooden handles.

"That's not my job," she said, surprised by the defensiveness in her voice. "I'm the masseuse."

"A *masseuse?* Of course." His dark eyes flickered over her in a thoroughly masculine assessment, nothing lecherous, just simple approval that made her pulse kick. She swallowed, realizing she'd been very wrong. The gallop girls would definitely notice this guy.

"We're one of the top therapy centers in West Virginia. Massage, hydrotherapy and oxygen chambers…for horses," she added, just in case he was a bit dense. The gorgeous ones usually were. "Are you with the construction crew?"

"No."

"Looking for a job then?" she asked. "Because Three Brooks is a great place to work." She didn't usually babble, but his sparseness with words was rather unnerving. "Wally's nice, easy-going."

"Obviously." His gaze flickered down the dirty aisle.

Her mouth tightened with resentment. Wally wasn't the most organized manager, but he was a family friend and genuinely loved the horses. And while it was okay for her to criticize, it wasn't acceptable for outsiders.

This man reeked of disapproval and probably wouldn't be good with animals either. Compassion could usually be sensed, and there was nothing coming from him now but sheer, autocratic authority—something that always bugged her. Worse, he was a cold ass, and those were the most dangerous of men.

She hoped Wally didn't like him either. In fact, maybe she could help with that.

Beaming a magnanimous smile, she unzipped her pack and groped for her keys. "Since you're in such a rush, I'll let you go first. I should take this stuff to my car anyway. But don't wait by the door. Wally likes visitors to knock, then walk right in."

"Really?" His eyebrow arched and his gaze bore into her.

Clearly he wasn't quite as gullible as she'd hoped, and the force of those laser eyes sent her into an unexpected fumble. Her hand jerked, knocking her pack sideways, and company supplements scattered across the floor. *Shit.*

She rammed the plastic bags back into her pack, annoyed that her hand shook. Wally wanted this trade-off kept under wraps. At least no staff was around, only this construction guy, and he wouldn't have a clue about horse dewormers. She peeked up, her breath flattening at his sudden stillness. It was obvious he was quite capable of drawing his own conclusions.

"What's your name," he asked, so quietly she wasn't sure she heard him correctly. Which was perfect as it was probably not a good idea to give her name.

"Could you help me with this please?" Her mind scrambled as she reached for a plausible excuse. "These supplements are past the expiry date. We're clearing out the supply room, getting ready for a big inventory, new owners...never mind. I have them."

She jammed the last bag in her pack and hoisted it up. Was so eager to escape she forgot her sore shoulder and winced at the stabbing pain.

An arm flashed. The weight disappeared. "You shouldn't be carrying around something this heavy," he said, tossing the bag over his shoulder with careless strength.

"It's okay. I'm fine." She glanced longingly at the door. "Really."

"Show me your car."

His expression was unreadable. Maybe he *had* swallowed her story of expired supplements. Best to humor him. Let a man help a little, and their protective instincts always kicked in. Use what you got, her father had always said.

She'd pick up her money tomorrow. Em would have it by Friday. Not a big deal, just a slight change in plans.

"This is so nice of you." She rubbed her shoulder, pretending simple gratitude as she accompanied him down the aisle. "My arm is rather sore."

"Shouldn't stuff it so full…while on the job."

She shot him a suspicious peek but his expression was unreadable, so she nodded as though he'd just imparted valuable words of wisdom. "You're absolutely right." She beamed another flattering smile. "Lucky for me you came along."

He opened the door, pausing to let her pass, but the corner of his mouth twitched again so she quit talking. Despite his solemn expression, she'd almost swear he was laughing. Her father had taught her to read faces, taught her about all the little 'tells' in poker, and a lip twitch was always a dead giveaway.

"My car's over there." She gestured at the green Neon, a mere twenty feet away. Normally the rust spots weren't so glaring, but today it was parked beside a powerful black Audi with spotless wheels that gleamed beneath the sun.

"That's the visitors' lot," he said. "Thought you worked here?"

"I do, but staff parks where they want. No big deal." Although no one ever took her customary space—on Wally's right—the second closest spot to the front door.

She glanced over her shoulder at the construction crew, anticipating their usual good-natured waves, but they were oddly subdued. She stooped, inserted her key and the compact trunk creaked open.

A blue bag of cans needed to be shoved aside to make space, and it was a relief when he finally maneuvered the pack of pilfered supplements between the clanking cans and her patched tire. Usually she was fairly cool with this type of thing, but today she felt jumpy. Hesitant even.

"So that's it? Nothing else to load up?" He paused, one big hand splayed over the trunk, watching her with an odd expression.

"Yes, that's all. Thanks." He seemed to be lingering so she reached out and slammed the trunk, hit by a rush of regret. He was rather nice in an uptight way, even gallant enough to load her car, yet she'd deliberately fed him with misinformation. And he might need a job as much as she did.

"You know, Wally's been a little stressed lately." She retreated around the fender to the driver's side. "Maybe it *is* best to wait until his door opens. But he's planning a big inventory and cleanup so needs to hire some muscle. I hope you get a job."

His eyes hooded as she slid behind the wheel. He didn't seem the indecisive type but definitely appeared to be thinking now. "All right," he finally said as though deciding something with himself. "Anything else I should know?"

"No. That should do it. Although it does help if you like horses." She turned her key. The engine sputtered to life. "Better hurry before someone else gets in line. Maybe I'll see you tomorrow. And you can help me...load more things."

He smiled then, a real smile that made her hands squeeze the wheel, and part of her fervently hoped he would land that cleanup job.

"What's your name?" he asked.

"Jenna, Jenna Murphy."

"I'll see you tomorrow, Jenna."

The raw promise in his voice jolted her as much as the Neon's aging clutch, and the little car bucked twice as it rolled from the parking lot. Definitely a cocky guy. But oh, so cool.

She chugged down the winding driveway, her heart thumping a tad faster than normal. Peeked in the rearview mirror, disappointed to see he was already gone. And that he hadn't even bothered to give his name.

***

ABOUT THE AUTHOR

Bev Pettersen is an award-winning writer and two-time finalist in the Romance Writers of America's Golden Heart® Contest. She competed for five years on the Alberta Thoroughbred race circuit and is an Equine Canada certified coach. She lives in Nova Scotia and when she's not writing novels, she's riding. Visit her at http://www.bevpettersen.com

Made in the USA
Lexington, KY
16 March 2018